LITTLE is LEFT to TELL

a novel

Advance Praise for Steven Hendricks

In *Little is Left to Tell* one scene is quietly illuminated and then that illumination glides to the next, equally quiet and wondrous. But the scenes are worlds and the worlds contain Fin, rabbits, a boat, and Virginia the wolf. Like a dream that inhabits an entire life, even a life of reading, this is a deeply rich and surprising novel.

—**Amina Cain**, author of *Creature*

"We need to kill the thing, but slow enough that we don't drop too fast." These words, spoken right in the middle of Steven Hendricks's *Little is Left to Tell*, invite us to consider the author's approach—rich, carefully crafted sentences whose elegance disguises the many types of violences that are happening within the stories being told by the storytellers within the stories told by even stranger storytellers. At the same time, the act of creating this string of stories seems to literally keep Mr. Fin, the novel's central figure, from dissolving into his own dementia. Bombs fall on the first page of the book, and when they drop they destroy villages whose ruins open up into bedtime stories for an apocalypse both environmental (dead animals and trees and villages) and personal (the dissolution of an isolated human creature). We go underground in this book, and keep digging, with hooves and claws, until we've surfaced into a timeless flood that absorbs all of the communities, animal and imagined, populating this entangled network of narratives that destroys yet refuses to stop regenerating.

—**Daniel Borzutsky**, author of *The Book of Interfering Bodies*

"What a wonderful, insane, and maddening book! I am amazed by what Hendricks is doing here—mixing children's fantasies and sadness with the same processes inverted in the fading mind of an elderly, decades-grieving father. The book's title out of old Sam Beckett is well-earned—we see death and pain, yes, but oh what language, light on its feet like a rabbit!"

—**Raymond Federman**, author of *Shhh: The Story of a Childhood*

LITTLE is LEFT to TELL

Steven Hendricks

STARCHERONE BOOKS / BUFFALO, NY

ISBN 978-1-938603-25-9
e-book ISBN 978-1-938603-26-6

General Editor: Ted Pelton
Cover Designer: Julian Montague
Rabbit: Steven Hendricks
Book Designer: Rebecca Maslen
Acquisitions Editor: Carra Stratton
Publicist: Cheryl Quimba
Proofreaders: Florine Melnyk and Anne Sondek

Excerpts from this novel appeared in *Brooklyn Rail, Denver Quarterly Slightly West*, and *Web Conjunctions*.

State of the Arts

NYSCA

This publication is made possible in part by the New York State Council on the Arts with the support of Governor Andrew Cuomo and the New York State Legislature.

Additional support of this project has come from numerous individuals, most significantly Frank Eannarino, Michael Hendricks, Alexandr Pashchenko, and Charles Buffington Radil.

[epigraph]

As silent as a mirror is believed

Realities plunge in silence by...

Chapter One

All the children of Mrs Rabbit had been healthy and happy, their rooms tidy, clothing and toys arranged in their places, sheets pulled snug, waiting to hold their bodies in the night, pillows where they would rest their heads when the clock sang time for bed. Ball, comb, sock, doll, slipper, hat, lamp: life had distributed the children a loving list of desires and objects that corresponded precisely, like the words and pictures in grammar books. While they danced or giggled or built with blocks in the house, Mother tended the garden, just in earshot of her little ones. She could stand from her work and see a few of them through the window. The light of the long summer evening reminded her of the peaches waiting in the kitchen.

When the bombs fell, mother ran for her children. Neighboring houses, crackling trees, the flat horizon itself became a vortex of slamming doors. She strained to focus on the tunnel of light and air between herself and her children, her feet dragging, nightmarish, through a blizzard of dirt and debris, her children lost in the clamor as her home disappeared.

The Rabbit children found each other in the morning when calm, clear air finally curled down from above and met the haggard earth, lacing through the smoke and ash, the zeppelin raid long concluded. They regarded each other and the world apprehensively, covered with filth, uncertain if they had truly lived. Eldest Brother and Eldest Sister kept their eyes down, not wishing to see too much, dreading what could not be forgotten, while the littler bunnies limped and stumbled dumbly into the wrecked yard, expecting their confusion to lessen in the hours.

Eldest Sister stopped and turned her eyes up. "The sky is gone," she said.

"I can't look," said her Brother, his body hunched and hunching.

All through the midday, the rabbits searched, at times listless, at times desperate, for their mother, Mrs Rabbit, Mama. They could not discern the original confines of the family garden. Fence-posts and smoldering beams lay scattered, the whole known planet unsettled like a puzzle squeezed apart on a table. They called to her, but their voices disappeared in the hot, ghost-filled air. They called to her, and that lifeless air, life inside out, that air clung to their lips and lungs, left cancers to creep along their drying voices. Soon, mama was the only thing, the only thing they had to say to the world. They fought the sick air with it.

On the second day, the sun, tireless, thrilled as ever, pushed them to sleep, and when they woke in the purpled evening, there seemed little reason to keep calling. Instead, they did what they had learned to do if lost at the market or in the hills: stay put.

Days passed. The weather was good. They moved things about, pried up sheets of wallboard, cleared mounds of roof tiles. Altogether too many things were piled everywhere, as if a neighboring village, chewed and torn, had been dropped onto the wreckage of their own. Where had it all come from? They didn't say to each other what they were doing, wouldn't say what they expected to find. The sifting was private, unspeakable, and automatic.

Eldest Brother said to himself, "My arms aren't my arms." There they were in the garden, maybe, but it wasn't like working in the garden. They moved about without chores or homework, no games to play and no rules. Everything was gone, but what was left was somehow real. They had no name for this sudden confrontation with pieces, parts, solids that were also absences. Reality was the opposite of itself, and they had no words for it.

Alone, the eldest rabbit stared, a full minute, at a wooden door—blown from who knows where, its hinges clutched the earth. Here, beneath such a door, he thought, must be something: a secret room, a tunnel, no, a secret house underground, the hidden fortress their mother kept, a mirror world, a kingdom. He thought he could feel the magic in the air, swirling and tickling with cosmic carbonation, and, as he knelt, the poor bunny thought he saw a brief spark of starlight deep within the crystal handle of the door.

He concentrated, tried to ascertain the faith inside, the special core of a child that sends one off to magical places, the part that gets one chosen for special missions in other worlds. He grasped the crystal knob in his fingers and lifted the door up, open, careful to pull it just so, as if it really was a door, and not just a piece of wood on the ground.

They were running out of edible food. Several bunnies ventured down the cluttered road, toward the neighbors', where they saw lush standing trees around the house of the young salmon couple. As they neared, they could see that the house still stood, nearly untouched, though something in the back yard smoldered darkly. The bunnies rushed around the bend but stopped, dryly retching, for there on the road lay the two Salmons, Mr and Mrs. They must have been running for home to protect their eggs. Their fish legs and torsos were in a mound, as if something had bitten them both in half, all in one go, from above. Insects busied themselves in the wounds, fell in love, madly danced like flying goats.

The bunnies ran back home, straight to their big sister, who scooped their little bodies up and hummed their favorite bedtime song. She could guess what they'd seen.

By that evening the bunnies had consumed all the food leftover from the house. Eldest Brother said they must ration for the littlest ones whatever was left in the jumbled garden. The two eldest children gathered handfuls of aborted carrots and hole-pocked half-charred cabbage leaves and hid them in the shadow of a faceless wall, each pile representing a day. Then the piles were gone.

At the end of a warm, beautiful day, the eldest of the bunnies, forgetting doors in the ground and faraway places, succumbed to the disaster of his greater intelligence and life experience. First, his comprehension of space and geography (recent lessons at school with colorful charts and papier-mâché landscapes) permitted him to understand the severity of their predicament, the impossibility of, say, reaching the sea or crossing the mountains. Lessons in history had opened the world to him, instructed him in the pains of war and the overwhelming force of their mysterious attacker. The other factors were his size, which made his hunger quick and ferocious, and, bravely, that he had refused to eat, even on the first day, even on the fourth.

Blanks followed timeless blanks. Bunnies are hungry, delicate beasts. There was nothing to do.

For lack of food or hope, then, the eldest bunny's body aggravated and numbed itself, divided and fruited the branches of his mind. He looked at his siblings with vacant eyes, all envy drowned in breaths of habit, watched them lingering in what was once their front yard, near the lane that once went everywhere, all the places in town and out, those nameless and named, and by the tree where they used to line up for school and mother would survey them, see that they had their lunches and books, those tired old books wrapped in pretty paper. Eldest saw them become white blurs among blurring debris, smears beneath a fog of gristle and gray, while deep inside, so much so that it was outside of him again, in the furthest open seas of the spilled galaxy, he wandered into that small place where breath cannot follow.

Their mother arrived from the air to rescue them. She said nothing, but her jaw worked like a vise to hold her heart inside as she saw them, went to them, gathered them. They were only capable of the slightest of grips about her shoulders. Bodies filthy and fur in mats, just the pink in their ears reflected the pumping joy in their hearts. They wanted to say something about those days, and about their brother, but could not. Could not say a thing. They had left him where they had found him, afraid to touch him, afraid to cover him over.

The children were raised toward the clouds, two at a time, up a sinewy rope hung from the winged ship that had brought their mother. On the ground, she loaded sacks full of useful things from the ruins of her home. She hoisted the sacks up after the children, into the open air for nearly half a mile, into the clouds, where long white-furred arms worked the other end, whirling hand over hand to run the system of ropes and pulleys.

The second eldest, now the eldest living bunny child, gazed up at the ship. It looked to her like a tremendous spider in the sky, the god of spiders. Its many wooden arms extended in all directions, some of them forever, branching spontaneously into green leafy wings, vine-wrapped spinnakers, chutes and broad moonrakers full of wind, all glowing caterpillar greens in the high warm sun.

She had never seen such a thing.

Life would continue as a dream.

Mr Fin busied himself in the garage all morning, cleaning and tinkering with his old boat, The Swan. For a break he fixed himself a grilled cheese and sat to work on his Harbor at Sunset jigsaw. Sam had left the puzzle for him yesterday on his way to the dock, and already the four corners stretched arms to form a loving rectangular window. Fin pecked his greasy fingers through the pile of marine-themed blotches and pale green backs, looking for the last edges.

The sun appeared in the late afternoon, so he dragged the boat out into the drive.

Nothing on it quite sparkled, but it gave off some shattered salt color from the outer spectrum, something perhaps only birds could really see, here at the prow, or along the ridges of oak. Old panels of wood around the tiny cabin had absorbed so much seawater, so many unseen microbes, so that every part of the Swan, an unused, rigid creature, a trophy, nonetheless teemed with half-lives and sea-ghosts.

Fin gave the fiberglass sides a once-over with the hose, dried it with several old cloth diapers, circles and petting. He stood back and adored the hull, rudder, keel, and cabin revealed in the sun, its form a compromise between a dolphin's back and the needs of a human rider working the wind. With the mast and boom stowed on racks in the garage, the un-winged boat lacked its true majesty, so had a look of vulnerability, a wounded or hibernating thing. He imagined the trailer disappearing and just the boat hovering there, a light, clear water filling the neighborhood—the Swan lounging in a magic element that overwhelmed the land, let everything float. He would moor it to the house with the garden hose.

The rain moved in quickly, so Mr Fin rushed to get the boat back under cover, tipping his body against it, huffing and puffing, anxious to keep it dry. The sun glared sharp from the west so that looking away from it, one saw plumes of gold brightening the wet trees and bejeweled windows catching the rainfall, and looking toward the sun, one saw a flat, black silhouette of knobby hills and bone-like buildings together in the earth.

The boat restored to the garage, Mr Fin hooked himself over the prow like a castaway clinging to the last timber, catching his breath. Idly, he jabbed behind him for the garage door button. It squealed shut while his old head swam with random memories, images cast up by the rush of blood. He let all but one go, because here he clung to his ship just as the young rabbits would have done, and he had not remembered them for some time.

Here they were, tumbling into the airship, saved at last, lives wiped clean to make room for adventures. He wanted to remember the stories, how he had told them the first time, the third time, the hundredth. He wandered, soaked in the dreary dream, to his study, where thoughts came so easily, and lowered himself into his wingback chair, waiting. His hand slipped over to the side table, fiddling for his reading glasses—he could write it all down—but he gave up, for his unadjusted eyes left him submerged in a dark envelope.

The rabbits would climb aboard, and their adventures would begin with the heroic Mr Crane and his flying ship. With each story, the world grew and changed, at first toward excitement, and then toward sleep. So many nights, bleary with exhaustion, Fin fell into this same chair after David had fallen to sleep at last, and Hart Crane, the rabbit, the poet, lingered there in his mind, sitting with one leg crossed over the other, fingers tapping the arm of the chair, well-kempt if a bit sweaty, impatient, eager to smoke. It would be fair to say that Fin knew little about him: he loved his name and the romance of his New York mysticism, and he was troubled by him, even then, his fall into the symbolist sea—his voice echoing the frustration of a hidden life, his crisis of verse summoning the azure priest of the Isle Ptyx, Stéphane: they both haunted Fin's invention. Hart, all suspenders and that weird mix of the rural and the urban, candy factory charm and Atlantean eyes: Hart Crane, one of many Orphic tragedies, was David's long-eared hero.

But now the lives of the bunnies and of their poor mother had shifted around the body of the eldest. He had remembered it wrong. The eldest bunny had not died, not originally. David would not have allowed that. No, Mr Crane saved them all in time. Hart Crane swooped down. Mr Fin could not see past this flaw in his memory, and couldn't rid himself of it either: Hart was too late, and Fin had no idea how he had got there, what would have delayed him, why he'd saved them in the first place. He'd plucked Hart Crane from poetry, made him appear to David as the perfect hero, quiet and indestructible, with no back story.

Mr Fin imagined himself and Mr Crane now, at sea, beneath a bright dome of pink and shell gray atmosphere. No sun or moon, but lit by a latent pearlescence in the air. Mr Fin narrated to himself: Hart Crane would stand and look out over the water from the deck of the toiling ship, and at the same time in the room, at the window, thrusting the curtains aside. Hart would agonize, push his rabbit ears back and pull them down in distress. He wanted to rage forth some poem, but found his mouth dry and empty. I wanted to help him, but I knew my words would hurt him instead: words, to him, were all curses and traps: one had to trick them into softness: an elegant language would be one that barely escaped the mouth, one as inscrutable as the mind.

The rabbit put his palm to his forehead as he stood by the rail, waiting for something to emerge. Mr Fin could see he was hurt. A thin line of blood trickled from his nose into his fur, and his left eye had swollen shut with lavender black skin. The rabbit snorted and spat blood at the sea, watching as the clot wriggled and flew off with the wind.

Mr Fin worried about the blood, the bruise. He tried to speak, "Are you alright," he would have said, but the rabbit stopped him, pleading the shush sign with his rabbit finger over his rabbit lips.

Hart sat down, stretched and twined his legs as in those pictures he'd admired of Mr Joyce.

Fin could see it in the rabbit's wounded eyes: this was not before, this was after, after the mistake. Hart already knew: Brother Rabbit had died. He had held the body himself, lowered it to the deck of his own ship.

The story had changed because of him.

Mr Fin wanted to ask questions, wanted to tell the story of Hart Crane the way it was meant to be: the adventurous rabbit. They would both see the story unfold in the room around them, and Fin would say, Hart readied his spear in one hand while the ship practically lunged through the air toward the attacking zeppelin!

He thought: that's all you need, a new story.

Hart stared at the ceiling or the stars. "All this foam: a mechanical diapason..." When Crane spoke the words were not slurred or stuttered, but hard won in some internal, mental conflict. "...Antiphonal in azure, the white torment of our sail...

"drawn from the abolished, silent nothing on the earth's table

"Where white choiring wings ascend, emit scintillating plumes

"to spend the suns about us, but too late."

He held his head like an orb on his hand's tripod.

The ocean, if it was there at all, was flat, despite the wind curling into the curtains. Fin could see their position on a map of the Sound, an island or two in view, but they were becalmed in the dark, a situation he adored, to a point. One gives up to the weather.

Eyes shut, Hart tried to compose in his head. "the... the... and..." He was all out of words. He pulled a book from the table, spread it open in his lap, scanned it affectionately. Mr Fin could see: it was David's book. Where had he got that from?

"the architecture... the entire world..." the rabbit said, naming the pages' constellations.

Mr Fin wanted to tell the story of the moment, to say, Hart Crane and Mr Fin talked about old times. Hart remembered things that Fin could not, and when Fin told the old stories, Hart blushed and changed the subject. And where were the bunnies now? They would smile. And where was the ship? In the garage, of course.

"The Peter Rabbit story?" asked Fin, his voice coming from elsewhere. It had been a favorite thing of David's to hear one pretend rabbit tell the story of another—the world of rabbits expanded to include them all.

Crane ignored him. He tore out a page in one smooth pull, unzipping it from its brittle glue. Mr Fin gave a start. "That's—."

Holding it in the light, the rabbit admired the fleshy paper, its two texts blending into lines and rectangles.

"That's—."

Hart shook his head: stop.

With the tips of his fingers, the rabbit pinched at the text and broke a number of pieces from it, no bigger than words, short words, medium words, and slipped them into his mouth, like bits of lettuce. He chewed them up thoughtfully. Now the page had holes where the words had been—a slug-sucked leaf.

"The boy," he said.

"No, no, it's not your fault."

Crane plucked more words and ate until the page was half gone. He pulled out another page and bit right into it, a whole paragraph at once, nodding to himself, as if deciding it was delicious after all. "If anyone could have saved me, it would have been you," said the words.

"That was David's. It's my—."

"Sails that cross some page of figures to be filed away," he concentrated as he chewed at more words, swallowed, ate another whole page. "...reabsorbed, not gone," he said. "No more will they triumph over strength, the desire to sacrifice. Who will carry? Hands join toward the one who cannot be touched." He chewed through the alphabet as if it were gum paper, sugar ink, until he was able to say, "The boy might wake up—as I have."

Mr Fin nodded eagerly, but even as he wished to return the story to its original form, he could feel his memory of it failing, seizing up like a chain contorted among its gears. He felt his cheek pressed into the upholstery of his chair. He said to Crane, "Bring him back. Don't give up. You're the hero."

The boat stopped being a boat. The sea was not the sea. He was sleeping. The room was itself again. No sea and no sky, but a wall of books within which Crane himself was still woven, a ghost among the leaves.

What else, thought Fin, were our bedtime stories but hauntings of what I've read? What is precious about the decline of the mind, he thought, is that one is erased in reverse. Lost things return: David curled perfectly under his arm, listening to their bedtime stories. He felt him in the chair with him, sleeping warmly, leaning back toward dream.

Now Hart Crane, the idea of Hart Crane, was eager to be on its way. "It is I who have helped you since. I was eaten by the world." He appeared at the window. He pulled the curtains open once more. The sea returned, crowding the window as if it were its only mouth.

"All the children of Mrs Rabbit," Fin said, softly to settle the phantom David to sleep in his arms, "Were healthy and happy."

Hart slipped one leg over the sill, then the other. His body released stray lines, almost a stanza, onto the frail and bustling wind. Some were lost while others catapulted into the room and roiled in the air, not as sound, but printed on the papery side of existence:

outspread   motionless
                    coasts the wind unwearyingly   forgetfulness rain at night
or an old house in a forest   a child
              white   white as a blasted tree

 bury the

Hart Crane looked once more at Fin from the other side of the window, his good eye piercing, his other sunken into bruise. A beard of blood surrounded his mouth, so his brief smile was grotesque. He said, "If anyone could have saved him... That's all I have left." The sea winds whipped at his body.

Mr Fin woke at once, bones locked in his chair.

He tried to blink the sleep away. Sunspots hovered where the rabbit's eyes had been.

The door. Someone was at the door.

A neighbor, bringing him several obscene squash and a small basket of pears from her garden. He had forgotten her name.

When she had gone—she went awkwardly—and he had sat back in his chair, not quite remembering how he'd got from the door to the chair, he couldn't picture the pears, whether they were red or green or something else, but he could remember the tight weave of the basket handle in his hand.

But what was her name?

He kept notes in a small composition book by the bedside. He fetched it, flipped through it. Sometimes ridiculous things. He tossed the book aside and slumped into his chair. Removing his glasses, Fin gave his nose an extended pinch, reciting lists of names, an alphabet of names, characters in books, but nothing attached to the woman with the basket of pears and an awkward departure.

Soon he'd forgot her face, if she had worn a hat or no hat, a skirt or a dress or slacks, floral print or stripes or solid colors—and why had she come, what business did she have with him, were they friendly, had he been rude?

He set the basket on the kitchen counter and laid the squash in a chaste line beside it. He ignored the dishes in the sink. He ignored the sticky notes on the microwave, on the coffee machine. He studied the pears, but they didn't contain her name. They contained details all their own: their red skin the finest felted wool, the way their stems had broken. He sliced one onto a plate. The pulp glistened. For a moment, he saw everything there was to see of the carved pear's white and moonish face. At the end of that moment, he was relieved.

From her porch, she could see one of his kitchen windows, a bit of his porch, and two upstairs windows. The house, to her, had a gloom to it, and she worried sometimes about her intentions, her morbid curiosities. She was not young, but she was of a different oldness than—whatever his name was, 'Fin.'

He had moved in not too long ago, and carried himself around with a bit of grace, even an imperiousness that made various lapses and errors seem the mark of a man with too much on his mind for the material world, for other people. That's what had appealed to her. She recognized a fellow misanthropic humanist. She had found him affable downtown, even walked with him a few blocks to make small talk. He walked, sat by the water: noble endeavors, to her mind.

She considered ways to invite herself over. Eventually, it was probably the afternoon, must have been early summer, late spring, she crossed the street, mounted the porch, and knocked, freshly baked bread swaddled in her arms as offering.

She waited, knocked again loudly. He had to be home. She had watched him return from his walk just ten minutes before. She straightened her cardigan over her top, tugging it closed. Another minute and she turned on herself. Poor man had hid from her and she had knocked twice, so desperate, so crude. What did she want with him anyway? She moved back a few paces from the porch, surveyed the façade. The recent rain drifted up from the house, the sun's heatless glare taking its vengeance by ricocheting everywhere.

"It's just as well," she said to herself.

She posed the bread on a chair by the door. "Crusty little orphan," she thought. "How silly is that?" Tucking it back under her arm, she rushed home, grabbed a pad of paper and a pen: "Hello! Came by today—had an extra loaf of bread, thought you might like. I'll try to bring it by later or feel free to stop by—I'd love to chat. Have a good day! —Viv—blue house (two down, across)." She scampered back up the street with the note pinched in her hand, tingling with the cocktail of mischief and flirtation—both wrong. She slowed herself, sobered her expression, tugged her skirt straight—it was getting warm— and climbed the porch steps like she meant business. She kept an eye on the neighbor's house, to see who might be watching, as she cracked the screen door, slipped the note in, and pressed it shut again.

"Hello?"

Her heart jolted.

"Ma'am?"

Held in his wicker chair, he let a paperback limp up and down at the end of his arm.

"Oh hi! Oh good!" She chirped, grinning as she gathered herself. She cleared her throat, "Hi," she needed to orient things, "Mr—?"

"—Fin. Hello to you." He set his book down neatly on top of another, but remained otherwise unmoving. "I recognize you." He waited. "Do you work downtown somewhere?"

She wanted to call him Huckleberry. She resisted. "Yes, we've... met, at the tea shop," still catching her breath, "But I don't work down there. May I sit?"

He nodded to the chair opposite.

She clapped her hand to her chest, "Bit of a jolt!" Snapping the note from the door, she sat heavily, waving the note in her hand, "I didn't see you..." Obviously. "I brought you some bread!"

"I see." He smiled.

She explained.

He explained. He had been out back, of course, "checking on my weeds," and had not heard a thing. He'd made that up, but it sounded convincing.

She wiped the sweat from her neck, but tried to keep her poise, not ready to relax. "I'm no baker, mind you. I've got one of those, dump-in-the-stuff and hit the button bread-makers, you know?"

Mr Fin nodded and kept nodding; he wasn't even trying to think of something to say.

She could tell she would need to press. "How is your house doing?"

"Fits me well," Fin stopped nodding, relieved. "Still lots of boxes to deal with. Just as well, I suppose."

"Life gets simpler, doesn't it?"

"Yes. Yes it does," there went the head, but he sent two fingers up to still it in what he hoped was a casual way.

"And you moved from where?" She worked at a hairpin, fussed it out and fussed it back in again.

"Not far. I'd been in a little place, by myself, for some years. But there was still too much to deal with on my own. It was on a bit of land. Too many chores—too many chickens, really."

"Well, you've been in the area longer than I have, then. But we both came here to slow down, hm?"

Mr Fin nodded and fidgeted a bit. One hand impulsively reached for his book, as if he was ready to go back to reading. He noticed and squelched the movement, instead leaning as if to get up, "Can I get you some water? Or something?"

"Oh, please don't trouble yourself. I wanted to say hi, not be a bother."

Fin sank back into his chair.

She struck the pose of one ready to be asked a question. It was his turn. She could tell him about her house, about her retirement, anything. He was very nearly immobile. He might be looking right through her. She couldn't catch his eye. She gave in.

"What are you reading?"

"Hemingway," he said, snapping up the book. He flashed her the cover, then studied it himself.

"Looks like it might fall apart before you're done. I guess you've read that one before?"

"Yes," he mused, "Probably a bit much, I'm afraid. But long ago. I was stuck in the high school circuit for a while."

"You taught English?"

Fin gazed down to the porch boards as if into a chasm. He spoke with solemnity, as if the past was way down there, beyond summoning. "Yes... to people who, by and large, would never touch a work of imagination for the rest of their lives."

She laughed, hoping that was the right chord to strike, "Someone's got to do it, I guess!"

Fin didn't laugh. He turned *The Old Man and the Sea* over in his hands.

She tried again. "So... have you been able to keep busy, in glorious retirement? I see you sometimes, sitting down by the water."

He pulled himself back to look at her. But she was already looking at him, and by the look in his eyes she could tell he had not really heard her. Oh, I've wandered into something, she thought.

"Park benches," he said.

How nice. She waited, readying some excuse to hustle home.

"Park benches help me think." His eyes were alive again. "I've always loved the benches with the iron legs, bolted into the concrete. Some parks will have tables or benches chained in place, and that, to me, seems to invite chaos. The benches keep me walking, though. I have a pretty regular route, along the shore, past the market, and then back. Easy. Keeps me going. I can read in the daylight."

She gave a big punctuating smile, but instead of leaving, she said, "I love to read. I could read everyday, sometimes, sometimes, I feel like I could just curl up with a book in my hammock and it would be like disappearing. Something about reading outside has always sent me. You know? I just love that feeling."

She waited.

"That's a fabulous book," she said, pointing to *The Old Man and the Sea*.

Mr Fin squeezed it in his hands. "His only good one." He felt threads from the chasmic past rise up through the book, remembering not just Santiago but all the young ears, the barely literate minds, waiting to be amazed or, preferably, amused. "Probably his worst. It was unlike him: full of, you know, literature."

"Really?"

"You know," Mr Fin shifted his posture, wetted his lips in thought, "after he wrote it, Hemingway almost killed himself on safari, crashed a plane." Now the porch had become his lectern, and he crossed one leg over the other. "He was a broken man, after this book," he wagged it in the air, "a pitiful fish tied to a boat... he was a parody of himself."

She knew a thing or two about Hemingway. "Really?"

"Well," Mr Fin shifted back in his seat, slipped off his reading glasses. "One could argue. I'm just..." He thumbed the book and said in a low voice, forgetting his point. "I don't know about Hemingway." Mr Fin padded his pockets like a man looking for his pipe. "I don't really care a whit for the man."

"I guess neither did Hemingway."

"I don't know." Distracted, sad to accept that he had no pipe, Fin settled down cradling his hands, one in the other, then the other in the one. Where have I put my glasses, he thought.

"A mess, though." Vivian could picture the blood, imagine the clean-up. She stood up, not exactly to leave, but to feel alive again, to feel the light and the shade.

"You know," Fin's face lit up and his knees gave a bounce. Something had popped into his head that enticed him, so that he spoke, at first, as if she wasn't there. "There's the old man *and* the sea; there's also the old man *of* the sea, grandfather to Achilles, a sort of water deity or monster or something. This old man—he's in Homer—wanders the beaches, and if one captured him, he would change form until his captor let go—he might become fire or water, or a serpent, or a lion, or a whale, or a horse."

"Is that part of *The Iliad*?" She sat again, now at the top of the porch steps, leaning against the white wooden post, calves in the sun.

"No. No, I don't think so. He's mentioned in *The Odyssey*. One of the other... guys, not Odysseus. Who was it who told the story to Odysseus's son? Maybe it was Menelaus—I think it was—who told Telemachus that, if you hold onto the old man until he weakens," Fin put out his fist, strangling the air, "then he'll return to his old-man form, and then he will answer any question you ask." He rested his hands back on his knees, enjoying the story wandering in his head. "Menelaus had done so, and asked about the other ships leaving Troy, about his comrades, forced the old man to say where they'd gone." Mr Fin scraped his shoe against the floor, as if smearing the fluorescent guts of a lightning bug into the chasm. "That's how he found out that Odysseus was still alive, living with Calypso."

"Anything to do with Hemingway?"

"Hm? I can't imagine so. But maybe they are connected, regardless." He waggled the book in front of him. "How can they not be—both odysseys, right? And in a few thousand years, they will seem almost contemporaries, teasing one another. Who would give a god, or an Odysseus, the fate of a Santiago?"

Fin set the book down, thumbs and fingers playing anxious games with tiny invisible strings. "I do wonder, I wonder how the old man of the sea was able to transform, and how he was able to answer questions," his eyes dimmed as he smiled to himself, mentally thumbing pages of books he wasn't holding.

She found his performance a little charming. "You said he was a god," she crossed her arms and let her head tip back, "Right, professor?"

Mr Fin could see the rococo shores as from a ship, twisted sweet almond trees falling over green rocks and yellow sage. He could hear, in the ancient air, the murmuring voices of the gods who haunted men's minds. "I think... I think it was because he used to be an island. A small island, visible from Athens as a little hill in the water, worth sailing out to for a picnic, nothing more, blue scrub, brown rocks, barely any trees." Fin stared off into the Aegean, shaping the island with his hands. "One year, it dissolved into the sea, and many years later, generations later, the island was replaced by a man. He appeared in the evening—some children saw him striding in to shore, not a ship in sight, not a mark on him, naked, no beard, like one of the old heroes. In the years before its return, the man—the island—had moved with all the currents of the world, snaring little wisps of itself on the sharp edges of the continents. In this way, its body had been strewn everywhere, like cobwebs, or a- a- thin net of consciousness, an immortal dust, clumps of it collecting and growing. It grew into port cities, or filtered into deep caves in cliff-sides, and it even entered the bodies of animals and became colonies of seals, gulls, orca whales, and tribes of men. The old man who eventually returned, striding in from the waters of the Aegean still felt the presence of his body distributed around the world. His nerves wrapped all but numbly into the fabric of the world."

She said quietly, in case it sounded stupid, "I wonder what that's meant to explain."

Fin went on. "You have to wonder what he—it—really is, was, a man or an island—not to make a cliché, but in the sense of his desires—or his allegiances. That is, we always have to wonder about the being that must be forced to speak, who won't give away knowledge for his own reasons, I mean for the sake of his values, sense of the good. Why must one be chained, exhausted—tortured, really—to answer simple questions? Why wouldn't he speak willingly? A man would. Does knowledge of a certain kind remove one's humanity?"

On more familiar footing, she said, "If he's got this amazing knowledge," she couldn't tell if Fin was listening, "And he's vulnerable, then it makes sense he'd be scared."

Fin could have placed his hand along the edges of the imaginary lectern as he felt his resolution emerge. "How many of us are really made of that same matter, descended from those infected tribes of men, like the caves and harbors that are the old man's ears, such that within us are threads of the inhuman, bands of that knowledge, depths of unwillingness to cooperate with our humanness, possessed of that immortal changeability? So he runs, escapes, hides." For a brief moment, Fin was all chasm, all a work of the past, in the past, in that awkwardly ecstatic way that left him anxious when it had gone. It wasn't always that he couldn't remember things, it was that he couldn't always feel the difference between remembering something and being something.

He watched the woman quiet on the steps. She folded a piece of paper between her fingers until it wouldn't fold anymore. She seemed content. She unfolded it to admire the grid of creases.

"What part are you on?" She nodded at the book in Fin's hand.

"Oh?" He looked. "Hemingway? About the middle I suppose. I—"

"Does he have the marlin yet?"

"Well." He fiddled with the book, looking it over. "I'm not going in order, exactly. My eyes don't allow long stints these days. So I check in with the book here and there and the rest I work up from memory, however I like."

"Oh I see. You and Hemingway, eh?"

"He's not much help, but there are lovely pieces here."

"Well," her tone signaled the end of the visit, "do you want a loaf of bread?" She rose from her seat and shook her long skirt loose.

"I'll trade you," Mr Fin said, brightening. He liked trades. "I've got garlic ready to dry... and I should have basil all summer, if you like."

She smiled, or she should have, or said something. Instead, she thought it over a moment too long.

"I'm sorry," Mr Fin broke in, "I didn't even catch your name." He tried to laugh a bit at his lack of manners.

"Viv—."

"I'm sorry," he said, his tone stripped of pleasantries. "I'm sorry. It's—"

Viv said, "No, don't worry about it. We're all getting older."

"No. I'm very sorry." Mr Fin screwed up his face a bit and hazarded, "it's just... we've met before, haven't we? And I've just forgotten everything? Have I just sat here like you were someone else? It happens. I'm in the early stages, I think, but it's enough to put you on edge, you know, makes it hard to pick up new names, so, I tend to— Maybe it's still the new place. Not enough time. Routine helps. But I'm sorry. I don't mean to be an ass. I—" He cut off. He didn't have anything else to say.

Viv took this in for a moment, letting her disappointment fade as a sense of responsibility, even vigilance, irrational duty, laid a plan out before her. "Well, hey. Why don't I bring the bread by tomorrow? Or something. I'm not sure the bread's all that good. And I'll take a head of garlic in trade. I love garlic. Okay? And you'll tell me more about your book."

Viv looked back before turning down the sidewalk. The sun warmed, merely, and everything that was still damp would stay damp, no longer reflective, but bright velvet grass, and the willow like a chandelier, and Mrs Owen's hydrangeas with fistfuls of color. In a newly painted world, Mr Fin, shadowed on his porch, looked like a dusty swatch of canvas, a smelly old book, she thought. She waved at him. She liked old books.

"I've got it now," he called. "Viv. Like Vivian."

Pairs of bunnies rose shivering into the sky until they could scramble onto the deck of the ship, where they rushed to join their mob of sibling fur. Wide eyed, they would risk scans of the world below them, the florets of darkening trees through the ship-rails, or the lightning-carved jaw of the mountains, and the sky itself, a sea instead of a ceiling, going everywhere, and the only sign of the zeppelins' destructiveness was the invisible ash and smoke clinging to their fur. Soon, they were all there together, except for mother and brother.

The tall rabbit at the rope and pulley system gazed down at the planet, letting the ropes hang slack, waiting. He turned toward the bunnies, who, as one, flinched back from him. His shape unnerved them. His body was somehow so wrong that his clothes bunched and sagged where they should not. As he came toward them, his legs moved as if he were just the back end of some larger creature. Was he even a rabbit?

He kneeled before them and bent in, his good eye and his missing eye taking them in. He counted them, a finger bouncing from head to head. As he finished, they could see his chin tremble the way a father's chin trembles. Then, in one motion, he pulled his arms out of his wool coat and swung the coat around them as a blanket. He hooked the black horn clasps, so they were all a lump of headless, legless man stuffed with fur. Some of the little ones giggled in the dark. He pulled the coat tight, to hug them with it. His eyes were filling with tears, which they could not see.

He stammered to them, "I-I'm sor— I'm sor—..." He gave up, let the words emerge, paper pulp dropping from his tongue, "We build our days with fin and hoof, with wing and sweetened fang. Distance again expands voiceless between us, as an uncoiled shell. Yet, love endures, starving and alone. A dove's wings clung about my heart each night with surging gentleness, as a blue stone, dipped in gleaming tides, blood and vine. We dare not share with us the breath released, brother-thief that we recall, because we take the wing and scar it in the hand. We must die to understand. We must—." He bit his lip to stem his speech, peered through the neck of the coat, then rushed back to his pulleys. He stared straight down at the busily crumbling world, watching for Mother, holding onto the loose, fuzzy rope.

The bunnies stayed swaddled together, anxious for their mother to return, for her to climb up into the bright evening of the clouds and be with them. They took turns peeking out of the greatcoat, being the "head." Down inside, they would grip each other and chatter their excitement or fear in the warm dark. When the little ones had settled down, the eldest sister poked her head up. She could fit her arms partway down the sleeves, and when she stood, the coat grew taller on her shoulders, so beneath her was a cozy room for her siblings.

She studied her surroundings. The ship itself appeared more grown than made. The smooth, jointless deck wrapped around a central hump with a cave-like passage leading below. She put her face into the coat collar and said to the others, "It's all one, like a flying tree."

She heard a mechanical rattling and looked up again to see the rabbit operating the pulley system, pulling rope over the side quickly and easily. After some time, his stringy, bowing arms brought up sacks of this or that. He slipped them from the rope and tossed them aside. Eldest watched him stand there still again, waiting. When he pulled again, this time straining, his boots pressing against the siderails, she felt it in her spine, the strain and the worry. Over the edge came a large bundle, all wrapped in mud-smeared white sheets and tied with twine. The rabbit detached it from the line and held it reverently in his arms. He looked where its eyes would be as he lowered it to the deck. Sister recognized her brother's body, wrapped in bedsheets and pillow cases.

"Stay down," she said to the little ones. She looked, looked for traces of fur, a bit of an ear to show beneath the wrappings, or some sign of a surreptitious breath behind the linen. She looked, and she tried to bring to mind a special thing to call him, but she could only think of him as "Brother," and now, "Brother who died."

All at once their Mother climbed onto the deck, tossed her sacks aside, and came to embrace her coat-full of children. Several snuck out from under the coat to smother themselves into her dress and touch her belly fur. They felt her love-starved limbs tremble, but in those arms they could leave the last few days behind. The bunnies were afraid, but not lost. Mother lowered herself into their midst, and they all slept in a pile.

Eldest Sister woke in the middle of the night and climbed from her wool cave. Mother had gotten up, and she sat apart from them with the odd rabbit, all the sacks and bundles were gone, even the one, and the two adults pointed into various distances as they talked.

The ship was moving. It lunged through the air, at times steady, at times trembling and tipping. Cold and damp swirled about. She heard Mother say, quietly. "I don't care where we go, but I must leave him in a proper hill of grass and dandelions. Somewhere safe. He'll need to be safe."

Sister returned to the coat and covered her ears.

All evening and into night, the ship soared, bird-like. It also grew. At the pace of an hour hand, it sculpted its sidewalls and deck around the bunny children to shield them from the wind. Waking warm in the eyeless morning, they found the wool coat gone, and next to them a fibrous, woolly, and, to them, giant bear. The sun had just tilted its head to reach the ship's deck, and light tangled into the bear's deep fur, etching acid orange light and bruise colored shadows around his frame. Some of the bunnies had already snuggled against the bear in their sleep. Its fur smelled of exotic mud and vinegar. The bear made a low grunt when it saw them squirming and staring. The earthy cave of its voice thrilled them, and those in the pile popped up to see. The bear grunted something again, this time a word, but none of them could tell what it was. The littlest bunnies admired the bear's bright button eyes and giant limbs, and they climbed up onto his legs and over his belly and into his arms, gripping his fur with their tiny paws. The bear made a few long low growls, laughing a bit, then panted to catch his breath. They giggled at the feel of his voice vibrating in their paws, the up and down of his belly and chest, and they chirped for more.

Eldest Sister held back, tucked into the newly formed wooden hovel, and she watched as the bear stuck out a giant paw, offering her siblings a mound of dried blueberries. All the little bunnies pounced. Sister found his posture wrong. He appeared weak, sickly. She closed her eyes and leaned into the lively wood of the ship.

The little ones stayed close to the bear all morning, and Sister kept lazy watch over them. Mother Rabbit brought more food for them all, brought a storybook, ribbons, a doll, marbles. She came to kiss her children, to nap with them in the warm afternoon, and she put her paw on the bear's paw to show her gratitude. She spent her other hours at her son's side, nursing her grief.

The bear pointed out parts of the ship—vines that were the rigging, knot-like formations that served as eyes, fleshy sails, and the barely perceptible beat of the ship's heart. He pointed out things down below that from up high looked suddenly foolish—the river, the monument to St. Peter, bicyclists, a flock of ducks in formation. He tried to tell them things that he knew from books, and sing little songs, in case they wanted to sleep. He said everything in a few words at a time, pacing himself, otherwise he would run out of breath, his words crack and garble, and he might fall into a fit of coughing. He said to Sister, when he caught her eye, "Your Mother would not rest—," he breathed in and out and in again, "Until she found you."

The bunnies adored the bear's voice and the tingling that filled his chest when he sang. As the ship glided west, away from the descending night, the bear's slow songs allowed the young rabbits to drift into dreams, not all good dreams, not deep or distant dreams, because life was already a dream, but into a half-sleep of visions that flowed along the delicate veil of his voice. Sister slept, too, and felt the ship taking hold of her, like a great hand around her waist and shoulders.

Sister woke in the evening and went to find her mother. She was sitting by the body, her hand on its shoulder. Sister approached carefully.

"Mama?"

Mother looked at her sleepily, her face exhausted and frightened for a moment, until she put on a smile.

"Come, dear." She held out her free arm.

Sister didn't want to enter an embrace, not so close to the body. She sat at her mother's knee. "Mama, are we going home soon?"

"Of course we are, of course."

"How long?"

"Not much longer."

"I miss our house."

Mother drew Sister to her by the shoulder and squeezed her daughter's head against her breast, leaned her lips and chin between the child's long silken ears.

"Sweet girl, my little girl" she said.

Yasha stiffened at first, but her mother's grip did not relent, and so she relaxed into the unexpected affection. This had the effect of opening something between them, a passage between their bodies, scratchy like twine, a granite cold. Through the passage, straight into her chest, Sister felt terror and anger, lifetimes of regret rushed into her body. Sister's breath came short. Mother wouldn't let go. Sister felt the unraveling of that anonymous pain between their two chests, forming knots and tangles, and she couldn't stop it. She was afraid of bursting into tears in front of her mother, and so squeezed her face tight. She counted to thirty. She thought about trees, roots, vegetables, fences. Every thought sank.

When her mother let go, at last, Sister hid her face and ran away.

At the other end of the ship, she encountered the Rabbit, emerging from the darkness below deck, a bottle of reddish amber under his arm.

"Hold!" he whispered sharply.

Sister jolted at his voice, then stopped, taking a step away as he approached.

He kneeled to see her more closely. He whispered, and Sister even saw a sly smile, "No running on deck."

"Yes, Mr Rabbit."

"Mr Crane," he corrected her.

"Yes, Mr Crane."

"Mr Hart Crane."

"Yes, Mr Hart Crane."

"Hart."

"Yes, sir."

"There's no where to rush to on a ship, young one."

"Yes, sir."

"Unless the captain orders you."

"Yes, sir."

"How is your mother?"

Sister wasn't sure how to answer. She knew how to be polite, but she didn't think Mr Crane was asking a question of politeness. And while she could picture in her mind how mother was, she didn't know how to say it, or if what she would say would be true. She realized that instead of answering, she was nodding, and that Mr Crane was nodding, too, as if they had understood something together. She remembered that when he had spoken before, it had been garbled, strange words like poems. "Your words," she hazarded, "are clearer."

Crane laughed a bit and looked back into the dark tunnel leading below deck. "I've been filling up." He patted his belly and gave a grin. Then his eyes widened and the humor was gone. "I'm sorry about your brother." He really was sorry. Sister thought he might weep.

"Thank you," she said. Dumb words, she thought.

"You've been crying. I'm really so sorry. I'm sorry I couldn't help him."

Sister backed away. She wanted to be with her siblings again. She was exhausted. She didn't want more of this.

"I'm going to do my best," he said. "I'm going to try to help him. I'll need you—and your mother—to trust me."

"Yes, sir. I have to go to sleep now, sir. Good night."

The rabbit Mr Crane nodded and waved her away.

Sister squeezed herself into a warm spot against the siderail, her heart thrumming her wide awake, her head propped so she could gaze out into the sky. Some of the bunnies roused, and the bear, half-asleep, still sang between breaths and snores. The flying tree moved idly through the crust of heaven, sails rippling, falling slack, filling, gasping with sudden lack or sudden lift, and, drifting back to sleep, the bear's body went silent. Sister listened to her brothers' and sisters' breathing, to the sound of the ship like a giant oak clicking and whirring in a storm, and its rustling wings near and faraway. Until she slept, she stared longingly below, looking for signs of the waking nocturnal planet.

Chapter Two

Vivian came by one day. All had been well.

He said, feeling bold, "Let's go for tea."

It was jacket weather, but sunny.

They walked side by side.

Mr Fin considered what he would write if he were to narrate the morning so far. It was jacket weather, but sunny. One of my better days. Felt like going out. Tea with Viv. Didn't worry about a thing. Imagined the city on a beautiful cliff over the sea; all these painted houses glow in the light, air is full of their vibrations, bouncing and sparks. Imagined I could build a model city out of spare parts. Remember playing all day as a kid. Blankets... all the usual stuff. Sorting buttons and bobbins on the carpet Saturday morning, the day stretching, stretching. I stared at the ceiling, the painted wood beams, the world composed of nothing but warm and cool spots, smoothing a marble in my fingers, feeling deep in the dusty wool shag, thinking, will I remember this? will I remember any of this? I did! But is that what I meant?

Around them, the best ribbons of the ocean air unrolled into silky brush strokes, painting the eaves of houses, the mystery of hedgerows, concrete, diamantine air. Indeed, he thought, it was also a cheaply ornamental day, torn from some ludicrous auntie's fat scrapbook. Mr Fin groaned, because what else was there to life?

He said to Viv as they started down the hill, "I was just thinking of what I would write about the day so far."

She hooked her hand to his elbow, "Well I know. Took walk with beautiful neighbor woman. How did I get so lucky?"

"Yes, that's it."

"No no. Tell me what, really."

"I would write... that some days are good days. It's enough, really, to be a kind of point in space, somewhere on a line, you know, a plot-able life." He glanced at her. "I don't mean to be depressing. I guess I'd rather be trite. I mean this feels like a good day. I really needed you to come by today. And you did. And... and I knew it was you, everything about you."

"Really, everything?" She gave him a look.

"You know what I mean. It's like I'm in the present now. Really in the present."

"I would think being in the present would be not worrying about the past or the future."

"No. No, being in the present is just the opposite. It's almost overwhelming. You know what it's like to forget something, like the name of an actor or a word. But I know what it's like to forget, say, the last decade, and in some sense the next decade—or however long. And then I'm stranded in this place, without time. And the names of people and things start dropping away, or behind, as if they used to sit in front of things, like captions, and suddenly they slip behind, and, even though I can see things, I can't quite know them. When the words come back—and when the little memories that make up a person, a feeling about them, when they come back, when memories are speakable it's like...like... being a kid in a candy store, it's like you've come back into the world from elsewhere. It feels amazing. It's not just the words, it's all the stuff bundled up with them, a feeling one has for them. I know it won't last, but it is something of a gift, from all of this... the miracle of the normal!"

Viv couldn't think of anything to say, as herself, in the face of his delight. She could only be dismayed. She took his hand as they walked. She thought about the balance of pity and friendship, how when we give we give blindly. She had not worried until recently about his safety, and part of her had assumed that, when things started to get bad, someone would show up to help him. Now here she was.

At Francine's they ordered chamomile mint and black vanilla, settled into the corner table among bright windows. They watched the steam and the steeping until each lost its form.

"I'm sorry," Viv shook her head. "I'm not the best company when I'm here."

Fin waited, knowing she would explain.

"I come here to be alone."

"Of course, I understand." Mr Fin lifted his tea strainer and let it drip into his mug. "Well. I'm the next best thing." He pressed his thumb into the swampy leaves and set the strainer aside on a napkin. "You do live alone, though, don't you?"

"Ha. Yes. But, you know what I mean. When I'm home it's different. Isn't it for you? When I'm home, well, I don't know, I guess I feel like I'm with the house and chores, and that's even somewhat who I am there: I manage the house. It's a costume, a uniform: I am house."

They drank their tea, listening to the other customers.

Viv tapped her spoon on the wood table. "So. Who do you write letters to?"

Mr Fin thought about this, thought, "to whom," and still wasn't sure he understood the question. "I don't really write anything. I just try to keep track of things." He saw her disappointment, grabbed for another subject. "I was also thinking about long afternoons, as a child, how days are so much longer." That experience of stretched out time does something to children that can't be undone, and he couldn't think what that thing was.

Viv nodded. "I had collections. I could spend the afternoon lining up maybe a hundred shells and sorting buttons and bobbins on the carpet, first from smallest to largest, then in color groups, all across our dusty wool carpet," she said.

Mr Fin put a touch more cream in his tea. "My son loved to take things apart; never put them back together, though: radios, clocks, toys."

"David?"

"What?" Mr Fin felt she was being suspicious, doubting him. Who else?

"You mean... David?"

"Sonofabitch." He hadn't forgotten anything. He was sure of it. He knew where David was.

Vivian was surprised. She clattered her cup down.

Again. "Sonofabitch— ." Felt good to get it out. Fin's head lolled in disgust and he pursed his lips. "Stop defending him. What is it this time?"

"Fin?"

"When will it stop? What more do we...? What? I've got to drive all the fuck out there, don't I? And then what?"

Viv looked around the shop to see who was watching. She leaned in. "Let's just take it easy, okay. Just breathe."

Fin adjusted his plate and cup, grabbed a napkin and wiped the table, clean, dry, polish. He stopped, palms on the table, "What did we do?" he wept a coughing, startled, weep, then choked it back. "Huh? Huh? What?"

"Shh. Please, just relax." Vivian tried to catch his eyes, to stare into him.

She looked strange. He'd missed her so much, yet here she still was, all this time. "I know you've never... you... I don't want to say it." Fin's hand plied the surface of the table, a wrinkled starfish somehow frantic. His eyes searched the room. "I can't live like this, with him, with us, like this."

Mr Fin patted his pockets for a handkerchief. "Damnit," he said. "When he—." He yanked another napkin from the dispenser. "I'll get him." He wiped his mouth and fingers. "I'll go and get him. We'll just sit him down, and... and... I don't know."

"Fin, you brought him home."

He nodded. "Yeah. Yeah, I did." He skipped a beat. "I did. I brought him back here." He looked at her carefully, more calm. He worked to piece her together, her hair pushed back, lips, eyes, cheeks and nose: all the pieces were there. Why were they just sitting here?

"It's me." She was squeezing his hand. Her mind was racing. She knew there must be magic questions, things to bring him back to now.

"He'll come back," Fin said.

"Fin, it's me, it's Vivian."

"He'll come back."

"I don't know," she said. "Hey," she insisted. "Hey!" She squeezed tightly. "Fin...? Your boat. Tell me about your boat. Tell me about The Swan. You've been working on it."

"Yes, I have." Of course he had. "It's ready. I've cleaned it up." He thought about this. The sea was the eye and the mouth of the only god that mattered. "You're right, you're right. We'll take it out. That's a good idea. Get out on the water." He could picture it in the driveway, but in front of the wrong house. Whose house?

"Really? I'll go with you. I know Sam would come, too." She didn't let go of his hand. She was trying to make eye contact.

"No, I mean, ...Not you. We'll..."

Mr Fin lifted his tea with his free hand.

She was asking... Not she. Vivian. Vivian was asking about the boat, and Sam. "No," he declared, as if it would cancel whatever had been happening. "No, I've decided not to sail again." Mr Fin looked around the room again. Tea shop. "Not the best idea."

"Oh, I thought— What are you going to do with it?"

"Nothing. Nothing at all." What was she angling for?

"Ah," she feigned disappointment. "Maybe you should sell it?"

Mr Fin felt his eyes here in the moment with Vivian, some part of himself alert to the dream of the moment, but his body was riddled with memories.

"No one would buy it. Maybe I can use the parts. Or not. Who knows?"

"You want David to have it? Does he sail?"

Mr Fin could only see David's bright eyes and hair, launching away, almost laughing at him, or shouting, no, instead, flat, apathetic. Sonofabitch.

She was still talking. "Is there something wrong with it?" She let go of his hand, and it stayed there on the table, subdued.

"Well," Mr Fin didn't want to sell the boat because he didn't want anyone else to have it. He didn't want it to exist. He needed it to strand him here as on an island, sail away from him, or with him, he couldn't decide—but the sea! "That boat is a..." He couldn't think. He pointed to her teacup. "Are you done?"

She wasn't quite done. "Fin, are you with me?"

Mr Fin didn't understand the question. "Nothing, I don't sail anymore." He laid their saucers together, stacked the cups. "I'd like some air." He stood, picked up the dishes to take them to the counter. Mr Fin balanced the clattering ceramic through the café. He dropped it all a bit too roughly into the bus tub. The noise embarrassed him. People looked. Old man.

He saw Viv standing to follow, and he shuffled outside, bundled his jacket against the cooling breeze. Scarf was there, found a hat in his pocket. Viv followed at a distance. They walked this way, separately, to the nearest park bench.

Mr Fin settled in, aimed himself right out into the harbor. Mr Fin had always liked park benches. Right out into the extended arms of the harbor. Mr Fin compared the two vertical peripheries: the frumpy cloud-creatures and the green deckling waves. He had always appreciated the enameled iron of park benches, fixed to the rolling world. The harbor considered every move, a slow and gentle giant composing tides of symmetry and drama between its conductor's arms, collecting scraps from the childish waves: a bone-like log the size of his own leg—bent at the knee, all the fish and the shells, a toy car, bottle caps, a sock, food wrappers, a copper pipe, someone's plastic wristwatch; all of these things Mr Fin observed in their places, where they landed or still drifted, undecided, as the city pressed on and the sea pressed in. The sea, odd feeling, the sea, which he had left behind, prepared something for him, under its roof of waves, from the currents beneath all the depths that concern reasonable people, from the water's continual night. He waited a bit longer until, sick of expectation, his mind stopped looking, stopped wanting, welcomed the return of a certain ease, felt words popping out of existence.

Viv stayed standing nearby as she lit a cigarette, waiting. Fin looked at her exposed knee, then back up, out into the water. He clung to solitude, but he needed her there for it to mean anything. "Fin?" She sat very near to him, checking his mood with her body. "Boats and benches," she said, trying to make him smile. He wouldn't lean in.

"Sometimes." Mr Fin felt things resettling, the continuous line of days. "The mobile and the fixed."

Viv put her head on his shoulder and smoked her cigarette.

"Shampoo and cigarette smoke," Fin said. He coughed unapologetically. "I'll have you to thank for my timely demise."

"Are you with me now?"

Fin nodded.

"You had a little thing in there, you know."

Fin nodded.

"How often does that happen now?"

Mr Fin couldn't think of the right answer, the one that changes the subject. "It's not bad," he said.

Vivian stood and lit another cigarette. "You want to tell me about David? I'd like to meet him sometime." She was digging—she should have met him by now. He should be here to help. He hadn't, wasn't.

"No. No I don't."

"Ok. Just... seemed like he set you off. I was worried." She blew smoke. She looked at her watch.

Already the sky was darkening. It must have been the fall.

"This was an okay outing otherwise, though. Right? I seem okay now, don't I? Normal?"

"You seem fine, just fine! ...Okay?" Viv pulled on the last of her cigarette. "Hey. Pop quiz!" she leaned over to grind the smoldering filter into the cement. "What's my name?"

Fin turned to her. "George," he smiled.

"See, Martha, you're fit as a fiddle!" Vivian tidied his jacket collar. "Haha. *Who's Afraid of—*."

"Yes, yes."

"Know what? I want to get home." She stuffed the crumpled filter back into the pack. "Looks like you're going to stay here, do your wave watching. Get home soon. Thanks for the tea. If I find you here after dark, I'll throw a blanket over you." She pecked him on the cheek, "Let's do this again, okay. Tomorrow morning! I'll meet you right here, say, 9:30ish."

Fin nodded.

Vivian gave him a good looking over. "Listen. I know you're doing pretty good most of the time, but I'm going to keep checking in. Seriously. I know you're not depressed or anything like that. But... well. We need to make sure you're— that you're not forgetting anything that's going to put you in danger. I don't want anything to happen to you."

Fin wasn't listening, and soon she was gone.

He thought clever phrases about the geese and the town, and he made drawings of his boat, The Swan, from different angles, in both calm and choppy waters. If he were ever to write a novel, it would be *The Old Man and the Sea,* but in his novel, the Old Man would rest peacefully in his seed-pod boat while the sharks had their feast, and in his novel, the story would continue long into the motionless winter. It would be the Old Man's story and the Sea's story, how they turned toward each other and then away again, how careful the Man would be to not want, and the sea, how it wanted everything.

He had not intended to be out so late. Fumbling his way into the unlit house, Mr Fin heard the rain tap on the porch, and then across the roof toward the back. He set his hat on the table and watched the first drops glimmer against the black mirror windows. All at once, the cup of tea, with the force of a gallon, surged in his bladder. He rushed for the toilet, shedding his jacket, scarf and belt and, to be safe, sat down.

He bent full over, fingers dangling down to the cold tile, forcing his belly up into his diaphragm, gasping as his poor organs flexed and burnt, tenderly negotiating bursts and trickles. There he hung himself, face reddening, for as long as he could bear—if anything else was going to happen, it would take time—then sat up to work on his bathroom puzzle book:

RYBFP FWR UOLWAO SYQR NWC'DD EW QLROA, UCR LWAXQPO QX SODD HWWE RYWCHYRX QX OMBD RYWCHYRX, QFE XIOQP FWR SBRY NWCA KWCRY UCR DBXR ABHYR SODD QDD XOFXO RYQR AOKQBFX. QFE RYOF BL NWC SBDD XIOQP, DWWP FWR YWS KCZY FWA YWS DBRRDO RYQR BR UO, SOBHY FWR SYQR BR BX FWA SYQR BR KOQFX.

He ran over the letters until they began to drop their masks, rotate in space, adjust their stems and bowls, and reassemble; when one seemed right, he pinned it to the paper with his mechanical pencil. Since attempting his first cryptogram, as a boy, he had always felt that one should be able, might indeed be able, to solve one by simply reading it over and over, that the brain would make the proper conversions, as it does with the senses, and the solution would appear whole in the mind, not as if it were read but as if its pattern could be swallowed, integrated into the body, that the pattern sufficed, even for Rilke, so that the pattern joined the blood. Now, he left them all half done—couldn't bear to fill them in once he sensed the impending solution. That was how it was: either too much or not enough.

By the time he'd determined the secret identity of just the Es and the Rs, his lower half had numbed so much that his entire rump vibrated, and he doubted he could get off the seat. He gripped the towel rack with one hand, the paper dispenser with the other, clenched everything he could, and lifted. For the moment, feeling legless, slightly paralyzed, he wondered, as he seldom did now, about the future, and about his body, a thing that for years had behaved in roughly the same manner while his mind, fatty and fuzzy, had so preoccupied him. What, then, if his body followed suit? Could he bear that? Was it better to lose the mind than endure the body's failure? He had once pretended that the loss of memory, of will, of self was a spiritual task. Now he knew: the mind abhors a vacuum. Failing to cease, the phantom will crowd every loss with mutations. Here he was, orange drops of urine escaping down his leg, his pants a perilous knee bend away. He tried to imagine the steps: one hand on the towel rack, bend the knees slightly, reach down, grab the belt. Should he sit back down?

The phone rang. "Good God!" His cry rang against the bathroom tile.

The phone shrieked again. He hazarded a bend, his fingers barely reaching his belt before he felt his whole bodily contraption wavering. He stood back up. The phone shrieked.

He gave up, peeled each shoe off, and yanked his way out of his pants. He forced his legs onward, each step on bright needles like the stab of a thousand sleigh bells. Ring. Bells lodged in his sphincter. He grasped the phone, found the button, and nearly shouted, "Hello?"

He heard his own breathing, various clicks of departure on the other end. "Hello!" Louder, as if his voice could break through the wires. "Sonofabitch!" He slapped the phone down. "Sonofabitch!" He smacked the wall, the counter, swiped the phone across the room.

Well, good, he thought, panting. We've come to this. This is how things get thrown across rooms.

Mr Fin woke in the middle of the night with an eye like a fish, its gasping slow, its thrashing nothing like a rhythm, nearing its end, no idea where the water was now. As it wriggled its way from his eye socket, he shoved it down against the deck with one hand. With the other, he grabbed a bottle of pills from the nightstand, popped the lid and peeled out a single white pellet.

For over an hour, the fish thought about the sea, periodically rousing itself, flexing its raw neck-body, nature's rough draft of the spine. Mr Fin ached and sagged as he waited for it to swim away.

He gave up, dragged himself out of bed, and retreated to the study. There, his medicated mind could wander invisibly among books, especially those he'd read a number of times, taught with again and again, until the life of reading resembled a slow killing of the mind, he thought, wandered on some heath, he thought, in the ambience of beginnings, and in the dross of my own reckoning. He saw that he was in his underwear and his button down shirt, a sign that the division between days had been lost.

He cracked a book and plucked out all the larger words with one eye, held them in his mind as a constellation, let the lines be drawn and redrawn. Frightened gills pulsed against his temple. The fish thrashed again, an eye lunging out, flipping back. Reading hurt. No, reading was impossible. Mr Crane, he said, what happened to the fish?

He tried again. Back to bed, more pills.

Some time later, awake again, Mr Fin wrapped his still aching self in its dressing gown and waddled, sour-mouthed, into his study to await a second medicinal dawn. Blurred around him were the ramshackle shelves of collected pulp and classic prose, leaning, bored mystics and symbolist poets stacked on each other's heads and bookended by crime novels, a dozen forgotten thrillers—a paper and glue nest of caved and rounded spines. At last, his head accepted a chemical peace, and Fin wandered invisibly among the shelves. He spied a book and scanned his memory of it, turned it over in his mind, picked another, made sentimental clucks of his tongue, picked another, saying to himself, the best authors are the architects of the mind, and the best writers are the barbarians. Such figures, he said out loud, The Old Man, Odysseus...are not characters in books, he lowered his voice, addressing his secret to the empty chair, but characters between books. He made a hand gesture to demonstrate: inhabiting the literary ether.

Mr Fin spoke to the chair across from him, wishing Hart Crane would appear, wielding at his absence a cloth bound Odyssey. You remember Odysseus, the first novelist, telling his own story to king Alcinous. The Phaeacians are no moderns. They only know one way to end a story, and so they help the hero, the artificer, the fraud, to return home.

A myth, he says, is full of beginnings. The book is merely a single enactment, one performance—a flat, flat shadow of the myth itself.

Begin here: the Trojans set fire to the horse.

Odysseus and his men were not long in deciding what to do, and they were lucky, though the heat tortured them and they were not uninjured. A few dozen Trojan warriors remained standing around the sprouting flames, having expected a bonfire and a night of drinking, roasted meat if they were lucky. The Greeks had gone in their ships. The ruby beaches were quiet. One was either dead or one was alive. The burning horse signaled their triumph and, at the same time, their indifference to conciliatory offerings.

Flames, ribbons of heat, smoke, popping joints of wood obscured, at first, the careful work of the Greeks to escape through the horse's belly. The searing heat and desperation made them perfect monsters, and the happy Trojans felt nothing but terror as the apelike forms tumbled from the blackening timber and flame. Death came easily as the ready alternative to knowing what monsters were erupting from the inferno.

Then what?

Signal the ships. Or had the smoke already composed the necessary sign? Clever, cocky Odysseus convinced the others, on the fuming tide of blood, smoke, and fury, to find entry to the city, over its stout walls, where they might carry out the original plan. But, already, things had changed inside Troy. The people demanded that Helen be brought before them. They wanted her image, and all the gold-threaded and fluted gowns and her sandaled toes. They wanted to see her cheekbones and her hair and her ringed fingers and pale wrists. They wanted her body. Some wanted her dead, wanted her torn apart and sent to all the Houses of Greece. Others just wanted to see her, to see her, and they said that she was a princess of Troy, and after all, what had they sacrificed for if not to look upon her, adore her, be adored by her.

Of course, she wasn't there. Had never been. Enamored with Cairo, she had remained in the low land of the Nile—as good as in the land of the dead. Perhaps she languished, or relished her privacy there, stretched on a linen mattress, waiting for Paris to return, or no longer waiting, but living free from all that. She might have a job, push a cart to market, carry a baby, shop at the expensive stores, beg on the street for coins, food, pity.

The Trojans, stunned by her absence, gathered in clots of conspiracy and shame, filling the streets of their quiet, tomb-like city. They heard the rain start up on the sand and watched as the same cold current that had filled the Greek sails dragged a storm overhead. The salty, tireless Wind poured over the walls, crawled through the temple and across the threshold of every house. Sharp air glimmered as Wind bent into the city, the shadowed hand of a newborn deity, a force of fear, with raging eyes, the breath of ruin. The people of Troy convulsed in the square, splintered into factions as they unsheathed swords, hollered curses while the rain broke above, and were gladly devoured.

Having gained purchase on the wall, Odysseus could observe the tumult in the downpour, could see how they tore at each other, at their lords, at their soldiers, at their gods. Odysseus could see how much more pure and eternal was self-destruction. He would have shuddered, sensing in the violence and in the seaside storm something of what awaited him.

In this story, Odysseus never makes it home. Nothing can stop him. He is too clever for every foe, too quick and sturdy for any danger. Nothing can stop him. He never makes it home because he loses the will to return. Instead, long before his lonely life with Calypso, he tells his men the story of their arrival on the beaches of Troy, invents the sorrows of Achilles, he tells them over and over as their ship stalls in the flat waters until, thirsty, confused, malnourished, he tells them, and they believe every word, of how they burned in that horse, how they felt the flames in their feet, how they felt the hair of their bodies curl and pinch like a million sparks inside their skin, how before they lost their senses they were falling among the coals, no longer desperate to escape the horse, but weeping to burn faster, faster, please, and how, at the last moment, how he had shouted to them, "We are quick to flare up, we races of men on the earth!"

All along, despite Athena's love for him, Odysseus did not suspect that he was the hero of a legend. All along he believed he would die alone, that his story, once told, would shame his family, and expose him as a thief, a liar, a coward, a fraud. Instead, he lives on as the blind bard, repeating his tale to be rid of having lived it. He lives on as the figure of all authors who transmute their speech into the dead earth of the novel.

She came by again, the same woman. He knew he knew her, knew he wanted her to come in, but he could only stand behind the closed door, wringing his memory, waiting for her to go. He could have opened it and enjoyed her company, but he couldn't find her name. He hung inches from the door, searching as she knocked again and waited a good long time.

Maybe her face would have brought everything back. But what if it didn't? He couldn't think. His head almost fell against the door, but he caught himself. He wasn't ready to give up. Give up my what? He wondered. My shame? Was that it? Or is it dignity one gives up, having to ask everything, be reminded to eat and walk and wash? It's not pride, he decided. Not exactly. He put his hand out for the knob, thought maybe his body could do it for him, swing open the door, naturally, just like always, say hi and smile, and whoever it was—it had to be her, had to be the same one. Who else comes to see me? It would come back, it might come back.

From behind a curtain, Fin watched her walk, in her concerned, looking back way, down the sidewalk. Finally, she was gone, invisible. He'd lost more than her name. He could feel the erased hours and days, and when he dared to open the door, any image he'd retained of her had turned well out of mind, as if rotated out of frame on a child's View-Master, replaced now with the opening, the door frame, the porch, the sky, the house across the street, nothing of interest. A basket of pears, green, at his feet.

He brought it in, shut the door and latched it. The basket in his hand, door shut, he tried to feel her on the other side and regain a picture, or the sounds of her name, but she was from another alphabet; she could be anyone now.

She had stood right outside this door, he told himself. I heard her shoes on the wooden porch beams. He knew it was the woman down the street. She'd been right here, he thought. Who else would do that?

Maybe she was his daughter. Did he even have a daughter?

Mr Fin cursed himself and paced across the room. He searched the pictures on the wall, pulled out one of the photo albums. A dry sweat itched his shoulders. Could he have forgotten his own daughter? Nothing brought her face to him, not the pictures, or her voice, or what he remembered of it, and the characters in his life's record, in the album, were familiar enough. He scratched his shoulders. He flipped pages. Back in time. Back in time again. Far enough. She wasn't there. He went to his study, looked for notes. Felt like his skin was peeling, damn eczema, turning him into gray paper. Why the hell doesn't he write these things down? He opened a few drawers, mostly office supplies, more pictures, file folders.

David's book was still on the table. He turned it over in his hands: tattered beyond reason, stuffed in that old duffel, worn out. Was it missing pages? He couldn't tell. He had not dared read it until a few years ago, and then haltingly, with difficulty, forced himself through parts of it. To concentrate on the original text seemed impossible, or pointless, because all he could see were David's underlines, his inquiring or bitter notes in the margins, the handwriting delicate here, chaotic there, the whole thing cracked from a thousand openings, riddled with annotations and scraps, pages from other books, notes, newspaper clippings. How could it not terrify?

He fell into his chair, listening to the rain, the book in his lap.

Was it raining? No, it wasn't. The sound of rain dispersed, became static, the furnace, the fridge, the hum of traffic far away, something else.

Sagging, Mr Fin stared into the window glass, imagining he'd locked eyes with one of the creatures from the story, a zeppelin, steering around the house, a singing whale hunting memories lost in the air, its mechanical eye trained on him whenever it passed the window. He closed his eyes and tried to imagine Hart Crane in the room again.

Said to no one, "Hart Crane hunted the zeppelins..." as if it were the beginning of a story.

But he was stuck already. The zeppelin circled the house, eating the gaps in his thinking, bits of memory. He wouldn't know what was missing, except that the zeppelin was always there, humming in the sky, sometimes faraway, sometimes right outside the window, its full, invisible stomach.

Fin set David's book on the table and, without much trouble, found Crane in one of those bible-paper anthologies on a low shelf, a few poems. His own underline: apparitional as sails that cross / Some page. He tore out all of the Crane pages and left the anthology on the floor. He opened David's book at random and folded in the Crane pages.

We loved sailing, he thought. If he could keep those memories while others fell away, that would be fine.

He went out to look at the boat. Idly, he grasped a pulley riveted to the fiberglass hull, then, feeling decisive, he snapped it off, spun its wheel under his thumb and slipped it into his pocket. It felt good to break something. Some page of numbers. He was wrong, perhaps, to think of the image of the zeppelin as a threat. Forgetting was a part of life, as it always had been, and he could break his way into the past, divide it up, sort through it like a box of papers. Cull phrases Apparitional as sails.

He'd whispered to sleepy, pajama'd David, "Once there lived a rabbit named Hart Crane, who was a storyteller, and when all the children were gathered around, he'd say, Now, my friends. He said it like a priest. His voice changed the air in the room."

That's how stories would start, because Fin, himself, had trouble telling stories.

Now, my friends, I will tell you a story I have told many times, one that you have probably heard many times.

The bunnies marveled that they understood him—he so rarely made sense—and they gathered close around him. The little ones were right up against Crane, as if listening with their whole bodies, or against the unmoving bear, all hoping to fall asleep there in the warmth well before the story ended, to be carried away, as if to bed, by their Mother.

It is the story of St. Peter: Peter the thief, Peter the liar; Peter the fearful, Peter the daring; Peter who passes through fences, Peter who... well...

As a child, Peter was warned each and every day by his mother not to venture near the garden of the McGregor. Why was he warned? Yes, because it was dangerous. Yes, because the McGregor would bake him into a pie. Yes, just like his father. What was the McGregor? That's an interesting question. No one knows what a McGregor is, or if there are any more of them. Does your mother have a garden? She did. Wasn't it beautiful? Yes, yes it was. Well, the McGregor's garden was even more so... imagine the biggest, most beautiful garden you can, and then make it ten times bigger, with vegetables and fruits you've never-ever even imagined but that taste so sweet and are so crunchy, and they just pop out of the dirt ready to eat! Well, that is why the children needed to be warned. Because even if you knew you might get baked into a pie for doing it... you might just think it was worth it to get a bite of some of those delicious veggies. Well, it's lucky there was the fence.

One morning, Peter's mother dressed him for the day, and all his brothers and sisters. She went to Peter alone, then, knowing that he had been staring out across the lane, at the fence, toward the garden, and she warned him again, and she buttoned up his beautiful blue jacket, right up to his chin. And what? Right, and no pants. Why didn't rabbits wear pants? Maybe because it was summer all the time. Yes, maybe they didn't have privates. Okay, shh. Maybe they just didn't care. Okay.

So. All of Peter's brothers and sisters were very obedient children, like most of you. And that's a good thing. But this story is not about them. And when I tell you this story, you can think about why we tell a story about St. Peter doing the wrong thing, and you might wonder what's so good about a little bunny who disobeys and... almost... gets... cooked.

His mother left, disappeared down the lane. Peter went right off. How do you think Peter felt as he crossed the lane and walked through the field toward the McGregor's garden? How would you feel? Terrified...guilty...worried... nervous? Peter felt none of that. But here's what I like to say about Peter. I told you about the vegetables and fruits he would find in the garden, and he knew about them as well. And he knew that his father had gone to steal carrots and had never come back. But all that Peter saw, all he really thought about as he crossed the lane and stepped into the tall grass, was the flat grey wooden fence around the garden.

He wanted to see it up close. He wanted to climb it, or get through it, or under it, whatever it took. He wanted to make it disappear by finding its weakness. Most fences meant nothing to a rabbit like Peter. Any gap was like an archway, a loose board was easily found and made a convenient door. In his father's time, there had been just such a flaw in the fence, but it had long since been repaired, and the McGregor was known to growl and stomp around the fence line, shoring it up against attack. Everyone knew that the giant McGregor's fence was not easily defeated. So here is the first mystery of St. Peter. How did he get through the fence?

The story ended with nothing like a calming effect. The bunnies who before had felt snuggly and dreamy now sparked with giggly energy. Mother couldn't enjoy it. She struggled to get them, one by one, ready for bed. She felt desperate for some normalcy, routine. The little ones weren't having it. That life had ended, and they scattered themselves all over the ship, complained, dragged their feet, wouldn't brush their teeth, distracted each other with manic tickles and chases. Some hid behind the twisting wood of the ship or tucked themselves into the bear's fur. Mother laughed it off while Hart watched, but she grew bitter, shooting harsh whispers when she had them to herself. She couldn't take much more of it.

The eldest, Sister, patched with brown in her black, tattered little overcoat, skirt, slippers, she ignored them all, stayed clear of the fray, and stared fixedly at the clouds. She knew exactly where on the ship her dead brother's body lay, how it thickened there, or thinned, how Mother doted on him, it, more than anything else.

The moonlit clouds formed shapes, dispersed, mutated as the ship carved past and through the silvered air, navigating dense white islands toward the changing archipelagos of cloud planets, cloud creatures, all of it hovering so close to Sister, in a realm that encompassed her but remained unreachable. Groaning in its belly and tilting through the wind, the ship stretched its leafy wings against the updrafts, taking pleasure in the muscular tramping, coasting, and tiny acrobatics of flight.

Once the little ones had begun to settle, Sister heard Mother saying, "You must take us to land tomorrow. We'll need food, after all. He needs to be at rest."

Mr Crane said something that Sister couldn't decipher.

It was true, Brother couldn't stay here like this. He had to go into the ground, into a warren. Otherwise, the body will smell, it will rot into a squishy scab on the floor, and it will attract the sky's equivalent of sharks or bugs—which might only be sky bugs. The closer to death, she felt, the closer to the company of monsters.

Mother went on in that awful tone of a parent's suppressed anger, the kind one hears from one's bedroom, and Sister felt that twinge in her chest as if they must be talking about her. She moved so she could see them from the shadows.

"...you don't expect me to sit by while the body of my eldest son rolls around on the deck, in the company of those creatures," she went on, and Sister heard the phlegm, flashes of grief, the world burning beneath them, friends torn apart, that nothing—she couldn't imagine—nothing would be as it had been.

In the village, she knew, the special hills called warrens held networks of tunnels that allowed rabbits to wander into crypts, to visit the dead. The clay hallways were lined with familial marks, not so much territorial, but careful, some elaborate crests, others built up over time, disorderly but magnificent tattoos for the earth.

Crane tried to hush Mother, to do something comforting with his hands on her shoulders.

She shunted his affections and stomped off out of view.

Sister had been in the warren on only two occasions. Because several entrances punctured the base of the hill, and stairs lead up and down, one felt that the hill was in fact an earthen office building, the offices of the dead. Walking past crypts, somber-walking, she had had the impression that the voluminous hill must be completely hollow except for the walls, and the walls, too, were full of hollows, and the bodies, too, resting in their hollows, were emptied in time.

They carried bright green grass with them, the children did, little spring clumps in their paws, their hands. They had been instructed to pick some on the way, to pick something nice and fresh, because the dead ate such things.

In the wall, beneath the names that were only names to them, a smooth little hole had been gouged into the wall, as if someone had stuck a long finger into the soft clay, down and in. One could fit some grass, a flower, a rolled note, a bit of lace. She had balled up her clump of grass and shoved it into her pocket, because she could only imagine the corpse's teeth just inside, snapping at the flush green grass, retched teeth desperate behind the hole.

Of course, Brother should be there. But what if there was no there? If the zeppelins had destroyed the hill? Is that possible? Wouldn't a destroyed hill just be a clumpy hill, and they would only need to rebuild? Oh, she thought, the tunneling back in...you would never want to tunnel back in.

All at once, Mother came from behind, grasped her Daughter's arms at the shoulders and squeezed. "Oh, my baby," she said. "My daughter," she said. The embrace was anonymous, extending from some impulse, merely—it used her. Mother released her and drifted to the back of the ship to sleep beside her son. Sister thought that she should cry, but it wouldn't happen. If only Brother had known that they would be rescued, that such things happened, he could have hung on. She had seen Mother, in the afternoon, holding Brother's body, like a baby. Later, she'd put her head on his chest, like a pillow.

Mother must be hoping to find another village with a warren. Sister had never been to another rabbit village. She wondered what they were like, what they would call each other. Were they all named Rabbit? Did they speak our language? Mother, Brother, Rabbit, Bear, Teacher, Neighbor, Salmon, Librarian, Frog, Dog. All these names puzzled the young rabbit. Here was this other rabbit, a strange rabbit, who was something other than Mr. Rabbit, with two other names, in fact, names which sounded like other creatures but somehow also described him alone, as if he were three blended animals: rabbit, hart, crane. He had a private name, singular, perhaps random, but with a meaning that did not tie him to any one thing in the world. The characters in books had them, names, but it was rare for a village rabbit to have one, in the real world.

Given this new life of sky creatures and escapes from destruction, given facing death, and given climbing ropes, and bears, and strange lands far below,

Sister decided that she, too, could have such a name, a name like "Peter," if only to speak it to herself, something other than Eldest, or Sister, Daughter!

Where did names come from? Were they all taken already? Should she become "Peter"? Or "Benjamin"? Or "Janet"? Or "Flopsy" or "Hazel"? Or "Fiver"? She searched for a sound she had never heard before, thinking it might be somewhere inside and that with it would come important prophecy or power. What could it turn her into? She moved her mouth around random syllables, working through an alphabet, ah, beh, see, day, eh, fee. She thought of objects she loved, foods, considered Bike-Chain, Soup, Pudding, Sissy, Tea Leaf, Sheshe. She considered other animal names, but these all felt goofy.

The deck had fallen silent, all of her siblings settling at last, most of them snuggled into some part of the sleeping bear, and mother was quiet. She could not see Mr Crane. Sister hadn't realized how much she had missed this sort of privacy, the kind one has when one is not the eldest and can walk home from school apart from others, can leave the busy house and hear all the neighbors in their grassy homes, see the gestures of the unfolding weather across the valley.

She wandered the deck, let her mind follow the air, felt the pulse and push of flight. Here, she thought, at this moment, no one on the earth can see me, and no one thinks of me but me. She listened for her name in the faraway air, along the limbs of the airship. I'm invisible, she thought, except to the ship, the tree-bird knows I'm here, and carries me. Almost without sound, the distant wings press down against the piles of sky between here and the turning world, lifting up through a cloud layer, woody arms treading the patient, obedient gravity. Sister focused on a branch full of green tulle wings, far off but not too far, and she watched them stir and cup the blue and cream nothing, and then heard in their remote gesture her name: yaaaaaaaaaa—shhhhhaaaaaaa. It was a chant, a drumbeat between the ship and the earth; she spoke it, "Ya-sha."

She spoke it into the depths of her body, but not out loud. Not yet. She tried to thread it through her memory, to name herself standing in the kitchen, helping stir the milk and flour, yasha, lying on her own bed, the sheets she knew so well with little stitches in circles and stars. She imagined her name called to her up the stairs, ya--sha, across the yard, in class, replacing every simple summons with her new, full, magical name.

To have such a thing did remind her of characters in books, so much so that she even sensed the chill of standing on a page, an illustration, now repeated on each of a thousand other pages, a thousand pictures per second, every pose articulated or every cross-section revealed in its intricate reds and blues, creams and browns, embraced by outlines that gave her form and inked precision, enough so that her movements felt real, that she could be animated by the ruffling of pages, to a new presence in the throng of pretend movement. She was living ink on living paper, and she was part of the conversation in the sky's humors, so that around her, crisply serifed letters relayed her thoughts to another world, told her story.

"You should be with the others," a gruff voice surprised her. She found the bear standing over her. No, not the bear, a different bear. This one was tall, sturdy, bright eyed. "I'm sorry," he continued, "I didn't mean to frighten you."

"That's ok. I didn't know you were there." Snapped from her reverie, Yasha tried to regain her calm.

"I'm making rounds," the bear said.

"Oh." She had no means of imagining what that meant. She tried not to shrink back into a simple child.

"And you?"

"Me?"

"Are you making rounds?"

"No. No. I don't..."

The bear seemed to smile and take in the fresh air. "You are not with my brother." It was either a question or a judgment, she wasn't sure.

"I'm just looking around." She gazed back out at whatever. He wouldn't go away. Sister tried to think of what she should do, what one does who possesses a name. "Are you all brothers?"

"Yes, we are brothers. I am his elder, and my elder is resting below, having been injured in the course of protecting the three of us—and this rabbit-captain."

They haven't got names, she thought, or he isn't telling. "Was your village attacked?"

"Bears do not live in villages. Eldest and I ventured out, when we saw the zeppelins, to help those nearby. Youngest stayed behind, too weak to travel. We wanted him home where he would be safe. We did not, honestly, know what we were facing, but we had to do something, you see. I'm ashamed to admit that my brother, who is so friendly to your little siblings, pleaded with us not to go. We knew about your village, you see, for it is not so far from our home, and we told him that the tide of monsters was rushing toward you. He was afraid to be alone. Maybe we were wrong to leave him. I don't know." The bear changed his tone. "You are a rabbit, like the captain, but not like him."

"I suppose. I don't know where he's from." Sister felt herself weakening. She told herself: ask, ask. "He's a friend of yours?"

The bear scanned the ship. "This creature," he began. He knelt, then he slid down onto his bottom, slouching eye to eye with the young rabbit. "This flying creature impresses me."

"The ship?"

"Yes. I love to fly. It's terrifying. I've never flown before. I love it," he looked wistful.

Yasha loved to fly, too. She said, "I was scared at first, but it's amazing to be up here."

"Gives me hope," said the bear. "It is more than a ship, more than a creature."

Yasha sensed the bear was avoiding something. "Did Mr Crane rescue you, too?"

The big bear buzzed his lips, laughing. He shifted his weight, and he said, "It's good that we encountered him. Now our brother is with us."

Two of Yasha's siblings skittered by in their pajamas. One held a cup and the other an empty flour sack. Before them, an exhausted beetle unshelled its wings to escape their traps. Its seed-like body landed with a click down the rail, a sliver of its gold and green belly visible as it made the leap. It had a moment's reprieve. It worked to clean itself, shells drifting apart and together like a sleepy eye. Spying the cup approaching once more, it arched its back open, released its silken gray wings, and zipped away. The bunnies lunged for it as it wrestled with the strange currents that swirled the ship. They wouldn't catch it, but Yasha saw how, despite its wings, it was trapped here, in this pocket of flight, and if it left the ship, it would be lost in a desert of sky, exhaust itself, and fall.

The bear continued, "You see, our young brother and the rabbit have made some form of compact."

Yasha didn't know what a compact was. She figured: friendship, a pressing together, closeness.

"Did Mr Crane rescue him? From the zeppelins?"

"Mr Crane...? I doubt Mr Crane has any idea what he has done."

Yasha thought of how Mother spoke to him, that he didn't seem to want to land. She lowered her voice. "Where is he taking us?"

The bear was thoughtful. "As much as I love flying, it does seem to bring us closer to the beasts, not necessarily farther from them. Does it not occur to you, little rabbit, that behind any cloud or hill, something might be waiting for us?" The bear cleaned one of his dark claws with another. "In any case, I believe you have asked the right question, precisely." He hoisted himself from the deck, grabbing the rail for support. "I must check on my elder's dressings. Get yourself some sleep. Let others take the watch." He disappeared down into the ship's belly. Yasha imagined a pocket watch, somewhere on ship, waiting to be claimed, waiting to be protected.

She pulled her coat more tightly around her waist, no longer relishing solitude. She heard the other bear, the one who never stood up, hardly moved, she heard him start to sing once more, his voice twined with the low sounds of the ship's chest. He was trying to get the beetle chasers back to sleep.

Yasha joined her siblings huddling next to the bear, on top of Mr Crane's wool coat. She settled herself in on their opposite side, into the welcoming curves of the ship's starboard hull. Now the bear's and the ship's smooth, wandering hums she could feel as much as hear. Peering down at the real world, she saw a forest let onto a high field, almost a plateau, a dark and speechless horizon.

Mr Fin woke in the afternoon, spread achingly across the bow of The Swan. With considerable effort, he dragged his body back into the house and dropped his bones into their chair, chest panting.

David's old book rested on the end table, side table, credenza. He roused himself a bit, took up the book, and opened its tangled pages—hectic margins. He didn't want to read it. He wanted to see the hands that had marked it. He pretended he had a pencil in his hand, rested on the page, ready. The two of them had always pinched their pencils in the same wrong way. He drew the invisible point along the underlines, followed the curls of cursive winding up the side of the page, taking note of the fibrous muscles at work in his fingers, his hand behaving like David's, occupying this space, right here, this same space.

Something was wrong: the movement of the air. He closed the book, waited.

The front door, he suddenly felt, was open, wide open. Someone was in the house. Someone going through his things. He pictured the bears, those two brothers, filling sacks with silverware, books, knick-knacks, what else did I have? What would they want? Parts, but I have none. I'll be stuck in this chair and they'll clomp in here, and me frozen, helpless, and they'd take David— they'd take the book—right out of my hands, break me here in this chair to die. No, they'd bag me up, too, and carry us, everything, off to some nightmare.

"Fin?" a voice, yellow and green confetti, burst into the room.

Fin gasped despite himself and squeezed the book in his hands, shoved it between his leg and the chair. The bears had come, searching the belly of a fallen zeppelin, gathering the wreckage from its stomach. They'd find him here, and their hands would wipe his eyes away, wipe the world away.

A body cooed and bent into the room while Fin's heart sent chemical shrieks into his brain. His chest heaved.

"How did you get in here?" He spat. But he wasn't really seeing her yet. All he saw was the blur of a someone striding into the room, a foul bear, bending around him, spying. He spat, "What do you want?" As he looked, the blur gathered into a real person, a woman he knew, a woman he liked.

He pinched his eyes. No bears, no beasts. He could feel the bulge of each iris behind his eyelids, twin bruises. He couldn't remember what book he'd been reading or how long he'd been sitting there, alone. "I'm so sick of this. I'm sick of this."

He watched her, caught his breath, let his vision clear. His nose dripped. She didn't leave. She sat across from him, on the floor, folding her legs together. He watched her. She looked up at him, then down at her lap. She reached into a bowl on a nearby shelf and pulled out a polished stone, passed it from hand to hand. She She She, everything she does, right now, what does it mean? What's she saying? Was his nose still dripping? He tasted salt. What does one do?

"Sorry," she said. "I knocked. It was open. I thought I'd see you downtown today. You didn't show." She let a soft agate roll across her palm.

Fin didn't remember the morning.

"I even sat on your bench for awhile. I thought you might grow right out of the curly green iron." She made the curls in the air with a finger, then left him a chance to say something.

She went on through her day. "I went to the tea shop—Francine's. I watched a ship come in, had some more tea, took a pee, had a scone and more tea. Learned how to knit a double bead. I wrote a letter. I hardly ever write letters. You stood me up." She smiled as she rocked from thigh to thigh on the floor and arched her back. "I got a little worried. I brought some pears, but you didn't answer the door."

Mr Fin raced through names, all he got was a basket of pears. What stayed with him now was the story, was Yasha and the bears and Hart Crane. He didn't feel them in the room. The bears did not seem real anymore, but he wanted to linger in the story, needed to return to it, the way one returns to a dream. Later. Later, he could read his way to it, turning his mind to his books would give the story its voice. Shyly, his hand checked for the book by his leg.

"What are you reading?"

"Nothing." He didn't know.

"Right. Not reading. Re-writing the classics, huh?"

He remembered having tea. Black vanilla. He gave in and tugged the book from hiding. He squinted at it for a moment, struggling to see it properly. "Oh." He saw what it was. He wanted to put it back. "This was my son's book."

"Which one?"

He didn't understand.

"What book?"

Mr Fin showed her the coverless front and said, "But I keep it because he wrote in it so much, marked it up. It was important to him. He took it with him everywhere, put all kinds of notes and ideas in it, too."

"Sort of a diary?"

"Sort of. An obsession."

She leaned back on her hands. "I knew boys like that."

"The boat," Fin said, trying to press on without pressing on. "I bought it for him and me, for us. He was a great swimmer, and he sailed very well, as though swimming and sailing were the same... the same thing. We'd camp out together, in the sound, when he was little. Seemed like he'd spend the whole day in the water, sometimes. So, I have some affection for the boat."

"Of course." Vivian waited. He couldn't easily resist her waiting, anymore.

"But I also... He. David, he would go away. Once even took a train to New York. That's where I was, the other day, I mean, in my head." He tapped his eye socket with two fingers, to show where he'd been. "Ended up in a—" he fished for the word, "a clinic. I brought him back, thinking we'd go sailing, you know, reconnect." Fin wavered, "He said that," weighing the book in his hands, "That my words were like needles. I wasn't allowed to speak. If I did, he would look at me like... Well, then, he took the boat. We found the car and trailer, of course, abandoned at the launch. And he was... well, you can imagine what we went through, for weeks, until he returned." He thumbed the book. "And then he left. I kept this because I found things in here that he'd said to me. I realized he'd been, I guess, journaling in here, preparing, keeping a record, scripting our conversations." He pulled out a handkerchief and used it to snag something out of his nose, stuffed it away.

"It's easier to say something difficult after you've written it, don't you think?" She waited. She knew he didn't want her to ask, but it slipped out under her breath, "Where is he?"

No answer. Fin leaned forward, elbows on knees, fingers locking around the book. He was elsewhere, fading. She didn't want to go through this again.

She took a deep breath and let it out, attempting to punctuate the scene, to move on, withdraw the question, all questions. Pretending to brush something from her jeans, she worked herself back to her feet, crying "Knees!" and wishing she hadn't eaten lunch. She went to a shelf by the door, grabbed a bookmarked book. "How about I read for a bit? Where were we?"

When Mr Fin saw her in front of the shelves, the image composed a warm echo: the light from the doorway, like fruit, the cool shadows falling behind her. How many times have we done this? But it didn't worry him. Instead, it brought waves of other readings, chapter by chapter, that shelf, her head tilted to find the book, her finger along the spines, her voice the substance of the story, the sea, the boat, the man, the boy—the way one searches a book for the last read lines, those lines that led into sleep, lost in the text until the right phrase brings everything back at once.

As Fin watched her slide down against the old wainscoting, her name dropped so lightly into his mouth that he almost spoke it right out at her. Vivian!

She cleared her throat in that beautiful way, transmuting her wet vocal chords, cheeks and lips into an instrument, something of wood and brass and wound copper wire.

"He did not remember when he had first started to talk aloud when he was by himself.

He had sung when he was by himself

                           in the old days   and he had sung at night sometimes   when he was alone   steering on his watch in the smacks

        ...smacks...that means jellyfish...

or in the turtle boats.

He had probably started to talk aloud,   when alone,

   when the boy had left.

   But he did not remember.

When he and the boy fished together they usually spoke only when it was necessary. They talked at night or when they were storm-bound by bad weather. It was considered a virtue not to talk unnecessarily at sea

   and the old man had always considered it so   and respected it.

   But now he said his thoughts aloud many times

   since there was no one

   that they could annoy..."

She read on, but Fin's mind already cast him at the shore, wading into the foam, barefoot, pants rolled, shirt untucked and flapping. He saw himself from a distance, not too far to hear, but he could not hear, not the waves, not his voice, and his body, as he watched it, alternated between still and heavy and then wild, sharp and twisting, a page turned back and forth— the gestures he could take as joy or rage, rage or joy, or both, one and then the other and the other and the one.

He wasn't sleeping, but he might as well have been when her voice stopped, and quietness awakened the room, drawing him back.

He could sense her readiness to leave. "The pears were delicious," he said. She folded the book shut, stretched to tuck it back onto the shelf from where she sat.

"Did you have any trouble this morning?" She tried to sound careless.

"I forgot some things. Yes." He looked at her eyes, then away. "I forgot you, too." He pressed his palms against his eyes. "I might be forgetting you right now." Fin showed a bit of smile. "Who the hell are you, anyway?"

"Silly," she said, "You can't really forget what's right in front of you—not yet anyway." Mr Fin thought, with a voice well inside, he thought: how could she be so wrong?

Vivian dragged herself up onto her feet. "Okay. This old lady needs to get going. You get some lunch and fresh air. Okay?" She pulled at her hair as she headed from the room, calling back, "I'm not going to be by for a couple days, but I'll tell Sam to keep you in line."

He smiled, but when he did, he noticed a trickle of drool draped across his cheek, so he caught it with his wrist and searched for his handkerchief. Finding it, he blew his nose and wiped his face. He let the hanky fall by the table.

"Really," he called toward the kitchen, "You know, I don't need Sam to—to— check on me... Vivian?"

She was gone.

"Vivian?" It felt good to call a name. He waited awhile, until confident she wouldn't hear from outside, and called again, "Vivian... Vivian!" filling the house.

Mr Fin gathered the book in his lap. Its loose pages made skinny triangles around the yellowed edges. He couldn't get them to line up. Anywhere one chose, the spine gave way, open, shut, open, shut, open. Here.

...innocence that was marvelously smooth on the outside, but on the inside composed of a thousand tiny edges of very hard crystal, so that at the slightest attempt to approach him he risked being torn by the long, fine needles of his innocence. He was there, slightly withdrawn, talking very little, with very poor and very ordinary words; he was almost buried in the armchair, disturbingly motionless, his large hands hanging, tired, from the ends of his arms. Yet one hardly looked at him; one saved looking at him for later. When I picture him this way: was he a broken man? On his way downhill from the very beginning? What was he waiting for? What did he hope to save? What could we do for him? Why did he suck in each of our words so avidly? Are you altogether forsaken? Can't you speak for yourself? Must we think in your absence, die in your place?

It unnerved him to sense David speaking to him, to be written to, read long ago—a book that reads me, he thought, strange creature. In such fragments, he couldn't place himself securely. Am I he? Am I you, am I we? So few words, and his eyes suffered already, and his mind could scarcely trace back over what he'd read. He saw the frictionless curve of innocence with its sharp, crystalline interior. If David sees me in this way, always saw me in this way, then no wonder, no wonder.

He went to the kitchen for coffee. The kitchen was clean. He couldn't remember cleaning it. And on every cupboard, every drawer, on the fridge, the oven, the coffee pot, the microwave, the kettle, the blender, the closet, the counter, the column, above the sink, on the phone, next to the phone, the little drawer on the phone table, on everything in the world were index cards, some whole, some cut in half with scissors, each taped with four strips of tape, long strips across the top and bottom that extended a few centimeters past the edge of the card, and short strips going up and down, like bandages, everywhere, each one with neat upper case letters, labels, notes, instructions, lists, reminders, in this cupboard, in this cupboard, this drawer, don't forget, first, then, if, only, for, with, in, don't.

He pulled some off, balled them in his hand. He worked at a few more, impatient with the tape, having to pick at it with his thumbnail. "Shut up," he told them. Instantly tired of the task, he dropped some crumpled labels on the floor, left the room and leaned into the soft woven wing of his chair, hands hanging tired from the ends of his arms, reached out and found a story he could hold.

Again, they escaped the burning horse. Leaving Sinon outside, Odysseus and his men climbed with stealth into the sleeping city at night, having slaughtered the few guards around the horse and a few who wandered, seeking friends left breathing on the beach.

As soon as they landed on the other side of the great walls of Troy, they felt like explorers on another planet, suited in armor that drenched them in the grim oxygen of their own distant, ruined land. At the sight of doorways, curtains, umbrellas, couches, shoes carefully arranged at thresholds, each, each on his own, in his own peculiar way, lost his bloodlust—at the sight of this foreign hearth, each man remembered home, and here they could touch it, as if it had traveled to meet them. They removed their helmets and breathed deeply.

Odysseus gathered them back by the wall to make plans. They clasped hands, laughing at the game, knowing it was not all game, still laughing as they climbed back over the wall and built costumes from the unassembled dead. Odysseus trembled as he worked, for he longed to get back into Troy, to become someone else. By morning, each was disguised and ready to take the place of a murdered enemy, eager to begin a new life acting as a Trojan.

So they came to live among kind, sorrowful, dark-haired Trojan women and their small children, among comrades who embraced when they met, and shared with them those weeks suspended in seeming peace, though none believed it would last. Odysseus himself, anxious to outdo other men, adopted several new identities: a soldier named Agenor whom he had slain by the horse, husband and father of three (to the children he jested, "Call me Phoenix!"); he became the priest Chryses, and spread hatred for Agamemnon; and clever Odysseus even haunted the tall and winding alleys of Troy as the ghost of Hector, rushing round and round in agony.

A month went by.

Odysseus's men met each other less often. In the streets, they failed to recognize each other. Each felt his bond to the city tightening. The deception lost its dimension of revenge, its irony. Odysseus, in Hector's voice, sang soothing ballads to the windows of the palace and along the pre-dawn streets.

The Trojans held markets again, travelers brought grain, chickens, oil, herbs, vegetables, tanned leather, and sweet wine. Trojan boys raced on their naked legs across the battlefields to get to the sea. Some came back with fish, half giddy with the sense of danger. Others crept among the dead, brought back gossip and tokens from the picturesque gore.

One afternoon, all the Greeks were in the market square with their families or their friends. Some exchanged sly nods, some dodged each other's looks. Peneleus, who'd sailed with the Argonauts, searched the stalls for his companions, and, near a rack of hanging fowl, struck up whispered confidence with a Trojan soldier whom he believed to be Odysseus. The Trojan drew his sword and grappled with Peneleus. The Argonaut quickly overcame the soldier and slipped a knife into his throat, desperate to preserve his secret. Nearby soldiers, among them Odysseus, Menelaus, and Ajax, restrained and arrested Peneleus. He faced trial before Priam's son, Polites, and was executed that day, not as a spy but as a citizen of Troy, a murderer.

Two nights later, the Achaen ships could be heard, creaking between the arms of the harbor. Other dramas had occupied them as they'd dallied around a corner in the wind; but now they came to write the end of the long war for Helen. Life in Troy spiraled into horror more than rage when they heard the Greeks rebuilding their camps, the flocks of soldiers calling and laughing on the sands.

Odysseus stood near the walls or strolled along the battlement in the early morning, listening to them dressing, greeting one another, preparing food, all tents and armor and fire. He longed for the dialect of his own tribe.

He passed a coded summons to his men, and on the appointed night they gathered once more at the wall. Together, they listened to the joyous noises of the camp. They said the names of their true friends and lovers and fathers. They imagined the impending battle, took pleasure in telling each other how it would unfold, the Greek stratagems, how they would flood the city—they knew just how to do it—and it would be theirs.

A few nights later, they all met a last time, and Odysseus told them what to do. Before dawn, they murdered their Trojan families and friends. Not one of them failed to do so. They murdered until blood drained from the doorways and bodies littered the promenades, and they walked through the open gates of Troy as if triumphant.

Whatever passed, Odysseus was still alive in the water, the empty ship a wandering horse-head of fairy tales on the endless sea; he watched it drift away from him, committed to floating until his muscles gave out, until some whim of Poseidon's overtook him. Poseidon's whim was that he should live, that he should return, that the blood should flow and flow.

Penelope's suitors were ministers, were her menses, were monsters. They were real, yes, but they were also not-real. They were her own lust and her own rage, wandering the house as she sealed herself in her rooms. They sprouted from her blood each month, a new heir, a new vile Oedipus, all abortions, half-men who drooled into their soup, saying Love, Love, Love. Her son, untethered, roamed the earth, no longer searching for his father, but only for Proteus, the Old Man, whom he wanted to wrestle, outwit, overwhelm.

Odysseus's return was a tragic rift in Penelope's well-earned silence. Having shed her last, she'd slipped into her quiet years. Mightn't it have been better if he'd never returned, or if he'd returned but left again immediately? And his poor son? Telemachus sailed home to greet his father, carrying with him a chest full of documents, keys to the Old Man's location. He leapt from his boat, a spry man, like his father, with a well-trimmed beard, sword at his hip, arms eager to embrace his rag-doll father of masks. Odysseus watched from the cliff. He had spent the morning slaughtering everything that came between him and his rightful bed, and once the last suitor lay in pieces, he rushed madly from the house, terrified of the indoors, and stood panting on the peering rocks. He saw his son as only another man. Without a second thought, he loosed three arrows into Telemachus's chest, caught him up with other victims like fish on a line and left them to dry in a tree. Telemachus hung there all day, gathering his life into his hands, weeping breathless pleas to his father's empty window. The father slept, drenched in survival, down on the rocks and sand.

In the night, Penelope cut her son down. She put her hand over his mouth as she yanked out the arrows. With strips of her own mourning gown, she staunched his wounds, stuffing each arrow hole with black linen. She lifted him up to his knees, cupping his jaw in her palms, she kissed him, then pressed him up to his feet. "Leave, my son, and never return," she said. He shook his head, but she begged him, so that he may keep his life, and so that his father would never know what he had done to his own son.

Odysseus woke before dawn, wailing on the rocks like a sea creature washed ashore, broken where the ocean's fingers searched among the rocks, lost in the tide he was a moaning hole, a thoughtless, trembling anemone, all stomach and all lung.

When he'd gathered his senses, Odysseus thought first of his Trojan wives and mistresses, their kisses and his Trojan children that were theirs, how they were scared of the sky, the horizon of the high walls, how they loved their city and hated Helen, how they loved Helen and hated the walls.

Late in the day, he raced back and forth on the beach, crying for Telemachus. Where had he gone? Why had he abandoned his dear father? By evening, he was a man again, having forgotten enough of his journey, having remembered his body and his house and his wife waiting on the high-buttressed veranda.

Viv Viv Viv. She didn't come by, she didn't come by. Mr Fin paced along the edge of the kitchen counter, pulled the curtain back and peered down the street. Viv: he had her name, he couldn't lose it now! He thought he should go out, but unsure when she might come by...he didn't want to miss her again.

Sam was coming, marching like a great big cartoon character down the street. He didn't want to see Sam. Fin locked the door and scooted out the kitchen door into the garage. Soon enough, he heard a knuckle wrap against the front door. And again a minute later. He'll never find me here, he thought. Pleased with his stealth, he climbed up onto The Swan.

The stability of the boat on its trailer was unnerving—boats were meant to sway, and he knew its surfaces in part as responses to his weight and his awareness of the waves and wind. Here, all felt inert, frozen in time. Nonetheless, even in the dark garage, the boat was its own established world, collaged hours tending rope, watching the ionic mobile of the weather, and the lazy embrasure of half-sleep cradled against slick steel rails round the enfolding lap of the deck. He hadn't much room to stand. Walking along the deck, he felt tangled in the tracks of the garage door and the low rafters and dust-filled webs.

He climbed down through the hatch. While the topside, on the water, extended his body into the keel, ropes and rudder, and through these into the air-sea continuum, the cave of the ship's cabin became a shell where latches, cubbies, sliding doors, radio dials, and portholes kept the world from him, provided the joy of living tucked into one's own form. He explored, opened cupboards and touched the various talismans of the seagoer hung about, bits of rope and shell and iron and bone. Some things were rotting, old muck getting older.

He could hide comfortably here for hours. He fitted himself into the rubbery couch and closed his eyes. Such a secret place: not the kitchen, not the bedroom, not the study. Here, his body would not be found for days and days and days, here, he was nearly lost to himself. If I fall asleep, he thought, I'll wake up as, for a moment, a different man. For how long?

He could wake up and believe that David was across from him, or reading on the bow, just beyond the door, or swimming nearby. As long as he held himself in that moment, they would be safe. It was in this reverie that his eyes caught on a corner of tanned paper showing from beneath the floor mat, stuck to the base of the cupboard. He pulled backed the mat. A mass of flattened pages were mashed together by time and water, plastered to the floor—not just paper, but pages. Fin tried to peel them up, just reaching his arm out from where he lay, but brittle edges chipped into pulp and shards. He got onto the floor and bent closer, tried to read the words, to see if any handwriting was visible. It was a note, a clue. It was a blood stain, a fingerprint, a voice.

The Swan, he thought, is full of secrets, evidence. He thought he could feel its breathing, as one feels the constant press of water beneath, its vibrations, even in its dormancy, that suggested a life concealed under its skin. He was Yasha wandering the flying tree, Odysseus tied to the mast. David slept here, read here, perhaps he cried, felt sorry, felt need, or love, felt dread, and he would have left signs of himself, and even more pages, as his letter to us.

"Oh, my dear, dear, Swan," he said, his hands now pressed against the floor, sensing the ribcage all around him, "You were always my messenger, and now I think you are the message."

He moved everything, pulled everything up, pried back all covers and casings, opened all doors. It didn't matter what he saw, what was there or wasn't there, he was moving, searching.

Some time later, having brought all that death home with him, Odysseus faced, in the night, the ghost of his mother and the ghost of bear-like Achilles. He was on the veranda, working up the nerve to speak to his wife, when, whispering from below, the ghosts delivered him twin messages: "the underworld has built a palace to hold your many faces," and "you will find the threshold adorned with love." When he turned to face Penelope, he saw a pearlescent orb in place of her head. When she turned to face her husband, she saw a ram's-head, its mouth gagged with a bloody scroll—cursed to speak without words.

Odysseus turned toward his ghosts and caught a glimpse of Achilles's shoulder disappearing into shadow. He followed after, anxious for adventure or death. He tracked the warrior through crags in the seaside cliffs and into winding caverns, through a narrow black hall that led down and down. Some hours later, the hall opened onto the landscape of the underworld, where the dead lingered in their collective tomb, hollow-eyed ghouls, the miserable in their torments, and the maids of the dead garden: Persephone's echoes, her charmed ashen fairies. These fascinated Odysseus, for they were as beautiful as Sylphs, with supple skin and bright green eyes. Whenever they willed, they could slip away behind folds in the air. He had lost Achilles.

Before him, paths like veins led to all parts of the cavern.

He said to himself, "Is this, then, my palace?"

Odysseus wandered a maze, one which, agonizingly, had no ends: every path only went on and on dividing, turning, branching back upon itself, leading onward forever in the endless hollow. The meandering left Odysseus addled, and soon he ran. On all sides, bodies lay devastated or languished as if merely tired or drunk. Some gnawed on their sleeping neighbors while others fought each other, vile but without vigor, so that their struggle might take decades of withering clawing and prying at each other's flesh. Odysseus stopped to watch them, when he thought he recognized an old friend or enemy. No matter the resemblances, their eyes were never their own. He saw young Elpenor and gasped, and the dead man reached out to him. When Odysseus approached, he saw that Elpenor's eyes were bored, even merciless, and though one hand reached as to a friend, the other clutched a nearby throat. Odysseus kept on.

Soon, in the distance, Odysseus spied a tree, the only upright thing in the wide horizon of leaning shadows. He made for it, not without difficulty, and realized at last that it was the tree from his own courtyard and, lashed to the bark and pinned with three arrows, Telemachus watched his approach.

Sweating happily, Mr Fin ripped and sawed at the boat, piling its pieces up in the drive like bones on a plate. He'd already made a good collection of naked, curving plastics, aluminum strips, fiberglass shells and hunks of foam, leaving much of the old wood skeleton exposed. He was of two minds: the first was to find more pages, traces; the second was to see what the boat itself could reveal, every part of it a tangled piece of a chain or a phrase from some new language, phrases locked indiscriminately in the amalgam that was "boat" or "Swan," hidden by a secret poetic grammar, readable only through destruction. If those were his two minds, then there were two bodies, as it were: in his chest, the need to bring something to an end, to forget, if possible, and in his arms and in his fingers, as they worked, a kind of murder, a vengeance against himself. He anticipated with equal relish the prospect of answers or of fresh pain.

He arranged paint buckets and empty pots and boxes on the floor around the boat and sorted all the metal bits, all the plastic gears and flutes and cleats; the screws and plugs and rings. He went back for more of these almost nameless bits. After he pried off or unscrewed a piece, he tossed it into one of the containers, one for machine screws and washers, one for plastic, no, one for bits that fit together, one for pulleys and hooks, no, one for things he'd touched with his hands, the others for parts that had always been hidden, no. David was everywhere, not just printed in the fragments of the boat's memories, but exposed in the room, all of his movements in those hidden weeks, obvious if still obscure, but he was there, in the boat, in the empty space the boat had outlined, in the new space outlined by its destroyed body.

By late afternoon, boat parts lined the garage floor and the shelves, collected in the pots or buckets or boxes or just on the floor, waiting, more random flotsam than not. Nearing its skeleton, the boat still outlasted Mr Fin, and in the early evening he dropped his pry bar, wiped his hands, and dragged himself inside for dinner.

He put something in the oven and leaned against the counter. Dumb tired, he stared at the drawer across from him, the last drawer on the left. He tried to guess what was in it.

No guesses. He gave himself a minute then pulled the drawer open. Among other things, he found 3x5 cards and a thick black marker. He wrote: "MARKERS NOTECARDS SCISSORS TAPE BATTERIES APPLIANCE MANUALS SCREWDRIVER ETC." He taped the label to the drawer front.

Mr Fin settled into his wing back chair after eating. Was it evening? he wondered. What had he eaten? Could he find out, if he went back into the kitchen? A pleasing muscular pain ticked all through his body, so he thought again of Odysseus, deliriously home. The old man and his ship, aching timbers, rambling through old hells. Homer was near at hand, spread open where he'd left it. Cradling the book, he stared into the words, wishing to feel a single line sing the way such lines once had sung, in his head, in the world in his head commensurate with all the things he'd ever known, even more. He put his hand over the page, as on the forehead of a sleeper.

He set it aside. If Hart Crane were there, they could talk. He could tell him the story of Odysseus, how his men tied him tightly to the mast, how they all filled their ears with wax. How, as they passed the island of Sirens, how his mind raged, how, to be honest, his whole being lusted embarrassingly for them, and yet, through it all, Odysseus heard nothing, not a sound. It was something he would never tell anyone except his wife, as they lay together on their death bed, still happy to be fondled under the sheets, feebly remembering things together and sharing those secrets one reserves for the time beyond time.

Mr Fin looked over the rims of his lenses, though he had lost his lenses. Mr Crane? Hart?

No response.

He went on. "When I picture Odysseus in this way," he told the chair, "I ask: was he a broken man? What was he hoping for? Odysseus, old as could be, bronzed by his long life, skin like bark, he would tell about his adventures as if he had been a great warrior, and Penelope would laugh, remembering his cardboard helmets, his ships built of chairs and blankets, how clever he was, always inventing. She would say, 'Oh, honey, you gave us a fright now and then, you know?'

"He would balk, and go on with another story."

Hart Crane would appear drowsy as Fin went on, but he would be listening. So after a long pause, Hart would say, "Odysseus doesn't know how to live, but he doesn't know why he shouldn't go on forever. His body is that black boat, that bridge, that strung lyre full of cries in the swarming air. Penelope went on weaving her silence, unweaving each night in dreams, and he could see that no matter how much he loved her, she would always be awaiting his return."

Mr Fin woke up with an eye like a bag of wind, like a lotus. He had slept the night in his chair, and his muscles were bitter.

He walked. It was early, quiet. It must have been very early. Rosy fingertips, he said. Sing muse, he said.

He'd wandered all the way to the dock, where he admired the clicking of lines on the silvery pale masts dallying above the pier, wobbling on the purple waves below, proud, dumb ducks. Retreating back to land, he settled on one of his usual benches, looking out at the water. In the half-light, he was pressed against the world like his hand against a page, not reading. The tide brought line after line of foam.

When he felt a gravitational pull on his attention, on his body first, his mind and eyes trailed toward the water, toward an unwavelike, unloglike form sliding in on the ramshackle tide. Leaning forward, he tried to open his eyes, open again, really see.

If somehow one's nerves could multiply and reach into all the miniature worlds of one's organs and flesh, weaving among the molecules of fat and tissue, coursing ever more finely into the rush of blood and more still to weave into the non-places between protons, neutrons, and electrons, sending out excitable quantum whiskers, all charged with feeding the same storm of attention, one would seem to float, mist-like, more empty space than not, feeling not thicker but diffuse, light, feeling all the lack of contact within oneself and between oneself and the world, a phantom, an opening in space, a hovering idea.

When he saw the head, he knew. By his count, at that moment, knowing full well the day of the week and the week of the month, having counted in his head and many times worked things out on paper, he knew that it had taken twenty years, three months, and twelve days for his son's body to wash ashore.

Mr Fin was little more than a perspective in space focused on the arrival of the head, the shoulder blades, appearing and disappearing in the unfolding water. He moved from the bench, not feeling his legs or his arms or his chest, susceptible only to the mutual tide of water and air, drawn to the coiling foam that gathered into itself, the infinite patience of the sea, until the sand broke the sway of his son's body, and Mr Fin ran to the water's lip.

He splashed into the water rushing up and back around his ankles, plying through loamy and sucking sand. He steadied himself, made himself strong, so he could reach down and hold the body still.

He lifted it into his arms and carried it up the hill. He mounted the porch steps, adjusting his hold under the knees and shoulders, kicking aside a basket of pears, and twisted his teetering way inside. Sweat lined his forehead as he dropped to his knees in the spare bedroom. Lowering the body, he noticed only now that the two of them were filthy with salt water, gobs and blotches of green and mustard algae. He undressed in the bathroom, gathered fresh towels, and layered them on the bedroom floor. Failing as a nurse, he nonetheless maneuvered the body onto the towels, using hand towels to carefully clean the body, just enough. Slumped against the bed, still naked, dazed, the residue of the sea that still clung to him became unbearable.

Freshly showered and dressed, Mr Fin gathered the pears from the porch, ate one of them, paced the room as he took even bites through its uniform density, careless of the juice on his hands, pacing as he chewed, feeling the fist of his heart against his ribs.

He put on the kettle and ate another pear, pacing.

He still had two boxes of his son's things from childhood. He slid open the spare room closet and pulled the chain on the bulb. It was all boxes, but he knew which two. He lifted responsibly, with his legs, took his time, breathing in circles to calm his heart, maneuvering boxes out of the way as if solving a puzzle. One was heavier than the other, mostly books. He set them both on the dresser. They had always been ghastly to him, two appalling cardboard blocks, reliquaries, really, full of wounds. Now he was here for them. The boxes were taped shut, perhaps for the move. Working his fingers under one flap he broke the tape, then the other side, and peeled the flaps apart down the middle. All at once, he caught the locked-in scent of the clothes. He hadn't expected that. Panic riddled through him, and he shut the box, covered his face, gasping for plain air.

Instead, he covered the body with blankets and eased himself to the floor next to him, the tattered book in hand. He tucked the blankets in close. "Listen," he whispered. The kettle shrieked, and Fin rushed to turn off the fire. He dropped a tea bag into his mug, poured the water over it, set the kettle back on the stove. All real things, he said to himself. He took a sip of the too-hot tea and left the mug on the counter.

He sat again, trying to get his knees to cooperate. So much water everywhere. The carpet might never recover. He took up the book, thumbing through pages, scanning for something to say. He could hardly see. He put the book down.

He picked it up again, searching as if for a spell. He landed on a passage scribbled at the end of a chapter.

Fin plucked a mosquito's fossil from the page and read out loud, straining to keep his eyes working, underlining each word with his thumbnail.

"I wouldn't suffer to wander in form and degree of knowing—And, therefore, I killed my desire graciously, and unfashioned its leash of longing—which absence led me by another thread to a state of pure knowing / to the other edge of the sea, the opposite of the shore, without form, where I learned to live more ghostly beside my wits and curiosities..." He read it twice over. It was either a comfort or a curse.

David, he said in his mind.

"David," he said aloud.

The body slept, the sleep of shock.

He arranged the book next to the body, as if David had fallen asleep reading it. He had always slept in this way. Not always. But often, he had slept like this, awkward, so that he should wake up in agony, but he won't, he won't.

Mr Fin squeezed the feet, touched the forehead with the backs of his fingers. He could hear David's younger voice as he would have read out the same passage, or something like it, some adolescent mysticism, all a bit slurred, a bit misunderstood, but serious. He would have copied it out sitting in his room, read it out loud to himself, deeply alone in his meditations.

Fin heard him as if through a wall, reciting.

When Fin had first come across the book, David had long been adrift in the muckish cold sea, but must have been on his way home, must have, must have truly felt the longing, felt the slow salt of his blood rise warm in his heart, drain and cool, rise again, as he drifted, the mere seed of a body floating at the gilded paper-thin horizon, a seed, growing, a heart sending cursive sound waves along the margins of air, repeating its stories.

Chapter Three

Mr Fin woke with an eye like a cloud, too big for his arms to gather it all back in. If he moved too quickly forward, it would drift behind him, leaving him half blind, disoriented. If he sat down, it would stay hovering above him. Only if he stood tall and still could he see clearly. He prided himself on the self control the cloud required—the will to stand in the middle of the room, bordering on miserable at times, resisting the urge to itch or shift his weight. Soon the cloud held distinct forms, delicately shadowed depths, wispy towers at its horizon and cumulus domes, and before him, a glittering soft city soon emerged, carved by the air in his evaporated eye.

The city's paleolithic arcades perched on the prow of a cloudy sea cliff. As it gathered detail, he took it at first for Troy, where his mind had been wandering the day before, but it wasn't the same. He watched as it gained modern details, electrical lines, sewer drains, windows, mass transit. People ventured from their doorways. One, in love, hung out of her third floor window, scanning about—she'd heard, perhaps, a pebble against the glass; another in her robe with a mug of coffee, her face in the steam; another yawning as he walked the street.

They shared the stretching dawn of squished shoulders and overbent necks, pressing through the tacky caul of sleep until, soundless, a white zeppelin emerged from the vanishing point of the central boulevard, its mouth gaping. It took soft sailing bites of brick cornices, window frames and balconies, a flying regiment of teeth, coming closer and closer, eating along the way. No one ran, no one panicked or cried. They went about their business and were devoured.

The zeppelin swallowed Fin's eye with everything else, trapped his vision in its belly, with its glut of broken mists. The beast sailed on, as if right through Mr Fin's head, and took the city and the cloud with it.

Fin saw clearly, plainly, and was relieved.

He went right out for his walk. His knees did not protest the downhill, and he turned away from the shops with a steady stride, toward the park. He scorned the protesting geese, made them disperse.

He watched the slow wandering paint-daub bodies of crows, feathery black hands that pinched this cornice, that stair, hobbling on the steady ground: if they ever gathered, it would be called a murder, or a storytelling, he thought, a winged hole in the street or in the air.

He passed a house he knew. Sam's house: he knew its peach shutters, its wooden door. Sam brought the puzzles, fetched things on occasion. Sam wanted to take him out fishing sometime. Fin did not fully relish the prospect. An image of Sam came easily: tall, bristle-haired, a singer's lips and whitened teeth. Mr Fin ticked through the basics until a deeper sense of Sam settled in, then again reduced him to his puppy dog voice and his ugly golfer's hat. That was a comfort, the ease of recall. Sam's house was small. He lived there alone, made paintings of the beach, of birds, of boats, of quaint buildings, maybe old restaurants—sold a small number to tourists.

Mr Fin arrived at the shore and settled into a bench. He'd never cared for fishing. Just for the water, the wind, the days of flatness and the strange hours among the waves. The Old Man would retire to his cottage, prepare it for the rains, for the cold. Throughout the first half, the Old Man believed that this winter would be his last, so the image of the cottage, of the repairs, of the impending cold, were images of the Old Man preparing his coffin, making it sea worthy. Mr Fin recalled the phrase, the opposite of shore, a guiding presence in the novel, echoed by the foam green piano wires at the horizon, staring back at the anonymity of the seaside hamlet, the accentuated lack of other places in the world, the phrase: "tell me no more," stories that please us by ending prettily.

The Old Man received news of the village from the boy less and less often, but then also from a mail carrier. The Old Man never received mail, but the mail carrier came by to talk, and they shared sips of whiskey from the mail carrier's flask, which he always kept in his sock. The mail carrier enjoyed reporting the bad news. So and so has lost his arm, so and so has drowned, so and so is sinking into poverty, so and so almost drowned, so and so has gone to war and his wife has taken another, and so on. The boy would come by, but very seldom. The boy, too, would one day be a bit of gossip, and before this could happen, the Old Man would refuse to greet the mail carrier. He would sit alone indoors, sober, quiet as dirt.

The figure of Hart Crane, the rabbit, watched Mr Fin from the water's edge, tiredly mocking the cavorting Old Man. He didn't look well, looked spat out. David loved our stories, he thought, when Hart was strong and adventurous. It wasn't easy. Crane would stagger from the forest, from the shore, from the desert, from the granite arcades of the damned, always surviving, only just. He looked terrible now.

Fin jolted, head jogging forward.

He remembered.

David came home.

He pinched his brow and cursed himself, cursed the simplicity of the morning, the damned routines that kept him sane, that boiled him down into this old man sitting here. He gathered his glove, hat, scarf, hat, socks, knees, glove, arms, hat, face, breath, stand upright. Go!

He passed by Sam's house again. Sam, he thought, was a breed of person he would have hated before. Not hated. Had no taste for. I'm better than this, he thought.

Mr Fin stopped for a moment on the hill, gasping, and looked back toward the water, imagining as best he could the figure of Hart Crane, placed him standing in the collapsing waves, looking spat out—how he clings to life! He would pace ashore, having escaped from some undersea prison, braving uncounted perils, now striding with purpose, oblivious to his own needs, to find the young rabbits and their mother, yes, weakened, near dead, he pressed on.

Mr Fin rushed through the house, dropping his hat on the floor and tossing his coat over a chair. He stopped at David's half-opened door. Will he still be there? Had he really come home?

He was, he had. Mr Fin lowered himself beside David on the floor, exhausted. They were quiet for a long while, late into the morning or long into early afternoon, Fin couldn't be sure. Here together in this room, though David had never lived here, Fin felt the pang of old times, though he couldn't say they'd sat together quite like this, but they might have, or when David was very young, certainly they must have gotten down to play on the rug, with bits of beach glass and old coins. That might have happened. Did he tell him stories then? Yes, he might have. They would have used driftwood and plastic animals, stuffed bears and pillow mountains, made them fly, talk, beat on each other like puppets, adventure to the far corners of the room.

Fin said, smiling, "I had a dream about Mr Crane." He thought for a moment. "I've been having."

He touched David's cheek with the back of his fingers, taking his temperature. He had curled up on the towels, like a little boy pressed into his blankets for a nap. Fin fixed the blanket over David's shoulders.

"You remember our old stories? Do you remember how Mr Crane met Mrs Rabbit? You remember? Hart Crane, the rabbit, swooped down and rescued her when she was about to be eaten by a zeppelin, pulled her by the collar into his wooden ship." He showed with his hands how the ship sailed up from the depths of the carpet. "She asked him to help her rescue her children, and together, they zoomed through the air to her village, and they gathered them all. That was how their adventures began. And Mr Crane would tell stories on the ship. And I would fall asleep telling you, stories in the stories until there was nothing left but counting or lists of colors and birds, and you would elbow me, and sometimes I would keep telling the stories in my sleep, and you'd laugh at me." He pulled a pillow down from the bed and fitted it behind his back. "Did we ever finish one? Or just go on to the next?"

All that day, Mr Fin wandered his house with the rescue scene on his mind, the rope always there with him, even when he thought and did other things, the rope was there, dangling from a light fixture, from the porch steps, up to the branches of the tree, whatever kind of tree, that whole day, just how it had been when he described it to David, the thing he had always pictured: oily hemp, soft and fibrous, like giant yarn. He worked in the yard while David slept. He tidied the kitchen, checked on David, ate a good lunch, or dinner, and wondered if David would be hungry soon.

It had been a good night for a story because, that morning, the so quiet little David had shrieked, in a rare moment of defiance, rare but bursting, "Get out of my life!" Mr Fin knew that there was some nut or fruit or, no, machine part that was the precise weight of that moment in the larger scheme of things, part of the machinery that wrapped his son up in its churn, arm, gear-catch, and clatter to the brink, to the inhuman brink. "Out of my." Meaningless in the moment. A bad mood.

He remembered that day as if standing outside the house watching, seeing himself and his family through the windows: David in his room; Mother in the kitchen, or back and forth from the den to the basement; he saw himself pacing across the windows, cleaning, running the vacuum for an hour. He saw himself ready to walk out the door and walk and walk and carry himself right out of life, but somehow in his rage, his how-dare-he, he saw himself in the days to come, the days that never really came, saw himself watch his weak little son cry and struggle and break down, lose all his anger, lose all his, yes, lose all his independence, and need him, give in. He saw it as the natural centrifugal process of detachment, break and reattach again and again, until the child spins off into adulthood. If I died, if I went to war, if I left them all, if I never spoke again, if I became a statue, if I refused to hear him, if I emptied his room and threw out his clothes, if I threw out my clothes, if I changed my name, if

I told him he wasn't mine. One side of a father's love is absence, the favor of disappearing, not needing and not being needed. And so it is, he thought, we enter the broken world.

Fin said to David that night, after things had cooled down, been passed over, "When you're older, it's okay if you hate me. It's okay if you don't want to see me or call me. It's okay."

"But I'm going to live with you and mommy forever." David made baby eyes and gripping baby hands. Whatever the tragedy of the day had been, David had forgotten. Children don't know how to forgive, they absorb and keep everything, but they easily forget.

"What I mean is, you don't owe me anything. I won't be hurt. I don't really have to matter to you."

"Matter for what?"

"I mean. You know. Did you know, if someone was... or, if there was some reason that you were going to die, but then I could save you by dying, then I would, and only so you could be happy."

His body reacted, but fantasy intervened, "But if someone was going to kill me, I'd just punch them and kick them."

"Yeah. That would probably do it. No one has ever tried to kill me, though. You know? That doesn't really happen."

"Dad, come on. Tell about the bunnies." They settled in. "What happened to the bunnies' mommy?"

"Don't worry, they won't be alone for long. One of them will see a rope falling from the clouds."

David still had so much of his boyish face, lost somewhat, in the difficult wreckage of years, but it was here, Fin could see it. The boy was here waiting for a story. Fin said, "Mrs Rabbit saw a strange ship approaching, steered through the falling bombs and explosions by a rabbit. When it came near, the rabbit put out his hand, and without thinking, she grabbed it. She was rescued! But she still needed to find her children." David was so quiet. He might already have been asleep, but really he was half-way. The sound of a story sent David's senses away, turned his eyes toward the invisible, silenced everything but the thread of the dream, filled the space around them with the contours of their imagined world.

Once the story was over, Mr Fin would petrify in his gloom, on the child-sized bed next to David, the rabbit world draped from his shoulders, and himself trapped there on the mattress, on a landscape of quilts, David and he were the somnolent deities of rock and earth, not a peaceful feeling, but the terror of being here, a body among dirt, seas and stars. Fin thought of the phrase "putting him to sleep" at bedtime, thought bedtime stories, bedtime songs, bedtime snuggles, slowing the world, darkening, that all of it was about teaching children how to die. I'm teaching him how to let go of the world, how to leave it. The window sent him to the wide world of objects and space, so much space, waiting for his mind to let go of knowing, to distract itself. His wife would say, of such an observation, "It's not about teaching them to die. It's reminding them of the womb."

"What's his name?"

"Who's name?"

"The hero rabbit."

"Oh. Of course." Mr Fin had to think about it. "We could call him David."

"Dad! No." David was severe about this. It hurt to have his name misused.

"Well, then," Fin took his time. He couldn't decide if he thought the bunnies could really be saved from such an explosion. Instead, he felt the story wandering away from the wreckage, that it would float off across a map of possibilities. "I think his name should be Hart Crane."

"That's a funny name."

"It's a poet's name, or his nickname."

"Is he alive?"

"No, not anymore. Now he lives in a tower made of pebbles, and all around the tower is a lake floating in the sky."

"Is he trapped there?"

"He was, and he had a son like you. But his son left him one day, and Hart was alone. He couldn't write poems anymore, just bits and pieces of poems."

"What was his son's name?"

"It was Anatole. And after many years alone, Mr Crane decided to swim to the edge of the lake, to go and find him."

Mr Fin watched David's exhausted body on the floor. He could lure David awake with stories, lull his injuries and time, time too, away, use their story as a summons, a bridge between mouth and ear. As he told him about Mother Rabbit, he would speak out loud the parts he remembered, but not all of it, and other parts would intercede, unbidden, as if from the air in the room, or from the pain that crept behind his knees or the twist-tied nerves around his skull, the story telling itself in flashes and murmurs in the room around them, around their two bodies on the floor. The rabbit world had ended when David got too old, decades ago, but here it lived still between them, lived, but not as it had been.

Mrs Rabbit's body was thrown down, covered with filth, buckets, splinters, branches. She woke, lunging from sleep into nightmare, unsure if hours or minutes had passed. She ran at top speed, intent to gather her children. But she ran the wrong way. The world had gone backward, or the poles had switched, or the dust filled her eyes and all she knew was that the great sheaths of sky were ripped and tumbling down as the bombing continued, zeppelins diving hungrily through the village. Wherever the bombs hit, houses and buildings were chewed and spat out by invisible mouths. Screaming vowels stabbed the earth, becoming thick, cracked consonants, with tongues of fire escaping the fissures, glass and wooden teeth shattered in all directions. For the ears of Mother Rabbit, it was a symphony of knives.

The end was only noise: of the bombs completing their arcs and unfoldings, of monstrous engines clawing back up into the sky and away, the remains of houses coughing fire and smoke. The wake of the last roaring zeppelins was a bone-rattling vibration, trailed by a long-bodied shark of air that prowled the bodies and debris, snaring lives in its teeth as it wound through the grim foam of ash and smoke.

Mother ran. In the bleary stumbling moments, she felt a new tremor behind her, something crashing, almost upon her. She looked back. It was a wounded zeppelin, a small one, its body tangled in its own greasy blood and the wreckage of a radio tower—a twisted, sprawling armature that had snared the beast. As Mother ran, she heard the zeppelin wrench free. It wagged itself up from the ground, smashed a chimney with its tail, and climbed back into the air. With a mechanical, open mouthed growl, it dove back down in pursuit of her, hungrily pecking at mailboxes and lampposts and flipping them back into its throat.

In another moment, it had caught her up in its teeth along with pieces of the children's school. As Mother tumbled into its mouth, the zeppelin began its disorderly gnawing on the fresh mouthfuls of civilization. With a lurch and a satisfied leap against the air, it carried its meal up high, straining to rejoin its fleet.

The zeppelin's mouth was a great cavern, a garbage dump, all mouth and stomach and head, a domed theater of broken props. Mother scrambled to avoid being crushed among the shifting dunes of half eaten benches, windows, brick walls, sidewalks, doors, fences, tomato cages, trees, carts, café tables, couches, shovels, chalkboards, picture frames, paper weights, books, playground equipment, sprinklers, and unidentifiable chunks of village life. She leapt under a battered school desk to hide. The giant trap chewed through rafters, lamps, and rocks as it trundled itself out of the village. The mouth couldn't fully close on its last bite, and Mother could see through the opening. She watched the village pan away beneath her, then emerald grasses, trees singing past, not too far below, some even scraping against the zeppelin's belly. When the curtain of trees flashed open, she saw the sapphire vein of the river. Around her, the clockwork of the zeppelin growled into action.

The chewing shook the wreckage all around her, and Mother ventured from her shelter, clambered up to the top of the shifting pile. A quick look and she saw no other rabbits, none of her children. But it was dim, and the beast was surging up and down, accelerating then colliding stupidly against columns of hard air. She yelled for them, grasping, she noticed, her own garden gate, she yelled for anyone, but heard no replies. As pieces of her village cracked and slid, crumpling when caught up in the teeth and gears of the mouth, she leapt onto whatever she could climb, deeper into the belly, yelling for her children.

The beast flew, working tongueless to close its teeth on its horde. "Eldest! Brother! Sister! Little Ones!" Gears squawked and clanged to eat. Mother had no time. She struggled back toward the teeth, waiting for a moment when the mouth opened just wide enough. The teeth ground down, twisting a lamppost, shattering glass and timber all around her. Almost shut. The mouth opened again—a burst of air. Mother leapt through.

A second later she was falling against a cushioning wind, thousands of ethereal hands that might carry her to the ground. A heartbeat, and the hands were gone. Mother spun through the blue-green void, up and down and sideways all juggled her body, whipped her, abandoned her. She had the presence of mind to come to grips with things, to say to herself: it was right to do this, to take the chance. I was trying to get back to them. Whatever happens, this was an act of love.

Mr Fin watched David's sleeping body. In the dark—no, in the light. He seemed tense, dreaming fitfully, when the front door shrieked four times from its wooden core—bombs, teeth, all around the house! Chomp-chomp-chomp-chomp! He could feel the zeppelins, cloud-like dream creatures, all pretend, but chewing, chewing, in the closets and drawers, just behind him, under the bed, under the windowsills.

Mr Fin hauled himself up, legs asleep, body aching with the goo of sleep. He looked down the hall. The doorknob rattled, twisted this way and that. Knocking again. His mind settled.

Must be the woman with the baskets. What was her name? Leave a basket and go, he thought. The knocking cracked through the air, blistering sound. Christ! He still pictured Mother falling toward the ground, the bunnies lost in the explosion. But the images were flat, dead, and the story wouldn't continue in his mind, he couldn't see the next pieces, couldn't make them survive. Knocking again, insistent.

He eased the bedroom door shut, a sleepy click, still too loud, and he limped on his beehiving legs, stepping soft. Even his buttock had fallen asleep. Leaning on the kitchen counter, he shook his legs. Had he shut David's door? Yes.

She's still there. She'll wait forever! He slid a dining room chair out, making as much noise as he could, and hobbled from it to the door, as if he'd just gotten up. He turned the bolt and cracked the door. Here she was, no, maybe, probably—who was it? What was her name? Really, it didn't matter. He just needed to get rid of whomever it was. "I'm sorry," he said, "I don't want to buy anything, and I won't convert to anything."

"Fin!" She laughed and walked right in, a basket under her arm, athletic shoes, hair a victim of the breeze. Hadn't someone already been by today? How many baskets does she have? Do they all have them?

Mr Fin remembered the real problem: David. Mustn't let her wander the house. He tried to think of an excuse to make her leave.

"I was just going to take a sh—."

She was stopped near the kitchen, noting the labels, the several remaining, the few blacked out, those torn down. Her face went motherly for half a moment, then she decided to let it pass. She scooped up the papers from the floor and slipped them into the garbage, put something from her basket into the fridge.

I'm not a child, he thought.

She toured the kitchen, assessing each item, surface, as if she might like to buy something, or she was making sure it was all there. Mr Fin could see that she wasn't looking at him, that she was preparing her face, trying to look natural, happy, happy. Fake.

At the table, she put her hand on the back of the chair and scanned the glossy oak. "You and Sam get some time together?"

The chair was pulled out at that angle, that angle at which one leaves a chair when getting up to answer the phone, the door, or get a drink. He had done that. But there was nothing on the table, no puzzle, no water-glass, nothing at all. What would she imagine—him sitting there pitifully, blankly? Stupidly? Maybe it was Sam. Sam had come by. He'd sneaked in and taken away the puzzle, the sunset puzzle. Or was this all the result of keeping Sam away? Sam brought the puzzles, set them on the table.

He saw it in her face, the concern, the struggle to formulate a question at once respectful, innocent, but probing, probing. What did she want from him? How many basket women were there?

"Have you had any lunch?" Now she was trying to catch his gaze.

He dodged her eyes. Mustn't let her wander the house. "I was just going to take a— to sit on the porch." Fin moved for the door, wishing she would follow him out. He could keep her on the porch.

From the open door, he watched her slide the chair under the table. She ran her fingers through her hair, taking a big, fussy breath. "How about a sandwich... or cottage and fruit?"

Without another word, as if she had some business here, she waltzed toward the back, past the guest room, and into the study. What was she up to? Had he closed David's door all the way? David would be anxious. He would want the rest of the story. He can't get to sleep after a cliffhanger.

Fin let the front door shut. His legs wouldn't work; skin swarmed.

She came back with a dirty glass in her hand. She was going to clean the house! She rinsed it and set it in the sink. The sound of glass on porcelain reminded him of cracking teeth. She rushed back to the study and returned waving a book at him, saying something sing-song. Which book did she have, which book?

What next? She'll barge into the bedrooms, looking for stray socks. Mr Fin panicked, and he was furious. If she was going to treat him like a mad fool, then he would act like one. "Get out!" he shot, stamping across the room. His legs were melting, but he trudged on.

She froze, shock in her eyes. Good.

"I don't need you people!" Mr Fin put on a face of wild alarm, pounded the kitchen counter. Act crazy, he told himself. He gripped one of those labels stuck to a cabinet, peeled it off and cast it down for good measure. Words like roaches on everything, he thought.

"It's me," she said. "What's happened?"

"Son of a bitch!" he yelled. "Intruder!" He smacked the countertop, avoiding her eyes. "You're a nurse, a fucking nurse. I don't need a fucking nurse! Get out of here!" What else does one say? "Don't you hurt me! Just get out!" He pointed to the front door and backed away from her, as if afraid. "Sonuvabitch!"

She went for the phone.

He shrieked, "Just go!" and held onto the sound, let it crack from his throat into a whine until he coughed. His knees went wobbly for a second. He pressed the counter to keep himself up. He gasped, "Sonofa-." What next?

She approached to comfort him. "Fin," she was saying, "Tell me about your boat, tell me about The Swan." She tried to say something else.

He pictured The Swan, saw it whole, launched into the waves, and saw it dismantled, ripped apart in the garage. Ripped apart in the garage! He screamed. He screamed for the boat to be together again, for it to fall apart years ago, both —everything. He screamed to be rid of it, to forget it. He yelled at her, "That fucking boat! That fucking boat! That fucking boat!"

He waved his arms up, slapped his knees, punched his temples with his fists.

She tried to approach again, to grab him.

He pulled open a drawer. Wrong one: forks, spoons, butter knives, antique egg beater. He brandished the egg beater at her, banged it against the counter. "Just get out! Why won't you just leave me alone! I don't know what else to do!"

He saw the confusion and sadness on her face.

He couldn't do it anymore. He waited, elbows on the counter, wishing his legs would wake up, glaring at her feet. "Why are you doing this to me?"

The woman backed away. He heard her feet against the cedar porch.

He limped to the window to watch her rush down the sidewalk, back to her mysterious basket garden. How many more of them would he need to fend off?

The phone rang a minute later. He was still standing at the window. He let it ring. He realized he was panting, his heart racing. He must have put on a good show.

The phone started up again, ringing seven times. For the next hour, it rang every few minutes. Who did she think was going to pick up?

He could have kept standing there, at the window. His legs were better now, like posts, pylons scabbed to the crust of the earth, his head was a tree house, a tower. But he felt the eyes of the world through the window. David's windows, too, might be open. He needs his rest, some peace and quiet.

Mr Fin closed all the curtains, graying all surfaces from room to room. He locked the back door, the storm door, and turned the bolts. For a time, he wandered aimlessly in the house, noticing how everything was arranged just so, how different each object seemed, shut off from the sunlight, concealed here with him. A bowl, a doorknob, a magazine, a toaster, a spoon, a pencil, chair, mug: tidy chunks of the planet floating in diffuse and dusty shade. In the thickened air, glowing threads of sea-green dust drifted wherever light crept in. He felt he might float there weightless, that in a moment, everything would be lifted by the eternal current. Each thing was itself and not itself. Here was the airless world of the sea, swimming deep underwater, camping in the tideless reaches.

He cleaned the kitchen, plucked and peeled at a number of the labels, ripped some off the cupboards, crumpled up the papers and left them on the floor. He needed quiet.

Evening went quickly to night. Feeling truly, pleasantly alone once more, Mr Fin thought of David, waiting for the next part, teeth brushed, pajamas on, the plot lines already inhabiting his body as he waited, tucked in, already entrancing himself by mentally recounting scenes, becoming all the characters, feeling them as if they were part of his own body. When the rabbit worked the pulleys, David felt his own arms working the pulleys.

"Do you remember the brave goat-boy? He and Hart Crane helped Mother Rabbit to find her little ones again."

"I like Hart Crane."

"Why do you like him?"

"He has the ship."

"Ah. Maybe the ship has him."

David mulled this over. "Is the goat-boy going to be the governor of his own island still?"

"Yes, eventually, he does do that. But in the beginning, he's been hurt, and mother helps him."

She said, "Hello. Hello. Can you hear me?" Then Mother said, "Be alive."

"Who is she talking to?"

"The goat-boy."

'What's he doing?"

"Just lying there."

"Where?"

"In the grass, by the river."

"Is he going to die?"

"No. Remember? No of course not."

"How did he get hurt?"

"Just listen."

The goat boy hummed in pain and rolled its—his—head on its horns, revealing the outset eyes and, upon opening, the rectangular irises of a goat. Tilting on its horns, vest torn, filthy with dried grass, the creature croaked bubbles of distress as it fell onto its back.

"What are you?" Mother took a step back, stricken as she took in the whole shape of the creature. It stopped moving, its breath bubbling from deep within. Mother persevered, touching a few fingers to the neck. She felt the regular beat of a heart, scanned the torso for blood. She could see no dire emergency. "You are some sort of goat."

The creature blinked at her, seemed to smile or grimace, or both. "I was a goat." It gasped, desperate, buzzing like a kazoo. Mother couldn't make out the words. "Now I am almost a boy."

"You poor thing." Mother came close again, kneeling by the creature's head. "I can't hear you very well. What happened to you? Can you stand up?"

"It hurts." Achingly, the creature nodded and raised itself up onto its elbows. "Did you see the elephants? They left me here."

Mother tried to understand, but realized that it wasn't the voice or the pain that muddled the creature's speech, but speech itself had fallen apart in him. Instead of words, it spoke some guttural animal language. She pressed her palm against its—his—forehead, felt what mothers feel in that way. She saw how young he was, saw it in his nose, his ears, the little nubs of soft horns hidden behind his bangs.

"Something has happened to your voice, dear. I can't understand what you're saying! Can you understand me? Nod your head if you can understand me!" It occurred to her that the goat might not really be understanding her, and, given their situation, given the slight hope she'd felt at finding a fellow in the wilderness, to be unable to speak to each other would be appalling.

The goat-boy nodded carefully. "I understand you." Then, turning away from her, looking at the air just past his shoulder, he said, "Perhaps you can speak with my friend."

"You understand! Listen, I see that you've been hurt. Your leg, it's— You were caught in the raid, yes? Many have... I am looking for my children. I- I've lost my whole village. It can't be far. If we find it, we'll find you some food there—and medicine. I can help you. Are you in very much pain? You must come with me. Will you?" Mother gestured to be sure she was understood, then made to leverage the odd goat up by the arms. He gasped as his weight shifted, blood shifting too, and she saw his pant leg and shoes were soaked.

The goat put one skinny arm around Mother's shoulders, and, awkwardly, the other out around the empty air. Mother moved to lower this other arm, but the goat waved her off. Somehow it helped him balance. They walked along the river. Whenever his injured leg touched the ground, he hissed with pain. She could feel his wavering fever in her arms. The goat kept changing his gait, searching for the right way to operate his misshapen body.

He was an ugly child. Most goats have an innocence about them, something this one still possessed in the eyes, but the rest of it, him, was malformed, rearranged. Mother hated to think what the poor thing must look like under its suit of clothes. How on earth did it manage to move its legs that way?

Mother steered them down river. Her mental map of this country was vague, but of the river she was sure enough. It would take them toward home. They made little progress before she stopped them to rest. In the dirt, as characters did in stories, she tried to sketch out for herself what she had seen from above, from the zeppelin: the course of the river, as much as she understood it, a series of hills, some short, some tall and rocky, a line of trees, a few distant landmarks, and she traced a line for them that avoided difficult passages. Staring at the finished map, however, she saw nothing of great use, no secret paths, no strategy, and perhaps she needed none, but she felt a loss, too, where the map should have offered at least the hope of clarity, a mere abstraction peered back at her.

Meanwhile, the goat-boy had worsened where he slumped, a child's doll propped against a boulder. His eyes studied the air beside him. "Why don't you speak to her?" he said.

Mother approached. "Are you okay? Do you need something?" He didn't respond. His head sagged. She stood over him, not sure what to do, rubbed her neck and arched her back. She wanted to get moving again, and here he was falling asleep. They had too far to go. She had too far to go.

The goat-boy's weight slid further down the boulder as his eyes, gold-leaf and gray, shut in a combination of sleep and concentration, and Mother heard this voice from nearby:

Please forgive me. Do not be frightened. You can't see me, but I am here with you, and here with the goat-boy, my poor friend, brother goat. He does not realize how difficult it is for me to be heard. See the pained expression on his face? I'm afraid he is lost and hurting inside. It is an effort for me to be heard. I am his imaginary friend. It is no trouble for he and I to speak and work together, but it is a great effort for me to communicate with others. We must repair his leg wound. Though I'm not sure it will help, in the end. Please nod if you understand me.

Mother nodded.

The goat-boy roused and gave the rabbit a pleading look. "You heard?"

Mother understood the look, the tone. "Your friend?"

She counted the steps they took through the remainder of the day, every ten, twenty steps calling to mind the granules of sand and dirt in her map, nothings of progress, and she wondered how long the goat could live on. She chose shorter and shorter destinations: that tree, that rock by the river, that patch of bright grass, all the while a joyous blue sky reminded her how the world stretched across marvelous distance.

Mother talked soothingly to him that evening. She tended his leg, or pretended to. What she could do was so little, she feared, for it was broken in two directions and bleeding eloquently by various wounds. Every step, she realized, must have been agony. As night fell, she collected material for a fire, and they both curled toward it and waited to sleep. As soon as the goat-boy was snoring, the voice returned, humming softly... and soon the humming separated into words, sung carelessly, often whispered and tuneless.

Mother smiled at this, sensing the affection between them.

When it stopped all at once, Mother had the sense of it turning toward her.

Madame Rabbit, it said. Please. The voice had moved closer, stretched across the low fire, please don't leave us.

Mother waited a while, then said, "My eldest, a boy, he loves school. He has been sprouting, eating up everything in the house, if I let him. He's like his father, in some ways, but really, I think he takes after me. Not like most boys. He really sees people, you know, understands their feelings. My youngests are just starting to babble, a few words each." She stopped, throat filling. "And they still tumble and play for hours. They still wet their beds. I do the sheets every morning. It's so frustrating, but I think I'll miss it, in a year or so, I'll miss the laundry. I'll miss them being so... I don't know. I'll miss knowing every bit of their lives, bathing them, when they grow."

The voice waited, long enough that Mother thought it was gone, that maybe it hadn't been listening. It said, When did you last see them?

"I don't know how long. We were separated in the attack."

But you think they will be okay?

"Yes."

And your village?

"I don't know." Mother tried to remember what she had seen, the number of zeppelins, the number of fires in the distance.

We can help.

"What usually happens? What are they trying to do?"

The voice came close and soothing. Mother questioned how she heard it, for it felt now as though the voice were her own thoughts, somewhere inside her, but still very real, very much not her own. When we find your children, it said, there are places we can go. We can hide. I will help you.

The voice was distant again, somewhere else. Then: I promise you, the goat-boy will be able to help your family. We are from a wealthy line of goats, and we are grateful to you. We can help.

David seemed dry enough to be put to bed. Fin had a hard time getting the whole body collected up in his arms—like lifting a load of laundry. He had pulled the sheets down, so now slipped the toes, heels, shins, knees down into the warm envelope of blankets, laid the back, shoulders, and then the head down, propped handsomely on the pillow. He positioned the head to resemble comfort. He drew the sheets up to the chest. He wanted to smile. He was trying to smile.

But he had to look away. He heard the story in the room around them, and felt himself in the role of Mother Rabbit, and David, his eldest, hovering between life and death.

He gathered up the wet towels and put them in the laundry.

He swept up David's book from the floor, let it fall open: "the subject is quieted when the object ceases," inky blue cursive at the top of the page.

The house was dim. The curtains drawn. Light oozed in from around them, the curtains and the shades, wounds of brightness that made everything, bookshelves, table, chair, all flat and thin, ghostly.

Many of the pages in David's book had slipped their glue, but the thing held itself together. He could never read it all. Perhaps, he thought, now, perhaps now, all that text, pointless text, could be carved away, leaving nothing but David's voice in the margins, and Fin could read his story, his untangled voice. He could scratch at it, pick the written words off and tug them free like loose strands of stitching in a hem, pluck them away and chew them, as Hart had done.

In the grey morning, they labored for every few feet, the goat boy leaning hard on Mother. His mouth hung open—a breathing tube, not a mouth—a sad extension of the lungs. The day moved slowly, and for every step gained Mother saw the steps she might have taken stretching out before her. How certain could she be, that the goat-boy would die without her?

In the evening, Mother sat up, stared across the fire at the goat-boy, waiting for him to fall asleep. She listened to the night and the small fire. She thought of her children. The goat and his friend were too slow. The boy looked bad. He might die in the night, and she would be free to go. She knew that it was cold to think this way, but she couldn't help it. Which was the greater weakness?

As soon as the goat-boy was asleep, the voice returned, humming at first, then it stopped.

Hello, it said.

Mother replied, "Hello again." She was surprised at how nice it felt to hear a voice, and she knew at once it was for two reasons, for companionship, and to say goodbye.

You are being a great help to him, to both of us, the voice said. Though at first it seemed to come from the goat-boy's body, or just behind it, now the source had drifted up and to the side.

"What do I call you?"

Oh. The voice hesitated. I'm sorry, I'm not sure... Mother kept trying to guess the age of the voice, but it was both old and young, and, as she listened, she was frustrated that it was both male and female, or neither, or something else.

"But where are you from?"

We are from this; I am from the goat-child.

"You mean the goat, himself, from—?"

Himself. I am from him. I think—. The voice halted. Mother tried to listen for breathing, heard none. I think it is possible that I am him. It's hard to tell, you understand, if there is really a place where I stop and he begins. It's difficult for me to say what I am.

We've always been together, as long as I can remember. The voice went on, taking on a warmth and moving a little closer to Mother's ears. When he was a child, I stayed very quiet. There was much to see and learn. I could have spoken. I could have helped him then, but I didn't. I think he still knew I was there. He knew I was watching, and he would say little things to me. He would stare about the room, trying to see me. He knew which things of his I liked, and he cared for them differently, held them as if for me to see.

The voice paused, but it was a pause without lips or throat clearing, or stray glances, and so it was also a complete stop, filled with spacious night and the fire pecking at the air.

At some point I began to speak clearly to him, to even, in some sense, know that I had to speak to be understood—that there was something different about our minds—it was after he'd learned how to play games... he learned how to stop thinking, to force me to do it for him. So he would move his pawn, then turn the board and wait. I couldn't help but work out the next move. He wouldn't do it. Eventually, I spoke out loud, in our way. Not in this way, as I speak to you. This came later. There is a new gap between us.

Mother prodded the fire with a stick and stretched out on the ground, her head resting on her bundled cardigan. "What happened to him, to you—does it hurt?"

I don't hurt. I never have. I am, first and foremost, this voice. It is only recently, since the attack, that I have found myself capable of substance. Something changed when the elephants killed us, I mean, swallowed us.

"What elephants?"

The flying elephants, the eaters, they snatched us up with our home, all at once. Our family, his family, everyone was hiding in the basement. But it didn't matter. They rip up everything. We were in its belly for weeks, alone, for the others had all died. At least, the others were dead quite soon. We were fine. For no reason. Nothing we could do, nothing we did that helped us to live. But there we were. I hate it. I don't even know if he remembers anymore, or if he has given me his memories, you know, of his parents and his sisters. I remember them in such great detail, but, really, I care little for them. He should have kept them, his memories, if he could.

Mother felt her eyes finally drifting, and she regretted letting the voice go on. She had hoped to reason with it, to apologize, tell it that she had to leave, but she would send help, and so on. Now she just wanted to sleep.

It was almost always dark, but never quiet, inside the elephant. The world melted around us in a riot of whining gears and oil and distant contractions. We were being digested, processed. The space, as much as we could get a sense of it, was huge, a great hall dug out of the air. Sometimes we were free to move, and we explored. Other times, we were pinned by crumbling debris, and trapped where we were. Beneath our feet, we never encountered the inner surface of the elephant's body, only more debris and heat, unpleasant. We tried to stay atop the material. But after several weeks, we were soon to pass down into the heat ourselves. The easy thing to do was to rest, to close our eyes. We talked to one another. We shared dreams, some good ones, some not.

We waited. When the heat was unbearable, he told me so, but I did not feel it, and so I sang him songs and remembered things to him, places we had been, good feelings we had shared. He tried to listen and say things back to me, and that was how I knew we had both changed somehow. As he began to lose his ability to think, and as the pain infuriated him, its patience, its small degrees of increase, I found myself feeling differently, as though the heat were turning my liquid being to solid, more solid. It might be better to say, turning air into something you can touch, or is that just wind? I don't know. I became more me, and less him. I thought he was dying, but he did not die. Perhaps he should have. It would have been easy to die, he would have welcomed it, at last, at least he said so, that he would prefer it to the beastliness of living through it all. But we survived, of course. We came out of the creature and fell to the ground. I wonder if this is what happens to everything it eats—is there a trail of its waste across the continent? I haven't seen one. But he is different, as you see, not a goat anymore, but a goat-boy. I would say he is a monster, but that sounds pitiless. I know he will die. I know. And I know it's selfish...

The voice stopped. It had left the past, had begun to speak in the present, but it seemed to have nothing more. The silence persisted as Mother studied the goat's withering form in the dark.

Do you think— it said.

I just keep wondering

A breathless, bodiless pause.

what's going to happen to me, when it's over.

They staggered on until noon. Mother had to stop.

She was terribly hungry. The goat-boy wheezed on her shoulder. She dragged to a tree near the river. "We haven't got any food," she remarked.

She left him against the tree and stomped through the grass to the river bank. Mother washed her face, soaked the bloodied hems of her skirts. All at once, she felt a kinship with this part of the river. How was that? Some smell? Some deep memory? Some bond made in a lifetime of closeness, drinking, washing, watering her garden. She was close. Her children were close. She should be there already. These were the last moments, the moments that, if wasted, would become critical, become moments of tortured hindsight. She could have been with them by now!

She rushed back to the tree. She used her wet skirt to wash the goat-boy's face, part of it. "Time to wake up," she cooed. His skin went loose, face empty. He exhaled sleepy moans.

"No... we've got to keep moving." Mother paced.

The voice was there, humming to quiet the dull moans.

"I'm not sure I can..." Mother said, but she couldn't finish, not yet. Her head spun. Putting some distance between them, she urinated into the mud, where the stream would creep, then she wandered into the grasses and let her bones down in the thick mulch. What would become of her children if she did not leave the goat to die?

She woke to the knotting of her gut, having cried in her sleep and been rained upon. She pushed some grass into her mouth, chewed, spat it out. Anxious, she dragged her body up and went to see the goat-boy, to see if it, he, was still alive.

She could tell that he was asleep, crumpled, and moreover, she knew that his friend was there listening, perhaps was watching her, though with what eyes, she couldn't guess. What anything, for that matter?

She decided the silence between them would stand as an ultimatum. I'll count to twenty, she thought, then I'll leave. I will have to leave them, if they have nothing to say.

Alright, came the voice.

Mother could see it was nudging the goat-boy, to wake him. She waited. Her head shook involuntarily. No, she thought, I can't keep doing this.

We're ready, it said. It was not resolve in the voice, exactly, but not resignation, either. I don't think he's going to wake. I can't watch him like this. Help me. Before you go, help me.

In her readiness to be gone, Mother misunderstood. "No, I've just got to go. You two can get along, I'm sure."

Oh, please. You must. I can't by myself. The voice stopped, and Mother saw the goat-boy's body shifting again, sliding slightly, his arm lifting, waist tipping up.

"Just let him sleep," Mother said. She sat down, despite herself. "Don't you see, he only lived for your sake! He kept you alive! Didn't you listen to yourself?"

The movement stopped. Mother waited while the voice gathered close to her. We're going to roll him into the water, it said, and be done, all done.

Now she understood. Mother would have rather just left them, whatever it might say about her. "I can't."

The voice came very close. Mother could sense it straining toward her ear. I can't do it without you.

"I'm sorry," she said.

You must, it said, pleading, you must. The voice halted, then retreated, hovering over the goat-boy. I'm scared, too. You understand? I don't know what's going to happen. How could I do it on my own?

Mother turned. She followed the river, toward home, she tried to close off her senses, to not hear or know what unfolded behind her.

I can't, said the voice. I'll be all alone, it said.

Soon Mother's heart pulsed, avid, opening her chest, dispelling her hunger and exhaustion, and she ran toward her village, toward home, to her children.

Late in the afternoon, a single familiar tree suggested the path that would bring her home soon, not soon enough, but she could imagine all the ways between here and home. She had camped nearby, many times, and climbed the tree for apples, in her youth, and one ancient branch had a crook that she and her siblings had called the throne. One could sit in the throne and lean back against strongly knotted branches, gaze at one's kingdom. From the throne, one looked straight off into the emerald country of the wild.

She ran again, charged with anticipation.

As she came over a rise, Mother Rabbit cried out. She saw, in the not too distant air of the bright sky, a shadowy, tentacled figure hovering, impossibly kite-like, more-impossibly tree-like. She turned and hid in the shrubs behind the hill crest. Still, the creature crawled through the air toward her—she could sense it sensing her.

Mother raised her head up out of the leaves and took it in: its tentacles were branches, some of which reached great distances. The outstretched limbs sprouted wide leaves very much like kites, intricate wings like webbed hands. A few subtle flicks of a limb sent the creature sailing this or that way. It tilted toward her, treading through the air as its quiet shadow consumed her, then left her behind.

It hovered idly for a few moments, then landed—the combined movements of a giant umbrella, an intelligent bouquet of flowers, a spider unspinning its web, a hundred year old bonsai tree returning to seed, a wooden ship arriving at port, unrigging, dropping sails, pulling in oars.

Mother knew she should run, but she couldn't help but watch. Seated on the grass, the creature appeared now to be a wooden skull, long like a horse's, resting on a nest of muscular roots.

Mother could just make out a figure standing on deck, shedding an overcoat. She rushed closer, suddenly hopeful, and when the sun hit the figure, she saw it was a rabbit, ears pressed haphazardly under his city hat, dressed in shirt and suspenders, navy wool slacks. Not from her village.

He waved his hand at her, beckoning her to approach. When he could see her eyes, he said, "Mechanical consid—" shook his head, "The route... the route to..." he pointed toward her village.

It was enough, and Mother hoisted her way up the side, lifting from one tangled root to another. She'd nearly grasped the bottom rail when the rabbit in the ship reached an arm down over the side, gripped her by the shoulder, too tightly, and lifted her quick as could be, turning her round until she was seated on the top rail.

Mother swung her legs onto the deck. She rubbed her shoulder and took quick looks at the rabbit's unusual form. He was taller than most, and not just tall but stretched, as if onto his tip toes, and his face was unpleasantly flat. Unsettling. Mother knew at once, but put on her unremarking face, but she knew, he too had suffered passage through a zeppelin, like the goat-boy.

"I haven't eaten for some time," she said frankly, "If you have anything... And if you would take me to my home, I'd be so grateful. It's just there, on this side of the village," she pointed and watched his glossy eyes follow her hand, "To the southeast corner. It will only take you a moment. And you can be on your way."

The rabbit nodded, overly calm, she thought, and turned to look down at something huddled into the siderail. There, the crumpled shape of some variety of bear, an unhealthy one by the look of it, regarded her with two marble eyes. She almost said hello, but decided there was no need.

The rabbit curled his hand round the rail of the ship and gripped it hard. All at once the wooden skull launched itself into the air, and Mrs Rabbit fell head over heels across the deck.

Fin stood at the closed door to David's room, found a small pulley in his pocket amidst a dozen or so machine screws. He fit his thumb against the pulley wheel and made it spin. As he wandered to the garage, Mr Fin remembered the scene, in the sequel to Hemingway: Santiago stoked the small stove with bits of wood, leaving the remaining few logs for a truly cold night. He checked the bandages around his palms—his wounds tended to absorb the wrappings. Twice he'd pulled off good skin along with old bandage. Why would you do this to me, he said, to the great fish, to the great sea. My stigmata, he said to his hands. My whale, he said to the hut. My giant, he said to the marlin. My God, he said to the sea. My ark, he said to his pencil. My disciples, he said to the sharks. David, so quiet in his room, was probably reading or listening to music or practicing holding his breath. Fin dropped the pulley into a bucket. He had prepared the boat for sea this way, on David's periphery, in the cool concrete of a garage.

He went into David's room without knocking. David slept. He kneeled to examine the shuttered, quiet face, looking for signs. He thought he saw movement, a tremor in the left eye socket, the kicking fetus of a dream, turning under its lid. "Go ahead," he said. "I'm listening. I know you want to say something."

Nothing, nothing.

Hart Crane would swoop down and wake you, you'd feel the rhythm of the ship's wings and another rhythm from within. Hart Crane would let you rest in the sun while he gathered supplies from below deck. He would stride toward you, smiling, tapping his ear as though he'd just heard a secret. "You need words!"

Mr Fin gathered David's book, picked and tore at it: words, bits of words, sentences. He assembled them on the mattress in front of David, a puzzle, an array of pills, an alphabet. The slips of paper had a mute brightness, something escaping the pounded wood fibers, carrying the luminosity of speech.

He tugged gently on David's chin, pulling down his lower lip, and from there too, a smooth glow emerged, the weak, passive glow of a fish's eye, of apple juice. Tenderly, he fed the paper, like medicine, like a secret message through a hole in a wall, into his mouth.

Fin slid his chair up to the bed and leaned his ear to David's lips. He held still. He had to be perfectly still and quiet. He held himself in place for several long minutes. His eyes pinched everything out of existence but the imaginary tunnel between his ear and David's lips until at last, barely detectable, felt as much as heard, a hum sounded between them, building into a slight wheeze. David was waking.

Mr Fin's heart pounded in his head, his mouth broke open, but he held still, listening with all his might, and heard the air that halted behind David's lips to form a quiet, questioning,

"mm?"

That was all.

His face boiled with joy, a terrifying joy, a joy that tore at existence, tore at all false things, tore at days and hours to reveal spired eternities, between his ear and David's mouth two decades of hollow silence now sparked into grand and gold-vaulted interiors of light, a cathedral of sparks buttressing into a cosmos that lit, now, the days to come, lit them with words.

The voice, that missed so long uttering mouth, its kerning to and fro, that little boy could speak.

Tilted neck, exhausted, he quaked down onto the blanket, feeling against his forehead that familiar shoulder bone, feeling against his hair the shape of David's jaw, the warming open space of his neck.

"I love you," he said. "Please stay with me." He tried to listen, but his pulse pounded and his chest wept.

"Mother Rabbit was in the airship now."

"With the other rabbit?"

"Yes, and the bear, and the other bears—but she hadn't met the others."

"What's wrong with the bear?"

"We'll see. He'll be okay."

"Is he the bear who ate everything and fell in the water?"

"Hm. Yes, but that was a different story, like a dream."

"Did they get the bunnies yet?"

"Yes."

"All of them?"

"Yes."

"Even the eldest?"

"Yes."

"He's okay?"

"Of course. They are all okay."

"I thought he was hurt."

"No, they fly off and start a new village. The airship takes root and becomes a house."

Mother scanned the worn out earth below.

Finally she pointed and called to Hart. All she needed to do was point, and the ship changed course itself. It stopped in the air, among the clouds above what was once her property.

Hart was assembling a mechanism at the side, a cross between a dumb waiter and a telegraph system. He waved Mother over.

"Why don't we land?" She tried to stay calm, but she was frantic inside, ready to do anything.

Hart tried to think of what to say, how to say it. Finally, he patted the ship as if consoling it, then pointed to several fires below: trees, gas lines, the old Canard place—blackened. He shook his head.

Now she felt it in her feet, paws: the ship's pulse was erratic, scared.

Hart gestured to his pulleys, ropes, and gears, then he gripped Mother rabbit by the shoulders.

His eyes went deep, open. He was trying to have a moment with her.

She was in her own moment.

Soon enough, she was on the ground and her children were rising up above her into the airship. She counted them as they went up, lost count. She started over with the first, way up in the sky, counting them down like knots in the rope. With the last little one hooked and rising, she knew: Eldest Brother was gone.

She scanned the rubble. She didn't mourn for her home when she saw its remains. She didn't think of the labor of surviving, building, maintaining for all these years. She was of two minds: fear blazing white, the one, and the other admitting to herself that she had no idea what she would do when she found him, but that she must find him.

She took in the town itself. It was all scabbed over but for a few houses down the lane, apparently whole, perhaps others at the distant edge of town. If there were other survivors, she would have some help, but the village, more and more toward its center, was empty, eaten. She called out for help, for someone. In the silence returned, she heard the absence of everyone she knew. No matter.

A rat slipped up next to her from under some garbage, and she smashed it under her boot. "Filth!" she shouted. "Mange!" She scraped her boot clean in the dirt.

Scanning for other rodents, she grabbed a stub of pipe, stomped heavily on the rubble to scare away whatever else fed and flourished in decay. Horrible creatures, she thought.

A large silver one scampered blindly toward her and she swung at it, just missed and smashed an already smashed lamp. It ran off across a pile of bricks and under a pile of smoldering velvet curtains.

Mother had to sit and catch her breath. The silver rat appeared again, sniffing, wet muzzle, groaning happily. It held a headless baby doll from the rabbit children's toy chest in its arms, and it mocked affection, chuckling at her. Mother waited for her moment and swung, caught its skull with the pipe. The old rat staggered, then fell heavily into the dirt.

She had promised she would gather useful items as she found them, so tugged an oat sack from her belt, all the while wielding her bit of pipe as a bat. The wind shifted, and she pulled her scarf around her face to block the drifting tar smoke and the angry, morbid air of bodies opened on the ground. Soon, the rats were keeping their distance.

Several small sacks of supplies went up the line to the ship. Mother continued to breathe, to work, to move, despite the world around her.

The fur of a dead rabbit is different than the fur of a live rabbit. It is the first change. Later the eyes and eyelids begin to dry, and the lips, and the nose. Very soon the gums turn pale. Rigidity sets in where it can, while deep inside and at the site of any wounds in the flesh, softness persists.

How should Mother come upon this changing thing? What would she not rather endure?

She saw her son on the ground, wearing the same little slacks and button up shirt as he had worn nearly a week before, when she had not said goodbye, not held him enough, not made his favorite breakfast. She neared him on stuttering legs. She wanted to look him in the face once and pretend, just for a moment, that he was still there, but as she approached, she saw that a horde of glistening insects clutched into his eyes. She dropped beside him and swept them away, crushing and swatting what she could. Lazily, indignant, they hovered and darted back at him, and she fought them off again. He must be protected, she thought. She raced into the footprint of her house. One corner of it stood. No roof in sight. The iron stove had tipped over, coughed out its coals.

She found several folded linen sheets, unburnt.

He was not light, but she was still his mother. She managed, harassed in waves by gnats and flies, to wrap him well, his arms cozy and his ears gently turned down against his neck.

She lifted the body, him, feeling its gruesome weight, solid and hollow at once, and carried it to the rope dangling from the clouds.

When her first son's body was fastened and rising ahead of her, a queer relief fell upon Mother, and she gripped the line herself, held on as it lifted her: there was nothing to say goodbye to, nothing to love left behind.

"I remember what you would say when I found you, long after bedtime, eyes stuck open in the night. You'd always say,"

"Tell me a story."

"Once upon a time, there was a little bunny named Yasha—"

"Good. I like Yasha."

"—but she had to leave her home."

"Why did she have to leave?"

"There was an elephant stampede, a flood of elephants. But she and her family all escaped in a flying tree with the unusual Mr Crane. Do you remember Mr Crane? It was Yasha, all her brothers and sisters, her mother, Mr Crane, and the three little bears. They all flew away from the elephants. But they weren't safe yet, because there were also flying elephants, not like Dumbo, but with mouths like whales and teeth like hippos, and they had no legs. Some of them had curling tusks. They would even attack each other with these tusks. And if they didn't, then their tusks would get so large that they'd be weighed down and crash to the ground. At this point, now, no one knew much about Mr Crane, and everyone was surprised when, upon spying one of the flying elephants moving, like a dark cloud, in the distance, he steered the ship straight for it."

"Why did he do that?"

"That's what they asked him. Yasha's mother was yelling at him. The bears came up from below decks and grumbled in their deep, petrifying voices, but Mr Crane wouldn't listen."

"Was he trying to kill it?"

"You might think that. But Mr Crane was not interested in killing anything. In fact, he knew an amazing secret, something that no one else in the whole world could have known."

"Why didn't he just tell them all the secret?"

"I think he was scared. He wanted to tell them. But he thought he might be wrong...or that they wouldn't believe him anyway. Or he thought it was just a secret for him. And you know, he didn't talk much, except to tell stories."

"So what did he do?"

"Well, he flew right at the elephant. It wasn't moving much. It didn't seem to notice them approaching. It just floated there, as if it were resting after a big big meal."

"What do they eat?" David pulled close.

"Well, they eat villages. In fact, they eat the ground-elephants that eat the villages, the ones that stampede in... the flying elephants swoop in and eat them up and all the bits and pieces of the villages that are in their stomachs."

"Gross." David's body wiggled.

"Yeah. So—"

"I don't like this one. Tell me the one about the bears."

Oh.

Ok.

Here is the one with the bears.

Here is the longest story in the world. It's so long, that even if everyone took turns telling the different parts of it, it would still be impossible to finish. It might be that no one would know how to finish the story, and so getting to the end is no longer the problem.

But here is the part I know because I was told it. It's about the bears. It comes from a daddy bear leading his cub into the wintering den, and the cub needing a long long story to hibernate with. And the daddy bear says, Long ago, when bears were just the size of ants, even smaller than ants—like dust... and the daddy bear takes giant breaths between phrases, his barrel chest singing out a low, slow rhythm... and there might be a million bears gathered around the tiniest puddle, and they would call it a sea. And there might be a million bears on a rock, and they would call it a mountain. A hundred bears could drown in a drop of rain... A thousand bears could sail across a puddle, all huddled into the half-shell of a pistachio nut.

The daddy bear says, Now you know why this is such a long story. With so many bears, and so small, the world is a very big place. This is the part of the story with all those tiny bears and the part of the story before we bears come to be what we are today. Even if we skip hundreds of thousands of years, and forget about many millions of important characters, we'll only get through part of the story. So, he says, I'll tell you what I can remember. There was a little tiny bear. We'll call him David.

"No. Dad, that's my name."

Ok. His name is Little Bear, because he wasn't just little like all bears. He was young and very very small. He was also the hungriest bear in the world. One time, even when he was still very little, he ate an entire blueberry, which doesn't sound like much, but if you imagine a blueberry that to you is the size of… say… an elephant. Well, this was amazing, but it could also be a problem. You know, that one blueberry could have fed a hundred bears for a week, and he ate it all in one day. After eating the blueberry in one day, he was bigger than anyone else, and he could eat more, so he ate two blueberries the next day. The day after that, he was so big, he ate an entire purple grape. Then he was even bigger…

In the morning, David asked, "How does the story end?"

"It didn't end. You fell asleep, little bear."

Fin set out a cereal bowl, hot kettle in the other hand. It was still dark out.

"But how does it end?" David laid his head in the bowl, eyes sticky, cheeks pink.

"Well. I don't know. You always fall asleep. I've never had to get very far."

"What do you mean? Don't you even know the story?" Yawn.

Fin brought a spoon. "No. It's a bedtime story." He stuck the spoon in David's bowl. "Every time I tell it I just try to make a really boring part to put you to sleep."

David grabbed the spoon in his fist and sat up. "And then you fall asleep! And I have to wake you up."

"Yeah. You want Os or Flakes?"

"No." He put the empty spoon in his mouth, then let it fall out onto the table.

"Besides, I told you it's the longest story in the world. What do you want?"

"Toast." David ran to the couch, grabbed a picture book from between the cushions, then spread it out on the table. He stared at it, but didn't read. "Why does everything eat everything else?" he said, closing the book. "I just want to know about the bear. What happens after he eats everything?"

"The ants." Mr Fin topped off his coffee.

"What do they do?"

Mr Fin took a sip. It was a bit gritty. "Well, the ants get inside the littlest bear. They eat!"

"Dad!"

"What? They eat and the bear shrinks, and everything goes back the way it was. It's a happy story." He presses the bread down into the toaster.

"But you would die if you had ants living in you. Yuck. What if some just crawled in your mouth while you were sleeping and started living in you but not eating you or anything, you're just like their house. Is that possible? And if you closed your mouth, they had to crawl out your butt to get food. That'd be so gross!"

"That's super gross. I'm going to spread some ants on your toast."

"And you would fart ants!"

What if the ants never gave up? What if they laid eggs in there? What if a single stray ant got in there accidentally and hatched an empire of little legs and teeth?

"To a tiny little ant," he told David, "You're like a whole continent... maybe even a planet."

"Well then they are pretty good explorers. They go all over the whole galaxy."

David lay awake. He wanted to speak, but all the words had slipped away into the water, dissolved.

Once upon a time, he said, just over his breath, there was Hart Crane the rabbit, and he came to me as if with a secret. We were together, on the sea.

He trusted words, Mr Crane. Words over things, over the mind, over reason. That's part of the secret, I suppose. But what else? You know, I don't think it was the sea, where we were. But he dove into it anyway. He dove in. Maybe that's why he loves you.

Mr Fin said, I see you need more. You look so calm. You've rested well. Can you see me? Can you tell I'm here? I could tell you the ends of the stories. Would you hear them? Would you dream them? Have you already? Maybe you are dreaming what happened to the poor little bear. Maybe I hear your dream the way the goat-boy hears his friend.

Mr Fin groaned and pushed himself up from the floor. His knees might have been broken for all they protested. He limped into the study and grabbed the book, leaning for rest against his chair. David had carried his book everywhere, tucked under his arm, rolled into his pocket, pride of place in his satchel. His father observed that, in general, young people obsessed with a book are so painfully quiet because the book has become their role model.

Standing over David, he pulled out a number of the loose pages. Held them up. Here was David. He had come back so he could speak, so he could explain. Why else would he be here? "What did we hope to save?" he read on one page, "What could we do for him?"

He placed the margins and the text on the body of his son. "Can't you speak for yourself?" the book said. David's marginal notes clung to him, miniature thought bubbles or dissection labels.

"Why did he suck in each of our words so avidly?" the book said.

Mr Fin stayed by David all morning and all afternoon. Fin kept talking, telling stories. Repeated everything over and over as he ran out of ideas. He kept the shades down all day, felt the light would be too harsh, kept his voice quiet, or stopped speaking altogether, letting the story go on without him. Occasionally, David's eyes would flutter or his lips part, and Fin would wait breathless for long minutes before continuing the story. He placed David's book on the bed, by David's head, tried to make it look natural there. He used his hands as ears, sitting listening. Yes, he remembered his hand on his wife's pregnant belly, and putting his ear against her, and saying hello to David in there, all the perfect waiting they did together.

Theirs was a good enough love, he supposed, and it was the chance that they might remember it that made separating so easy, that it would not end but was ended, wrapped round itself and tucked away. Not for later. Otherwise, every look between them was a scar set backward in time.

In the evening, Mr Fin made himself some tea. When he returned to the room, David's hand was on top of the book.

Fin nearly dropped his saucer. Instead, porcelain rustling, he set it aside on the shelf and hunched over the bed. He placed his hand on the hand on the book and hovered close.

"Your book!"

The fingers were slightly bent into the soft cut edges of paper, as if about to draw it open.

"You want to read it..."

He urged David's fingers into the pages, pretended he was just watching as he turned the book open. "You're doing it," he told him.

Together, they leaned in close to the page, their eyes not meeting but staring together off into the same text. Between them, the book gave a dry pulse—of air between pages, of spine resisting and yielding, and Fin saw it clearly: it was a single vein, the text was a vein scrolling through the book, tangled, knotted and barbed with David's words, marginalia like tributaries and capillaries harshly pulled to the corners—but one long flow of blood without a heart.

David said, syllables all a clatter and tangle, stuck together: Memory that I am, yet that I also wait for, toward which I go down toward you, far from you, space of that memory, of which there is no memory, which holds me back only where I have long since ceased to be, as though you, who perhaps do not exist, in the calm persistence of what disappears, were continuing to turn me into a memory and search for what could recall me to you, great memory in which we are both held fast, face to face, wrapped in the lament I hear: Eternal, eternal; space of cold like into which you have drawn me without being there and in which I affirm you without seeing you, knowing that you are not there, not knowing it, knowing it...

He went on speaking, deflating, words coming more dryly until his voice trailed into a hum, into a possible hum, in the walls or in the distance.

Mr Fin was beside himself, desperate to hold his son and not to lose a single word of what he'd said. He clutched his forehead, made his own notes in the margins of David's book. He sat still for hours, going over the phrases he remembered, committing to them. It was late in the evening that Mr Fin felt, in place of the voice, a calligraphy of shadows possess the room, a net of words carved by light holding each artifact in place, or taking it to another, naming or changing it: the words themselves, the story itself, wrapping the two of them together.

Mr Fin eased his hands into the first box: t-shirt, jeans, graduation jacket, necklace, hat, summer camp shirt, book, book, letters, pictures in frames, blue ribbon in something. The smells were intoxicating, but everything, now, was intoxication. He tried not to think, just lifted each object out from its place and laid it somewhere else on the end table, dressing table, or on the chair, or on the bed. He had the feeling of being two places at once: this room, where things were uncertain but where pain had turned to hope, and David's childhood room, where, he supposed, the opposite was true.

The second box was all books, and at this, Mr Fin was at first bereft. What an idiot he had been to save such things.

Nonetheless, he set them on a shelf, and they surprised him with a new game: he thought that he might be able to remember the order they had taken in David's collection. He would not have arranged them by author, but by theme or value or size or by the sequence in which he'd read them or intended to read them. So Fin changed the order around a few times, testing the possibilities, and pulled their spines right up flush to the edge of the shelf, altogether, shoulder to shoulder. Yes, these were cherished friends. They were not like the book he had written in, but from another time. Perhaps they were the world of books that followed after the bedtime stories. In these, David's internal vision had sought new refuge, all the rabbits and bears and goats took on new masks.

He went to the bedside to tell David, to tell him how his room was coming along. But there was a problem. Fin heard rattling sounds. From the look of the eyes and the pallor spreading up his chest and neck, across his cheek, Mr Fin guessed that one of David's lungs wasn't working, had broken in the rush of words, or had slipped out, maybe in the shallows, in the sand, or on the sidewalk, or in the sea.

He would have to find it.

Mr Fin went out immediately, in the middle of the night, or whenever it was, it was dim. A lively, art-deco sea was drawing within feet of the concrete barrier, among the rocks and petrifying trees, the night parade of floating bodies, living and dying, going out and coming in. He rolled his pant legs above his knees, rolled his sleeves, and slogged in. The water was shockingly cold, but he felt it only from a distance. His mind was elsewhere. He flipped on his flashlight and searched the water. He could imagine the lung catching on a branch or caught up with seaweed. After half an hour, he began to despair. Of course, it could have washed back out, or never come in at all. The tide was moving, though Fin couldn't tell which way, which way was walking in, which way out. He was up to his waist, and then a few steps later only to his knees, and then to his waist again. He kept going. Keep going, he told himself.

He couldn't see the outline of the port anymore, or any trees. Just waves and piles of waves, ephemeral shallows wandering the sea. Finally, he came to an island of rocks, and in their midst was calm water. He waded in. Something warm in the water tickled and bit him around the knees. He stabbed his light into the depths. The water was full of lungs! It was a colony of lost lungs, taking refuge from the tide. They were difficult to grab, and several fell apart in his hands, but eventually, he snared a large, slow lung and brought it up in his palms. The lung trembled in the cold air.

A little bear cracked out of its porcelain egg, growing, growing bigger than any bear had ever grown before. While other bears were scarcely larger than ideas, this little bear ate and ate until he was the size of an acorn, then he ate and ate until he was the size of a plum, and then he ate and ate and ate until he was the size of a cantaloupe, and he kept eating and growing, so much so that he believed he was the only bear in the world, and felt very much that he was in a world of his own now, a world unlike the one to which he'd been born, because here were things one could grab, here was something more than the bumping and gusting of microscopic life. Now there were colors, leaves, textures, soft and hard places, airy and dense places, temperatures, and what's more, there were new things to eat, and he was hungry: he was all mouth. In not too many years, he was a hillside of a bear, and it entered his mind that, someday, he might be able to eat the world itself. But a terrible thirst possessed him. He had been so focused on eating and was still not used to needing water, so he had not drunk a thing for years. He maneuvered his mass toward the ocean, rolling a bit and scraping his claws into the dirt to steer, nibbling away as he wished: sweet and bitter trees, quick lizards, crunchy rocks and velvety gardens, wiggly rabbits, long noodly ivy, crunchy birds' nests. Not just those but also snake eggs, cattle, small houses, machines, vegetable carts, the silly elephants, and more.

Hart Crane paced and gestured as he told the story.

The ocean was not nearby, but he could smell it as he approached, eating everything he could along the way. Finally, from the crest of a mountain, he could see it. All he had to do was roll down, and his momentum, he figured, would take him all the way to the water. He hadn't heard about salt water. But that's not important. He rolled and rolled, taking bites out of the mountain itself and then, at last, splashed into the water. He kept rolling, but he didn't mind, because now he drank and drank and had no doubt that he could drink the whole thing. But he could not. He sank into a very deep part of the ocean, beyond knowledge of the sun, still drinking and eating, sucking in fish and sharks and whales and walruses and kelp and shrimp and seaweed and more and more until finally, gulps gulping tightly packed, a little painfully, it was too much. He was hardly a bear anymore. He could feel it. He could feel that he was, compared to the things he had consumed, that he was a very thin shell, a kind of atmosphere around a world of trapped and uprooted things, slowly living on. He had thinned out into an ozone, a gathering, no longer a gatherer. He closed his mouth. He closed it tight. He waited.

Mr Fin found his way home at dawn, having carried the lung all the while in his cradled palms.

He pulled a chair close to David's bed and fitted the lung in place. He was no doctor, but he knew the body would adapt.

He stroked David's forehead, hummed a soothing tune.

"Sweet boy. Just relax. Picture this: picture all the beautiful pearls of oxygen hidden in the air, and when you breathe in, breathe in slow, from your tummy, all those pearls are collected by tiny little cells, like little fish swimming around in your body, they suck up the little pearls of oxygen and carry them around, to your blood, to your bones, to your muscles. And when you are relaxed, the fish bite down on the oxygen, it bursts like a... like a... tiny water balloon, full of... of. It's full of numbers and letters, and the numbers and letters sing a little song for your body."

David was awake, turned his head and clicked, "Da—"

Mr Fin made a cry of joy he'd never heard from himself before.

"Da-da-da-da-da-da-d-a," David said. His lips moved, searching. The body, too, made slow turns, a subtle dance. "Th-ba-be-bo..." He was working so hard. Fin pulled the blankets back down to David's waist to give him room to move. David's body gestured and babbled through a strange alphabet of dregs, saying at last, "Th bear, th bear nnn th heart," and he was exhausted.

"It's okay. I'll tell you the story."

Chapter Four

The sky had turned a fleshy yellow as evening wore impossibly on. The bear worked to explain, in his uncertain, tiring manner, his not always well-chosen but hard-won, dry or drooled phrases, that the ship chased the sun. The bunnies, four or six or eight, sat in a circle, big eyes and straight ears, attentive to his words and hand-signals.

Yasha found it easy to understand his charades and mumbling. She knew what story he would tell, for he pointed first at the distant green mountains, then gestured to his bear heart.

She understood that bears evolved from trees and once were cousins to the roots. Repeated destruction of delicate bark by wild hogs had led the mother trees to grow the small, fierce, root-like bears above ground, wriggly and aggressive, with simple claws and teeth. The first bears were like living branches, eating whatever tried to scratch or scale the trunks to which they were bound. They protected the seedlings well enough, but these clumsy, tethered monsters were themselves eaten by the parachuting father leaves, by cunning hunters in the air, and by those who climbed from above instead of below. One season, the bears learned to gnaw through their own woody umbilici and thereby separated from their mothers. Some managed, unhappily, to mate with one another, and began to change. Pitiful, but free. Wandering, the bears faced more danger and, what's more, shirked their duties.

This would not do. The mother trees, forgetting why they'd grown the bears to begin with, were desperate to protect them from harm. Their rippling bark, which had the capacity of what we now call muscles, grew wide-walled skirts to contain their new brood. It took centuries, and sweet, aqueous mother blood or mother milk rivered down their chests, across their linked arms, forming lakes in the interior labyrinths of their bodies, or down their backs, to the ocean, a weird alchemy in the tides. They gorged on the earth and the sun, growing into living towers, fortresses to protect and keep their monstrous offspring. Having lived for millennia as a majestic forest, protecting the small trees, loosing the ravenous fathers in the wind, sharing the sun and the soil, they ended an age so they could prevent the suffering of their soft, vicious dropplings. What promise did they imagine for the sad, toothy, hobbling little bears?

This was not much of a story to tell. The bear was humble about this. But it was the first story, the first letter of the alphabet of stories.

Though he was clearly tired of gesturing, the bear went on, more quietly, amusing the patient bunnies. But now he told a story of adventure that Yasha only gradually understood. In her version of the story, she saw the bear as the hero, venturing into the wooden mountain of mother trees, deep into its carved passages. He carried a spear. She imagined this was the story of how he became what he was, how he was weakened once and for all, and how his elder had been injured. She couldn't be sure. Before he finished the telling, he fell to sleep amidst the assembled bunnies.

Mother was sleeping again, her head resting just shy of the long bound legs of the wrapped up Brother. Tomorrow she would lie there again, but an inch further away, and another inch the next, and another, until she had to lie with her arms out above her head to reach his toes, hands and ears, ever lingering around his absence, as if waiting for him to wake or finally go to sleep or drowsily to seek comfort in her arms. Yasha gazed at it, her Brother, all still in the linen, in that place beyond sleep, before birth. The more she thought about him, now, and who he was days ago, wandering the house and the yard, which she could scarcely picture with clarity anymore, the more she feared that he was rolled up and dead but still thinking in there, listening, waiting to go in the ground, and that all she had to do was cover her face, roll up in a blanket, lie still, and she, too, would be dead, stop for good, or worse, that the longer she stared, the more likely it was that he would say something, ask her to unwrap him, for somebody to please help him up.

Yasha couldn't sit still. She explored the ship. At last, she would investigate the dim hall below deck. She knew the other two bears stayed down there. She was curious about the middle brother, who seemed interested in talking with her, and she thought he might know more than he admitted about the rabbit Hart Crane.

To get below, she only had to walk down a ramp descending through a humped archway at the back of the ship. If when landed and unwinged the ship was a horse's skull, then it was a cyclops of a horse, and this was its eye socket. Her eyes took time to adjust to the shadow as she descended, so Yasha listened carefully. She didn't have anything in particular to fear, but she didn't have reason not to fear. Happily, at the bottom of the ramp, she saw a rather simple tunnel lit by several pear-shaped lanterns grown from the walls. From the tunnel, seven openings like hollowed knots led to small rooms, alcoves really, four on one side, three on the other. Only one room, on the far end, situated at the back of the ship, was hidden behind a solid black door. Everything was wood, so that she felt she was inside of a tremendous tree, with the distinction that the interior wood, unlike much of the deck and the arms, was smooth, as if sanded and polished. She thought the bears must find this either absolutely peaceful or terrifying: like a womb.

Each of the side rooms were nearly identical small hovels, room enough to sleep. Some held bags or boxes of food or supplies or the things Mother had collected. She stepped into one, thinking she might claim it as her own. Despite small air vents like portholes, however, she found the air stuffy and unpleasantly soggy, a slow-pulsing breath.

Yasha noticed the bears, the two bears, huddled together in one room, and she approached. She was about to say hello when she saw that Middle Bear was drawing a knife along a swollen wound on Eldest's side. The wound drooled milky blood, and the stench of vinegar and yogurt hit Yasha hard. She covered her face and rushed to the end of the tunnel, where the tarred wooden door was shut tight, but without a lock. Yasha knocked and urged it open with care. Inside, fresh cool air was cycling around and, filling much of the room, bound into it by tubes and fat and tendons, a bulging, gurgling wormy flesh worked like a bellows.

All at once the room was aglow, and Yasha couldn't tell what was happening. She heard the door shut behind her, and she spun in alarm. It was Hart Crane, holding up a dull orange lantern. He regarded her with a momentary suspicion, then reached a hand for Yasha's shoulder, to hold her still. Hart studied her face. With his gaze he led her eyes to the weird organ treading in the air.

Kneeling, he set the lantern between them. He spoke and made explanatory gestures,

"Monarch of the air through whose pulse
I hear, counting the beats my veins recall and add,
revived and sure. I entered the broken world
to trace the visionary company of death,
its voice an instant in the wind.
Above my world I poured visible wings of silence
sown in azure circles, widening as they descended.
The matrix of the heart, unwound
from the eyes which shrine the quiet lake
and the commodious, tall decorum of that sky
unwinging her earth, reflected in the broken wake of a singular dive."

Yasha understood that he was kind. She nodded. She understood that something connected Mr Crane with the ship, that it truly felt, saw, thought, lived. The thing was its heart.

Crane demonstrated putting his hand closer to the heart. Yasha did the same. She could feel it working, vibrations caught in her palm, tickled into her wrists.

He encouraged her to move closer.

As she did, the rhythm surged in silken waves, walls of sound that felt commensurate with the size of the heart and swallowed her whole arm in their mumbling. A chorus of smaller waves rattled in her chest, suggesting that inside the heart were dozens more, or at least numerous small passages, working in a complex coordination that was not entirely rhythmic.

Yasha closed her eyes and hovered a little closer. Now that her hand was inches from the heart and the sound was overwhelming, filling her chest, she felt she was, for a moment, a conduit for its rhythm, that it was about to say something through her, move her body as if she were a paper puppet. She held on, though the rhythm made her head feel funny, busy, and she felt as though it might overwhelm her, fill her up and even stop her heart, that she'd forget to breathe, be engulfed within it.

In the moment she pulled away, she heard, saw, felt, what the heart was saying. She saw a skinny tower of rocks in the sky, and a lake suspended around it, as though a cloud had thickened into water and become stuck there, unable to fall or drift on. All at once, she was in the water, descending to its lower edge, and beside her was a rabbit not unlike her own elder brother. They swam together, squeezing their lungs shut, until all at once, their hands broke through to the air, they splashed through, gasping, and saw the world looming far below. With a shout, Yasha pulled herself further back from the heart, and the image was gone.

Mr Crane moved his whole body very close to the heart but not touching, and he turned his head, his ear just shy of against it. He held himself very still, eyes closed, face passive. He hung there as though he longed to embrace it, and the heart gurgled and mumbled its liquid thoughts.

He stepped away. Miming to Yasha, he tapped his ear, as if something had been hidden there, and led her out of the room, closing the door tightly behind them.

She said to him, "My name is Yasha," and took his hand. She noticed that, though Hart appeared content, his hand was not responsive. He was weakened. He took lurching breaths, and with trouble, as if caught in smoke. She felt she was leading him as they walked past the hovel of the two bears. Hart looked straight ahead. Yasha peered into the bears' alcove. Eldest's leg and chest were wrapped in stained rags and string. Wet with sweat, he panted in a very gross way. Middle Bear stood at his side, eyes fixed on a high transom growing in the hull, where a moonlit cloud raced by.

Now David was sleeping, but all evening the stories had arrived in their halting way, a voice that hovered between them, tracing from David to the book to Mr Fin, or from the book to David to Mr Fin, or from the book to Mr Fin to David, or from Fin to the book to David, or from Fin to David to the book. Fin knew the story was an echo of David's time on the stolen Swan, and his time in the hospital, and his time elsewhere in secret, and he saw how the work strained, how it made do with borrowed objects, and he saw, as David grew tired, that the paper words in his mouth and on his neck were wearing thin.

Mr Fin set himself up on the porch with his coffee, with David's tattered book ("At these times, he talks very fast in a sort of low voice: great sentences that seem infinite, that roll with the sound of waves, an all-encompassing murmur, a barely perceptible planetary song. This goes on and on, is terribly imposing in its gentleness and distance").

He scanned two pages, reading what pleased him, pulled the sheet away from its brittle spine and laid it down in a stack, tucked a little way under his thigh. Two more pages, one more sheet. He worked through the book in this way: first, find some pages with notes and underlines; read them, tear them out; when his eyes were tired, as they frequently were, and he could read no more, he would tear the margins from the sheets, bit by bit, careful to preserve the writing, discarding the blanks; then the text itself he would peel into strips, as even as he could make them.

The wicker chair creaked and popped like a dwindling fire; there was no wind, but the stillness shifted every now and again, west, east, west. It was good air, the kind of air one finds when secured in a hiding place, under a dense bush, alone in the weeds behind the brick chimney. Even this moment, thought Mr Fin, is part of his memory.

The mother of the three bears, who was a tree and part of the ancient tree-mothers who now formed a range of mountains, told each of her boys that they were the best little bears in the world. She had had no real children, as tree children could no longer thrive in the darkness of the forest, though some still sprouted (from who knows what), gangly pollen-besotted bulbs whose desperate existences could do little more than feed some desperate mammal. In the depths, recesses, and rocky feet of their mountainous form, the trees no longer found it necessary to grow protective bears, so the three boys were precious to their mother. The first son was strong and brave. The second was wise and sharp witted. But the third, called Youngest, just as soon as he left behind his roots and grew his first coat of fur, the third acquired a deadly infestation—a species of ant that sought to live in his bones, and they worked like mad.

Youngest's mother sealed him in sap for months to suffocate the ants. Relentless, the ants dug their way out of the glistening tomb and back in again. His mother bled herself into the ant architecture, wrapped her bark around the body of her son, warmed him, fed him, cut away his fur and sealed him up more thickly again until the colony's corpses littered his frame, his bowel, his marrow. Still, they built their cities. Doctors were summoned, experiments and tests performed, sun cures and starvation. Finally, the colony weakened. The queen's slaves staggered and got lost when they were out. They were easy to catch. The two older bears would snatch them up and pick their legs off, shoot their segments across the patio like marbles.

Finally, mother gathered the last fathers of the season, possibly the last ever, crushed them in a crucible, and stuffed her child with the pulp. Youngest gagged as the fathers raged inside him, living screams of affection, until at last the ant queen crawled up through his throat and, pressing out between his jaws, her damp head emerged: an angry, shiny plum between his teeth.

She faced the mother tree, defeated but defiant still. She surveyed Youngest's room, where he had been kept through the months of sickness, sap, and bark. Standing on the crumpled little bear, the ant queen regarded the last corpses of her failed colony and addressed the ancient mother in the tongue of trees, "Tall one, still one, shade-maker, ladder to heaven, dying breed, womb of monsters, noble goddess of the forest, my enemy, my giver, my murderer, we greet you in our defeat. I am a queen with no grand hall, with not a slave at my side, with no army. Have mercy on our memory. We wanted your son's body as a home for our children, who would have numbered in the millions. For that we do not apologize, for the lives of millions outweigh the life of one miserable beast, and what gifts we are granted with which to make our lives we must use, and these are the same by which we perish. Life is sweet and precious for us all, mother tree. Now I give mine, the worth of which is gone, to the air."

With that, she destroyed herself in a cloud of pheromones. Youngest, there on the floor, watched the greenish blackish fog of the ant queen hovering, seeming to roll into itself, then slipping across the room and out a window.

To him, it was beautiful.

Youngest was special in that he had been saved, and because somewhere in the world, the cloud of the ant queen's self-destruction contained, so his mother would say, her apology to him, and from this he possessed a kind of luck. His brothers, in their innocence, had all along wished that he would just die, and that the trouble with the ants had not taken up so much of the family's energy. They made a point of ignoring him, leaving him behind, treating him as though he were still wrapped in sap, and they called him filthy, called him Sandpile, Ant-shit, Colony. He couldn't deny that he felt dirty. Aside from being weak, tired all the time, hungry all the time but too tired to eat enough, breakable, he itched on the inside.

He wanted to be rinsed out. Some nights, he would lie awake and imagine a great tree-hand that lifted his body gently into space and, piece by piece, pulled him apart, in layers, in chunks, its ghostly fingers disassembling him and creating a new species. The intricate silken branches of the great hand would run over each bone and joint, cleaning, straightening, strengthening. Each muscle would be bathed in a running river and rubbed with oils and blood, and when shaken, they would snap like lizard tongues catching flies, abalone scales stretching and sliding back into place.

He stared into the space between his breath and the ceiling, able to dream, but scarcely to really sleep. He knew, but never spoke it to anyone, that his weakness, his misery and his miserableness were caused not by the ant queen, not really. It was his fault, it was living that had damned him.

When the ant queen first left Youngest's body, he felt relieved, yes. But two distinct losses struck him immediately, without his really understanding them, without having words to describe them, not even inside-his-head words. The first was the loss of the queen herself. He had not thought of her as a companion but as an invader, a parasite. That seemed true, as true as anything. But objectively, what did that say about how he should feel at their separation? He realized that all along, as he suffered, as he went through cure after cure, as all the little jaws dug through him like tiny shards of glass, that the queen's mind had also possessed him, not just her mind, or not her mind in the limited sense, but her mind that included her signals, and not just the signals that made the others work, slave really, but the extraneous signals that no other ant understood, or perhaps other queens alone would understand, but no other. Youngest didn't understand it. It was a something inside that he thought had been a part of him, part of his insides, of who he had been, and now it was clear that it had been something else entirely, altogether another—and he wasn't sure what remained.

The second was the loss of certainty. He had faced death for nearly half of his life. No. Not exactly. One can not face it. Rather, he had not had to regard living as an option. Had no prospects. Immune to hope. Life was a routine of being eaten alive.

Now, empty of what he thought was part of himself, the future stretched out before him. The unending future menaced him. How long could it go on? Why should I live this way for a day more, let alone a year, or years?

That was his condition.

One morning, he sensed his brother in the room and opened his eyes. It was Middle.

"Good morning," he said, for he could get several words out at a time, without taking a breath, at this stage.

He still lived in his bed. Sometimes Eldest Bear was sent in to observe him. Middle Bear would bring things to eat or drink. Mother seemed to be there at times. Of course she couldn't really be there, because she was a skyscraper of a tree, fused with other skyscraper trees, all forming a tremendous mountain, reclined above the green valley where the three bears lived. But at times, he felt her there, apron tight on her waist, maybe a spoon in one hand. She'd just been fussing in the kitchen, folding warm laundry, making jam. She was love incarnate. He came to think of her as the cottage itself. It was part wood. He came to think of her as the pages of books; these were made of wood and leaves. He came to think of her as the dusk and darkness, as though the darkness that soothed his room at night had been delivered from deep within the mountain's shade, fresh darkness, like fresh water, tumbling down into the valley, filling the corners up, never running out, no matter the number of nights given to the valley, always sufficient darkness.

Middle didn't respond. He was standing at the bookshelf, snatching every third or fourth book by its head cap, turning each over in his hands, flipping the pages under his thumb.

"What are you looking for?" Now Youngest would have to catch his breath.

"We're running low on food for you."

Youngest had forgotten where their food came from. He wasn't sure he'd ever understood. He thought there was a garden, maybe a store in town. But was he on a special diet? He had not thought so. Had he been getting some unique substance, something rare in this region? Something difficult to store? He imagined the silos, once filled to the brim with Youngest Bear Feed, now hollow, their doors agape, farmers ho-humming, hands in pockets as they walked their fallow fields.

"But my books," he said.

"Our books, brother. I'm sorry, we'll need to sell them for food. Books are valuable." Middle had not turned to look at Youngest, but studied the books, now eight of them, stacked in his arm.

"I like to read those." Youngest really did. Mother had read to him, every night, when he was sick, as he struggled to sleep and when he woke gasping, she held him in the bathroom steam and cooed little stories from some musty book— or was that father, the screaming poultice of photosynthetic love, his curly veins? Sometimes all that existed were the words' magic leaping from the page, a string of melodies, and the images, the characters, not all understood, some not at all, but they were everything he had, at certain times, when all he could do was lie shapeless in someone's arms. How did all this happen, he wondered, when mother was a tree among divine trees, and father drenched in sky?

"Look here." Middle turned and held up the books, nine in all. "I think this will give you ten weeks of food. Think of that. Ten weeks of life! What else can I do?" He left the room.

Youngest heard Middle loading the books into a satchel, heard him slap an already-saddled horse, leather reins unknotting from around the metal rail. Off he went.

He counted the books still on the shelf. It took a few tries. Sixteen left. Sixteen.

The next time he woke up, Youngest saw Middle in the chair, reading a book.

"Hey there." Middle slapped the book down on the bookcase.

Youngest smiled.

"Listen, I've set some things out here for you on the side table. Can you reach?"

Middle grasped Youngest's arm and made it move about like a puppet's.

Youngest smiled. It was like a game.

His brother laughed, "ha-ha," then maneuvered the arm as if it were reaching out for something on the table then bringing that something to his mouth. "Yes. Good. Might have to roll a bit to get everything. But you see that? Food enough for a while. And a glass of water. I put a straw in it for you. And here." He turned back and grabbed the book he'd been reading, laid it on the blanket, on a very flat part by Youngest's hip. "Something to read. So. Eldest and I are going on an expedition. You know. We're going up the mountain a ways."

"Up the mountain?" That was an incredible idea. In fact, Youngest had never thought of it before, though it was obvious. Just walk up the mountain.

"Are there caves?" he asked. Wouldn't caves be a miracle?

Middle screwed up his eyes, "No. No, we're bringing tents. We'll be back in about a week. Maybe I'll bring you something. We saw one of the zeppelins fall, right about the snow-line. We're going to check it out." What Youngest did not know, had never had a chance to see, was that behind their cottage were two large barns, each brimming with items his brothers had collected from fallen zeppelins.

Now Youngest was feeling a bit confused, and he was thinking simultaneously about the expedition and about the book by his side, whichever one it was, and he asked, "Monsters?"

"Ha ha. Yes, lots of terrible monsters. We'll bring you back some magical... um, stuff!"

"I can read about it," Youngest said, having lost the thread of the conversation. He worked his arm from under the blanket and cast his hand onto the book. He recognized the texture, the split corners. "I remember, in this one, there is a mountain. This is not the monster one." He was breathless, but went on, speaking without air, just a muttering that rose and fell from sound, "this is the one with the sea creatures, the sea creatures, and the giant killed by the boy, and the boy, the boy has a sister or a daughter of a sister or an uncle of a daughter of a sister's daughter, I think, and there's a whole city, a huge city above the sea," and as he went on he managed to prop the book up on his chest and to prop his arms there to hold it in place, and he began to read at whatever page was opened, and he would remain on that page reading again and again, until he felt he had the energy to turn a page and the wherewithal to remember everything from those first two pages. "Thank you, brother," he said.

But Middle had gone. The night was spilling in.

The house was silent. Everything held still except the curtains. And as he breathed, the blankets moved, and the book, as he breathed, bobbed up and then down again. Everything still except the curtains, the blanket, and the book, and these all in communion.

Here was the page about the fetus, "resting in the cave like a seed in a pod." Youngest swooned at the image of a cave, once more, facing him as it had in the world, but now, from the book. The character, a one-armed weaver named Pim, crept into the cave's night, on this page. Pim had lingered at the mouth of the cave, in dread, on one page. To him, the cave was an image of death, a tomb. But this was wrong, Youngest knew, and the weaver quieted his nerves, as if dimly aware of his reader's calm, his hope. The Weaver sought the left eye of a fallen god. On the facing page was a god, in the womb of the mountain, in the mother, and the eye itself was also the egg of the god's rebirth. This was how gods were made. The cave equals the mother's womb. To see a cave this way, in a book, was a secret symbol, revealing the deeply mysterious architecture of the novel. But Youngest knew the world did not work in that complex way, that the world, in this sense, was flat. There were no caves in the mountains. The world was not a mother. The words did not care. He did not have words, of his own, for this knowledge about books and the world, but felt it in the transformation of the book, the world of the book, from the flat page. Where the book was flat, the world was full of depth, and where the book held meaning, the world was empty handed. I live, he thought clearly enough, on a page, under a bed sheet, so my life is flat in both directions.

Thoughts of this kind produced a melancholy in the youngest bear. He longed to get up from the bed, but it was terribly dark, not a good time for risks. He couldn't read the book anymore, but could linger in the imaginary cave, approaching its terminus riding on the shoulder of Pim the Weaver, taking the place of his lost arm, feeling the weakness in his calves as he took those last furtive steps toward the sphere of the nascent god, raising his spear with that good arm, imagining the dagger point digging into its circular iris, and the little bear dreamed that he was the phantom limb, and that he would reach out and touch the egg sac, and that his touch would shiver through the child god, warn it, welcome it, whatever happened next, comfort it, whatever happened. Pim began the slow puncture of the eye, the egg, putting his weight into it until the gelatinous womb gently enveloped the blade, producing a cataract, a cloudy amber that tumbled onto the cave floor. Through the emptied shell of the eye-become-egg, the Weaver sees not just the curled form of the growing god, but also the head of a man, teeth gripping the amnion, chewing its own way toward the fetus.

Youngest woke in the afternoon. On his shelf were three books, each with the same style of number on the spine: one, two, three, while on his chest was number four, which altogether formed a series. How thoughtful his brothers were. In the months to follow, brothers in, brothers out, he kept these last four and read through them again and again, each time striking new upon the closing chapter of the fourth book, which promised that the fifth and last book was still to come. What he would give for that last book, for the closing words of the world that had filled his room and all the hollows of his mind!

One day, as Youngest lay in bed, he listened to the sounds in the other rooms of the house. Things were being gathered. Decisions were being made. Voices were low. The little bear stared at the familiar ceiling. He stared at the familiar window frame. He was thirsty. He hadn't eaten since the day before.

A screen door slammed. Heavy feet padded toward his room, and he heard the door, the familiar door, open in an unfamiliar way.

He loved the soft yellow and orange pattern on the curtains. The cotton had thinned in places, and he loved the light and air that came through those exhausted fibers.

Eldest Bear stood over him.

Eldest Bear's face was a burl of emotion.

"As for you," he said.

Littlest Bear said nothing.

"All our lives. No one wanted you, and then we put up with you, and then you got sick, and it was all about you, every thing was poor you, special you, needy you, suffering you..."

The young bear tried to read his brother's face. He thought maybe one could see murder in another's eyes, real hatred. Maybe there were clear signs. If he could read the signs, maybe he could figure out what needed to be said. Though he wasn't too good with words.

"Thank—."

"Shut up." Eldest Bear put a knee into Youngest's diaphragm. This was a tender spot for Youngest, who was already, in general, quite tender. "You know what?" It really seemed, for a moment, that eldest was full, entirely full, of emotion. "When you were little, we didn't like you, but we started to think it was ok to have another brother, that three would be an ok number, after all. And then you got sick. And we were relieved. We thought, 'good, now he's going to die, and we won't have to worry about having another brother.' Think about it, Little Bear... two is enough. Two is enough. And when you got sick, that proved it, and everything would have been ok. But you didn't die."

Littlest Bear was struggling to breathe. He heard other footsteps enter the room and then stop. This was middle brother, standing at the threshold, holding a pot of honey.

Eldest continued. "You should have died. You were supposed to die. You were so sick no one wanted you. You thought our mother wanted you, but she only did what she thought she was supposed to, cause you're supposed to love cute little weak little bears, so she tried to save you. But she never thought you'd really live. She was just going through the motions. She was hoping you'd die. Every day. Every day. We'd all sit around and talk about it. About how good things were going to be when it was over. You..."

Middle Bear had set down the honey and moved closer.

Eldest spat, "...you thing. But here you are."

Middle Bear put his paw out, "Brother," —he meant Eldest—"there's no point." He gave Eldest's shoulder a gentle tug.

Eldest moved aside, leaving Youngest gasping for air.

Eldest Bear retreated toward the door. "I'm ready," he said over his shoulder. He swept the remaining books from the shelf into the crook of his arm, snapped up the honey pot, and walked out.

Middle Bear kneeled next to Youngest, pulled one of his quilts up straighter. "Are you comfortable?"

Littlest thought it was obvious that he was not. He thought to himself that he had never, to his mind, been comfortable, not in the way others are, but he suspected that to say so would provoke more difficulties. He tried to fill his chest with air. The air was full of bees.

"Eldest thought we should smother you before we go." Middle Bear sighed, "I thought we should give you a choice, don't you think?"

Little Bear nodded.

"So? What do you think? I mean, you're just going to lie here, right? And, it's true. You should have been dead a long time ago. I mean. We're your brothers. We feel sort of responsible for you. Just leaving you here, starving? It seems a bit cruel."

Littlest Bear wasn't sure what to say. He thought he should live. Didn't everyone want to live? Wasn't living the only choice? But Middle Bear was always so smart, and he seemed to really care about what happened next. He must have a plan.

Littlest Bear nodded, but immediately realized he'd forgotten what the question had been. So he shook his head, for good measure.

"It's not a bad old house," Middle Bear said. "But I don't know if anyone will want it all stinky with a rotten corpse!"

Little Bear smiled, because that would be really gross.

"Let's get you out into the sun," said Middle Bear.

Littlest Bear was not sure about the sun. When his body had been infested with a colony of ants, hard-working ants, the doctor had recommended a sun cure, a cure intended to, in effect, cook the ants out. There had not been a lot of study about ants, about whether they liked the heat or liked the cold. It stood to reason, though, that it would be a rare colony of creatures that could take being in the hot sun for days on end! Certainly the queen, for one, would find this unsuitable, and she would leave. In this phase of Littlest Bear's treatment, he had been given cold water, just enough, to drink, or just on his face to cool him down. He had appreciated the ease, after two days, of sleeping. It was easier and easier to know nothing, to disappear. Maybe that's what would happen now. Maybe that's what death was, and it would be a relief when it was finished. He could not imagine choosing it, but he could not imagine denying it, either.

Middle Bear drew his brother out of the bed and draped Littlest's arm over his own shoulders, not easy work for Middle Bear, who was not the strong one, but he did not mind, for now, the hardship. He even smiled at his little brother, reassuringly, as if to say, don't worry, I can handle it.

"I could read..." said Littlest, reaching for his shelf. But there was nothing there. His last books, one, two, three, and four: they were gone. "My books?" he asked. "Have you got the fifth one?" he asked Middle. "Are they all together now?" It might all be a kind of surprise. They knew, they must have known all along how much he wanted it, how happy it would make him. He thought of saying to them, if I could read that book, you can leave me wherever you like, I could be done with, but I'd like to read the last one, the fifth. But by the time he'd gotten to the end of the thought, he'd forgotten how it had begun, and they were squeezing out the front door together.

Eldest Bear was already outside, and he was tightening straps on their largest wooden wagon, which, under the strapping, was piled with boxes and bags of things from their house and from the barns. He watched Middle and Littlest emerge and gave a dismayed look.

"Come along, brother. Let's set him up against that rock."

Eldest slipped his big arm around Littlest's chest and took on most of the work. Even a wasted bear is not a small thing.

They guided Littlest toward a large, boat-shaped rock. His books weren't there.

As they neared it, Littlest said, "Oh I know this rock. One day, I was spread across its top to dry, by our mother. I found it fit my back, bumps and ridges, there, held my neck, for hours. My books...?"

The two brothers stopped and let Littlest down on the ground with just his head and shoulders propped against a pocked and buggy jag of the rock.

Little Bear tried to speak, but nothing came out.

Eldest was already walking away.

Middle looked down at him, brushed his hands together and gave his neck a stretching turn. "I think you ought to be okay out here for a while. You'll have a few nice days, I should think. Really is beautiful. You can see the forest, can't you? Can you turn your head a bit? Well. I'm glad we brought you out here. You're lucky we did."

Eldest had got the wagon rolling, and Middle ran to catch up.

Littlest's head tipped toward the road, eyes following the sand and dust as the wagon descended a slight hill, ascended again, a much smaller road, and he saw where it disappeared at last into the trees that surrounded the base of the mountain. He watched the convergence of road and mountain until he woke in the morning. He had always felt uncomfortable in the grass, and numerous critters had entered his fur for the night, after the others, who had come in for the day, had left. He suffered this quietly, but not well, and he cried for himself, and regretted his tears, which drained him all the more.

Some days later, zeppelins loomed close in the evening air, maybe seven of them all in a group—Youngest had trouble getting a count as they crossed each other's paths and turned through space. He was amazed and delighted by them. They lumbered through the sky, their attacking finished, they dawdled home, or to the next place, coasting restfully through the evening, and they were beautiful, so close to impossible. Youngest saw how their gray skin clung to them, walruses in the air, some tipping forward or backward as they flew, some twisting ever so slightly, as if to expose some part of their bellies or backs to the cool air, or to a warm draft, or to turn their strange eyes up toward the few stars that had leaked into the eastern blue evening.

Before they had passed from sight, the zeppelin in the lead made a booming call or siren sound, a signal. Within moments, they had all formed a triangle behind the leader, and they flew with more severity.

Then, as if it were part of the same maneuver, several of the zeppelins released something from their bellies, defecated really, and these turds tumbled from the sky, turning, odd-shaped things, and as several disappeared behind the tree-tops, Youngest thought that he could hear the slight thumps made as they landed. One of them came rushing down very near, and he saw it crashing into a treetop and plummet through the leaves, catching on branches, more like a sack of turd than a turd, which would simply break apart then crumble to the ground.

It wasn't a turd at all, and as it raised itself from the ground, Youngest saw what it really was.

Hart Crane was now a different sort of rabbit. He had been eaten by an elephant, one of the zeppelins—war machines—monsters. It was a migration that voided memory, he would say, in the belly of inventions that stone the heart, an unspeakable bridge to spent suns, to the floating Atlantis of the sky, beyond time, where an arcing spear, bloodied by a toiling star (drained of its infinite flame—orphic strings mapped the sidereal phalanxes, auroras of pity, antiphonal whispers sucked through the gear-teeth of night and flung about by the blue flywheel of the ocean), gushed from the azure moon.

Such was his soliloquy as he stumbled from the trees, sputtering, chilled to the naked bone. He saw the house of the three bears, he saw his own paws, hands, and he heard the brushing of his strange legs moving queer in the drying leaves. He was naked, but unashamed. He pronounced to the trees still around him, though it seemed to him they were dispersing or gathering behind him, he orated to them, because here was a world that seemed, to him, for the moment, void of idea, void of names...

He was astounded that his words did not follow his will, or if they did it was in some secret way, so to speak of his confusion, the difficulty of gathering what had happened these last few days, he said, "So was I turned about and back, much as your smoke compiles a too well-known biography? That evening spear was the river... and have I walked the dozen decimals of time? My memory I left in a ravine—among apron rocks, congregated pears in moonlit bushels—and only wakes in an alley of trees, a trough beneath a glittering abyss—the abyss is a serpent sunning itself, drumming its tongue against the not-abyss, the fountain: what icy speech through the walls? What rustle of scales, of water, of paper: memory committed to a broken page."

When he was done speaking, he heard the young bear's weak summons. He wandered to him, and without question or greeting, joined him, leaning sleepily against the stone beside him, as if that were all there was left to do.

Little Bear said to him, much later, when they both happened to be awake, "They took my books." He let a tear tip from his eyelid as if on command but without further expression, not to let emotion tire the body.

Hart said softly, like the last lines of a bedtime story, "I think the air has thrown itself upon me and been answered, at least in part, and I believe I am a little changed—not essentially, but changed and transubstantiated as anyone is who has asked a question and been answered. Now the form of my life rises out of a past that so overwhelms the present with its mutant shades and visions that I am at a loss to imagine real links between that past and any future at all." He tried to meet Little Bear's eyes.

Little Bear's eyes showed delight, and he said, "I'm so glad you're here with me. You are more book than rabbit!"

Hart said, in agreement, "The bottom of the sea is cruel...'" and he went on and on.

When Hart fell quiet they both slept, although, in general, Littlest would have found it hard to determine what was sleeping and what was waking as they sat together, so peaceful was he, and so delightful a calmative were the words and stories Hart recited. He seemed to do it, tell stories, the way one hums a tune—unconsciously, following the breath, wandering wherever, perhaps thinking his own very different thoughts as the stories scrolled pillars and bridges from his mouth.

Waking to a pause, Little Bear remembered his books and told Hart Crane, as efficiently as he could manage, about the end of the last but one book in the series he had been adoring for that last year, or since the absence of his mother's voice. It took days for Little Bear to tell Hart the stories, and he digressed often to discuss his feelings for the characters and his feelings for the objects, and his feelings for the things that were neither. When Littlest was done, Hart sat up and told the stories back to Littlest. At the same time, he sewed himself some traveling clothes and a sharp, soft hat, the kind a farmer might wear to venture outside the valley of his birth for the last time.

With shapes made of his fingers and a few mimes, Hart said, let's go fetch your books and find out if the end is to be had. Myself, he indicated, I could never finish a story or a poem, and whenever I came close, everything would be changed again, and the words would be nothing but dried webs in my hands.

Little Bear indicated the mountain, where his brothers had gone in their wagon, presumably to fleece the stomach of another fallen beast.

Sam was approaching.

Mr Fin stopped mid-rip.

He slipped his glasses off and gathered the loose pages and pieces into a neat stack. He fit them back in the book, nestled them in. He searched for his pipe.

He remembered early in the Quixote just such a scene. The knight reclined, newly caked in his armor, not yet so foolish but very out of place, on the side veranda, and the priest or the barber approaching, prepared to mock or jest, as if the world did not, all its own, bear proof of its enchantments.

"Nice day!" Sam put one foot up on the second step and wrapped his broad, too-hairy hand on the railing. Mr Fin could smell his bottom-shelf scotch, his shampoo, and his tattered boots. Sam worked his body back and forth, testing the railing or testing his arm. "Up to no good?"

"I'm alright, Sam. You?"

"Been good. Been good." Sam mounted the porch and sat down, nothing more needing to be said. A minute passed. "Give me that," he said, reaching out for the book. Fin obliged. "Aww. Well, I can fix this for you. Little bit of glue is all. Have it back to you tomorrow, good and readable, alright?"

"Alright." Mr Fin felt his hands emptied.

"How's the old boat?"

Mr Fin thought of the boat in the garage, like Schrodinger's cat. "It's all clean." He should have kept the book.

"That was a piece of shit old boat, alright. You gonna sell it? Someone would buy it, maybe I would..."

"I don't want to sell it."

"Is it in okay shape? I could help you fix it up."

"I don't want to sell it." Mr Fin, gazing down, said, or thinks he said, "At midnight, on the stairs, the image of swirling ashes continued uninterrupted through the mirror. Nothingness departed. What remained outlined the castle of our purity."

"Well, listen, old Fin," Sam drummed his knees, "I know you're not much for sailing now, but how about a little flatboat-fishing. You and me, some early morning near-about? What you say?" He back-handed Fin on the arm in a gesture of camaraderie.

Fin grunted. "Sure," he said, not really caring, not believing the day would come. The two men sat nodding for a few moments, approving of the weather and of the handsome stillness. There is also, he considered, the old man against the sea, the immortal, sinking maelstrom of the word.

Without the book, how would David speak? How could he tell me what's happened? The hollow feeling in his hands was the inverse of a sudden presence in the house. David?

Sam went on, "... You ever checked that thing on the water heater, little valve thing; holy shit! I found out the thing could blow up if I didn't check it; and when I did it starts dumping all over the floor, 'bout ruins a box full of pictures... all my records and old shit got wet!"

Yasha heard her mother screaming.

Hart Crane was rushing around the deck. He gathered a satchel, threw various things into it, hitched a long knife into his belt. What looked like a pile of gears, plates, and rope he slung to his back. Unwinding rope from the contraption, he tied one end to the ship rail, hitched the other to a long barbed spear. The body of Yasha's Brother was there on the deck, hung on the rail like a dry-cleaned suit.

Mother continued to punish and even pull at Hart, but he ignored her. When she reached for her son, he pushed her aside.

Yasha heard a strange singing in the distance, mechanical, wiry voices, shrill rotations in some deep chest. She saw it, directly in front of them: a zeppelin. It was alone, lolling crooked in the air, as if sleeping or injured.

Mr Crane's ship was cruising toward it, wings and arms eager with wind. The gathering speed shook the ship until a last muscular pounding of its limbs brought it close enough to lock branches to the zeppelin. As they collided, down went the confused little bunnies, slipping and scratching on the deck. Mother rushed around to lead them all below. Yasha avoided her, held tight to the rail. She could see the fleshy metallic shell of the zeppelin, wrinkled and filthy. A long wet gash marked its side. Its awful jaw hung ajar, snapped or dumb.

From his position spread limp in the deck, the youngest bear watched Hart without expression, then he nodded knowingly and shut his eyes. The other two bears struggled up from below decks. Middle was carrying Eldest bent over his shoulder. Middle yelled for Crane, "Rabbit!" between gasps, "Crane!"

Hart finished his preparations, threw one leg over the rail and hooked his foot onto a short limb.

Hart scanned the emerging bears, then stared a moment at Yasha. He almost turned away, then looked her in the eyes. Concentration filled him, desperate to speak.

He said, "I heard the sea in sapphire arenas of the hills."

The ship groaned with effort, long arms struggling with the zeppelin, working to ensnare it as it turned its mouth against them. Hart called loudly over the din, "I was promised an improved infancy!" He shook his head, disappointed.

Hart gathered rope and spear in one hand, braced himself with the other, and cast the spear into the side of the zeppelin, where it stuck with an awful sound. He turned once more, gathering the body of Brother rabbit up under his free arm.

"Cobblestone the heart, unspeakable bridge!

Thy pardon for this history, Anemone,"

He looked elsewhere, everywhere at once. He was wild with readiness.

"Now, while thy petals spend the suns about us, hold,

Atlantis, hold thy floating singer late!"

Just then, Mother returned from below and went for her son. Half moaning, half screaming, she leapt even as Hart was heaving his bulk over the rail. Hart shoved off from the ship, but too late, and Mother got an arm around her son's legs while the other scraped against Mr Crane's grip.

Middle Bear had dropped eldest against the ship rail and reached for Crane, but the rabbit slipped away from them both, flailing as he zipped into space, and the body of Brother Rabbit tipped back onto the deck. In a moment, Hart had planted his feet on the zeppelin, amid the stream of black blood in the beast's side. He clung there panting and pondering. Mother, caught in a dry-weeping panic, Yasha steadying her, rushed with her son down into the ship's belly.

Crane stared back at his ship, watching the rabbit boy and his mother. For the moment, the zeppelin was distracted by the pest on its side, but could do nothing about it.

"What's he doing now?" the eldest bear shouted. His voice was dreadful, pained but full of menace and stone.

"I don't know, but I think we've had enough," Middle grabbed the rope and even as he stared straight at Mr Crane, gave it a vigorous yank, hoping to rip the spear and Hart himself right out into the open air. What he accomplished instead was to freshly upset the zeppelin, which gave a swashing turn against the tangle of branches and began to work its crippled jaw into the wood.

Hart, frantic, reset his hooks to slide himself back to the ship. Middle Bear had already pried his fingers into the knotted rope. In a moment he held the loose end, like a leash.

Eldest chuckled when he saw. "Let the sunuvabitch go!'

"Goodbye, Mr Crane." Middle dropped the rope. Hart fell several meters before he regained a grip, and there he dangled, strung from the bending spear in the zeppelin's flesh. The zeppelin had torn free of all but one tree limb, and it chewed menacingly on the broad leaves, eating its way toward the deck of the flying tree.

Middle grabbed his brother's paw and held him up steady against the rail. He inspected his leg. "You've gone and opened it up," he complained.

"Look at this," Eldest pointed.

Hart had made it back up to the zeppelin and was traversing its side, toward the mouth.

"He's climbing in!"

"Ha!" Eldest smacked his forehead, "You said he was mad."

"What's he up to in there?"

As they watched, Hart Crane's hind feet disappeared between the tremendous teeth of the zeppelin.

The creature made a powerful surge of effort toward the ship, bending the branch that held it and clamping its teeth onto another. Even so, the ship continued to bend more limbs toward the creature, some wrapping round it, others wrapping it with their rails, while others reached vine-like fingers into the mouth, searching for Mr Crane.

Middle cried out, "We'll all be killed if it doesn't let go of the thing!"

Yasha returned to the rail and stared out at the beast. The spear protruded from its side, the rope plumb from its end, drifting parallel to the stream of black blood. Hart was nowhere. "Did he fall?" Immediately, by the bears' expressions, she knew he hadn't. She shrieked with fury, "You've killed him?"

No one answered her. Cycling winds and grumbling guts and gears and gnashed branches filled her ears.

Middle Bear was examining their options.

"Where is he?" she cried. And then, all her attention on the behemoth, she uttered, "What is it?" To her, the zeppelin seemed both machine and animal. A black knob to one side of the mouth seemed to glare at them. The mouth was full of bucket-like teeth.

"He's gone into the mouth, the crazy bastard." The Middle Bear paced.

"He's okay? What is he doing?" Yasha clung to the ship, waiting for Hart to reappear as the struggle in the air shook and tilted the ship.

Eldest chimed in, almost chuckling, "Has it not occurred to you, little bunny, that we're all about to die? I don't think you need to worry about-"

The zeppelin gave a sudden and vicious shake, like a shark tearing meat from bone. Yasha and Middle were thrown but caught the rail. A limb came off in the zeppelin's mouth. It chewed and spat the green wood, ripping apart the vines that had curled into its mouth. The ship bent a fresh, broad-sailed arm into position to press the creature away.

Yasha realized what the bear had done. "You let the rope go. That was his only way back! He's gone to kill it somehow, but you've thrown over his rope."

Middle Bear growled at her, "Don't be stupid. That rope tied us to the beast. It would have dragged us all to our deaths. If that was his plan, then good riddance." Middle Bear ignored her now and rubbed his forehead. "How on earth do we drive this ship?" he searched the deck, the places where Hart would stand. Middle was powerless, appalled.

"But he must be coming back. Don't you see? He was trying to save us from it!"

Middle Bear turned on her. "Hush, child. The son of a bitch was going to feed your brother's corpse to the creature and get us all killed in the bargain. He's mad." He stomped below deck.

Yasha called out at the zeppelin. "Mr Crane! Mr Crane! Hurry! You can climb back on the branches!" The air between the ships was ripping up and down as the zeppelin made shrieking rotations and worked its jaw. Yasha called again. Her voice went nowhere.

Middle Bear returned with a hatchet. Reaching over the side, he swung at a branch that still held the zeppelin.

"Stop!" Yasha rushed at the bear as he prepared a second swing. Wary of the blade, she flung herself at him and dug her fingers and toes into the bear's arm. The branch had already begun to crack and split down its length, and with one more explosive crack the ship lurched onto its side. Middle and Yasha fell headlong and rolled across the deck. Youngest Bear slid to the portal and held himself there while Eldest dug his claws into the rail and pulled fiercely upright.

Yasha slammed into the far rail and for an instant thought she was going to roll further, roll right out into space. But she stuck there. Something heavy battered her legs. It was the hatchet, slipped away from Middle. Without missing a moment, she grabbed it and threw it over the side.

"Filthy rodent," sneered the bear. The ship righted itself, and the bear lunged for her, took her by the ears. Yasha had never been lifted by the ears before. It was unbearable, as if they were tearing off. She shrieked and grabbed for his wrist. The bear lifted her to glare into her face, and he growled like an animal. His breath heaved against her. Yasha closed her eyes. If he throws me over, she thought, maybe the ship will catch me up in its green hands. I'll reach out...

Instead of tossing her after the hatchet, the bear flung her through the portal. She slid and tumbled down the ramp, her head rioting.

Eldest Bear had taken matters into his own hands. He'd shimmied down one of the ship's branches. He didn't have far to go, for the zeppelin was tacking its head toward them, a wet, hungry engine thrilling from its depths, mouth already closing on a long arm and wing, chewing its way to the deck.

Eldest gained footing on its back, scaled to the gash in its side and worked his hands into the wound. With a cry, he yanked it open, releasing a gush of black blood and a jumble of gore. The creature groaned like thunder as Eldest scaled back to the zeppelin's spine, grasping for the branch, dragging his infected leg. Before he could get hold, the zeppelin wrenched free of the last branch and let itself float away, its gears crowing, squealing like sirens from its muddled head. Eldest nearly slipped but held tight to the zeppelin's flesh. The machine exerted a last shriek of will and the distance between them multiplied. Eldest clutched ahold with his claws.

Middle was beside himself. He called to his brother. He shook himself against the rails. His cries were a boyish song. He leaned on the rail and wept and coughed, staring at the shrinking form of his brother, just visible as an insect on a leaf, adrift.

Middle's eyes turned to stone as Eldest slipped from view, down, his silhouette falling like a drip of water from the zeppelin's belly, straight through the sky and on and on to some invisible place.

Sam went on, but Mr Fin shut out his voice. He could feel it: Hart Crane had returned. He was peeling open the door to David's room. He could feel it in the stories tracing through the house, branches, tar-black doors, zeppelins, bodies: the revisions.

Empty handed, Hart could only have come to gather words and sympathy. He had meant to carry Brother Rabbit through the zeppelin, to let it transform him, but here was another body, David, awaiting him, quilted in the bed, drifting to sleep or drifting awake. The rabbit stepped reverently to David's side, set his hand on the blanket where it rounded the scapula. He wanted to climb in, to be embraced by the sleeper. Oh, to be a stuffed rabbit, and not a real one, he thought.

Sam was saying, "The boy and I fished together but only talked when necessary. We talked at night or when storm-bound by the weather. They say it's a virtue not to talk unnecessarily at sea. Well, I don't know. But you know, lately I talk and talk with no one else in the boat!"

"Sam, I've got to get inside."

Sam smiled as if Fin had said something cute. "No. Let's talk. I need to make sure you remember—."

"It's too warm out here." Fin patted his pockets, "I need to get my..."

"It was no accident," Sam said, and he leaned in as if he had a secret, one hand raised to hold a picture in the air. "It had come up from deep down in the water as the dark cloud of blood had settled and dispersed in the mile deep sea. It had come up so fast and absolutely without caution that it broke the surface of the blue water and was in the sun!"

Fin knew that Crane would lift back the quilt, expose David's skin to the air. Fin felt he would burst unless he pushed himself out of his chair, "I need to go in."

With the quilt folded down, Hart despaired. David was not well, and though he could see how handsome a young man he might have become, he saw the failed joints and sea-worn bones.

"Do you remember me?" he asked. "It's Mr Crane. I was waiting for you, but you swam away. So I kept waiting." He put his head next to David's, so that their noses nearly touched.

"I waited a long time for you, so long my lives confuse me now." Close as they were, Hart breathed David's breath. "Can you speak? Do you want to come with me?" David roused slightly.

"Fin, listen," Sam put a hand out for Fin's shoulder. "Just settle down. I'll get you some iced tea... you got any iced tea in the fridge?"

"I'd better keep the book," Fin said, reaching.

"No, listen, that doesn't make sense... it's all torn up, I know you can't read it, anyway." Sam held it behind his back and grinned. "You'll thank me later, trust me."

"Come by tomorrow, then," Fin worked to appear calm, "with the book, all fixed up. Bring it tomorrow." Yes, in fact, it was safe with Sam. Who knows, Crane might eat the whole thing.

Fin kept moving: screen door, wood door, lock the bolt, tired groan, he strode through the house to the guest room. The door was shut.

David's hands floccillated the edge of the quilt.

"You're cold!" Hart cooed and pulled the blanket up. The hands kept working. Hart heard the footsteps, leapt up and twisted the lock. Fin tried the knob and banged twice. "David!" he cried.

Sam rattled the knob on the porch and peeked into the window. "What'd you say? Hey, I'll call you later, okay? Take a nap or something, okay? Just don't... don't leave the house, got it? Or try to drive again, okay? ...Shit." He knocked on the window. "Hey, I'll send Viv over soon. Okay? Y'alright?"

Sam slumped down the porch steps, turned and looked at the house. "Shit."

Hart returned to the bedside. The lips were struggling, cramped shut. "What is it? What is it?" Hart framed David's cheeks between his palms. "I'm here," he whispered. He kissed David's forehead and a gasp of breath lifted David's chest.

"WHERE'S MY BOOK? MY BOOK!" David's eyes, flashing open, tinged with jaundice, raged about the room. His neck didn't work. "MY BOOK!" he said, eyes leaping.

Mr Fin pounded on the door. "Listen, David! I'm coming in," he said. Hart could hear his footsteps recede, a kitchen drawer yanked open.

"We've go to go," he said to David.

"MY BOOK!" David, locked in place except for his mouth, except for his eyes and hands clambering, repeated the cry over and over again.

Hart moaned. "I don't have your book," but David, croaking, would not hear a thing. Terror locked him up and whipped through him.

Fin stood outside the door, listening, hand to the knob, listening, slowly pressing the key into place. He eased the door open. Crane was bent over to embrace David, who still screamed in feeble bursts, parched syllables spilling, spouting. "MBKMBKMBKMBKMBKMKMBKMBMKBK!"

Fin knelt next to the rabbit. He whispered in David's ear, "Listen. Once, Hart Crane was in his flying ship, leaning into the azure wind, and they flew toward the nest of the zeppelins…"

As his father continued the story, David ticked and tocked until all that was left was a pulsing moan, and soon he was quieted. Once Fin was certain he was asleep, he leaned his head on Hart Crane's shoulder. "Oh, Stéphane," he said, "the Book is gone. Sam took it."

Crane sat back on his ankles. "None of us know the color of the sky… each our own end of nature." He looked at Fin, said with his eyes: the rabbit boy is dead. I couldn't bring him. I won't have another chance.

"That's not important," Fin said.

Hart didn't understand. How could that not be everything?

"The story is here." Fin put his hand beside the rabbit's beside David's. "But the book is gone."

The rabbit was already on his way.

Middle Bear searched the ship. He believed some secret control lever, a wheel, or pressure points would make it move, wake it up.

It wasn't long before he gave up and hid in his room below.

Mother wasn't talking. She sat with the children in the main tunnel. She had had enough. She hadn't slept properly since the attack, so she slept with her eyes open, arms taut.

Yasha and Littlest Bear stayed above deck. Yasha watched for the zeppelin to return. She watched for a dot resembling Hart on the ground. She tried to operate the pulley system that had brought her here, but soon realized that parts of it, in particular the rope, had gone into Hart's other machine.

The ship remained where it was or drifted this way or that. The whole body, arms and belly, visibly sagged, lacking will. It merely treaded the air.

Yasha said to the bear or to no one, "I think the ship is waiting for Hart! It thinks he's alive."

The bear nodded, signaling both that it was true and that it was a sad truth. Little Bear was used to this lifestyle.

Occasionally, Yasha would hear Middle below, approach or cross the ramp, and she would prepare to move, to rush to the other end of the ship. She didn't want to have to look at him, didn't want him to look at her.

It was night soon enough. Yasha couldn't sleep. She felt her eyes were bursting open on their own, and she tried to squeeze them shut with her palms. She imagined the ship dropping its leaves and falling like a stone. She saw Middle standing above her, picking her up and throwing her out into nothingness—he might, if she fell asleep, just pick her up and drop her. She might wake in mid-air, body tipping in the shadowy flood of wind, not knowing up from down, or wake with the awful mouth of a zeppelin upon her.

To calm herself, she crawled across the deck and fitted her body between the bear and the side of the ship, hidden in his fur and shadow. His body adjusted to hers, and he made a sleepy hum in his belly. Yasha lay there awake, supremely warm, for another hour and didn't wake until the sun sparked over the side.

She could tell by the size of the trees below that they had gone neither higher nor lower. She listened for activity below deck. It was a cave down there, and the sun was not likely to wake anyone who didn't want to be awake. She tiptoed down the ramp, stared at each dim cell until she was sure no one was coming out, then, on all fours, scampered to the end of the tunnel, to the door. She opened it just enough, wincing at the sucking gasp of air that shot through the gap. She pulled the door behind her and held it shut. She listened for Middle. After a minute, she decided he must be asleep, or uninterested in whatever she was doing.

There was the heart.

Palm first, she moved toward it. Its pulse was different, slower, and the murmuring pulses from within were chaotic, slight, and simple all at once, an orchestra of distant drums being tuned, a faltering crowd. She positioned her whole body just next to it, wrapping her arms around its form but careful not to touch it. The heaviest pulse filled her bones, but she couldn't hear anything, nothing like a voice, saw nothing. She tried speaking. She said, "We need to leave here."

"It's time to land."

She lied, "We have to land, to find Mr Crane. You want to find Mr Crane, don't you?" And, "I thought you would take me home."

She really meant it. She had thought the ship wanted to help them all, that it was saving them, that it liked them, or at least the children. "You know me," she said. "I'm named Yasha. What's—" she felt a little silly, but she meant it nonetheless, "What's your name?"

"Please," she was whispering. "Wake up. Let's go."

She listened, she held still, perfectly still, she heard every vibration, every gurgle of tubing, but none of it meant anything to her, and nothing happened.

She left the room and climbed back up the ramp.

Little Bear was there. He smiled at her.

"Any change?" she was a bit breathless, looking out at the sea of clouds, down to the sea of land.

The bear understood her, shook his head.

She slumped next to him.

"Hey..." Yasha popped up again, alert. She walked toward the ramp and back again. She walked to the other side of the deck and back again, taking stiff, even steps. "This isn't good. The deck is shrinking."

Not only was it shrinking, but it had begun to tilt up. The entire structure of the ship had begun to fold itself in like a flower. Later that afternoon, it was difficult to stay on deck, and after leaning against the interior wall as the deck folded in on them, Yasha and the bear finally settled in the portal's mouth.

"It's going to get dark," she said.

She heard Middle behind them, down below.

"What the hell is happening? It's the middle of the day."

Yasha looked at him and looked away.

He got as far as he needed to see for himself.

"Oh my god. Oh my... are the wings still working... are we just going to drop? What is this? Some kind of trap? Is this how it lands? We'll all be crushed in the fall!"

He scrambled out the portal and climbed around the deck, looking over the edge where he could.

He returned. "Okay. I think if we need to, at least, we can get on the roof. I don't think it will be covered. The wings look fine... unless the thing doesn't want to drop them all until it's done imprisoning us. Okay. I'm going to gather some things. You tell me if it starts moving any more quickly." He disappeared below.

Yasha wanted to trust the ship. But Middle had a point. The ship might think that they'd be safe; it might be dropping, turning into a seed and planting itself, for all she knew. It might not care about any of them. She patted Youngest Bear on the shoulder then rushed back down to the door.

She stood as close to the heart as she could. Very tenderly, she touched it with her palm. It was warm, damp, leathery. She didn't bother saying anything.

She stayed with it as long as she could. She thought about the tower and the floating lake in the sky. She thought about Mr Crane, caught inside the zeppelin, and Eldest Bear trying to save them and falling all that way down. She tried to put her thoughts into her own heart, to make them travel from the air of her mind through the air of her lungs and pass into the liquid world of her blood, to become part of the rhythm of her body, to speak with the rhythm, keep living, be with us, keep living, be with us.

When she came back out, it was nearly pitch black in the tunnel. The lamps had gone out, and just a dim glow made it in from above. Little Bear was still there, at the mouth of the tunnel. Middle was bustling just out of view beyond him, grunting and straining with something.

"This isn't going to work! This is—"

Yasha heard a fibrous crack.

"Oh, damn." He came down below, dragging Little Bear with him. He let his brother sink against a wall. "That's it. We need to kill the thing, but slow enough that we don't drop too fast." He headed toward the ship's heart.

"What?" Yasha backed toward the door. "No!" She spun and slipped through the door before Middle could get there, pulled it shut, wishing for a lock, a bolt. Holding the door shut, she yelled at the pulsing room, "Come on! COME ON! Do something! Tell me what to do! Why don't you just do something?" She peeked to see if Middle was upon them. He had stayed in the tunnel, talking with his brother. "Come on. Please." She held the door shut with one hand while reaching toward the heart with the other.

Middle drew the door back, heedless of Yasha's efforts to prevent him, then stopped. His younger brother was saying something.

Middle turned to Yasha, smiling, "I guess he wants to do it."

Yasha heard the bear groaning as he lifted himself from the ground.

"No! What?" She tried to yank the door closed again, but Middle gave it a shove that sent her to the floor.

Yasha shot back up and wrapped her arms around the heart. She shook it. "Say something! They're going to kill you!"

Littlest Bear came in, gripping the door, panting from the effort.

He looked at Yasha as she broke into gasping tears, suddenly beyond her strength. She stayed on the floor and leaned next to the heart.

Middle handed his brother the dagger.

Balancing as he shifted closer, the little bear put one hand on the heart.

"Hello," he said.

"Hurry up," Middle was standing in the doorway.

"Close the door," said Littlest.

"Just hurry up." Middle stayed where he was.

Littlest smoothed his hand across the heart, as if comforting an injured dog.

Yasha pleaded exhaustedly up at him, said there must be another way, that they can't kill such a thing, that there's some way to speak to it, they just need to figure it out. Said she believed he must have some compassion in him.

Little Bear grabbed a knotty root in the ceiling to steady himself, exercised his grip on the knife.

"What are you doing? Where's my daughter?" Mother appeared just behind Middle Bear. Seeing Yasha on the floor, her dire face and tears, Mother's eyes lit with horror. Though small, she leveraged her weight and fury and shoved Middle Bear aside.

"Mother, they're going to kill—"

"Stay away from her!" Mother yelled at the bears. "Both of you," she gathered up Yasha, "stay away from all of us!" She carried Yasha out of the room. Yasha protested, but weakly. For her, the fight seemed lost already, and a tempest choked her insides. Mother rushed them into an alcove where the other bunnies were huddled. This room, too, was dark and shrinking. Yasha heard Middle Bear urging the young bear on, berating him. What was taking so long? Yasha felt sudden hope. It's all a trick. The young bear has compassion for the ship, and for us, for Hart Crane, but he finds it hard to betray his brother, but he will, he will stab him, stab him and save us all.

She did not hear the cutting sound, but she heard the thick slosh of blood spilling. She listened. It was far more blood than would come out of a bear. She wrested herself up and ran to see. Even then, the tide of blood had nearly covered the floor, and it increased in waves, pulsing waves of more blood.

Middle Bear high stepped from the room, shook his legs as if to get the blood off his boots, but it was all around his ankles.

"There," he said. "I'm going to take a look at our progress. You'll want to tuck yourself in somewhere." He marched up to the deck. He had to work all four sets of claws into the wood to climb his way to the rails. Yasha could not see him but knew he must be peering over the side.

"I think it's working!" he called, straining to hold himself up. "I think one of the limbs is weakening already! Ha!"

The younger bear stepped from the room. He leaned the door shut, but the tide forced it open again. It flowed quickly. It didn't slow down. He grunted something at Yasha, shaking his head, and dropped the knife into the pool of blood. Yasha wanted to retch at the sight and smell. It was well above her ankles now.

Mother had gathered her children in her hammock arms, held them all up high in the corner of their hovel. The children clung to each other, a knot of fur.

Middle called again, "It's working! The leaves are drying up." Yasha heard a crack, felt the ship tip slightly in one direction, the blood sloshed as the ship righted itself. "You see? A limb just came off! We're coming down already!"

Youngest Bear dragged his feet through the blood, held Yasha's shoulder, tapped his shoulder with his other paw, grunted something, inviting her to climb up.

Yasha shook her head, no, stared at the doorway. The black door lolled open. The heart was a spring of blood, a sputtering mouth. It wasn't letting up.

Middle called from above as the process went on. "It's working!" he would cry. Then, as if on a wild river ride, he would laugh and yell when the ship rocked from side to side, slipped down through layers of sky, catch itself up on lively wings and wind. Below deck, the blood was rushing everywhere, against one side, then curling back in a wave. Yasha let herself be covered over, thrown off her feet in the vicious little currents, her fur was thick with it. Finally, she climbed up the bear's arm. He held her there and held himself against a wall, bracing his arm. Yasha heard Mother's shouts, the young bunnies weeping, a few of them letting out rhythmic, unthinking shrieks of alarm with each sickening lurch.

The ship was dropping, as Middle had said. As the ship's wings struggled to keep it up, the heart beat faster and emptied all the more.

Yasha nudged the bear and pointed up the ramp to the deck, saying, "Let's go!"

She called to her mother, but Mother was already inching her way toward the ramp, pinning herself to the wall, bunnies in her arms and clinging to every side of her, just above the red surface. The young bear strode to her and with careful claws plucked bunnies one by one from her arms, perching them on his high shoulders.

The ship was calm for a moment, and Yasha leapt off the bear to the ramp. Mother was treading now, and the bear pulled the last of the bunnies from her shoulders so she could swim. A lurch sent the bear to his knees and gave all the bunnies a jolt. One slipped off and disappeared, ripped away by the diving torrents. Its ears popped up a few yards away, and Mother dove for it, grasped the ears, and hoisted its horrified form above her head. She swam back to the bear holding the bunny above her, kicking desperately. The bear swept it up. The child gagged on the wash of blood in its mouth. The bear gave it a good shake, then scrubbed its face against his chest. The bunny gripped in, wide-eyed and tight-lipped.

Mother was able to stand again once she'd found the ramp. The bear, dropping to all fours, could climb it with some ease, catching his claws into the wood. At the top, they were finally out of the blood, which continued to rise and tumble as the ship bucked through the air.

They were all filthy with it, pinned between the edges of the portal and the nearly vertical deck, clinging as the ship's fall quickened. Mother caught her breath. She checked each of the little ones, stroked their cheeks with her thumbs. She smiled at Yasha, stroked her head, pushing her ears back affectionately.

"I have to find your brother," she said. She dove into the blood.

Moments later, Middle called out, "Brace yourselves!"

When the ship hit the ground, there was an awful crunching of limbs buckling under, the sides of the ship straining and cracking, then the grumble of warm blood searching with trapped force as the ship collapsed on its side, spewing everything out onto the blank field.

They had to struggle not to drown in the outpouring.

Little Bear was spent. Spread on his back, he wheezed, arms adrift in the red pond. Mother was already up, stomping through the mess with her son on her shoulder. She tipped him onto the grass and strode back in to gather up bunnies, increasingly frantic that one might be small enough to disappear.

Yasha rushed to help, found several siblings and hoisted them up, carried them to dry green grass.

Once all were gathered, she watched the ship. Its limbs dropped and splayed, its dry and severed arms littered the valley, and its last few green wings crackled into ash. Its body, its horse-skull body, still drained blood as it closed itself into a cracked wooden egg, closing but not healing.

Mr Fin faced Sam's house.

He needed the book.

He knocked. Sam did not answer.

Just as well, he thought. He wanted no trouble, and he would have had difficulty explaining.

He had rehearsed, "I need my book back..."

"I'll fix it myself, I think..."

"I just can't wait to read it..."

"I like loose pages, actually..."

He knew Sam would have none of it. He'd keep it to fix, but really, he would never get to it. It would sit on a shelf and rot next to decades of half-broken electronics, right on back to his kid's wood-burning kit and broken Christmas ornaments.

He pretended to hear something on the other side of the door, for the benefit of a passerby, and he turned the knob. "Oh, okay, I'll come on in!" he called.

He tried the knob. Unlocked.

He called loudly, "Sam!"

Nothing.

Sam's living room was organized around an old recliner, draped in a plaid wool blanket, positioned just so in relation to the fireplace, the television, an old card table at its side piled with mail, small tools, brushes, empty and not-empty jars, a corked liquor bottle, dishes, light bulbs, a few books, a small phone and its coiled cord.

A peculiar smell seeped up from the warm shag carpet: seawater, cats, smoked salt, stroganoff. Mr Fin hunted for the book. Kitchen, no, bedroom, no. The basement remained—likely Sam's shop and studio.

He pulled the door and called down the unlit stairway, "Sam!"

Nothing. No switch.

Mr Fin spied a flashlight hanging on a nail and took it. He couldn't see the bottom of the stairs in the light beam, thought maybe he was seeing as far as a landing and a turn. So close to the shore, such a basement ought to be knee deep in water.

Mr Fin did not notice, but his body was terrified. As he took the first few steps, his heart raced, his eyes locked open, and his legs clamored to turn, to climb away. Fortunately, he found, on a second landing, a single page that had slipped from David's book. He gathered it up, held it like a talisman. He ran the flashlight's yellow blobs along the stairs, hoping the rest was nearby. He saw nothing, nothing but stairs going down. The flashlight beam, wherever he aimed it, ended in a gray cloud, a stairway, a cloud, as he continued down. Finally the light hit something not cloud, a shifting and glittering black floor.

He could see that, in fact, the basement was flooded with water, water that rushed about in little wavelets and currents. Boxes and bits of memorabilia floated, shadows immersed in shadow. Mr Fin wandered the surface with the flashlight. He could make out water everywhere, but nothing standing in it that would indicate its depth: no laundry machine, no water heater, no shelving, no skis propped up, no windows, and no walls. Just dense black air and gray water. The book would be in there, somewhere, but soaked, destroyed! He didn't know if he would have the nerve to wade in after a page, or even after the whole book, should it float by. Water in the darkness, he thought, without a way to finish the thought.

The light struck something large, stuck out of the current, perhaps snared between branches—no, there wouldn't be branches. Mr Fin was already holding his breath when he realized it was a body. It was not Sam, and it was not David.

It was poor Hart Crane, come to recover the book! Drowned in the cellar!

Fin panicked back up the stairs, up a flight and turn, gripping his page, up a flight and turn... desperate for the orange glow of the kitchen. He couldn't look back into the dark well. Finally the stairs glowed, up a flight and turn, and a rectangle of kitchen glowed above him like a sunrise. He caught the door frame and yanked himself into the light, pulling the basement door until it latched securely behind him.

He rushed through the house, stumbling back out into the day. Pacing in Sam's yard, Fin clenched his face and hands, strained to hold his mind back tight to the real world, or at least to the one where lives go on as they should.

Back home, he hid in his chair, and drowsy, frayed, he read the page he'd rescued, the last available words:

at an earlier time wasn't I always near you, this light, avid, insatiable desire to see you and yet, once you were visible, to transform you further, into something more visible, to draw you, slowly and darkly, into that point where you couldn't any longer be anything but seen, where your face became the nakedness of a face and your mouth metamorphosed into a mouth? Wasn't there a moment when you said to me: 'I have the feeling that when you die, I will become completely visible, more visible than is possible and to the point that I won't be able to endure it.'

These words were Hart Crane's message to him, or his plea, or his curse. Mr Fin couldn't tell, had no idea who was you and who was I, who was dying or seen and who could speak and who desired. But he clutched the paper like a long awaited letter.

The last few lines fit with some difficulty. The mouth was dry, the natural impulse to swallow or chew, for David, was limited. But it all fit, and Mr Fin pressed the gray lips together. As he did, he heard breathing, a sound not unlike water running through pipes in some other part of the house, but rhythmic, a bit low, a bit wheezy, strained.

"Just relax," he said, stroking David's forehead, "It's from your book, just like you wanted." He drew his finger down David's throat to encourage him to swallow. "It's just a part of it, but that's enough for now, right? You can speak this way, just like Mr Crane—reciting stories, or his crazy poems. These are the lines that connect you with him, and with who he was before, and before. That's how I know you." Mr Fin laid his head on the chest, nuzzled his wet nose against the quilt.

Breath leaked from somewhere in the chest, but not as much as before. After a time, he left the body there, on the bed, and paced in his sitting room. David's breathing continued in his ears, but to Mr Fin, it seemed all inhalation, nothing captured or returned, the body nothing more than a passage. All over the house, he could still hear it, tiny throaty hissing, a gurgle in a distant cavern, a pipe in the ceiling suddenly compelled by the distant water tower.

She focused on the moment, the elation of freedom, the capacities of her mind. Oh, there was light and sun and fresh air and all the beautiful devices of liberated feeling, but none of these drew her attention. Her body, which before she had thought of as voice, as being near or far from the boy, had its own intricate wonders. She could move it, change it, feel air and water push against it. The goat-boy's imaginary friend came to some realizations. Standing over him, in the river, she tried to feel the torn place in her mind that had once connected them, but she could not. She felt whole. What's more, she felt larger than she had been, and older. She felt her past, the strength she possessed, the knowledge of the world that had been clogged up by the goat-boy, and her thoughts, her private thoughts, thoughts like the elements—pieces of a grand and infinite puzzle. Her body was a cloud of its own patterns, of signals that she controlled, signals she could send out in any direction, not any distance, but far, quite far.

She marveled at the love and companionship she had felt with the goat, with the goat-boy. Part of her worried that the pleasures of living she'd felt through their union would be impossible now, or, more precisely, that they were only possible if she reduced herself, poured herself into some form and began again, ignorant, quiet, subservient. What a distraction that existence seemed, and it pleased her to see him in the river, to know how his form would dissolve and float away, delicate, quieted pieces of that simple life. Was he still in there, and was she now free? Or was he also somewhere in the air; were they both locked in their own quiet, airy minds? No. He was this thing beneath her. Incredible, she thought, that, freed of all that organic machinery, she felt more fully, more completely the world and herself within it. So much effort goes into flimsy organs and flesh.

She tested her limits, letting her form drift into the distance. Though at times she felt dangerously thin, the extent to which her form could expand without breaking was potentially unlimited—she could become a thread of particles stretching, who knows, around the world. She was so much more, unfolding, refolding, aligning, spinning and expanding into new constellations, some of which were thoughts, some memories. In fact, wherever she relaxed her form, her body would take on its own patterns, show her pictures of the past, recount the story of her life. She played with relaxing completely, letting herself be pulled into whatever shape by memory. Soon, thoughts glimmering as if around her waist returned to her the life she'd lived as the queen of ants, and her colony. She saw the colony grow and grow, moving from host to host, and soon enough, she remembered their destruction and the brown deflated bear on the tile floor, the windows and the tree-mother, the vicious brothers, so unfit for existence. She was more than alive now. She could wander among all the lovely objects of the world.

Chapter Five

Mr Fin woke with an eye like a great iron church bell. When he rolled over, the bell clanged and clamored, shook his skull. The heavy iron brought him headlong to the floor. He reached for his pills with one hand while the other worked as if to cram the bell back through his eye socket.

Much of the morning, because of the bell, he had to crawl along on all fours, backwards like a dog at tug-o-war, at first, and then, his neck filled with vigor, he stepped his arms and stepped his knees like a workhorse hooked to a cruel load, neck curled to make a regal hook. By noon he had fallen asleep, face flattened spongily against the bathroom floor, body splayed behind.

The bell melted, turned to drool and sleepy tears. Waking, he had to gasp to inflate his chest. He felt textured waves of ether sweep through him every second, then every two seconds, three, five, eight, and then pleasantly uncountable intervals expanded as he lay.

He played himself the scene in *Quixote* in which Sancho woke his master by accident, in the process of sneaking off toward the cellar for something to eat; they were at an inn of some kind, and the knight woke fully steeped by dreams, in his delusions, and said, feebly at first, still quite asleep, but moving from sleep to waking without transition or interruption, he said, "Sancho, my sometimes loyal squire! Though you yourself possess nothing of the courage and dignity of knighthood," now he was all awake, and went right on as if the dream and the moment were one, "I see how my influence, even the nobility of my destiny, ignites some hidden vittle of valor within you, and now provokes you toward foolish bravery. But you must not face the dark wizard of this castle. That is my task, as a knight, and a burden proper to my station, but I do thank you, for I believe I might have perished here on this unholy ground, either from my wounds or from the accommodations. Now tell me—what part of this castle conceals our foe, for I must leave you and face the fiend immediately!"

Sancho, hesitating only a moment, suggested, "In the barn, master, just a moment ago, I saw an unholy orange glow in the windows!"

The Knight of the Lion looked perplexed, irritated, then he understood. "Ah, Sancho. I was confused. Consider, as you may, that the world is like a saddlebag. If, every day of his pitiable life, a man should be satisfied to reach into the bag on his mount—or at his side if he walks along by his mule, or, because it is not elemental to the moral of my speech, you may imagine him reaching into the pack slung over his very own shoulder—and when he reaches there to find and to consume the sandwich or block of bread or bit of meat he has stored for himself, then indeed, we may call him lucky, and every day he shall be satisfied, fed, and nourished. But let us imagine that he goes through all his days in this manner, each morning replacing what was taken the day before, ever satisfied, until, dreadfully late in life, the old bag gives up its ghost, that is, the bottom comes unstitched and everything falls from it in a pile. There on the ground, Sancho, lies the sandwich of the day, the very one he packed that morning, believing it to be the sole contents of the bag, but now he sees that it lies atop a pile of gold, or jewels, or—"

Sancho laughed. "I suppose, old fool that he is, he thinks the gold or the jewels had been lying on the ground, and himself lucky to find his sandwich fallen there. In other words: he who stumbles upon riches won't mend the holes in his pockets."

"You've missed my purpose entirely, Sancho, and I haven't time now to mend your thinking. Stay here, my friend, and be safe."

"Or you might remind him, you may be a man if you've got a knot in your back, but you're a mule if you find another's brick in your sack!"

"I can't hear another. Listen to me, Sancho, and heed what comes to you now from the lips of your master: you may wish to cover your ears with that blanket, there. In the coming battle, I face as many torments as my adversary, and you will hear my cries amongst his. You will quail if you hear but the least of them, and your heart will ache, your mind will reel about in anguish at the terrific clamoring of our struggle. But fear not and do not weep, Sancho, for I will be victorious in the dawn, which, in the divine scheme of the day, is the season of the just and possesses the right aura for great victories, and you will see how different the world appears when that sorcerer is cast out from it by the thrash of my shining blade."

In the barn, Quixote encountered farm animals that he took for monsters of legend. He moved to slay the fierce griffin, but in a wild swing embedded his sword in one of the barn's rafters. A startled horse shouted and bucked, fueling the knight's delusion, for now he saw smoke and flames gathering around the figure of a bronze-skinned centaur who brandished a whip like lightning. Soon a hellish choir of startled creatures pitched the knight toward frenzy, and, reeling, he tangled himself up in tack and collapsed into a pile of hay sweepings, his head finding the edge of a smith's anvil on the way down.

He was fortunate in that moment that a goose approached, for she appeared to him as a Swan, an emissary from fair Dulcinea. In his befuddled eyes, the bird was surrounded by rose and white ether, which, in all the stories, is the sign that the hero is suspended outside of time, in a cocoon of mystical light, and is thereby welcomed into the congress of the gods and goddesses, bidden by them to receive a message or a vision. "What do you bring me, Swan of the gods, or Zeus's rapturous cloak, in this dark and terrible hour? What consolation for this weary knight, what slim promise or hope to ignite or at least fan the last sparks of my being? What word from my love, fairest Dulcinea, have the gods allowed you to transport and deliver to my remaining, untorn ear?"

Sleep, Quixote.

And so it was that Alonso Quijano seemed to lie down with a swan, and as he embraced the divine bird, it grew and seemed to him like a living couch, so that he was both curled around and riding on the swan's back, and together they floated for a time, on a small lake full of liquid pre-dawn light, and when the swan leapt into the air the knight sat up briefly, for that was all his stomach could bear, but he sat up and saw from a height the rotund expanse of the country, and he felt his blood rising and falling through his entire frame as the silver wings shuddered and lunged against the veil of appearances.

How shall I begin to get up? Elbows? Knees?

The bridge was just a quarter mile from where the river joined the sea. Fin was in lunch-hour traffic, the day was warming. The bridge had four lanes and a pedestrian crossing, large for the town because it fed the nearby freeway and served as a junction for commuters. The bridge was industrial but approaching lovely. It had a name.

Mr Fin stopped the car a third of the way across. Immediately, cars stacked up behind him, there was a moment of patience, of heads tilting to see what was going on. A distant honk. Drivers began to whip their cars out from behind him to take the other lane. Still, they stacked up, and the other lane became halting and cluttered with lane changes. The opposing traffic flashed by.

Fin pulled the parking break, left the engine running, and opened his door, careful not to swing it out too far. Turning his body, he pulled himself up and out. The honking was fierce now, except for a few cars directly behind him. He glanced at the woman in the first car in the line. She had clearly accepted a little wait, and now looked both annoyed and concerned. The man in the next car had cracked his door and poked his head up to see what was happening. Mr Fin tried to take stock of it all, of all the responses, and then to forget them, to not care. He was not part of their world.

He couldn't remember which lane to cross. He imagined himself back in the passenger seat, the sound of the door, yanking and furious and the denim of David's jacket, silver radio dials, and the bumpy steering wheel, moments ridiculously detailed. Why hadn't he driven himself? He heard in his memory a slap on the hood as David lunged around the car, yes, then Fin had turned to his right, scrambled at his own locked door as David paused at the stark headlight.

The pedestrian walk was on the right side, across the frustrated traffic. Everyone was watching him, even those hustling to cut around, so he didn't worry about stopping and looking. He fixed his mind as if to a singular purpose, though he couldn't name it, didn't want it to be his own, instead a waiting, a passivity, a disappearance into the action.

He had to climb a low barrier to reach the walkway. He laughed at how slow he was, but he ignored the little pains and protests, tipped over as he landed, but held firm to the peeling green and rust-marbled rail.

He wrapped each hand around a wire as he peered into the quick, pinched water below, heavy development and pylons on both sides, just as it angled toward the embrace and confusion of the sea. Fin leaned as far out as he could to feel the untamed air, the gravity and the distance down, sensed the delighted watery updraft.

He pulled himself back in and headed toward land along the pedestrian walkway. Once he'd passed the first three or four cars, no one minded him, just another pedestrian. Metal grate stairs offered access to the water below, a disused dirt path, unceremonious. He found a spot where he could reach into the water: knees in the soft bank, one hand on a rock. The cold rush of it horrified him. He immersed his hand, pressed the wet cold against his closed lips, pushed it through his hair.

Not exhausted at all, he walked along the river until he was home again.

They washed in the river.

But it wan't enough to clear the blood.

Middle marched downstream, as if he knew where to go, and everyone else followed, with nothing better to do. Held between Mother and Yasha, the younger bear could drag himself along on all fours. When they got too far behind, Middle stopped and picked his claws, or drew water from the river, washed his face, all of it impatiently. When they caught up, he was off again.

They walked until evening. Middle was a mile ahead.

Mother stopped, a hollow gasp filling her face with terror.

"My son," she said. "My son." She was frozen. Her mind reeled at the hours, each hour of numb forgetting, and she imagined the weight of his body on her back, how slow she would be, every step she would need to take to retrieve him. Much of the night to get back to him, perhaps a whole day or more to get back here, under his weight, here, which was still nowhere. Without another word, she turned and walked the way she had come.

Yasha, Youngest, and all the small bunnies stood wordlessly, thoughtlessly, then sat and waited. In the morning, they found things to chew, fetched water.

In the morning, Vivian came by. She knocked ceaselessly.

With a cold damp cloth to his forehead, Mr Fin cracked the door, putting on his most miserable face.

"Oh, my, you look terrible," she cried, distracted momentarily. She'd been about to stroll inside.

"I'm ill." Fin said. "You shouldn't come in." He glanced toward the back of the house. David's room was open. Casually, he set his foot to keep the door from opening further.

"Well, I wanted to bring you..." She laid something on the porch before the door, large, flat, and black. "This!"

"What is it?"

"It's a, you know, a welcome mat. See?" She demonstrated standing before it and knocking on the door. "Hello!"

"Did I need a welcome mat?"

"I just thought... um." She took a moment to decide. "Honestly?"

Fin waited.

"So, it's supposed to help keep you from taking off when you're not really remembering stuff, you know, in case you're off a bit."

"It's going to stop me?"

"Well, supposedly, when you open your door, you'll look out here, and then you'll see that there's a black, um, pit in front of the door, and you won't want to try to get over it. You know your eyes aren't so good."

"Oh!"

"I know it sounds really stupid. I'm sorry, I was worried..."

"No it's okay. That sounds... fine." Fin gave a cough and a sniffle. "I like it. Thanks. That will be..."

"Okay... we'll just see." Vivian smiled and peered past Fin into the house. She jerked her head back, aghast. "Oh, god, Fin, what's that smell?"

"What?"

"Is everything okay in there? I could do some dishes, if you like. Since you're ill... maybe you need someone to... oh, god... really, what have you got in there? If... if you're feeling sick, it might be from... that, whatever it is. Can't you smell it?" She covered her mouth and nose with her hand and backed away.

"I'm just not feeling well," Fin said, "Come back tomorrow!" He shut the door and bolted it.

Minutes later the phone rang. It was Sam.

"Hey bud. Listen. I'm going to take you out on the boat, like I said. This Saturday's good for me, and I know it's good for you, so I'll come by around... uh, say, six. Alright? That's A.M., of course. Okay—and I've got two good poles, so don't worry about a thing. Bring yourself some coffee or something, though, and maybe a snack. It's gonna be cold."

Mr Fin agreed and hung up. He sat with his head and his ear nestled into the wing of his wing-back chair. Tired chair, tired flesh, when all the books have been read. He loved old upholstery, the sweet smell of fibers that have touched so many faces so many times. Where a banister smooths from too much touch, upholstery wears down, yes, but also sweetens. Sweetens from too much. From too much what, he wondered.

Fin was on the water for days, his version of camping. He'd put away the sails that morning, watched the clouds, stood in the sun, napped below deck, ate little, felt himself draining into the day's progression, his life stringing forward in an aimless line instead of a cycle of predictable moves. He thought, what if I stop being hungry? He thought, what if I don't sleep?

This was the last time on The Swan. Was I moping? he wondered. How did I get back? That was. No. It was the fourth day, after the third night, swimming in the morning.

That was a glorious morning. Nothing disturbed me. I stripped naked and dove into the permeable earth, into its true soul. I spoke that way, to myself, after a day or two on the boat one does, and I knew what vastness floated around me and beneath me. That was how it felt, that the water floated, on itself, on the impossible bedrock of the soft planet. I could hold my breath. David got that from me. I suspended myself below water, forcing my eyelids to open, to accept the stinging water, saw beams of light wiggling around the boat.

He had to move or freeze. He kicked off the boat and down, into the immediate dark, immediate cold, saw nothing in the thickness. Whirled himself, stretched himself, tried to work his whole body into a sea creature, sweeping, orchestrated turns, nothing to do but stare about, process oxygen, move blood. As he ran low on air, he tried to disorient himself, to float as if in space, ignored the pull of the surface and the push of the deep. He wondered how long he could stay. He wondered at the cold licking his body, pressing beneath his skin.

I came to the surface, hand up for the rickety ladder, and he saw himself on the deck already, putting up the sail, readying for home. He stopped in the water, bobbing hand out reaching for the ladder, stopped treading, watched himself so dry and smug on the deck: he had shaven this morning, made coffee, there was a breeze, he was almost beautiful, putting up the sail, ready to go. I let myself submerge again, as if to make the world blink, reconsider.

Underwater, I could hear the clicking of the turning hull, aching as the wind and the waves competed for it, heard the rattling lines sliding through their pulleys. Back up, I saw The Swan on its way.

I waited, trying to accept that I was already gone.

Mr Fin got home late at night. He parked the boat in the yard and stumbled inside.

The next morning, he cleaned out David's closet, emptied David's chest of drawers, tidied and dusted and sprayed. He remembered the figure of himself in the water, stranded out there. They'd never found the body. He loaded David's things into boxes, collected more boxes from the grocer, packed his own things away, whatever he didn't immediately need, gradually accepting that he was leaving his home.

Yasha was cold, but she refused the company of her siblings, who all huddled into Youngest's fur. Bears are all butchers, she said to herself, selfish and dumb beasts. When she thought the bear was asleep, she stood and paced until she cried.

"I can tell you about Mr Crane." The bear's voice was an insect in the night.

Yasha gave him a reproachful look, his button eyes gloaming in the dark, but she knew immediately that he wouldn't care about, probably wouldn't notice, her anger. She couldn't even be sure her face was displaying the correct emotion; who could tell what anything was in this anonymous field?

She wanted to know about Crane, so kept quiet.

"Hart was born long before any of us. His father was a well-placed clerk in an architectural firm, and his mother ran the house. She died before he really knew her. He told me he had no actual memories of her. Can you imagine? So he had nothing to mourn, had not been alive enough as a child to understand what had happened, had lost all memories. It would be nonsense, anyway. So it was Hart, his older sister, and their father. But his father was not as interested in his children as he was in finding a new wife. Hart and his sister spent most of their time with grandparents, in the country, eventually all of their time out of school they spent with the old grandparents, in the country, or not so much with them as in their keeping, well outside the city. It was not a farm. Nothing like that. It was a country estate. The grandparents were not wealthy. The house was all they had. Brother and sister were passionately close, though the sister was ten years older. She doted on him, and he thought the world of her. They had most of their time to themselves, outside on the lawn, playing among the arbors and by the dry well, in tunnels under the masses of bending blackberry vines, among old walls of river rock they found in the tall grass. Hart was a boy firmly lodged in fantasy, and some of it felt very true: that they were orphans, held captive in a mansion, that all of their kind were gone and they had to survive in the wild, that she had found him, a lost baby or puppy, abandoned in the woods, and it turned out he had magical powers. These might have been small moments, long afternoons among the doldrums, but to him, now, then, they made up the entirety of his early childhood. She never outgrew him. Even when she was a young woman, she never had a harsh word for his errors and stupidity. When she fell sick, her father and his new wife came to stay, and for Hart, their presence was the end of the insular world that brother and sister shared. Through every day of her illness, he shut the door to her room, drew back the curtains and opened the windows, carved the space out from the stain of his father's air, and he lingered with her, wishing that air and soul were one, waiting for her to get better in his care. He was with her when she died. She was not without energy up to the end. She would listen to him and speak with him and laugh, and she would stay awake even when they sat in silence. It was not her mind being killed, it was something deep in her body. In the last moments, which the moment she spoke he realized were the last moments, he'd said to her, 'You can't die. It's not possible.' She replied, 'Don't think about life. Let life be as unthinkable as the rest.' As she was dying, he heard the horses ninny in the yard, below the window, and the leather saddles being slid from their backs. He could smell the ice of the coming winter in the air, despite the sun. He wished her soul was a white bird, and he would see it rising, but it was not. When he spoke of her, much later, he called her his poor young phantom. He said it as if she were something he had invented, a figure from the literature of his life. When he was of age, he denied anything his family could offer him and established himself as a storyteller in a large town far from his former homes. Young, idealistic, priestly, he attracted families to his afternoon tales and serious men of letters to his evening recitations. Soon, he was married, and had a child of his own, and another. The second one, a boy, died quite young, he would not say how young. Not another day went by that he did not think about his phantoms. It was not the feeling of death pursuing him, nor the feeling of some mortal hour approaching, it was a sense that death had come so close to him, beginning with the dreamy closeness of an unremembered mother. His sister had died as he watched, in mid-conversation, as if she'd willed him to see her go. Now his own son, the loss of whom was unspeakable—no story, no verse (his verse was shattered). Death surrounded him in space. He could reach out an arm and his fingers would dip into the underworld as into cold cream, his feet were made damp by the puddles of the Lethe. The entirety of the unseen world was the other world, beyond his periphery, hidden in old traveling trunks, the hollow between walls, the interior of the body, the thick shadows of a cold fireplace at night, all of it was, to him, a lattice of open graves. None of this caused him anxiety. During his recitations, he would stand before his acolytes and speak with his eyes closed, learning as it crossed his lips the language of death, the language of last words, to pronounce from that cold place the warrant of life, an eternal obsequy, founded less in the meaning of words as in their weakness when intoned by one so near to the end of things. He did not want to die. He was confident enough that he would die. He refused to separate the joy of living from the presence of death. He did not always look the way he does now, and not long ago, he was a rabbit like you, and like your mother. He told me that, later, when he was a young man again, indeed, as if he was a character in a book, that he spent time on the ocean and in deserts of snow, and he spent his life sick with love, sick because his love was infected with shame, and desire was a crime, especially in the cities, where crime was part of life. He wrote all of his stories down, but in the city none of it was understood, everyone was silent about stories. He went to the ocean in search of the language of last words, of what had been so close to him before. He watched the seabirds sail drunkenly between foam and sky until the ship was beyond birds. He wanted to stop writing, stop speaking: he wanted to be no more or less than a letter in the great book of the ocean. There was a shipwreck, and he described being sucked into a maelstrom, and he told me how, deep in the mouth of the storm, his hand caught upon something that would save him, from being sucked down, and he said, he told me, he couldn't decide whether to hold on or to let go. He told me that he didn't remember any of this until the zeppelin attack. When his town was attacked, eaten, he was eaten as well, swallowed alive, and it was the same feeling, as he was pulled through the guts of the zeppelin, and the decision was impossible still. I watched him fall from one, and walk out of the forest naked, transformed, unable to speak as he used to, barely able to think. He saved my life. From that moment, though, all he wanted was to change again, or change back, to be transformed again, to become what, I don't know, or maybe, at last, to die, but I don't think so. I think now, after all that has happened, that maybe he should not have lived, and I should not have been saved by him, and maybe somehow you all would have been safe together, more safe than you are now. That's what Hart and I have in common: we can't help living."

It took the bear most of the night to get through the words. Yasha waited until she was sure he was finished. In that pause, she negotiated between hope and grief and said evenly: "Do you think he's okay? Do you think he might come back?"

"I'm no good at guesses."

"Why did you do it?" she asked.

"I had two reasons. I believed my brother would kill the ship without compassion. Not to say whether it would suffer more, but that there would be no friendship in the murder, no tenderness or regret. Second, I thought that it wouldn't matter. I thought, no one speaks with their hearts, therefore, it was not, truly, a heart. I thought, too, trees do not have hearts, they have roots. So I had hope that I was not killing it but was only taking its voice, if it truly had one. Was that two?"

Yasha was unmoved. Dawn came, matter of fact. "That's— I saw it. I heard it speaking to Mr Crane. I felt its voice myself. It told me about a place that used to be, or something that Mr Crane had imagined, and it knew his son. The ship knew him. You killed it. You took its voice. You drained its blood. After it saved us all."

"Yes." Youngest left space around the word. "I think I may have been wrong. It all reminded me of something I read in a book once. That's a third reason, I think. I've never been very good at making up ideas. In the book, everything seemed very pretty and right."

He heard something in the air, as if just outside the window, or in the attic, like a hummingbird. He'd once held a hummingbird in his palm, victim of one of the cats. The bird's heart raced, but it played dead as long as it could bear, waiting for the right moment. In his palm, it was like a living swatch of silk, wings made of dense air. It zipped away. The breath. The breath was diminishing, straining. David was sunk further into the sheets, the words were rotting in his mouth, others drying on his skin. He needed something more.

Fin saw the rabbits, all nameless and drenched in crusting blood, exhausted polyps on the prairie earth. He mourned the collapse of the wooden ship, which he knew David had enjoyed. David had drawn pictures of it, placed himself on the deck with Hart Crane.

The ship.

Fin gathered the buckets of boat parts from the garage. Strips of sail cloth draped around his neck, he lugged them into David's room. He made several more trips, arranging the broad and long woods and metal strips by the bed. Finally, he bundled into his arms the old halyards and sheets and all the little lines and bits of line resting on shelves.

"Look, David," he said, "I can build us a ship."

The ship, now a seed, sank a bit into the soaked earth, its shell softening in the rain and splitting in the sun. The invisible friend, the ant queen, surveyed its crumpled walnut flesh and its aching chest. She reached out to it, as she had learned to do, speaking its language, or rather, speaking her own language, the essence of language that all creatures must succumb to. She told it to stop bleeding. The released blood had already formed a shallow swamp, cracking at the edges into filthy streams. She found that messy. She advised the ship to heal its wound.

She had a good feeling about this creature. She could sense its age, and though it said nothing to her, she thought she could understand its attitude toward things, which was not unlike her own, written in its organs, the fingerprint of this grotesque moment. Its scattered limbs grieved her, and she wondered, with the parts of her that reached into the wooden bird, so in a sense, speaking her thoughts to it, she wondered why it allowed itself to suffer in this way. Why must you suffer like this? She could not read its thoughts or its memories easily, but she became aware of its mood. Searching further into the ship's body, she could tell it was waiting for someone. She told it to be patient and to not destroy itself for the sake of another. She knew it heard her. She tried to hold it, to send it soothing thoughts. The fountain of blood stopped. Splintered and chopped shoulders smoothed.

The imaginary friend spotted something on the edge of the swamp: the wrapped up body of a rabbit-boy, dead. Perhaps that was what the ship mourned, its child or its sailor. She lifted the body—such actions were still not easy, but it was easier than moving the goat, that heavy thing, into the water. She carried the rabbit to the ship. The ship did not respond. She placed it on top of the ship, balanced the body on its curving pod-like roof. She unwrapped the body, threw the sheets and rags to the ground. This must be it, she thought; she remembered the shape of pity.

She grew frustrated with the ship. At least tell me something, she demanded.

She learned the rabbit's exterior. Must be it. The scenario seemed more and more accurate: the ship was waiting for a rabbit, she could see it now, in its pain, and here was the rabbit. This must be it. The ship was silent.

Tentative, she pressed herself a tiny way into the prone body of the dead rabbit. She would occupy it enough to make the ship believe it was alive, to draw it out. She reached around the rabbit's arm, made it move up and down, reached into its other arm, made it pat the ship. She could feel the cold of the rabbit's body, its soggy internal decay. The muscles were difficult to maneuver. She sent ideas to the ship through the rabbit's mouth.

"I'm here!" the mouth said.

"Wake up!" it cried.

But the words were not so crisp. She had to use her own voice.

"I'm here!" she called.

"Wake up!" she cried.

Everything in the bunny was collapsing. She slipped the rest of the chest on—like putting on a coat made of rotten fruit. She put her arms around the ship and suddenly felt it, the heart starting up in the wooden chamber, a rhythmic acknowledgement, but also a question. She wanted to be the answer to that question. She leapt fully into the body, meaning to climb into the ship as the rabbit. She wanted nothing more than to swim down through the blood to the heart—did she really, did she want this? She shook, urging the dead rabbit to climb.

But she couldn't. She was all in, and now the body floundered and snapped rigid around her. She was trapped, and they, the dead rabbit and she, fell from the ship into the blood below.

She remembered this feeling. This was how life had felt before she'd spoken from within the goat-boy: to be held deep inside a body, no means of detaching from it until the two voices, hers and his, could know each other as separate. Here, inside the dead rabbit, there was no one to talk to. She had lost control of the limbs. Curse bodies, she said. Curse that ship. She had eyes to look from, a mind, shrunk away from the world, but a mind nonetheless. She waited. Was this the way she'd been fooled before? Trees! She laughed to herself. It can't be for long.

You need a name, she said to the rabbit.

The rabbit wasn't there.

That was how Mother found her son. So, again, she gathered sheets and rags and towels, blood soaked as they were, and wrapped him. She had no choice but to hoist him onto her shoulders and begin the long walk to rejoin her other children.

Mr Fin didn't go into the house.

He sat in the garage, examining the boat.

His wife was just inside. He could hear her performing innocent tasks. Pure and beautiful sounds, salt shaker placed on the shelf, a cupboard opening and closing, walking to the other room, moving a magazine from here to there, quiet as she sat down, but he could imagine the sound of her work shoes sliding off over her nylons.

The boat looked almost new. He'd cleaned it the week before.

Fin tipped from his stool and sat on the pavement. He stretched out on his back under the boat, so that it soared above him. He couldn't imagine his mouth opening ever again, because the next words that had to come out of him...

Because she would leave him, and he wouldn't care.

Because once he said it, he would have to believe it, and he would never be free of these hours.

The ant queen searched every corner of the rabbit's corpse, expecting to find some kind of exit. Why should it be—she kept going over it—that the death of the goat-boy released me, but a dead rabbit can trap me again? She had already realized the answer, but it horrified her all the more: she had become part of the goat boy by accident, almost completely disappeared into him, for years, she hardly even knew she existed. She had become capable of differentiating from him because both had recognized the subtle gulf that divided them. The zeppelin had done something more to them. What had destroyed his body had made hers all the more real. But now she had become a dead rabbit, and there was nothing in the rabbit to recognize her, to see her as foreign, to name her. She was a corpse.

She could spread herself evenly through the body, feel its surfaces and all its organs. She found it to be a satisfyingly complex space, but death was not kind to bodies. Distant memories of the bear's body came to mind, and though the rabbit body was much smaller, there was something similar about it. Could she, perhaps, still summon a colony of ants? Could she bring them to her now to carve a home in this rabbit? Could they help her to escape imprisonment? The more she considered her strange presence and her abilities, the more convinced she was that her life as an ant, that it, too, was temporary, that all creatures were small and simple compared to her. She was an essence, the invisible space between speechless minds, she rode the air, could guide others in all they did, and even if she was only a fragment of the net of thought, it was being cut off from the rest that made her free. She was a dictionary, the invisible tongue of nature.

She sensed something happening, even in the thick confusion of the body, she could sense that it had been lifted, and she and it were being moved. It was the shift in fluids and gravity, what stretched and how the thickness of the landscape bent and trembled. She searched out all the boundaries of the body in contact with whatever carried it. She wriggled her form between tissue and among molecules and, at the barrier between the dead body and the living, she stretched herself toward the void. Something like a wall stopped her from going further, but she went against it anyway, speaking, shouting, nothing in particular, just hello or put me down, or whatever, only hoping for a response of some kind, a counter-signal, a change. There was no way out, and no way to send her voice out of the body, which came to the same thing.

She spent several days curled up in the skull as the body was carried. The skull fit her like a good chair. The movement of being carried soothed her some, the gray room somber and quiet, so that she listed often to a kind of sleep, a waking dream that sent shivers through the body. She would be patient, as before, taking her time in death with the rabbit as if she were a child carried in its mother's soupy, dark womb.

When Mother returned with her son, wrapped and everything charred red on her shoulder, all red, they did not move on. Mother slept for a day and a night. When she woke, she washed in the river, then set herself to cleaning, arranging. She told all the bunnies which rocks and shrubs were the corners and walls of their new home, that the river was where they went and where they washed, and she showed them how to do it properly. She arranged weeds and dry grass into beds, and she gathered sticks and stones and stray objects that resembled household tools: can opener, butter knife, trowel, knitting needles, spoon, spatula, doorknob, telephone, bedside lamp, keys, shoe rack, hatstand, alarm clock, pantry shelf, tea tray, kettle, saucepan, hot pad, magazine rack, ashtray, pencil sharpener, dishrag, and so on. Each thing she held before her assembled children, and they recited each name after her. She observed them carefully, showed them how to open doors that weren't there, chided them if they passed through walls.

Each morning, the rabbit children were all expected to wake up, tidy their beds, and dress. They were given lessons in grammar and mathematics. Though breakfast, lunch, snack time, and dinner were all pretend, they sat through them dutifully, obedient to the forced play of comforts, and though at first it was only for Mother's eyes, the palliative routine absorbed them. After lunch, before snack time, they were sent outside to play, but not too close to the river, not too far into the deep grasses.

"Look, children," Mother said, "Mrs Salmon is coming to visit. We're going to make a proper meal, and she and I are going to play cards while you all do homework." Some of the little ones were better at pretend than others. Every problem of addition or subtraction had details, steps to take, along with the memories of classrooms and teachers, name tags and paperclips, and the promise of reward when turned in, a bright letter or a sticker with an apple on it. These lucky bunnies kept busy. Some got stuck. They would try to work, but, with no alternative, find themselves staring into space. Mother was exceptional. She had a grand time with Mrs Salmon. The playing cards had texture, bright colors, and the game was fluid and always within reason.

One morning, Yasha told her mother, "I need to go to proper school today," and she wandered out of sight and sat by the river for hours. After several days of school, the littlest bear met her out there. He'd left on the second day, but it took effort to reach her.

She asked him why he was there.

He said, in his slow way, that he thought he could tell her things, stories, things he'd learned. Like real school. It was up to her. Obviously, she could go somewhere else, and he could not easily follow. He would be here, in the grass by the river, trying to remember all the things he'd read.

"Have you read a lot of books?" Yasha asked.

"Yes. It's all I did."

"How many did you have?"

"At first, I had almost a hundred, and more, because my mother told me things that weren't in books but were like books—just like them."

"At first?"

"We had to cut back. For a while, I had sixteen that I read over and over, and then just the four I loved most. I know them the best. Then we had to sell those."

"What were they about?"

"They were about humans, and they had adventures. And I know some other things, too, but not as well." He wanted her to ask.

"What other things?"

"Mr Crane's stories. He told me some."

"Ok."

This conversation had taken much of the afternoon, because Littlest needed time to work through such sentences. Yasha liked the pace. She felt it was a fine pace for the world. She tried to think as slowly as he spoke. She couldn't decide if this made the days longer or shorter. Was time gaining finer detail, texture and nuance, or losing it, becoming smooth and distant?

The next day, a funny thing happened.

Yasha left for school, and she encountered the bear not two hundred paces from home.

"Why did you move?" she demanded.

"Move what?" he asked, surprised at her sourness.

"We're too close!" she said. "Mother will see."

"I didn't move," the bear said, "you can see that I'm in the same grass, next to the same river, and these rocks, here, are the same, and I can smell, not too far off, not far at all, where I've been peeing."

Yasha wasn't sure.

"We need to be further," she insisted. She looked back and saw her mother's head bobbing behind a shrub. "Catch up." She stomped off through the grass. Littlest found her as evening fell. "Would you like to hear a story?" he asked, lying down, exhausted.

"No. I've got to go home. School can't go all day. I'll come back in the morning."

The next day, it was the same. Yasha walked no more than two hundred paces and came upon the bear.

"What are you up to?" she demanded. She was harsh with him. How stupid could he be?

Yasha found another location for school, this time, much further from home. She did not see the bear again until she was on her way home, in the evening. She told him, "There is a dead tree next to a rock, near the river. I scratched an x on the tree so that we know which one it is. If you move to another tree, a closer tree, then I'll know." It did not occur to her that the bear could scratch an x into a tree with his claw, but it did not occur to him, either.

The next day, Yasha woke up, and even from where she lay on her grass mat, in her room, next to her reading lamp and her slippers, she could see the tree, she could see the sickly ears of the bear poke out above the grasses. She ran to the bear and woke him.

"Something very unusual is happening," she whispered.

They resolved to stay out all night by the tree. Yasha told Mother that it was the weekend, and that she and the bear were preparing a science project for Monday, and that it involved studying the constellations late at night.

Mother consented, saying, "Don't tell the little ones. I don't want them to start getting ideas. It gets cold at night. Wear your hat."

Once everyone was asleep, they hid in the grasses and waited to see what would happen. While they waited, the bear told her a story from his favorite series of books.

Once upon a time, there was a weaver, named... No, not that one. There was a princess. What should her name be?

Yasha took her time, then said, as ambivalent as she could manage, "Yasha."

Well, when the story starts, see, it's already the beginning of the fourth book, the Princess Yasha has been captured. It happened near the end of the third book, and she was going to be executed, but then they couldn't until the stars aligned, and so they waited, and then that book ended when the

Spider King was destroyed by the farmer, who married the Princess's mother, the Queen, but just as they were married, the Queen was turned to dust by a sorcerer whose name I forget, it's all surprising, and he escapes, and the farmer, the new King, finds out that his only daughter—Princess Yasha— heir to the throne, has been imprisoned by a wicked Lord G-something, who has been secretly scheming with the sorcerer to overturn the kingdom. The Farmer King rushes home to gather an army, but finds his castle and township already overrun with Lord G—um, Lord—

Lord Gum?

Alright, Lord Gum has already taken the castle. Of course he still has allies, but he must rally them, and the third book ends with him all alone, pursued by Gum's mercenaries, racing on horseback through the forest, trying for the safety of a nearby village. The fourth book is very long, but it all happens in one day! It is the day of the Princess's execution. A lot of other things happen, too. But Yasha is in prison, working out an escape plan. She digs around in the straw, looking for cracks in the stone or weaknesses in the iron cage that surrounded her, and then something happened that had never happened before: she was holding tight to the iron bar when instantly, where her hand touched the bar, it turned to powder, dust. She dropped the black dust to the floor in amazement. Where her hand had been on the cage was now a blank, an opening. It was like a glimmer of freedom. She grabbed the cage again, well above the gap so that the two gaps would remove a whole length of iron. She held tightly. She focused. The hour of her execution approached! That's where the book ended!

The fourth book begins with the infancy of the world, the world is a mouth, a kiss, and out come monsters and storms and myths. But later it picked up right there in the dungeon. Yasha tried to dissolve more of the cage, but to no avail.

Then, it's her father telling the story and we find out what had been happening for him. He has reached safety: he assembled a small team of friends, each with special skills, and sought out the mercenaries that had trailed him. Eventually they capture the mercenaries and kill them, all but one. The last one they sent back to Lord Gum with a message. We don't find out what it says until later. Now, with this same team, the Farmer King heads for Gum's castle, where the princess is being held—you see now it's that same day again, even though it's full of things that happened before, but only those things that the characters remember on that day.

Princess Yasha was frantic to recreate the magic of that singular gap. She wondered if perhaps the gap had been there all along, and she only dreamt or hallucinated that she'd made it. She might have been grabbing at air, felt the dust of a crushed spider. All for nothing, because the executioner arrived. Lord Gum himself had come to watch over her death, since it was the symbol of the complete collapse of the old kingdom. You see, only very few people knew about the Farmer King, for he married the Queen in secret, so the Princess was, to the rest of the world, the rightful queen, and her death was the death of everything she stood for.

What no one else knows is that the Queen had a brother, who would therefore be Princess Yasha's Uncle. And his name was Uncle Fin. Uncle Fin was a wizard, which was considered a rather bad thing to be in this time, and so he lived in secret in a small village on the edge of a forest, quietly tucked away from much of the drama of the world. But now that we see what kind of wizard he is—he can change his shape—we can begin to see that magic powers must run in the family. It's also obvious that the way that Yasha turned the iron into dust resembled the way her mother, the Queen, turned to dust immediately after marrying the farmer. Well, Fin the wizard lived alone, and even the villagers knew little about him. He did nothing extraordinary for anyone, never secretly used his magic for good or evil, and generally kept to himself. He did, however, have one mystical project. Every so often—the villagers realized this—he would disappear for days at a time. No one knew where he would go or what he was doing. But they would see that his house was empty all the time, and he did not go for water, and his roof was without smoke or steam. When we read about all this, we don't really know who he is, that he's related to the Princess or the Queen or anything, we just see this old man. So one day the old man leaves his house, and finally we see that the old man wanders into the woods, carrying nothing but some bread and sausage wrapped in a napkin, and soon reaches an unusual cave set into the bottom of a hill, in fact one of a series of hills, quite renowned hills, which everyone says looks like this or that from various angles. The hills were one thing only: the corpse of a fallen god. Once inside, we see how the mysterious old man is building a workshop out of the god's dried up interior.

So, the Princess is being led to her execution. She is supposed to have her head cut off with a sword. Of course she will survive. The Farmer King and his crew do not arrive in time. No, but you can imagine what will happen. The executioner twists his body, his wide sword poised behind his shoulders. Yasha is chained to a short stone wall. A crowd is gathered. Lord Gum looks on from a nearby window. The crowd is breathless. This is not your usual criminal execution. This is the stuff of history, of legend. And much more than that, because when the sword wheels into her neck, wherever it touches her, it turns to dust, and the executioner spins nearly out of control, and the far end of the sword spins off ferociously into the crowd. Everyone blinks, someone screams, then a kind of madness boils through the throng, delight and horror, rage and dread steam and fuse. Without pause, the executioner grabs another weapon and swings it, a bit more restrained, but with the same result. Yasha, with a surging heart, yanks against her chains, and now these, too, dissolve away. She is loose, but far from free. From this theater of cruelty, she might make it to a nearby alleyway, but then what, with a whole city of people looking for her, having seen what she'd done?

Well, here comes her stepfather, swinging grandly across the boulevard, he scoops her up, and lets their momentum hurl them onto the roof of a building. Disguised as locals, his band of friends created more confusion, some leading hunting parties in the wrong direction, others setting off small explosions of flashing lights and smoke. Well outside of town, not without fierce battles and narrow escapes, the rescue team meets in the woods. The Princess, of course, requires explanations the whole time, so that her stepfather must convince her to trust him, tell his story, and prove that it is the truth all while rushing through the city, battling guards and dodging mad crowds. It's very exciting. The Farmer King was a well-loved character, and his return was very exciting.

But they have no time to rest. Lord Gum will not give up easily. So they are on their way. After a few risky encounters, battling a monster, some thieves, and a band of Gum's mercenaries, they finally arrived, serendipitously, at the village where Fin, the old wizard, lived.

Yasha silenced the bear. She saw movement in the house. A hulking shadow walked among her siblings' beds, gathering up things as it went, putting whatever it found into a sack that it carried on its back.

"Let's get closer," she said.

Little Bear whispered, "I'll wait here."

Yasha crawled on all fours through the grass, staying close by the river, zipping from dead tree to rock to dead tree.

Now she saw more clearly in the moonlight. It was Middle Bear. His sack full, he hurried off down river, toward school, then stopped just short of it. Yasha crept closer. She saw Middle Bear take everything out of the sack and arrange it neatly in the new place. When he was done, he ran back for another load. Once the entire house had been moved, Yasha watched Middle creep off some distance until he found a hiding place, a nook in some rocks by the river, and he curled himself up inside, exhausted.

Night after night, the same thing happened.

Yasha could not help but think there was some menace in Middle's behavior, but she preferred it to Mother's immobility. So, each night, she and Littlest would stay up with another installment of the story, and they watched as Middle moved the house and all the bunnies down the river.

That night, Princess Yasha and her Uncle Fin wandered the workshop in the dead god's body. It was not easy to tell that it was the inside of a body. There was no gore, no smell. The bones that were visible could easily have been soft pale pine worn smooth. The head, as was reasonable, was where Fin kept his most prized magical artifacts and was where he had the most hope of harnessing something of the mystical power latent in the corpse. The most disturbing feature of the head was that one eyeball remained fixed in its socket, dried like a locust shell, dangling siphonophoric nerves as if frozen in mid-thrust through the skull. On a table beneath and on the mud walls and bone-nooks around the eye, Fin had assembled talismans, magical dolls and materials, symbols scratched and painted on bark, bundles of herbs tied with string. A semicircle of powder and moisture stains on the floor marked out a territory around the eye and its nerves, clearly a space not to be entered lightly.

Uncle Fin offered the Princess a seat on a wooden stool at one end of the skull. She surmised she must be perched just above a buried ear canal. She studied the room. Indeed, it appeared the god lay on its side, its ear beneath her, resting on the rocks below, the other ear up toward the sky, its eyes gazing straight west, as if it had stretched out to watch the sunset. Fin was examining her, adoringly, as a long lost uncle, and adoringly, the way an archeologist examines a fragment of delicate stonework.

"You are not a wizard," he said.

This did not exactly surprise her. Her power was different from any she'd heard of.

"You are something else..."

"Something?" She was amused.

"My dear niece," he said, proud and sad, "you are the end of the world."

Middle was at it again. From where they huddled, they watched him stomp by with everything slung over his shoulder. He grunted with the effort. Yasha could see that her siblings were in the bundle, their sleeping bunny shapes pressed against the sackcloth.

After Middle had passed, Yasha said, "What does that mean?"

Uncle Fin explained. The Princess was one, the last one, of a line of women of incredible power. To one extent or another, each had control over the very substance of matter, control, in some cases, over the forces that bind things together; in others, the capacity to move things at will without touching them, powers to create or destroy. That power had been growing over the centuries. In her, in the Princess, it had culminated in a force that would eventually infect the world, that would overreach even her ability to control it, and it would erase the world, making room for another to emerge from the dust.

Yasha was horrified. It was a curse, not a power. It was evil, not renewal. She wept and demanded that her uncle tell her how to change it. He could not.

"It is the order of things, the order of the cosmos, that such eruptions should spring forth. You are a gift."

"The gift of death?" She was appalled. "How can I live another moment?"

"We all die eventually. Worlds, too," he said. "You do realize, you have a very long life yet to live, and what's more, in that time, you'll be able to control your power, for the most part. It's when you near your end that the force of dissolution will spring forth, and the world will... well... it will all just sort of dry up."

"I will destroy myself before that happens. Why shouldn't I?"

Uncle Fin smiled, "I see what a good heart you have, and that is part of how I know what this power is," Fin sat and was almost wistful, "because before the end of things, if you live long and work hard, and seek to control your magic, then you will create a beautiful peace in our world, a golden age like no other, an age worthy of your arrival." He would never see that world, himself, but he stared as if to see its seeds in her eyes.

The Princess thought it over. "Well that's clear enough," she said, "with the dawn of a golden age, when there is peace, then I will end myself, and I'll not let my power escape me."

Uncle Fin shook his head. He had no reason to doubt that some prophecies could be evaded, or that fate could be vague, or that his exegesis might be wrong, but he knew the difference between what is called magic that is part of the world and what is magic that is part of childhood and morality tales.

Middle had finished his work by the time Youngest had breathed out the story's conversation. He said, "We're almost to the end of that book, and then there's just one more, and we're waiting for that last one, the finale. I don't know if it's been written. For me, it is the story of the bird that carried us, the awakened god, and it is my mother, or perhaps my father, an idea I have difficulty understanding. Do you wish to know what happens to the Princess? I wish I knew. All I know is that her dear friend, Orpheus, was coming to see her, much later, and she will ask him to take her to the land of the dead. And then a strange thing happens to her uncle. This was the preview, on the last page of book four: Fin is all alone, in the body of the giant, and he is doing something with the giant eye, so that it begins to glow, and Fin stands under the eye, and he presses his head up into it, as if it's some kind of telescope. But then his body gives a lurch, and he is stuck there, in the eye, and it's as if the eye has become his head, a great orb on his shoulders. And the strangest thing is that his body comes off and falls to the floor. It's not gross. It's all very... dry. And then his head, inside the eye, grows numerous black legs, like a spider, from his temples and under his ears, and, trapped within the eye, he weaves a cocoon."

Mother looked rather confused, or concerned, Yasha couldn't tell which. The bunnies, in general, seemed convinced that they were home, that the pretend walls were as real as the ones they remembered. Mother's eyes saw both, and Yasha guessed that she was beginning to take note of the nightly changes in their surroundings. Truly, the landscape was, in general, very bland and very much the same wherever Middle took them, but distant objects were shifting, the mountains turning like moons.

They were all there in the house, playing, while Mother stood outside the window, worrying in her imaginary yard.

The youngest bear slumped in an imaginary corner of the room, an oversized novelty toy. He said, "I know the next part of Peter's story. Hart told me." The bunnies arranged themselves in a semi-circle in front of him.

Listen, my dears, he said.

Peter made it to the other side of the fence, and he feasted on the miraculous vegetables he found there. He ate his fill twice over, and he fell asleep among the cabbage leaves. It was only the MacGregor's spade crashing into the soil beneath a nearby cabbage that woke him. The weapon could have taken his head off, like plucking the top off a dandelion with your fingernail. Peter was lucky. He woke. The spade struck again, closer still, and Peter scrambled away. Instead of running toward the fence, and home, Peter ran toward the shed, and he almost made it there without being seen at all, but he was seen. The MacGregor spied his fluffy, pantless tail and the two tips of his ears disappear into the shed. Peter heard the terrible rumbling of the MacGregor and searched for a place to hide. He slipped under a flowerpot, but it was too small, and his feet stuck out. He threw it aside and slipped under another. This one would have fit, but he found soil caked all over it, and he was covered with grit. At last, he found an empty pot and slipped under it just in time.

Through the single eye-hole at the bottom of the pot, Peter caught glimpses of the MacGregor. It was a monster! It sniffled at the air and wiped its lips. Then, laughing, the MacGregor pulled the shed door closed. Now it was too dark to see clearly, and Peter had no escape. Silently, Peter lifted the bottom of the flower from the ground and peered out. The MacGregor had its back turned. Peter flipped the pot over and scrambled toward the door, but it wouldn't budge. The MacGregor hadn't seen him yet—it was inspecting the pot.

The only light in the shed came through a dingy window. It was Peter's only chance. He made for it, bounding up onto sacks and boxes, up onto the wooden table, scattering seedlings and tools as he pressed himself on, faster, faster. The MacGregor saw him and swung the spade. Lucky for Peter! The spade smashed through the window and missed him. He leapt through the jagged hole, only tearing his jacket as he went. He flipped through the air and landed pell-mell in the grass. One shoe had fallen off, so Peter peeled off the other and ran, digging his claws into the dirt, springing on all four paws over rocks and bales. The MacGregor was already back outside and charging after him. Scrambling through the tomato vines, Peter lost the beautiful button from his coat, which had already been torn by the glass, and now the coat trailed behind him, snagging on things as he ran. All of a sudden it caught on a nail, gave a rip, and held him in place. Before the spade came down on his head, Peter slipped out of his jacket, and, naked as could be, he ran on all fours toward the fence.

The MacGregor didn't give up. With a roar, it threw the spade like a spear. Peter had reached the fence and begun digging when he felt the steel blade—SWACK!—it cut the tip of his ear clean off and chomped into the fence board where it stuck. While the Macgregor tried to pry his weapon free, Peter scrambled with all four legs and dug a hole under the fence and squeezed through, the MacGregor's horrible claws grabbing for his hind legs even after he'd popped out the other side. Panting and stunned, Peter ran all the way home.

Mr Fin was on the smallish boat with Sam. Sam had the oars. Mr Fin was breathing steadily, and he would, on the inhale, fix his gaze onto the horizon.

Sam could see that he had paled. "Lost your legs."

"Yes."

"Won't be long. Just don't puke in the boat."

It was the morning, and cool, which were good features of the experience for Mr Fin. The sun would have nauseated him more. Sam was rowing only very casually, now and then.

"You mean we're heading back soon?" Mr Fin knew this was not what he'd meant.

Sam laughed. "We'll be there in a bit. Nice spot, really. I promise, we'll catch something."

Mr Fin had a thermos of coffee that he clutched now, opened, sipped, twisted, clutched. Morning birds appeared on the far shore, where the light fog had lifted, catching bugs. The soundscape had shifted now, no shore sounds, no foam or shifting sand, no collapsing waters. Now it was boat sounds, air sounds, air on his ear and in his clothing, boots on wood sounds, the oars pouring in and out of the water, burbling fingers at the tips of waves.

"Oh, you know, I haven't fixed that book for you yet. Thing's a mess. You know it's missing quite a few pages."

"You don't need to bother, really. I'll just use a rubber band. It's fine the way it is."

Sam smiled wide. Sam was the type of person who, at the end of a one-sided conversation, smiled wide to let you know that whatever you had said was irrelevant, he was moving on. "Viv been by lately? How's she?"

This was a challenge for Mr Fin. He knew, for certain, who Viv was, he could even see her face and her shoulders as she had stood there in front of the book shelf, preparing to leave, or stay, that was her, indescribably her. But what else? Pears, yes, that was sticking with him, and other visits he knew were her, too, but, he thought, these were thin, even if perfect. He pictured her again, at the door, in the kitchen. In every recollection, her voice was missing. He could not hear her or recall anything that she had ever said. Her mouth: his mind could project very close to her mouth so that was all he saw, and he really saw it, then, the little pinkish and somewhat dry vertical lines that composed her lips, the u-ish, v-ish dip below her nose, the little bit of powder she used, the creasing of her skin as her mouth moved, talking, expressing, reading to him, insignificant freckles, a pinpoint of a scar on her lower lip, left of center. But no sounds, no words. The absence of sound pained him, and he held his breath against it.

"Fin?"

His blood arrived in his brain somewhat oxygen-poor, all images scattered, his world again was the wooden boat, streaked green and gray old wood, the sound and fog. They were approaching an inlet or an outlet, and the water was thick with weedy and pustule-like greenery. He breathed again. "Oh, she's doing quite well. She comes by."

A motorboat whined in the distance, after which their boat was shaken and turned by its wake. Sam let them drift, and they approached the inlet, or outlet, or channel, whatever it was.

Mr Fin looked admiringly at Sam for a moment. He remembered why he was friends with Sam. They drank beer and talked boats, water, fish. Mr Fin hadn't cared much for such conversation but had been consigning himself to it, adapting to his new town, new lifestyle, enjoying his beer. Sam had looked at him after a good forty-five minutes of such talk, and Sam had said, "Man, I hate talking about all this shit, don't you?" Mr Fin was never sure if this was true, if that was how Sam felt about it, but he admired that Sam had said it, either way, and perhaps more so if it had been a friendly lie. Because after that day, they talked about boats and water and fish and rope and the weather and wood stains and blade sharpening and deck paint and hooks and nets and all kinds of terrible things, quite often. Conversation was an excuse for proximity, something to accompany the beer, the standing or sitting in place.

Now Fin could imagine, superimposed on the rowboat, the dimensions of The Swan, easing through the lulling cavity, tired from the ocean or anxious to be in it. Also on The Swan sat the Knight of the Sorrowful Countenance, of the Missing Molars, still suspended in the air. He could see that the mysterious Swan was bringing him at last to his esteemed Dulcinea, and he rehearsed several eloquent speeches: a speech in the instance that she was disappointed in her knight, a speech ready in case she was too overwhelmed with desire and chaste words were in order, and a speech designed to soothe her spirits if the sight of her knight, so mistreated, put her to fear and sorrow. But The Swan delivered Quixote to a hole in the earth, a deep round hole, the throat of the hole lined with stones, like teeth. The hole was carved out of a modest hill near the sea, and the wind whipped around our hero as The Swan retook the wind and vanished from his sight. The knight was amazed. Here was a final quest. All at once he knew the place: the fabled Cave of _____, its wolfish mouth.

"Lord!" he said, "how deep it is! Born melancholic that I am, the only way to keep afloat is to stay within the story. Stop, and I sink down, down... if I sink further I shall only... I shall only reach—nothing, there is nothing for any of us. Reading, writing, disguises, people, even children are useless in such a place."

Mr Fin recalled the evening before, working tirelessly on David's ship, his Swan. Look, he said, not quite saying it, but it happened in his mind, in that hollow they shared where the stories appeared, unbidden, Look, the mattress is the air and the clouds, and you are the wooden hull and tunnel, the heart and lungs. Your eyes are everywhere, and you can grow whatever you need. Wings of rope and sail will hold you up, and your body will be flight, pulse, and voice, absolute elegance in the air, and you don't even need to speak these words, because they'll be a part of you, and you can hum them to Mr Crane, and the ship will carry you, you will carry you and all our rabbits and bears, forgive them.

"Where will they all go?" Mr Fin asked. "What would become of the ship?"

David had no answer, at first. His body trussed by metal stripping, rope lines taut or loose extended from his limbs to the curtain rod, light fixture, other furniture. Pulleys made the lines criss-cross his chest, where springs, levers, and plastic joints were puzzled together like clockworks. Sailcloth strips mingled with and rose above the quilt and wool, a flowering of kites for which Fin had opened one window, to see it gesture and receive the air. The wooden keel and rudder mechanisms formed noble fins, the latter fixed to the bed frame, and the former carefully secured to wooden arms and metal ribbing so that it extended up from David's chest.

Mr Fin, arms a harbor in the air, felt the voice deep within the structure. He could read its mood in the sails. The story that emerged in his mind was echoed in the operations of David's new form, which, at last, said, "The world was a mouth turned inside out, eyes shedding light in through your bedroom windows at night, its hollowed and expansive stomach roiled chemical dice in the atmosphere of centuries, its teeth waited in all the doorways. Should we have stayed inside, each our name and place, rather than face such terrible dreams?"

Once they'd passed the narrowest part of the inlet or outlet or channel, Mr Fin recognized the area—a particular island, hooked toward the shore, large rocks on its hillside crest of bright yellow and green, a few wind-shaped trees, blue scrub, brown sandstone. He wanted desperately to walk there, to sit for hours, to be stranded.

Just audibly, he said, "I've been through here."

Sam had no reply.

Vivian was already in the house, scarf pressed against her mouth and nose, weeping at the threshold to David's room. She dropped her box of cleaning supplies, squeeze bottles and cans of powder, brushes, gloves and sponges, let them scatter in the hall, and she ran outside.

Chapter Six

The sun sinks. One sees landscapes encircling creatures who want only to leave this cold night. I have resisted grain and water enough to die before the week is out. I disperse like angels around a grave. Solemn rail, it sheds black hair, such feet, such a purse, hairy cheeks, a pacifist's chin, before a banquet of dust... in slippery satin, sea-green women condemn me... a square upon the oblong... here are the stones that wither beside the smooth stream, where fish sink, sea-smitten, almost gods, bearing fruit and blossom. I take them from you, mended to the sky and to the distant shores, my fortune, my fortune of stones. I watch the cool wells, I walk the roads. I will remain in this landing between stairs, looking out upon dead lands, where nothing moves. I will hold on, I will not let go. I will consume and be consumed. From the air that forms in the heart of the earth, into the air that forms the breath of me, I cast my stones, my curses.

Virginia the Wolf was a fractal. If one looked closely (if one were able) at the composition of her flesh, one would find them, hundreds, millions of wolfish jaws gaping, and there in their throats, a veritable plague of bacteria-like Virginias, smaller than small and wandering about, prowling and sinister ornaments that knew all she knew, waiting in their own wild orbits. Every moment, a nation of them was sloughed off, scraped against a wall, shaken into the distance when she was cold, when she scratched, and they formed infinitesimal piles of life all over the house and grounds—every moment, yet they would never be used up. The whole world might already be filled with her, inside and out.

So, to meet her was to meet an earthly deity, though her manner was restrained, even withdrawn. Withdrawn as she sat at the window as if waiting; withdrawn as she did her typing, in the early dawn before breakfast and from the close of supper until darkness had risen. The deity appreciated the echo of her own slow keystrokes. She gave her commands to the elders among her many servants, who all obeyed a formalism of task and communication that kept them occupied: this, that. The few with whom she spoke hovered on her words, as if her breath were delicious viscera. Picture them in brown, male or female, shiny as Labradors but with noble, dispassionate eyes. Many of her commands, she would admit, were useless, that is, they were already the daily machinations of the house and grounds, but in maintaining her right to command the details, to alter them slightly, to be the finest but most decisive gear in the watch-works, she maintained her authority in the house and her right to anger at whatever she pleased.

Here she was, seated at the window, in the window seat. Virginia forced herself to remain perfectly still, to not move a single muscle but to keep her body in a uniform slight tension. This was the worst hour of the long evening, knowing that later she would need to write.

A minute, maybe two whole minutes, perfectly still, balancing the dizzying epochs and dynasties of her novels against the current moment, the last sentence, the next waiting image.

Virginia thought about her daughter, for she needed to think her way through the strange city she'd drawn from Jinny's own stories. Whatever she'd taken she had made her own, but still, as much as her work was her escape, her meditation, she was haunted by her daughter's creations, and they made her book a troubled thing.

Jinny's city would easily sigh into morning, bustling, and one could ease toward it with a few prepositions, coasting on the opening of a chapter where spires took shape and an urban architecture both familiar and foreign. Virginia's mind could range over the city as if she were remembering it, where laced throughout its boulevards and private rooms were her daughter's words, everything was frozen and clear, but these days, nothing would happen there, there was no story. The walls and windows and faces and flags and birds would all turn to brittle clay. When the novel was finished, and if she wrote it well, carried Jinny's dreams through its pages, would she come home?

Years ago, Jinny hid in her closet and listened to the house, the house without her in it, just the others, stepping from here to there, picking things up, grumbled conversations. Jinny had written everything by hand. Forever ago, when she was a little girl, after lights out, she sometimes replaced her sleeping form with pillows so she could hide in her closet: a pen light, notebook, pencil.

She anticipated being missed, relished the coming moment when someone would say, "Where's—?" She studied her new surroundings, eyes open wide in the weird light of the closet. Then she closed her eyes to hear every prick of life in the house. When at last they called for her, she did not make a sound, though she was surprised at how riveted her body at once was—nearly lunging at the call of her name. To restrain it made her giddy. They kept calling, and she had to keep from laughing. When they searched, she didn't fidget. They went through phases: curious, irritated, worried, patient, irritated, nervous, speculative, angry, scared, desperate, angry, angry.

Jinny wondered how long it could go on. She had no excuse to reveal herself now, nothing to assuage their seemingly real feelings, and whatever they were doing seemed less and less real to her. Her family was a distant land, a story in a book. As she listened to their growing fear, their panic to find her, she felt that maybe she could never return. She would stay here, in her corner of the closet, forever, and the dark clothes and boxes and shoes would be everything—it would be easy, because her mind would fill the void with spirits.

Voices raged upstairs then down and out in the yard and on the phone, but they were just noise to her. A vast city grew in her mind, surrounded by a countryside of brightness, so much room, acres and canyons and skies. In a moment, her mind was erased by light flooding the closet, and she felt severe hands under her arms. The hands yanked her out of the closet, her hair tangling in wire hangers, her left arm against the vicious door frame. She tried to stand but managed to give the brass doorknob an electric crack with her kneecap. Her toes scraped against the landscape below as she was flown away. They would be angry until she'd wept for what she'd done. Virginia had pulled her daughter out, and furious as she had been, she'd secretly adored her daughter's secret.

As Virginia rendered it in her novel, the city resembled a lizard clinging to the edge of a cliff, sails, wings of reptilian flesh stretching out from it to feed on the wind, especially that warm breath that rose constantly from the abyss, the nameless sea. The lizard's horny head was a palace of jewels and silver scales, a dozen dome-eyes, and pillared arcade teeth spiraling around a peak. Jinny's own descriptions of the city were simple and of course childish, borrowing from board games or fairy tales—inconsistent. Virginia had refined those elements from Jinny's notebooks into a substance that reminded her of her daughter's unique imagination. She believed that everything could end in Jinny's city, that her characters would all arrive there one day, and perhaps the end would present itself. But now, these days, lately, the dry, immobile city said nothing to her, gave her nothing to do, no way to imagine what could happen. So she wandered the frozen boulevard, expressionless marketplace. She could see, feel, hear, taste any detail of it she chose: it surrounded her, it obeyed her; but the city was a trail gone cold, abandoned.

A noise from the hall brought her back to the present. Virginia twisted her ears toward the source. She listened for him, the sound of feet approaching from behind. He's coming this way, she thought.

The city faded. To Virginia, it seemed to drift physically from around her head, up into the curtains, wallpaper, window, its geological strata visible as if cross-sectioned, its buildings swallowed by shadows, or else they floated semi-transparent in the light. The cliff and the reptilian sails that captured the wind merged with the wallpaper, the fine and luminous pattern of urns and monstrous flowers.

She didn't look his way, but her face gathered and steeled itself to resist sensing any more of him: Pim, his musty scent, the urine dribbling ineluctably into his undergarments, his anapestic staggering. Any moment, the air behind her would carry the vibrations of his voice against her back. His words would ricochet in the stairwell, cling to her, fill her nose and ears and mouth like fumes.

"Mom?" he said. Pim was still in his awful pajamas—haggard, faded monkeys and bananas, stretched to the limit. He had a handful of pencils, and in his other arm he cradled a roll of hand-drawn maps, scotch tape, and scissors.

Young Pim was a prodigy of everything. At four, he'd drafted full-color diagrams for a complex and enormous house, part underground, part above the clouds, and part in the ocean, and soon after that, a richly detailed sketch of a cathedral that extended into space and surrounded the moon, ending the need for space suits and rockets. Weaponry, transportation, flying machines, mind-reading headsets, frictionless boots, hologram-recording devices, brain-preservation jars, gloves that gave one super strength... all of this, prepubescently, he'd designed, built paper models of, demonstrated the usefulness of in commercials, in dramatic plays, and in clandestine operations on behalf of a shadow government that had tracked his efforts since birth. Though he received no public recognition for his work, he kept at it, inventing every day, drawing obsessively in his study.

He had a large head, and he believed this to be, in part, the cause of his genius. The house held an enormous library, three rooms of which he read with vigor, not all the words, but many, the ones that seemed most important, that caught his eye: he knew all the names, all the capitalized ideas and bold places.

"Mom," he said again, now that he could see her. He hovered at the top of the stairs, noticing her posture: private, menacing.

"What is it?" Virginia hadn't seen Pim for several days, as was usual. His requirements were, in general, met by the staff. She looked him over, his bleary eyes, his awkward, pointless plump. His general condition she deemed acceptable. His face unnerved her. His voice. His breathing. He just keeps going, she thought.

"I can't find one of my books." Pim had stopped a good ten paces from his mother.

Virginia thought this over. She knew what this meant, but refused to allow him his evasions. "I don't see how that's my business."

Pim mustered, adjusting his materials between hands. "It's just, well, I'm pretty sure it's—uh."

She wasn't going to help.

"I think it's in her room."

Virginia held still. "I see."

"In Jinny's room," he said pointlessly. No, because he wanted to say her name.

"Yes, I see."

"I can get it myself." He was eager to, but restrained his tone.

"No you will not." Virginia waited for his protest.

"But..." He knew he wouldn't get far.

"Don't." Virginia thought: patience, patience. "I'll have it left outside your door by morning. What's the title?"

Soon he was gone.

Virginia's brain was swirling now as it had not done for some time. Jinny is a ghost, she thought. She is gone and she is everywhere. Without a picture of Jinny to hand, Virginia felt a sudden panic. What would she look like? How tall is she? Still not her full size, but a growing girl, growing so fast. Virginia held her hand out flat to guess Jinny's height, if she were standing beside her on the landing, by the window seat, in the twilight and the blue dust, or in the entryway of the house as it once was, peeling off her fashionable boots, hopping, then leaving them scattered there, smiling in her socks.

She put out a hand as if to pat Jinny's head, but it didn't seem right, not right enough. But there was her hand, atop the imagined head, close to the imagined cheek.

She snapped it back and regained herself.

Instead there was Pim.

She returned to the city, working to imbue it with the biology and psyche of her fantasy world: beginning with edge-of-the-map monsters and rudimentary fish, its tools, knot-work, and its hives—pollen-like bees, hive-like flowers, hearts and minds that sparked and died in a loom of light and shade. Everything here exists just before that last moment, everything about to disappear.

Virginia knew most of the imaginary world very well. She had chronicled centuries-full and continents-full of its stories in her series of thick fantastical novels, thick with adventure, romance, and fable, what she was not embarrassed to call door-stop novels. She loved her audience. But the secret of her novels was that they awaited just the one reader. Her novels were a summons that, so far, must have come out all wrong. She had reinvented Jinny's heroes, made them venture in and venture out: Orpheus and Eurydice wandered the Caves of Ice that formed the border between life and death, trapped, but together, but numb wherever they touched one another. Virginia sat perfectly still and let the reptilian city fan out from her body.

A long, limitless death, followed by a leap out of the water, to the bridge, the inverted scream of interrupted death, his face in his hands after such a leap, such a miscalculation, but the fingers at his shoulder, that sudden touch that received him, that yanked him from the bleak water, possibly reached all the way into the ocean in search of him, and that hand and those fingers wove his mind back toward the image of his own eventual birth, and he lived his life as a familiar story thumbed from end to beginning, attentive to the pleasure of movement, of holding his breath, forgetting, of slipping closer and closer to wordless ideas, phantoms instead of faces, a rustling, infant world of noise and skin.

As he settled into a bench, Mr Fin noted the spray of water from passing automobiles lift and spread into a fine mist... hang in the air, fog for a moment, settling. He wrote everything down in a kind of frenzy, racing to the end of the moment, as he understood it, to see how, when put to words, it would conclude, and how its sudden wholeness would elate him. He couldn't read his writing, but he knew it was there. He hoped the clouds would hold firm until he got home. He had not been at the shore all day, but off and on again, and not always at this bench, but others, too. This day, he felt, had had one of the better tide readings, a sense of symmetry and drama all at once, the kind of tide that brought things in.

It was raining.

Mr Fin stood from his last bench of the day, gathering as he stood the rumpled drapery of his overcoat. He slid his hat into place atop his head, considered his umbrella for a moment, but left it shut, tapped it like a cane, a dialogue with the heavy drops on the felt of his brim. He followed the sidewalk where it led him. Mr Fin was slowing down. Getting himself up the hill felt less of a certainty each day. Things used to get easier the more he did them. He watched his shoes pad the wet cement while his knees juggled around in his pant legs. Halfway up the hill, he stopped a moment, rested his arm on a parking meter and wheezed at the town below, the bay over there, his hand pulsing. He opened his umbrella.

Scrutinizing the building as he approached, Mr Fin tried to put it, too, to words. I'm thinking like a book, he would note. He heard gutter-pipes drooling, saw the clammy fingerprints of illness; he smelled the hovering mold on the porch, touched the unwinding wicker and barren pots; he watched himself reaching for the door: appeals to the senses.

Having passed through the ornately tooled double doors, Mr Fin lingered in the entryway, where hints of marble and wood were yet visible, though faded from the damp and heat and the bugs and no doubt from the toxins of human breathing.

Grumbling for his shoulders, Mr Fin unwound his coat and hung it below his hat, shook his umbrella out the door and left it leaning in the corner. He retrieved his notes from his coat pocket and opened the next set of doors, revealing a more spartan room, narrow, perfectly empty, once white. Here, he removed his gloves and allowed himself to hum a tune as he bent to undo his laces. Presently, he replaced his shoes and socks with the proper slippers.

This room let on to another smallish entrance, one with the grace of tinted windows, which allowed light from the interior to mingle with exterior light falling in from either side by narrow, crinkled glass in the walls. He removed his tie and rolled it, unbuttoned his shirt, removed his cuff-links and pulled his sleeves off. Over his undershirt he pulled a clean day-gown.

The new door in front of him announced the building's name, date, etc., and it allowed him access to the arterial hallway, a hum of invisible activity all around him, the opportunity to go left or right, a strict line of doors extending in both directions.

He opened the door to his room and set his notes on the credenza, his curled paper ptyx of the day's scratchings. Where had David gone?

Mr Fin sat on the edge of the bed. He loved the yellow and orange light that fell through the curtains. He could see that the curtains were warm still, despite the rain. He rolled on his back, and sent his arm out for his bedside book, set it on his chest.

The book was a wound, a wound he could see through.

"What's that you've been reading?" David said.

Mr Fin smiled. "Oh, nothing. But I should tell you about... you know... the wolf and the—"

"I'd really love to get outside for a bit. Could we?"

"Of course."

Mr Fin gathered the wheelchair from behind the door and opened it by the bed.

"Let's see... should I...?"

"No. I've got it." David lurched up on an elbow, wincing a bit.

"I could just—."

"I've got it!"

David's hand grasped the green plastic arm rest. He tipped his head, all the way over, toward the chair, then lunged, and his body followed, a sack of grain, until it all fell together into the seat. After a few moments, he was able to speak again. "Alright, let's go."

"You're doing so well," said Fin. "I'm so proud of you."

Out they went.

"And what?" David said to the air. "Where have you pulled me?"

Fin would offer the beginning of a story, but David would say, "What hounds me is the long darkness before my birth! Why did I scream so? And what was my mother?" He remembered falling out of the sea.

Soon he was asleep. The fresh air was too much for him, intoxicating.

Fin rolled him home, slipped back under the sheets, pulled them up tight around his shoulders. After a moment, he got out of bed, retrieved his notes from the table, and sat in the nearby chair.

"Listen. I've remembered more today."

Pim was Jinny's brother, alone in the house more often than not. Sadly, he was infected with the disease of matter after a secret sabbatical at age eleven. As a reward for his service to the Shadow Government, Pim was offered 3 hours of impossible travel, outside of time and space. All he had to do was craft an accurate model of himself to act as an avatar in real space-time—otherwise he would be unable to return; his existence would be replaced with anti-matter. Pim chose a collection of wires, wooden toy pieces, and bicycle parts to create the armature of his model. The size would not affect the quality of the avatar, but Pim strove for something close to his actual dimensions. He crafted bones, organs, nerves, and veins out of a homemade dough and fitted them to the infrastructure. It was the surface that confounded him. Skin and hair were difficult to represent, and his face never looked right, especially the nose and ears. After a week he had created something that would fool an observer from ten or fifteen feet, in the dark, but was it enough to fool atomic particles? Enough to fool his own existential matrix? He hoped so.

Surprisingly, the portal leading outside of real space-time, the closest one, anyhow, was through the back fence, had been there all along, in fact. A fence board had been loosened by agents in the field to mark Pim's path.

On the appointed day, he ran through the backyard, through the chicken yard, and toward the back lot, where the grass was as tall as he was. In the shadows of the trees that defined the edge of the familiar world, he followed the fence-line, tapping boards. There. The loose one. As soon as he stepped through, time and space would unravel, and the mysteries of the universe would unfold before him, he would accelerate beyond light speed, he would observe the universe as a non-dimensional being, which is the same as to say a being of infinite dimension.

He didn't make it back, not all the way, and the failings of his anatomical model were from then on his own. Back in his room, dazed, his skin hurt, his eyes bugged, he felt greasy, stained, he threw up. He panicked—I'm dying, he thought. He gathered his favorite things: drawings, his stuffed bear, his collection of worn down pencils, marbles, a hundred year old postcard, and he arranged them on his bed, smoothed out his quilt, and curled around it all, waiting. This is how they will find me, he thought, in this tomb, and they'll go through everything and realize just how brilliant I was, and maybe then it will have been worth it.

He got bored and went to find Jinny. Her bedroom door was locked, no answer. He did feel sick, really. He wasn't imagining it. Something was happening. He felt like he was getting smaller, not shrinking exactly, but un-growing. He found his mother, typing. He said some things that she didn't hear.

She focused on her work, scratched her ears.

"Where's dad?"

She stopped. She turned her body toward him. "Listen, Pim. Your dad moved out. He's not coming back." As if that wasn't enough, she said, "He has a new family." She turned back to her work.

Pim couldn't respond. "Where's Jinny?"

"She's gone to your grandmother's house. You'll be asleep before she's back." Jinny hated helping grandmother. They both did. Jinny must have done something bad.

Pim ached. "I'm sorry," he said. His fingers and toes stung.

"What?" Virginia eyed him over her shoulder, as if he were a suspicious bump in the night.

"I'm. I'm going to take my bath."

Jinny had left for grandmother's house at dusk. She would visit until grandmother fell asleep. Grandmother's house was in the woods, on the other side of the village—about two miles.

Grandmother might say to her, "You've been chewing your nails."

Jinny had learned to respond simply, "mmhmm."

"Your mother had no discipline."

Mmhmm.

It was easy to ignore her, some nights.

Grandmother watched Jinny tidy the jars of jam and spices on the counter. "You are not all wolf," she said, one eyebrow up, one down, "I can tell."

"Mmhmm." Jinny was thinking about her father. His absence was blanking out acres of her world.

"Not even half, I'd say." Grandmother snickered in her throat: it's all teasing, it's not teasing at all.

"Mmhmm."

"I could eat you in one gulp."

"Mmhmm."

After Jinny finished chores, grandmother settled down. They sat together in their chairs, listening to the sound of the fire, the day birds finding home, and the night birds sallying forth. Jinny would have to sit perfectly still, to unfocus, to not want, not see, and in that austerity, grandmother would fall asleep more quickly. Once she heard the rhythmic, gut-driven breathing from the other chair, Jinny watched the fire, slid closer to feel its warmth on her toes, knees, fingertips, weakening her eyelids, and she woke up, having not noticed herself sleeping.

"Where is my blanket?" Grandmother shivered in her chair, its wood like parched bone, faintly creaking.

"Right here, up to your chin."

"Is this the good one? The one my mother made?"

"Yes, Grandma, it's the good one your mother made. Why don't we get you in bed?"

"Too cold to go to bed. I feel a draft. I need my nightcap."

"I've got it here." She slipped the cap over the old dry ears.

"Gentle, darling."

"There you go."

"It's so cold. You didn't latch the window properly."

"Okay, grandma, I'm sorry. There, is that better? And the curtains are tied together."

"Don't let the fire go out, dear. Though I suppose If I don't freeze you'll burn me down."

"The fire's fine, grandma."

"If you say so. I hear them you know, all kinds, outside. They try to get in at night. You better latch that door good, you hear?"

"Yes grandma, I will."

"And I suppose you ought to run through the woods. Don't stop. Not for anything. Don't even look behind you. Little thing like you."

Later.

"Grandmother?" Nothing but a glow on the hearth. For a moment she could not tell if grandmother was still in the chair opposite or not. The wool rug was cold.

Her eyes adjusted. A string of light marked grandmother's forehead, her nose—a stretched and somewhat battered thing, and a deeper hollow filled her mouth. Her ears were black orchestra pits.

"Grandmother?"

Still sleepy herself, Jinny hadn't been hearing, but now she heard: a slow snore grumbling in grandmother's head, in the unsettling hollows behind her eyes.

Jinny struggled to stay awake until grandmother roused, from a dream or from the cold, or from some pain or other. She coaxed her to the bed, tucked her in. Hum.

Hum. She checked the windows, stoked the fire. Hum.

Jinny wrapped herself up, taking deep, fortifying breaths: hat, scarf, cloak, boots, belt, mittens. Once she opened the door, the cold would surge in. Once she closed it behind her, the iron lock would drop into place. She took a breath, as if it were her last, and dove amidst the towering trees. The end of winter: the moon was bright but the woods were dark. The path was not wide.

She ran, as if escaping, as if something chased her already, then stopped, panting in the moon.

Now tonight, she said, my body rises tier upon tier like some cool temple whose floor is strewn with carpets and murmurs, rises, and the altars stand smoking; but up above, here in my serene head, come only fine gusts of melody, waves of incense, while the lost dove wails, and the banners tremble above tombs, and the dark airs of midnight shake trees against amber windows—how thin and mottled like some sea-bird's egg. I could worship my hand even, with its fan of bones laced by blue mysterious veins and its astonishing look of aptness, suppleness and ability to curl softly or suddenly crush—its infinite sensibility. Immeasurably receptive, holding everything, trembling with fullness, yet clear, contained—so my being seems, now that desire urges it no more out and away; now that curiosity no longer dyes it a thousand colours. It lies deep, tideless, immune, now dead, like the child clutching at words—A, pits of air through bodies, B, paste and powder, C, the caul of sleep, D, ways of naming death. But now let the door open, the glass door that is forever turning on its hinges, for the shock of the falling wave which has sounded all my life, which woke me so that I saw the world in its last throes, no longer makes quiver what I hold.

A week later, Pim watched her go, eating his bedtime snack, and he felt jealous of her independence, even though it was couched in punishment. Still, to go out at night! He watched her tuck her notebook into the bottom of her basket, pears piled on top, muffins wrapped in a dish towel. He didn't say anything, none of the things he used to say to her. He hadn't told her about his disease, that he was dying, that he'd made a mistake. Did it even matter now? They hadn't spoken much, certainly not about dad. He wondered if she knew. She was heading out the kitchen door.

"Jinny," he whispered to her. He thought mom might be in the dining room.

"What is it, Pim? I've got to go." The wintry night air came snapping in.
He wasn't sure how to keep her attention.

"Can I come?"

"No. Of course not. And why would you want to?"

"Yeah. No, I don't really. But—I just. Did mom tell you? About dad?"

Jinny was caught off guard. "She told me."

To Pim, she looked suddenly exhausted. "When is he coming back, do you
know?"

Jinny drew herself back into the kitchen, closing the door behind her. She
sat down across from him. "What do you mean, Pim?"

"Dad. When's dad coming back?"

Jinny stared out the kitchen window, holding something in her mind like a
piece of ice under her tongue. "Pim, dad's gone. Really gone."

Pim allowed the impossible, though it choked him. "Like... like dead?"

"No, not dead, really, but, to us... to us, I guess so. And mom, she..." Jinny's
head shook. "You just need to take it easy, okay. You're going to be fine. I'm
sorry, Pimmy. Just don't think about it." She left quickly.

Jinny brought her notebook because the evenings had gotten longer, and
grandmother would wake more often in the dark. Jinny couldn't just leave her—
she would wake up and be terrified. She would bob through sleep in her chair, but
she couldn't get her to bed. Once it was late enough, Jinny put out all the lights but
one, arranged everything, so that, when grandmother woke up in the night, she
remembered that Jinny had gone, could feel sure that Jinny had bolted the windows
and the door, closed up the curtains, filled the stove, and put an axe near at hand,
by the bed. Until then, she was in and out, unsettled, Jinny had to assure her, in the
moments of waking, "Look, look, grandma, the window is bolted just right."

"Where is my blanket?" Grandmother shivered in her chair, its wood like
parched bone, faintly creaking.

"Right here, up to your chin."

"Is this the good one? The one my mother made?"

"Yes, Grandma, it's the good one your mother made. Why don't we get you
in bed?"

"Too cold to go to bed. I feel a draft. I need my nightcap."

"I've got it here."

"Gentle, darling."

"There you go."

"It's so cold. You didn't latch the window properly."

"Okay, grandma, I'm sorry. There, is that better? And the curtains are tied together."

"Don't let the fire go out, dear. Though I suppose if I don't freeze you'll burn me down."

"The fire's fine, grandma."

Grandmother tipped back in her rocker and stayed there, her slippered toes just touching the rug, striking a balance, her mouth drooped open for air, though she'd always snore. She was out again. They had eaten the muffins. The pears were too hard. Virginia slid her notebook out from the bottom of the basket and opened it in her lap. Given the cold, she wrote: walls of ice. Given the delicate frost on the windows, she wrote: crystal medallion: a map of the world. Given the firelight and threads of black smoke, she wrote: shadow creatures. Given the woods, she wrote: lost. Given her grandmother's more-than-asleep expression, she wrote: land of the dead. Given the pears, she wrote: fruit of the underworld. Given herself, she wrote: the young princess is doomed to live on.

Little Bear had told the story to Yasha. The glistening ice walls hummed like a crystal goblet as ancient draughts dragged through the glittering caverns, muttering ghosts of wind against their ears. Daggers in hand, Orpheus and Eurydice advanced between the mirror-walls of ice, straining to see their way in the shadowy blue abyss of reflections. Their hearts raced. None had lived to tell of the Caves of Ice, but Legend held that there dwelled two manner of beasts in the caves: the first, a cruel distortion of nature, the twisted evolution of the Untaka tribe, famed ages ago for their spells of protection and healing, they had become vampires of warmth. Caught in the Flow, they used their powers of healing and protection with such craft and desperation that the magic entered their bodies, changing them forever. Like the undead who breathe only once a decade, these blue-skinned, hairless wraiths steal the living warmth of trespassers. With a touch, they kill to live, leaving their victims frozen. These tunnels were their hive, their warren, their tomb. But the shadow creatures were far worse. Beings from the Unreality of reflection and dream, they sought minds to inhabit, minds weak and willing to do their bidding. They waited to escape the walls, like dim reflections of their vampirical counterparts.

Orpheus looked to Eurydice, as if to say at once "we'll make it," and, "we won't go without a fight." In that glance, the humming ceased, the winds calmed. Fearing the foreboding calm, they moved more quickly, down this corridor then that, guided by the map projected from the crystal around Eurydice's neck. Soon they found themselves in a large frosted well of a room. One hundred men high, the ceiling glowed brightly with refracted sunlight and dripped a thousand elephantine stalactites. This was the way out... but how? The corridor ended. The walls, frosted over, admitted nothing. Eurydice held the crystal to her eye as she searched the room.

"There!" she shouted, pointing. Nearly a hundred feet up: a rabbit hole in the ice.

"Is that our only choice? Is there a way up?" Orpheus glanced around, cornered and sensing that staying in one place would only encourage lurking foes.

Eurydice nodded and made for the wall beneath the opening. A dagger in each hand, she dug into the ice and began to pull herself up the wall. Orpheus followed behind. As he dug his blades into the ice, now ten feet from the ground, he gazed into the wall where Eurydice's climb had rubbed away the frost. There in the clear ice, he saw their faces. Shouting, Orpheus leapt from the wall, leaving his daggers behind. Eurydice looked with a start to see what was the matter. She lost one of her hand holds, swung perilously a moment.

"Shadow beasts!" Orpheus cried.

Eurydice, hanging from a single blade, gazed into the wall of ice. There, behind her own reflection, she saw their faces, grisly and inhuman, swelling through the wall like bruises until one pressed forward, its gaze even with hers, and opened its crooked maw. A scream shot from Eurydice's spine and she covered her eyes with one hand. She didn't let go of her knife, but all at once, it dissolved in her hand, and she fell, the wraith trailing from her eyes, clinging to her soul.

That's not how it had been. For Jinny, it had always been the hero, Orpheus, who went up the wall, suffered, braved. But now, for Virginia, it was Eurydice, many-named, many-faced: the young bride, the virgin, the princess, the daughter, the maid, the abandoned child. She suffered, died or almost died or died and lived again or gave birth to dead children and wept herself to death or was fed upon by the dead or herself descended, accidentally, into the tunnels of the dead, by secret stairs or bone-ladders in old wells, wandered among graves, cell to cell in the underground prison where the moon shines black, married the dead, was kidnapped by death, gazed into the eyes of eternal sleep and sorrow, lost, lost, lost.

The beautiful Eurydice, whose life would end with the end of the world, who was once trapped and left to die in the dungeons of the Wicked Grinspoon, had, since then, been trapped once in an undersea kingdom, sealed in a glass globe, locked in a tower, buried alive, thrown into the river.

"David? Are you asleep yet?"

"No."

"It's very late."

"I'm scared."

"What are you scared of?"

"The wolf."

"There's not really a wolf."

"I know. I just can't stop thinking about it. I feel like I'm going to have a nightmare."

"Try to think about something else."

"I know. I can't."

"Well... just imagine that you're there with the bunnies, with Yasha. The mother wolf is there, but she's actually very nice. She only eats vegetables, and her son is older than you, but he has really cool toys, a big big room full of toys. And all the butlers are funny looking dogs in tuxedos. And, one night at dinner, you're all having lasagna, and the wolf says that she would like to tell a story, because she's a famous writer, and she hasn't gotten to tell a story for a long time. And her stories are all about a very strange kind of creature. Do you know what that strange creature is?"

"What?"

"People."

"Ha ha."

"Try to close your eyes. In the wolf's stories, because all the characters are people, every story is extra weird. And instead of being called Mr and Mrs Human, they all have names, sometimes many names. So, the wolf starts telling a story over dinner, and it's about her favorite two characters, Orpheus and Eurydice. She's written several books, and these two characters are the heroes of the newest one. They are heroes in the old sense, like Hercules and Theseus, and all they like to do is go on adventures. Sometimes they kill monsters, sometimes one of them is captured, and the other must perform a rescue. Sometimes the stories are funny, sometimes scary, but they always end well. So, at the dinner table, Virginia says, "I'd like to tell a story." She stands, everyone is quiet. She's about to start, but then all the little bunnies jump out of their seats and huddle around her chair to listen.

The wolf laughs a bit and clears her throat, saying, "Once upon a time."

"But dad?"

"What?"

"Why does she have to be a wolf?"

Once night had fallen, Virginia climbed the stairs from her study to her chambers. Her servants undressed and dressed her for the night. Tea steeped on the night stand. A dish of placid cream waited warmly. Still, sleep was hard won. Characters and lines of plotting turned about her head. If Jinny came home, she would be free of the task; she would give it up. If she finished, there would be nothing left to do but wait.

Virginia held herself very still in her velvet chair: a species of chair unlike any other: a platypus of a chair. Her mind raced through the imaginary world. The whole sweep of it was there, but some things remained invisible to her: rather, she sensed hollows, holding nothing or hiding something, and these drew her attention. In these little absences, she thought she could sense her daughter waiting for her, missing her. She held herself at the window: box window, an extension of its own nook on the landing between two long-enclosed flights of stairs, which gave the feeling of being in the turret of a tower, perched in a tree. Wood framed it all, a variety of poplar, stained too darkly, and cut into ornaments that matched the banisters, the pilasters, the runner, the amphibious aspects of the chair, the way the curtains fell, and all of it, as one, designed to summon the long forgotten age before. She was older still.

From there, she observed the dot, the small clump, of the several creatures emerging from the sharp horizon. They had no where else to go but to her door.

Jinny.

She summoned a retriever with a click of her fingers.

"Have someone wash Pim for me. Remind him not to speak unless spoken to. Prepare a cart. Fetch them. Fetch them."

When the dog bowed in acknowledgement and began to step away, she halted it with her hand, "Stay."

She fixed her eyes and ears and nose on their approach. Her heart was a whirlpool. The clump of travelers would soon show itself in kind and number. An hour passed. The vague gray shimmer of creatures finally became more or less discernible for what it was. Virginia held still, shut her eyes. Her disappointment, for a moment, followed a single stretched nerve into the city she shared with Jinny, and for a moment, that world was animated by the fresh wound, something Eurydice says to Orpheus just before she changes form.

"Prepare rooms," Virginia said. "One large for the children, one for the mother, another for the two bears. Tell the kitchen."

The dog bowed its head again and strode off.

Virginia put her face in her hands until she had recovered. She heard the muffled assignments and conversations ripple through the house as she watched the figures resolve, the sun tipping against their slow approach. They slowed, sat, and continued. Now some of them were heaped upon each other while others straggled feebly on. Soon, all had dropped into the grass. How precious, she thought, how perfect.

"A wagon," she said. She couldn't be sure if her labrador was nearby, but someone must have heard her.

The bears were taken to a basement room. They were smelly, matted, and bad tempered. Virginia didn't want to see them. She decided to greet the rabbits the next afternoon.

"Bring them to the southeast patio in half an hour," she said.

She dressed in faded gardening clothes, a scarf covering her head, weeding-knife in hand, working the edge of a stone patio.

She gave the impression of being a comfortable and lively woman of means, all easy smiles, tall glasses with ice, bright sweat on her cheeks, lemon slices. She had the rabbits brought to the garden to see her, bade the children explore the paths, pick flowers, if they like, "see if you can find any carrots!" she called to them, delighted by their simpleness. She doubted there were any carrots.

She changed into a skirt and blouse while they were given iced water with mint and sugar by the fountain, and then she took them on a tour of the grounds, the manor, her art collection. Timeless anecdotes rolled from her mouth, all designed for the children, about fairy sightings and secret passages. In one massive hall, stone statues of men and women seemed frozen in panic. Dominating the room was a strange vessel made of stone, much decayed. "A god," Virginia said, "one of the planets, took issue with a sailor and turned his ship to stone." She took them to the highest balcony, where they could look out on the garden, really see the plan of it, its many symmetrical curls, grand staffs of music swept here and there, all composed of hedges and small orchards, walkways, and riverstone walls. The bunnies could see, in the distance, the darkening flat horizon from which they'd come.

She let them dash here and there on the broad balcony, listening to their exclamations, how they teased one another and giggled. When she could take no more, she clapped her hands and said, "Please, your attention: if the children would all line up."

They were all on their best behavior. Mother made sure of it. She posed them each by the shoulders until they were a tidy row before Virginia.

"Good. You'll be pleased to know that we'll all dine together this evening, and I don't think you'll mind if we have a little inspection to prepare ourselves. I heard the state you were in yesterday," she gave Mother sympathetic nods, then looked to her no more, "and my heart goes out to all of you. I feel that, much as my staff might have been of assistance to you in freshening up when you arrived, there might be more we can do. Yes? Please children: arms like this, yes, chins up, very good, and turn when I ask it of you."

She took note of their condition, one by one, and called prescriptions to the waiting labradors, much like a dentist notes the condition of a row of teeth. Grind this one, pull that, ears on number three, scrape here...

The alphabet had been jostled in the dead rabbit's brain. She felt cold and groggy. She stretched out across the neck and chest and hips and legs, the space so familiar now. The movement stopped, but the whole corpse was oriented differently. To move herself from the skull to the chest, for instance, she could feel required a bit of a climb against gravity.

At the chest, the alphabet had felt a new kind of pull, a rush. At first she thought the rabbit boy was gasping to life—it was thrilling, but she soon saw that fluid from all over the body was coming down in a cold swelling, ice melt rippling around organs as if down a mountainside. Parts of her that lingered in the blood she had to gather in to keep together. The flood soon slowed, but then a rift opened in the chest, space rushed in, organs moved about. Someone was digging about in the body! She had to think quickly. She still could not extract herself from the boundaries of the body, but these were clearly changing, and perhaps she could change with it. She stretched out all at once, everywhere she could, inspecting the limbs. Ah! Then the head was gone! And some of her with it! What would become of it? Was she still there? She couldn't think straight. Now something else was gone. Which was it? The left arm? The right? What next? Where was she? A shriek of metal filled the air. The alphabet twisted and lunged, avoiding the strike of a saw, the dig of a knife. She compressed herself near the spine, then reconsidered. Hoping that this might be her chance to escape, she spread her body as evenly as possible through the rabbit's body and held still, waiting to disappear, or be free.

At six o'clock, Virginia stood at the head of the dinner table in the grand hall. The plates had been set, and she encouraged the bunnies to pass the bread and butter around, not to dig right in, though she knew they must be famished, but to pass everything around once first, counterclockwise, and be patient, my little ladies.

Mother, for one, found the collection of foods surprising: skinless pickles, raw bacon, wheat rolls, cucumbers, a stew of shrimp and potatoes, a platter of small birds still in their feathers, wine and tomato juice, fried bananas and a bowl of olives.

"This looks lovely," Mother said to no one. Virginia's attention was fixed on the candles.

When the serving bowls and plates and spoons and forks had come to rest, and each plate had its menagerie, Virginia smiled broadly, "Doesn't this look delicious!" Above her plate she demonstrated to all the bunnies how to unfold their napkins and spread them in their laps.

Her hand hovered over her fork, then returned to her lap. "No," she breathed. Some of the bunnies were reaching for cucumbers, "Hold!" she snapped. "We can't ignore it." She sighed and worked up a bit of grin in the corner of her mouth. "I see some of the house is missing."

"Ma'am," Yasha ventured, "I beg your pardon, I think the bear brothers are really not well. Please forgive them."

"No. I mean, of course. What I mean is, yes, I realize. My own doctor has seen to them. But— well, you're a smart girl," she lingered on Yasha, feeling clever, "tell me what you see."

Yasha looked around the whole room, and then around the table. "I see there are three empty chairs."

Virginia adjusted the alignment of her fork and spoon, "Exactly." She spoke as much to her plate as to anyone. "Two places to acknowledge our guests, in the wish that their health and hygiene permitted them. But the other... well, the other," she passed a look to each of the five servants in the hall, "I find inexplicable and, well, embarrassing."

She sat up straight in her chair as if to wait, hands in her lap.

"How long shall we give him?"

No one answered.

One of the servants rotated on his heels, or what would be in the place of heels on a dog, and he drifted from the room.

Virginia's groan of displeasure came from all around, as if the dining hall, and not her chest, were working to crush out the air.

Another minute passed. Virginia said, sincerely, "I'm sorry," and pushed her chair back. "We'll just have to try this again. Everyone return to your rooms. When you hear the bell, you may come to the table. Take all this away," she gestured at the table. Give it to the pigs. Bring something else. Clean plates. A fresh napkin for that one, no, for everyone, the white ones. I hate these candles. Never liked them." She addressed the bunnies again. "I know you must be very hungry, but—."

She froze.

Pim had entered at the other end of the hall. He limped to the empty seat across from his mother. He struggled a bit to get himself situated, to pull out his ungainly chair, failing to keep it from moaning as it scraped its limbs against the chalkboard floor. Still he had to squeeze himself between the seat and the table, his whole body an abused erector set of limited possibilities.

She snapped up her napkin. Her attendants had approached the table. She waved them back to their places. She sat, smoothing her napkin once again into her lap.

The young wolf sat.

The bunnies waited, waited for a bomb to drop, for fire to consume them all, for jagged cracks of black lightning to form in the ceiling, for a scream, a flash of light.

At last, Virginia lifted her fork, and the children reached for theirs. They could eat.

Yasha's gut felt pinched so that each swallow was work. She sipped her tomato juice, both hands around the goblet, horrified that something might drip. Most of her siblings were oblivious, except one next to Mother, who cried silently into her disinterested shoulder.

"I apologize," Virginia's effort at grace had returned, "We live a simple enough life..." She abandoned her thought and started over, "I am an old woman: I allow myself the privilege of certain expectations. You understand."

Halfway through what was on her plate, Yasha felt she could hardly go on. She liked so little of it. She was relieved when Virginia stood, dabbing her lips with her napkin, magnanimous again.

"Melon soup, I think," she said, as if it were a comment on the state of the world, a truism. She remained standing. The young wolf stood, too, slipping some piece of bird anatomy into his mouth, then returned his fork to plate. His napkin had fallen from his lap, so he ducked for it, smeared it across his lips and stood stolid before his chair. Mother and all the bunnies followed suit, and the dishes were cleared by the waiting dogs.

Virginia begged them all to sit, but remained on her feet. "My dear guests, I think you haven't met my son. I call him Pim. He is deeply apologetic for spoiling the first part of dinner. Please forgive him. We've been too informal of late."

Mother stood and nodded to Pim. "Hello—," she began.

"Pim, greet Mrs Rabbit."

Pim shimmied up awkwardly and stumbled through his words. "Hello, Ma'am. It's truly pleasure and have you in our guest in our house, I—."

"That's enough. Don't tire her."

Pim sat. Mother sat.

"Well, since the soup may be a few moments, I thought I might say a word or two. First, I beg you to ask for whatever you may need to be comfortable during your short stay. I understand many of the things you came with, your clothes and soiled things, have been taken to the Wash House for cleaning. I hope—."

Mother Rabbit stood.

"I'm sorry, Mrs Rabbit, did you need to be excused?"

"Kind Madam w-Wolf," Yasha had never heard her mother's voice like this. "I carried my unfortunate son with me. I supposed he had been left outside the grounds, but I have looked and I could not find the place where, thank your graciousness, your, um, staff found us, and so I think perhaps his..." she looked for the word, "...remains might also have been collected, and I wish..." She staggered through a few phrases, but couldn't finish the sentence.

Virginia was disappointed by the distraction. "I see." She clenched her bright teeth behind her licorice black lips.

Mother was utterly torn between her fear, her attempts at decorum, and her desperation to know where the body had gone. Her night had been filled with visions of him devoured by rodents, or dumped into a river or eaten by hogs, or simply lost, never to be found, to rot for years and be nothing but bones in the field. "Your words gave me hope that—that he might have been discovered and taken, as well, to the... the..."

"The Wash House," Pim suggested.

Virginia's eyes snapped at him. "Yes," she enunciated, "Surely he would be in the Wash House. Thank you, Pim. Please, however, mind yourself and let us converse." Virginia surveyed the assembled bunnies. "You're all so young," she said. "I had no idea the grief you carried. Perhaps," she directed her tone to the dogs posted about the room, "I might have been informed." Virginia pulled herself together. "Please," she beamed, "eat. And I will try to continue where I left off, assuming that you are satisfied, Mrs Rabbit: I am quite certain that you will find all your questions resolved as soon as you like, after the meal.

I will place you in good hands. I promise, there's no reason to worry." Yasha watched as Virginia moved through a number of stray gestures, her hands idle, her eyes, looking for something to anchor her thoughts, a direction in which to move. "I trust..." she started. "I suspect... Ah! The soup!"

Carrying several bowls each, the servants were stealthy and precise as they delivered the cold, green liquified melon. The bunnies nearly drooled. Mother Rabbit lowered herself back into her seat.

"Very well, then. I trust your rooms are adequate. I trust that you will respect that, in a house such as this, there are guest quarters and public rooms, and there are those private spaces for myself, my family, and the staff. I beg you to mirror my hospitality with your discretion. I'm sure there is plenty for you to explore. Please also understand that, as has been demonstrated, my son Pim you may not count among your hosts. For his sake, I ask you not to expect or request anything of him. He very much needs his privacy throughout the day."

Virginia tried to make eye contact with some of the bunnies. Funny little beady eyes! "Good! That should all be very clear." A girlish grin punctured her face. "You've arrived at a happy time. After quite a long two years, I am scheduled to release the final volume of the series of books for which I have gained a portion of fame." She let that sink in, let it occupy, in their minds, the wealth around them. "In just a few short days, I am scheduled to offer a public event, a reading—you know, how they like to generate some excitement for new releases. Of course, you'd be invited excepting that the event is not open to... em, well, there just won't be any more tickets. So... in preparation, as a special treat, I thought I might tell a few stories with our dinners together, for however long you may stay." She passed a smile over the table. "I might be a bit rusty, after all. So, a story, and then to bed with you all."

Once, she intoned, in the land of humans, there lived a weaver, and his name was Pim. He is one of the heroes of this story. But he did not start as a hero, nor did he have any desire to be one. Weaver Pim lived in the age of machines, and when I say he was a weaver, I do not mean he sat at a loom all day, or spun yarn or made rugs and tapestries. No, he worked in a tremendous building the inside of which was taken up entirely by the weaving machine. All about and within the machine were stations where the workers would stand, pumping this, checking that, each doing something that the machine could not do for itself. Pim was one of these, and he was very good at it, or as good as one can be at such a task, and by this work he supported his two children and his beautiful wife, who had within her his third child.

Pim was clever and ambitious in his work. And though it seemed at times to the neglect of his children, he spent many hours in his barn, putting together this and that, assembling mechanical arms, devices that, though made of metal and wood, could move on their own when given a turn. Eventually, he interested his employer in some of his devices, insisting that they would improve the weaving machine. He was well rewarded for his cleverness, and with his budding wealth he enlarged his home, provided for all the needs of his growing family, and acquired new tools for himself.

Then his fortunes turned. The modified weaving machine indeed worked better and faster than before, and with fewer men. But the machine had also become more dangerous. Another weaver, by the name Boris, was caught by Pim's invention and lost his life in a gruesome fashion. Pim, desperate to repair his pride, attempted to demonstrate how his machines could work safely and that he could correct any errors, and in the process lost his own arm....Virginia trailed off.

The youngest bear had crawled across the threshold of the dining room. His breathing was harsh as he pulled himself into the room, as much rug as bear. Virginia waited, guarding her nose discreetly. It took several minutes for the bear to maneuver himself to the empty chair, climb his legs up into the seat and hang himself, like a bulky sweater, upright against the back of it. He wheezed deeply as he situated himself, then panted wetly from his efforts. He was obviously a bit dim from exhaustion, but he stayed awake. Yasha could see he was anxious for the story, not for food, and in fact his eyes seemed full and bright. A servant, labradorian, moved to get the bear a dish of soup. Virginia stopped him with a wave of her hand and tidy shake of her head. No no, she said, of course not.

She went on, poising her napkin close to her lips and nose.

He was now out of work, disgraced, reviled by his peers, and in almost every way that mattered to him, he was incapacitated. Terribly saddened, though his wife and children still loved him, he, in an effort to change their fortune, sold everything they could, packed them all into a cart, and set off for anywhere.

Along the way, they encountered a dreadful scene. A man was hung upside down against the trunk of a tree. His body was bloodied, by man or beast they couldn't tell from afar, but clearly he lived. Pim made his children hide their eyes as their cart approached. He pulled his horse to a stop and climbed down. He saw that the condemned man could see him, and as he neared, that he was strong as an ox, and that his bronze skin admitted no imperfections save for a few remarkable scars. A heavy chain coiled around him like a python of iron, but left no bruise or scrape, and scarcely pressed in upon his skin.

Pim was cautious, but full of pity. When he saw the eyes of the man, bright as morning, he was in awe, and he asked, "Are you an immortal god?" for there were still gods among men in this era.

The bound man said that he was none other than Orpheus, the accidental child of a god and a water nymph, but alas, he was all too mortal. "Even today," he said, "I have died three times on this tree. And last month I was swallowed by the earth, and before that, incinerated twice by witches, and before that, when I was but four years of age, I was poisoned by my father and stabbed by his mistress, and later smothered by my mother's rightful spouse; I was drowned twice in the same war, when I was just a babe. So, my one-armed friend, I am eleven times more mortal than you." Orpheus gave him a wink. "I think I may go on dying the rest of my days."

"Who has chained you here?" the weaver begged, not forgetting to look around in case the god's foes or family waited nearby.

"The Enchanter, Hades, jealous Lord of the Dead and Prince of Angels."

By this point, Youngest Bear had begun to breathe excitedly, still rather limp in his chair, but his floppy face showed clear delight, a kind of happy shock.

"How many men is that?" Pim asked.

"Just one—many names."

Pim examined the chain. "My lord, I doubt I have any means to free you."

"Worry not for me. You must instead find my wife, Eurydice, whom the Fanged Worm has taken."

"And who is Fanged Worm?" Pim asked, horrified.

"Same as the others. He lives now in the tallest mountain of the North Range, where he studies the source of his power on earth, a Titan's eye, stolen from the belly of my father's father, an orb which shows him the thousand-fold paths of fate and will birth a monster that devours worlds. With it he will rule the earth and never return to his proper dominion, and I ...I shall be without my love."

Pim shook his head, despairing. "I'm sorry. I don't think this is a task for me, an ex-weaver with one arm. You'll have to wait for a better man to come along."

Virginia languished at this crux, savoring the looks on their faces. Though some clearly had not understood the tale, many of them were filled with curiosity, a delicate tether between them and her, and now, the room having been full of her voice and her world, she had crafted this silence in which their need could take root.

"That's enough for one night," she said. "I must retire." She left her full soup bowl at the table and regarded only the clock as she left the room.

Mother told her bunnies to get to bed immediately, to close their door and be as quiet as could be. They were dutiful, made happy by melon soup, but also as close to melancholy as bunnies can be, surely ready to keep their own company. The little bunnies hoisted the bear together, like a horrible rug laid over their collective heads, and helped him back to his rooms. All along the way, he mumbled things at them and threw his head about as if he'd lost something. Yasha helped them to get washed and tucked in.

Mother was met at the table by a well dressed young terrier, not too tall, who offered his elbow. "I'm terribly sorry for your loss, Madame," his tone was so sincere, she felt she had been sung to. She rested her hand on his arm and walked beside him, quiet for a number of steps, feeling that he was leading them along but that the rhythm and speed of their progress was hers to command.

"How far is the Wash House?" she asked, looking up at his thin jaw.

Without turning his head, he pronounced, "The Wash House is just over nine hundred feet away. As soon as we're in the garden, you'll hear the sound of the water wracking stones, for the river is high and quick. We'll go along the west garden path and through the corner of the orchard, and we'll meet the river in another hundred paces. The path continues along the river, which will now seem noisy, high and quick, so that we'll not feel like talking, and we may feel a breeze, the kind that dips down between banks to cool itself against the mountain currents. Just as we begin to tire and as the twilight seeps away, we'll see a clump of trees that, as we approach, will resolve into the Wash House, its arbors and deciduous shade. The path will wind away from the water, among the trees, and up to the house, where it will branch. One branch leads straight to the stairs and the immaculate blue door of the House. The other branch leads around and down to the lower levels of the House, where servants and tradesmen enter and exit."

They mounted the steps. The terrier pulled open the blue door, and ushered Mother inside.

Virginia slipped a fresh sheet of white around the platen of her typewriter, adjusted the carriage to target the center of the page.

Orpheus did not struggle.

He hung on the tree for years. Eurydice grew old while Pim wondered what to do and Orpheus waited.

One day, Pim came upon a turtle in the road, wedged in a rut in the hardened dirt. He lifted it, carried it to the grass, and sent it on its way. He was glad of what he was capable of, that he could rescue such a lovely creature. A little further along the road, however, he saw two turtle shells crushed, one across the back where a wheel had run it over, the other by a hoof driven straight through it to the mud. The splintered and fractured pieces of shell littered the path after them. Pim could see that he would not often be in the right place at the right time. He became an old man with property and successful children, many grandchildren. His wife was strong and wise. A satisfied if simple creature, it pleased him to sit on his porch at dawn and study the horizons, if one can think of many horizons, or the horizon, if we think of the edge of the world as a single cut across the eye. He knew that in some distant cave and on some ancient tree, fabled beings were leaving the world behind. There.

None of this was part of her novel, but Virginia enjoyed seeing her characters act out these plays, as if moonlighting in the alley behind the grand theater of their lives. A different story tomorrow. Pim bored her, the boy hung on his namesake, and the story already exhausted itself in the obvious.

Instead she described the city, typed it into existence five different ways, made Orpheus wake up in an antechamber of some mud and brick compound. The ocean, far below, roared continuously, and the wind, far above, echoed its brother. He had arrived. He knew, sensed, felt, felt the dread in his heart of hearts, in his head, his head of heads, that Eurydice had perished, died, fallen, been lost, been taken, possessed, and that all he could do was carry her body to its raft, carry it to its raft.

All that would remain was revenge, but against an enemy that had adopted her skin, sickened her soul, that hid behind her eyes, that shook her limbs like a puppet, that moved her thoughts and words with strings. Was there still flesh behind such a wound?

He would find the city strange. Its denizens were silent, slow moving. Their cream-marbled eyes said nothing but, "leave us," "leave us." He found his way to her, where she was being held, and where hooded priests worked to salvage her soul from her body, mined for it, unstitched her form to discover the pattern of the stitching. Orpheus watched as they arrayed pieces of her body on tables, an encyclopedia of anatomy, and Orpheus was more fascinated than ever by his love.

Eurydice would survive, and though Orpheus carried her mind, in the form of a book, her body would be led away from the city by a child, a child sent by her uncle, and her body would take refuge in a small village nearby, where she was cared for faithfully and forever. Her uncle, now fused with the spider-legged eye of a god, could weave slight strands of hope and dream before her, so that she would wake each day and want to live.

Her mind was in the book, but her power?

All this she typed: including variations, lush descriptions, terse dialogues, complex characters enameled and brushed, for her, not for the reader. She showed and didn't tell. Omissions were eloquent. Only chapters to go, and for the moment, she ignored how, in the back of her mind, Jinny was approaching, finally reflected in the morbidity and in the romantic impulses, approaching in the wandering figures: a poet, a book, and a body.

Her eyes itched, bloodshot. Her fingers, numb from hitting the bony keys, craved... She cracked her door and listened to the house: quiet, quiet enough. She descended the carpeted stairs, sat momentarily in her window seat, but could not settle.

The house was old, almost as old as she, and to wander it was in part a wandering in its history, all its functions, through peace and terror, the passage from age to age. In the cool of a plush and satin parlor lined with leather books, Virginia felt herself the librarian of a different collection, so long had she wandered these rooms, having witnessed every change to the structure, redesigns and reconstructions, each break another text, she knew the seams, the abutments and layers that no one else could see, and she felt it was in this private knowledge that she was most herself, most secure.

In her study, she listened to the night lamps sipping their oil into flame, into vapor, orange and supple air that curled up and came cooling down among the shelves, settees, tables. The light stained whatever it touched with artifice. She remembered the diurnal and the nocturnal dance, the grim laws of the forest, before gaslight and electricity, when she herself was a child, even when she was a grown man, when this very room would have been a forest of eyes, and she was he, the master of the pathless places.

In that classical age, Virginia the Wolf wandered the woods naked, and she was a he-wolf, on four legs or two, as it suited, his long jaw wet and tireless, his horrible eyes white orbs in the leathery night.

Murder was a formal endeavor. First, he ate a deserving child from each village. Then he waited, watching the villagers in their glowing dens. They would put on defiance in small ways: purchase locks, sharpen axes, hold hands. Some would grieve desperately, but everyone knew the kids deserved it. The wolf starved on the smells of their cooking, waiting for more children to brag, wander, trust. If more than a month went by, he might take a chicken or two, sometimes slaughtered a dog in the process, gnawed its bones.

The anger and grief of the villagers would swell. The scent of their outrage entered his body, even as he watched them carrying torches into the wood, wielding forks and rifles, their lust for his blood was delicious, and stoked that deeper emptiness, the one that ached to eat something sweet, pure, untarnished by curiosity or lust. He couldn't wait for long, then.

He would take an innocent. The fairy tale ended, the tragedy took over, and the villagers swarmed into the woods. The inescapable smells of their nervous and sweaty limbs charging about, clenched, the crevices of their muscular bodies, their perfumed and oiled hair: the ripe gases of life made his black nose flare, and, riding on the fumes of mothers and fathers and hunters and farmers, he fell into a joyous rampage, always pursued, from village to village: paws pounding, legs leaping, jaws snatching up infants, right from their cradles, even from a breast, if he liked. Nothing else tasted like a fed baby.

In one story, he grabbed a child and just shook it to pieces in the street, beside himself with joy and adventure. He laughed at the mess, slipped to his haunches, worn out from days and nights of chase. Perhaps someone had tricked him somehow; it didn't matter, there he was, delighted, exhausted. A crowd formed, yokels and yapping dogs encircled him, pale faces, stout men trembling but inching forward. Virginia the wolf laughed harder as he picked a few soft, blonde hairs from his teeth. It had been a riotous run. He giggled irrepressibly, a tickle on his lips sending tremors through his body and a new laugh from his gut, a laugh like a hiccough, jarring his frame. His stomach lurched, and in a violent guffaw, a laugh and a cough and a sneeze and a retch and a yell, out came one of the children he had just eaten. It landed in a lump before the crowd, wriggled there like a worm. It tried to stand, but slipped and fell on its bum. He laughed some more and imagined that one might come out his nose, like milk, and then out sprang another between his teeth, and another, and more, and even one he'd eaten months ago shot right out of his mouth.

They all had blood and other filth on their bodies, but they sat up and looked around, stunned, no doubt expecting to see their mothers and fathers. All but two of the children were in a foreign village, and a chorus of wailing and tears erupted. Some of the villagers rejoiced while others just stared. Several women moved in, picked up the children, wiped their awful faces. Was there a lesson here? Was this the orchestration of the gods or just the filthy eructation of monsters?

It was not Virginia's first maddened crowd, but she remembered it well, and felt, in this moment, anticipating the coming night, her eager readers, that the crazed village was among the first of her audiences, hanging as they did upon her every move, attentive to the slaughter as to the well-turned phrase.

One villager held up a toddler and gazed at it, trying to recognize her own. "You devil!" she cried at Virginia. Then she turned the child toward the crowd, "It's a monster!"

And some brute behind Virginia whacked off his head with a well-swung shovel.

That same village dissolved in the years, returned to valley, left no evidence of itself so that the melliferous brook of flowery banks could babble on, where still she could wander alone, until, one evening, its course wound about her, arched up from the ground, at once a typhoon and a python of water—and a song, and a horse—and they held each other, and from that there was Jinny, and from another evening there was Pim, and some mornings it came to the door as a man, and left again, unhappily and unhappy, until, in her life he was no more than an occasional voice, and then a babble again, and a river, and a dumb one that only ran its course, and he was dead in the water or had rushed his way to the soundless sea. In this century, most of the forest she'd once charged through fell to the city, the theater, the lights and spectacle of modern living.

Virginia remembered wincing against the iced air while beside her, hooked in her arm, her daughter danced, goofy and gangly on the sidewalk. They were on their way somewhere. On her other arm, Pim hung and hunched over his billowing blue shirt and damp wool coat. Each a speechless inner world, out of sync but together. Her daughter seemed so happy, so strange. Virginia felt the yank of her dancing. She heard feet slap and glide on the glossy cement. One such moment must have been the last one of her daughter's decent childhood, when she could still hold her in her arms, though who could say which moment, or if there ever is or was decency in children, or for children, a little more betrayed by the world every day. That day was exactly like all the others. Jupiter's storm has preserved itself for millennia.

Did Eurydice hope to die? to hide from her fate? Had she found a way to undo the curse?

It took the whole of the day to descend. Though Orpheus was tempted to curl their bodies into a hovel or under an outcropping for rest, he would not have forgiven himself if, in the end, it was only time that condemned Eurydice's soul. It was as he found a path down to the tree line that he felt the flow of Eurydice's blood tickle against his back. In the warm blood that left her body, Orpheus thought he could distinguish the cold, black bile of the shadow beast worming its way between them. The warmth was encouraging, as he could not always feel her chest working for air, but the cold crawled down his back, and in the grim, jumbled moon above ancient cedars, Orpheus wondered if it was not seeping its way through his skin, in search of his own heart. "Bring her back," the wizard Fin had said, "you must bring her back."

The dying sun sparked through elephantine mists. Dew shuddered and monstrous roses drooled. The lifting clouds gradually revealed a landscape disorderly, jagged, and twisted. The ground heaved here, not dramatically from the depths, but in the tumbles and crashes of a raging river made into rock, pale dirt, sage foam, and fish like roots lurching for safety. Beyond the tumult rose the secret city, its buildings bright scales layered from the sea to the cliffs of a towering bedrock, its mysterious sails reaching up and out into distant drafts from ends of the world. The waves of the sea drummed far below as gulls called to no one, swooping among cabled bridges and sharply falling waters.

Even as he made his way to the city, Orpheus hung from the tree, dying over and over, useless, a thin sheet between the tip of his blood-warm skull and the infinite depths. The book, stuffed with phrases, had fallen to the ground. The stars, she said, draw back and are extinguished. No more words, but pages to be swept away.

The next morning the little bear crept from his room, using what was left of himself to carry his eyes through the shadows of the house, looking for Virginia's library, or her study, or her typewriter... wherever he might find the fifth and last book of the series. His hands felt strong with this mission, wiry and free, and having lost so much of the rest, he found it easy to pull himself along the smooth wood floor. He had hoisted himself up some stairs in the night, and he spent the morning crossing the threshold between the public rooms of the house and the private rooms of Mrs Wolf. He was eager to hold a book, any book, but one most of all, and he was delighted all the more that, once he had it, there would be stories to tell the child bunny who had grown to hate him. He had no thought of penance, nor need to apologize anymore, but he wanted dearly for her to have a story to listen to, to finish what they had started, and himself to wander again into that hatred with the gift of a peaceful end.

Chapter Seven

Mrs Rabbit settled into a soft chair in the Wash House, near a well-appointed tea service. Steaming water was poured, plates with lumpy bread shapes offered, sat cooling and clumping on the table. The kind terrier had gone back outside, waiting, she hoped, to escort her to the main house once she had her son. She would not allow the dog to carry him. Her wait seemed interminable. She might have dozed as she sat, she couldn't be sure, the light changed, but the balance of shadow, lamps, and the odd hue in the window indicated little beyond an eternal dusk or dawn.

The reception room of the Wash House was a formal affair. The couch was well stuffed, the walls were pantheons of oak moulding, crowns and spiraling horns stained blood red in the corners, elaborate arboreally legged tables next to floor lamps of painted iron, all together forming a polished and gilded forest of typographic abstractions.

Given a ceremonial position in an alcove just behind Mother, between the two halls letting into the rest of the House, a nearly full-scale image presented a fantastical scene. A human woman with sweetly braided hair, wheat brown and fine, dressed in a blouse and skirts of silken earth tones, chalk blue sleeves, reptilian green brocades climbing across her chest, a finely woven trim slid around her neck, which, strong and smooth as can be, presented a perfect fusion of arch and angle to hold her head just so, her face allowing only the mythic sadness of a tragedy repeated a thousand times over, anticipated for centuries, necessary.

Her green, blue, and rust-red skirts fell from the shadow of the assemblage in her arms, rather, in one arm, balanced with the fingers of the other hand. She held a lyre, bright as a coat of arms and elaborate as a grandfather clock, but as much of the earth as a tortoise shell, and upon the strings, placid and pale, the head of Orpheus, according to a label, crowned silver and wreathed in his own blonde curls, hovered in a gray sea foam instead of blood, sinking into the strings of the lyre.

She was either a maiden, come upon him after his rending, appreciating the last sorrowful, impotent expression of the god's love of the world, or she was, at least for a moment, Eurydice, returning his desperate, adoring, murderous glance.

Bunny clothing, tightly folded, was brought before Mother Rabbit, presented, as if for her approval, then wrapped in paper, tied with string, each on its own, and labeled: sister's nightgown, little one's jumper, a pair of fuzzy socks. Soon all the clothes the bunnies had been wearing, crisp, colorful, were wrapped in brown paper and stacked handsomely, like gifts for some sad holiday, on the credenza near the door. Next, perfectly folded sheets were presented, tidy as decks of cards, wrapped, placed. Soon there were three such sheets, pearly white without even a hint of old brown or bleached blood, as if new.

Mother stared at the stacks of laundry. She missed her home, its shelves and tables, all the places she knew to put things, and the knobs on the children's dresser drawers. Another emerged with another sheet, and another, more sheets until it was all of them, as if all that was left of her son was sheets, flattened and folded. Mother sucked her breath as a rage filled her. A dog appeared with several stacked kitchen towels, held them in front of her for perfunctory inspection and glided away to wrap them. Mother set her tea aside and stood.

"Stop!" she shouted. "I don't need any of this. You don't understand. I just came for my son. He was... wrapped in the sheets, these sheets! He needs burial. If you have him down there... you must bring him to me immediately. If not, please just tell me where he is." The dog gave her nothing else to react to, but nodded, blank faced, and trotted back the way he'd come. She called out again, but she knew it was useless.

The terrier returned from outside.

"I'm terribly sorry," he told her, "I've been told that the body of your loved one was taken further down river, to the Stable House. It was assumed that, at the Stable House, they might have the means to properly prepare the remains for burial, assuming that is your wish."

Soon, Mother and the terrier were on their way again, now in the chirping night. He led her by lamplight to a small dock, explaining that the Stable House was some distance down the river, and that they would need to travel by boat. "We meet the boatman at the Bridge House, there." A grim shed, almost in the water, sulked in the near distance. They would sleep for the night on this side of the bank and summon the boatman in the morning. The terrier curled himself into a patch of long grass and shut his eyes. Mother watched the river. She turned and watched the amber lights of the main house, knowing her children slept in one of the dark places.

"Why is it called the Bridge House, when there is no bridge?" She was feeling conversational, it being night, and the wait inevitable.

The dog roused only slightly, saying "Once was a bridge. You see the old house across there?"

She hadn't until now. A small house, more a cottage, was set well back from the River in a clump of grass and trees.

"That's the River House. River didn't like the bridge much. Prefers the boat, now." He licked himself idly, but Mother sensed the action was designed to put her off. She fixed her gaze on the cottage now. "Someone named River?"

"The old father. He stayed. It's not so much the bridge. Things weren't good."

Pim's mother spent the next day typing. She must be so excited to have an audience, he thought, after so long in hiding. She got this way before book releases, in the old days. She called to him, but when he came to her, it was one of her labradors, dangling a hanger full of clothes for him. "You'll bathe and dress after dinner," said the dog.

"Yes, sir," said Pim. He could remember her calling repeatedly to Jinny, "Get your coat, Jin, it's time!" and the two of them would be gone to her reading, signing, workshop, whatever, and the house would be delightfully empty, echoes of nothing resounded, and he fell in love with invisibility. Now, he regretted everything and felt only Jinny's absence, not the peace of his sacred irrelevance.

Early, the dinner bell drew them all to table. Pim was there, dressed neat but simple. He kept his eyes lowered over his plate. The bunnies had learned how to sit patiently. The table was set with silky bone-china dishes. Decorative bands of relief images wrapped around the edges of the plates, cups and bowls, revealing farm scenes, familiar folk tales involving spears, cities, oases, lakes, maidens, birds, boys, bags of gold, claws, and fruit.

The bunnies gazed hopefully at the empty dishes. One was clearly muttering to herself, "melonsoup, melonsoup, melonsoup..." Yasha hushed her. Yasha did not relish her position as eldest, and as she gazed at her nameless siblings, she couldn't imagine gaining control of them should they become disruptive, or helping them if they were troubled. It had been easy before, at home, to survive, to cope with changes, strange as they were, even death. Here, life was not falling apart, but building something barely comprehensible around them. How would she keep up?

With a bit of pomp, two retrievers hoisted into the room a giant tureen of soup between two rods, as if it were a princess in a sedan chair. A third followed behind with a ladle in one hand and a number of bowls in the other. Through an elaborate juggling of soup, china, and steam, he delivered portions of the brothy, chunky mixture to each guest and the two wolves. As soon as he smelled it, Pim quivered with a horror and desire that exhausted him, tilted the entire room. He put his face in the steam and panted.

Virginia herself made a show of waving her long nose in the aroma of the steaming bowls, her eyes going drunk with anticipation. When she raised her head to the bunnies, her smile was toothy. "Please... begin," she said, balancing her spoon.

All the little bunnies scooped and slurped eagerly. Yasha peered into her bowl, studying the grainy and oily surface, pale chunks and soft strings. She sniffed it. "Pardon," she said, "but what kind of soup is it? I mean, it looks delicious..."

"Oh, I'm not sure," said Virginia, lips wet, "Perhaps chicken and rice?"

Pim held his tongue. He realized Virginia was eyeing him, and he brought a spoonful to his lips, making a show of agreeability, an enthusiastic slurp. He couldn't help but enjoy it.

"I'm sorry," Yasha said, struggling to get through the sentence, "I regret that rabbits don't, well, it's not in the norm for a rabbit to eat meat."

Virginia smiled sweetly as she took another sip of soup. "But look," she dabbed her lips with her napkin, "all your brothers and sisters just love it. I promise, it's quite nutritious. It can't do you any harm, you know."

"I'm very sorry," Yasha put her hands in her lap. "I just can't."

The little bunnies went on eating, oblivious, and Virginia smiled at this. "There will be salad," she said to no one in particular.

Once all the soups but Yasha's were finished, the bowls were cleared and two long-haired dogs entered carrying between them a rotund wooden bowl. Behind them, another pair rushed in with an iron tripod, which they settled under the bowl as it was lowered. As those four dogs trotted off, a new pair of elegantly groomed retrievers waltzed in wearing crisp white aprons. These two gave the bowl a spin.

Virginia applauded briefly. It spun very well.

One of the retrievers produced a decanter of golden oil and another of black vinegar, and these he tipped above the bowl as the other tousled the bowl's contents with a goose-neck fork. Their focus was beyond description.

"Would you look at that!" Virginia cooed.

An assistant arrived with plates, and, with the bowl still spinning, the two retrievers began to assemble a salad on each one, piece by piece, plucking each torn green and carved vegetable from the bowl and tapping it into place, all with quick, bird-like maneuvers of sterling tongs.

"Thank you, dear, no! Not for me!" Virginia waved her salad away as the others were served. She stood, hands clasped, and smiled broadly at her company, "As I'm sure you can detect, there is something special about our dinner tonight, for tonight I shall be off to the big event, to reveal to my undying fans a glimpse of the final chapter of the great saga. Before I go, I would like to leave you all with a last tale," she almost hit whimsy, "something that could happen in my novel, but in fact has not. I had to cut it, you see, as one must do from time to time, even with something dear. So, a special treat— really, a secret! Are you ready?"

Once upon a time, late in the life of Pim the Weaver, whom you will remember, he did a terrible thing. You see, each month, under penalty of exile or death, he was required to deliver goods to the king: three baskets of this, three of that, three of the other. One year, there was just enough grain to fill three baskets, and just enough cabbage to fill three more, but the insects had not been kind to his trees, and there was just a little more than two baskets worth of pears. What could he do? Well, Pim had many grandchildren, and many of them were bright and adventuresome, but one in particular never spoke and hardly left the house. She was strange and lonesome. Pim decided that he would hide this grandchild at the bottom of one of his baskets. She could eat the pears as much as she liked, and once the baskets had been stored, she could sneak out in the night and return home. It would seem as though half the pears had been eaten.

That was how...oh, let's call her Pearl. That was how she ended up in the kitchen of the castle. All day and night, she heard activity all round her, and so she stayed hidden in her basket. Every now and then, the lid was popped off and a pear removed, but no one noticed her hidden beneath the fruit, not until the third day. One of the cooks saw the core of a pear that Pearl had eaten, and she cried out in anger, "Oh, come and see, Martha!" she cried, "We've got a rat!"

So they dug through the pears and found not a rat, but Pearl.

"What on earth are you doing in here?" they shrieked and laughed and cooed and puffed their cheeks all amazed.

Pearl said nothing, but kept her eye out for a door to leave by. There were no doors.

"It's a pear-child," said one, for people thought such things back then.

"It's an orphan," said another.

"It's a bastard," said one.

"Whatever you are, you'll work in the kitchen now. Here you go!" and they put her to work, and they called her Pear. Do you see? From Pearl to Pear? Well, the poor girl took to the name, and soon forgot the name she'd been given.

Pear enjoyed the work and soon seemed quite happy in the world of the castle kitchen. She was friendly with the other maids, but not friends with any of them. She never went outside or looked outside, for there were no windows in the basement kitchens, and she was not allowed to use the stairs.

One day, she met the child prince where he wandered in the weird lower halls of the castle, and the two of them were fast friends—both somewhat sullen and dark-willed, but happy together, together imaginative and serene. They grew up as secret playmates, teasing and pretending in the dusty and unused halls of stone, becoming each season more dear to each other's hearts.

One day, observing the loving eyes of the prince, who lingered looking down at Pear from atop the servants' stairs, the other young maids grew jealous, and so spread rumors about Pear, about how she boasted she could cook better than Cook, how she was an orphan because her real father was a king on something-or-other mountain, and how, though knights and heroes had failed, she alone could slay the Ogre of Montesinos, a creature who had ravaged the countryside and now hid in the deepest caves beneath Mount Arador.

Pear was called before the king, but she refused to go to him, afraid to climb the stairs. Mystified, in the mood for a lark, the king marched down to the servants' hall and demanded to see her. "Show me this proud and fearsome creature!"

Pear was brought before him, and something in her look amused him and probably saved her from instant death.

"I am told you claim to be the finest cook one could find. Is this true?"

Pear said nothing.

"Your silence may cost you," said the king. "Cook for me the finest meal I've ever eaten, or I will put you to death."

He gave her three days. Pear wept in the kitchen, pondering what to do. In the night after the first day, she began to cook, but everything she tried burnt, or oozed, or dried up, and it all tasted awful. She tried again the second night, with the same results.

On the third day, she decided to give up and escape. Her heart swooned to leave her prince behind, but she fantasized that perhaps one day he would find her. Pear chose the least-used stairway and crept her way to the ground floor of the castle. Her knees felt wobbly, as if she were on some ship of stone, and all at once her eyes were dazzled by the harsh beams of light casting about the chamber and the nearby halls—the sun falling through windows. She headed directly for the nearest door, but along the way stopped short, for she saw a different kind of light, the easy glow of color through a stained glass set into a chamber wall. It drew all her attention, and she walked toward it, floated, really, and touched the jewel-like surface. In the glass was the image of a woman, young and beautiful, and she was in chains before a mad crowd.

Suddenly a voice came through the glass. "Girl!" it said, severe, but not unkind.

She pulled her hand back in fright, but didn't move away. She thought it might be the characters in the glass speaking to her, or yelling at the chained woman, but then realized that someone was hunched on the other side of the window.

Pear whispered, "Who are you?"

"Please, my girl, don't worry about who I am, just do as I say!" came the voice.

It was an old woman, Pear was sure, and she worried that she was encountering a witch.

Pear could see the old woman's silhouette sharpen as she leaned her head closer to the glass. She tried to stare through the purple and green, but it was all shadow on the other side. "Listen to me," said the woman, "I will give you what you need to live through the night, and when you have survived, you will give me whatever I ask for." Pear could see the head nodding to itself.

"I—."

"Do you agree or not? Do you want to live or not?"

"I do. I agree."

"Thank you." The woman's shadow tipped away again, blurred and wavering. Pear had to strain to hear her next words: "Find the meal that will satisfy the king in the empty pear basket, my dear, and then, at midnight, come here, to me, at this window."

The figure was gone. Pear rushed downstairs and resumed her work until evening came. The king commanded that the meal be brought before him. She rushed to the pantry and checked one basket, then another, finding them full of pears, and then opened the third. There it was. Steaming aromas of butter, honey, peppers, and oils filled her head. Packed neatly in the basket was a fabulous and ornate meal of the finest ingredients. She brought it to the king, and he spared her life.

At midnight, she went to the window. At once, the old woman's voice came through the glass. "Leave me a lock of your hair, there on the window sill."

Having no scissors, Pear yanked out a lock of hair, tied it once, and set it on the sill.

"Now go."

The next day, she was called before the king. No longer fearful, she mounted the stairs.

He said to her, "Precious little maid, your boasting in at least one respect has proven true, and so I am eager to see how you live up to your other claims. Tell me, which would you rather prove to me now: that you are the daughter of a king of some mountain," he gave an arch smile, "or that you can slay the Ogre and bring me his treasure?" Snips of laughter passed among those assembled.

The king's son, Pear's dear friend, stood next to his father, brow furrowed with fear.

Pear said, "The Ogre, sir," her voice shrinking, "I'll slay the Ogre."

"She speaks!" the king spat, amused. "Off with you then!"

"Father," said the prince, "I would be happy to accompany her, so that, upon failing, she returns to your mercy, or, should she succeed," he put on a sarcastic smile, "I might relay the story of her deeds to your ears myself."

The king allowed it, and together, Pear and the prince prepared to leave the castle.

The night before they were to go, Pear crept up the stairs and to the stained glass window.

"Hello?" she said. She pinched her lips and eyes through the long silence, listening.

The voice came so suddenly, she nearly jumped, "Listen carefully! I will leave a sack in your chamber with three things. The first is a waistcoat that you must wear at all times. The second is a small wooden box that you must not open until you are in the presence of the Ogre. And last, a crystal bottle with which you must collect some water from the river three times, once at each crossing. Do this, and you will live. Do all this as I have described."

Pear touched the glass where the woman's shadow showed her cheeks. "Who are you?" she said. "Why are you helping me?"

The shadow wavered, as if to leave, then the voice said, "Return. Return to me here, when you have finished."

Out on the moors, the prince was beaming with his cleverness and told Pear how they would run away and build a cottage and live together with simple means, happily ever after.

Already Pear missed the kitchen, the dank corridors, and she found the sun intolerable, and she found the old woman's command inescapable, and that whatever they faced, it might be worth it to return and discover her identity. "No," she said plainly, "We'll go and slay the Ogre of Montesinos, and then return to your father. I'll do it myself, if you like."

"Don't bother returning," the prince said, "I'll tell my father you died foolishly, the death of a boasting orphan girl who doesn't know her place!" He stomped off, assuming she'd follow and weep. You'll be glad to know that not an hour later, he tripped on his own laces and popped his little head open on a sharp rock!

So it was that Pear came to the first crossing alone. She uncorked the bottle the woman had left her and tipped its lip into the stream. Water leapt in. She corked it and continued. She wore the vest when she slept and when she bathed, usually under a more feminine shirt or dress. She did not see that it did anything in particular, but she grew fond of it as of a second skin.

She came to a second crossing, and finally a third, and after filling the crystal bottle, she could see the gnarled and fetid entrance to the cave nearby, like a tumor in the mountain's side. At the cave's entrance, she smoothed her vest over her chest. She gripped the small wooden box in one hand and the bottle of river water in the other. She had a short sword at her waist, but she left it there. What good would it do her?

The air in the cave was nothing but the trapped breath and odors of the ogre itself. On all sides, jagged rocks like warts protruded through the mud. Pear stepped warily in on her toes, lightlessly down into the dark. With nothing better to do, she called into the deep, "Hello? Ogre!"

A gurgling and grumbling groped somewhere in the darkness. In her fear, all she could feel was her own thirst, and so, trusting her instincts, she uncorked her bottle and drank down the entire draft of river. All at once, she was unafraid. But without her fear, exhaustion took her, and she lowered herself to the cave floor and soon fell to sleep.

She slept for days. When she woke, she was warm, in the deepest nodule of the cave surrounded by the golden orange of a fire. She was naked. Her vest had been removed. She threw her cloak over her shoulders as she sat up, and she searched for her sword. As her eyes darted helplessly in the half-light, she heard the garbled breathing of someone nearby: the ogre was just to her right, dozing against a rock.

In search of her sword, her hand fell upon the wooden box. She was in the presence of the ogre, so she opened it. She couldn't see inside the box. She felt around: it felt like a fat, damp frog. She thought it might be some kind of ogre bane, so she slid the box toward the ogre and waited to see what would happen.

It wasn't long before his eyes burst open, and seeing her there, he roared and shook his fists. She could see that the ogre held her vest in one hand, and he shook it at her, shrieking his horrible, tongue-tangled caterwauls.

Fire-lit tears filled his eyes, and Pear's fear disappeared. She lifted the box toward him.

The ogre took the thing out of the box, held it in both hands, nestled it in the waistcoat, and shook his head, confused. At last, the ogre shut his eyes and slipped the frog-like object into his mouth.

As Pearl watched, the ogre's sickly scabby skin dried and broke from his body like the shell of a hard-boiled egg. His tortured muscles relaxed and shrank until, crouched before her was nothing but a pale old man, clutching the waistcoat.

He held it out to her. "I made this for you," he said. "And you brought me my heart."

"How do you know me?" Pear asked.

"I am Pim, your grandfather."

Pear considered this. "Who does that make me?"

"You are my little pear, but, if that's true, where is the water from the river, the song of Orpheus?"

Pear felt afraid to answer truthfully. She said, "The water spilled, when I came into the cave. I was so frightened."

Pim shut his eyes. When he opened them, they were again the eyes of an ogre.

Virginia coughed. "I forgot to say..." She let go her composure for a half second. "I'm sorry, I thought someone was asking a question." She pinched her eyes a moment, scratched her ears. She laughed at herself. "Where was I?"

...The eyes of an QKVB. XB IQOYJ XPCB BPWBZ TBPVY...

"I'm sorry," Virginia cleared her throat.

DA DW XPJ ZQW RBBZ AQV WXB QYJ IQFPZ, IXQ IPH, QA SQOVHB, XBV FQWXBV.

"I-."

Virginia excused them. When they'd gone, she slumped in her dining chair, pressed both palms against her ears. She put her energy into her lips, and mouthed words, got her mouth working again. Enough. The hour was approaching.

Yasha rushed to their guest room, but when her siblings came flooding noisily in after her, some crying, others climbing in bed to hide, she left them, preferring to wander alone. Pim caught up with her among the statuary. "Little rabbit," he said.

Yasha didn't respond but halted and nodded politely.

"Come with me," he said. He rushed to a nearby door and held it open for Yasha. She peeked inside. It was the size of a ballroom, littered with bizarre contraptions, rolls of paper, bottles and boxes of materials natural and strange, shelves crammed with pieces of this and that, a century's worth of books in every size, shelved and stacked with studied chaos, half museum, half pharaoh's tomb. "Come on in. It's okay." He led her inside, then turned to face her. "I'm so sorry," he said to Yasha, "I'm so sorry." He pushed the door shut. "I was scared. I didn't know what else to do." He ran to a marble sink in one corner and spat and splashed water in his mouth, spat more. "I feel just terrible," he said, slouching back to her, looking mournful.

"What are you talking about?" Yasha stepped back, one hand looking for the door handle.

"The soup!" he cried. "The soup!" He moaned and spread his arms, "Your brother!" He tugged at his ears in confused despair. Yasha rushed out the door. Pim caught up with her in the hall, where the stone boat heaved against stone waves. He caught her by the arm. He begged and pleaded and soothed her until she promised not to confront his mother.

"You have to admit," he said, "It's somewhat natural."

Yasha punched him in the teeth. Her knuckles screamed. She called him names as he led her back to his room.

"You remind me of my sister," he said. "I like you."

"I'm going to be sick." Yasha was on all fours. Pim brought her a bucket.

"I'm concerned about your mother," he said.

Much of the day, Mother and her terrier guide waited for the boatman.

First, the terrier had lit a torch at the end of the dock. After they observed no activity on the river or the other side, he lit another. He called, barked, and howled a combination of complex phrases, but to no avail. He was neither apologetic to Mother nor impatient. In the afternoon, he said, "Ah, now, there he comes."

A sketch of a creature, tall and long armed, had appeared on the opposite shore. Mother could not make out what it was—a breed of dog, a wolf? It was tall enough, she suspected it might be an exotic—a giraffe (she'd never seen one) or a cat, perhaps—awful things. The terrier observed the creature and nodded with some relief, relaxing on his haunches with his eyes shut. A blue crack had formed in the brightening clouds. "Don't drink the water," he said, and made ready to nap in the warmth.

Impatient, Mother shouted to the boatman, hands, paws, cupped around her mouth. The terrier growled low at her, placing his paw on her arm. It was hours later when the boatman made another move. He had stepped into the boat—Mother hadn't seen it happen—and now he drove it toward them with a pole. The river was quick, but the boat never strayed from the course drawn by the boatman's eyes. He was an ape, bearded and slim. His meager fur clung haggard to his sickly skin. His eyes were not so much held in his skull as balanced there. He was nude, which Mrs Rabbit found grotesque.

With one hand on her guide's wrist, she balanced her way into the boat. She didn't bother trying to greet the old ape, but crouched down so that she could stare upriver or scan the opposite shore. Distracted in this way, she didn't notice that the terrier remained on the dock as the boatman pushed them back into the current. "Sir!" she called to him, but he sat facing the other direction, cleaning his knee with his tongue. She didn't call again. Her singular purpose was enough to prevent her from caring what else happened on the way.

Pim said, "I will take you to find her. I know the best way to get to the Wash House. But we can't go until morning. I've got to-."

Yasha was hardly listening, but she'd heard enough. "I'm going now," she said, and she rushed back through the house and out into the garden.

Pim washed himself, got dressed. He sat absently at his desk, examining his various projects, secret formulae, and the notes he'd made toward curing his disease. Hopeless, he thought. Hopeless. He brushed his teeth and went to wait in the foyer for his mother. Virginia appeared, her hard shoes hammering down the hallway. She was tight-lipped, trembling. Pim could see she was terrified, and she ignored him as she gathered her jacket and scarf. He followed her out the door.

She said to the waiting retrievers, measuring her words, enunciating, "I'll be riding alone. My son may take a different carriage or walk, if it suits him, or stay here. Here we go." She mounted the family carriage, a horse was whipped, and Pim watched, standing alongside the remaining retriever, who scratched his crotch dismissively.

"I'll walk," Pim said, and he padded into the grass.

He didn't get far before a voice shocked him from the shadowy trees. "Hey!" it called.

Pim scrambled and twisted back toward the house. Someone was about to grab him, stab him, slide a bag over his head! He willed himself to run, to leap for the lighted windows of the house, for doors that lock!

"It's me!" The voice sang now, and he really heard it. "Pimmy!" it said.

It was his sister. Pim nearly bounced, nearly peed, and when Jinny squeezed him, surrounded him, smothered him in a strong hug, he felt ready to explode. They pulled out of the warmth of their hug, and Pim stared through the shadows, looking for all the ways that she was the same and all the ways she was different. She wore clothes he'd never seen, she was tall, her face was bright and still so strangely smart, like an owl's or a mole's, but her mouth was sharper, moved and smiled in new ways.

She said, "Come along. We're going into town."

"Mother's just left! Why didn't you come sooner and ride with her? She'll be—She'll be..."

"Exactly. We're going to meet her—after. It's a big surprise."

"After her reading? It's going to be late."

"Mmhm."

"Do we have to wait?"

Jinny didn't answer at first.

Pim saw her switching gears, changing faces. "We have to." She took his arm. "I just want to be with you now, Pimmy."

He couldn't tell what was happening. She had never sounded like this before. If only I could tell, he thought, if she was tricking me. They walked through the woods, by the water, into town, from dirt to gravel to paved roads. Jinny said nothing at first, but she was excited, humming and clicking her tongue. They stopped at a crosswalk. There was no traffic. Normally they would just walk on across, but Jinny stopped and waited. Dusk fell, in the form of mist. She put her arm around Pim. "She thinks I'm going back to school here, but no way. Can you imagine?"

This was a surprise. Pim could imagine. He didn't appreciate it when she and mother fought. "What'll you do?" Pim thought of his room, his laboratory: escape.

"I'm going to sail around the world!"

"Sail? You can't sail."

"Shut up." She took her arm away. "What do you know?" She didn't laugh. "I learned to sail at camp."

"Oh. Can you really just do that? Just go?"

"Sure!" She gestured at the size of the world. "Well, I can. I don't know about you." It was a real jab.

They crossed the street. "Why don't you want to finish school?"

Jinny thought about this. A streetcar whistled and shrieked somewhere in the distance. "It's not just school." They walked through a neighborhood, cute little houses, bright yellow dining rooms busy with children and parents sitting or standing at the table, and dishes of food steaming as they passed them around, families leaning in and leaning out from each other as they talked. Outside, street lamps stood in flickerless rows, no stars above.

"I was really scared when you disappeared." Pim had never told her this, the times before.

"I didn't disappear. You were just scared I wouldn't come back for you? Ha."

"No." That wasn't it at all.

"You don't need to worry. I was fine." Jinny's eyes darted around, as if she was mapping the area. "That was stupid anyway. Don't you ever do that. Ok?"

"Do what?"

"You have to stay with mom, at least for a while."

"Ok."

"And if you stay... if you're patient, you'll see dad, too."

"How?"

"He's around. I've seen him. I traveled with him. That's where I was some of the time."

Pim was speechless. He didn't quite believe it. Jinny had lied before. "What does he... Why?" Pim knew, without wanting even to think the words, he knew what he was about to ask. He bit back the words and tried to remain simple. "I want to see him, too."

"Like I said. Be patient. But Pim." Jinny looked at him, really looked, stopped him in his tracks. "Just don't fucking become him, okay?"

"Oh."

"Or her."

"Ok."

"Don't become anyone, P." She smiled, she yelled happily, "Don't become anyone!" Her yell filled the darkness, filled space, sound waves possessing the darkness like a constellation, turning night into a solid.

They walked through the last lamp-brightened walls of suburbia and joined the main road. As they entered the town center, they could see elaborately silked, cloaked, and haberdashed creatures choking the entrance to the theater. Their mother was inside, about to begin her talk, and then her reading, and then answer questions, and how she would look divine, sound divine, a lovely doll, a mythical creature, a product of the audience's adoration.

Orpheus and Eurydice came to a bridge spanning a majestic river. Beneath its blue and green ruckling surface, a thousand memories swam and swirled with the current. The bridge drew a lonesome wooden line across a near ocean of consequences, narrow enough that they could walk with each hand on a rail. The slats were firm, and though it stretched out of sight toward the distant bank, it did not move or shudder in the least. The memories clamored below, some thin, some like fireworks, some like iron anchors crushing the water's surface. Orpheus was immortal, and he was a visitor to the end of things. He did not risk emptying himself into the river, nor did he have anything to gather. Eurydice was different, and he said to her, "You wait here, for now. I will cross, make certain that your passage is protected, and then return for you."

Orpheus moved quickly out into the void. Eurydice waited, for the rest of the day, through the night, and into the dawn, and then decided to follow after him. She'd taken no more than a dozen steps before, looking back, she saw that the land had disappeared. Nothing but bridge remained behind her. She looked down into the water, and there it was, confused in the rolling water, her memories of the land behind her. More memories followed. She watched them disappear into the river. She was amused that it didn't hurt, not at all. They kept pouring out of her, and she marched on.

Meanwhile, Orpheus at last reached the middle of the bridge, marked by a change in the wood, a sequence of joints in the side rails, and, as he passed through that point, marked by everything else. The bridge wobbled and swayed furiously beneath him, the waters below were emptied of their memories. Now waves like saw-blades flew above the current and broke around frothing rock. The long bridge before him snaked in the wind and moaned for every year of its eternal vigil. He could see the end, where a massive gate pinned the bridge to shore, a short gray thread of land on either side. He gripped the rails and moved forward, every muscle in his body straining to keep him in place with each small step. It was not long before he knew that he was defeated, the maelstrom gripped him, turned him round, the river of chaos conspiring against him. Crossing the center line again, all was as before, bright waters, an airy, taut sidewalk to where he'd begun. The memories below seemed horrible to him, and he longed for Eurydice. He raced to her, gathered her up in his arms and hurried them both to shore.

"I'm sorry," he said to her. "I am not strong enough for this passage."

"I'll go alone," she said, secretly giddy with her fresh, loosening mind.

Orpheus couldn't be without her. "No, there's another way. We'll go through the mountains."

Jinny led Pim down an alley and through a side entrance, where they were recognized by a well-stuffed security guard. They rushed down a queer, damp concrete hallway, up metal stairs, past the catwalks.

"Are we going to—"

"Sh!" Up again, and then a ladder, tight turns, a small door—opened it with a clunk. They stepped out onto the roof.

Jinny stretched and felt the relief of having arrived unseen at a secret place. Jinny said how gorgeous it was, but it was cold and stank of pigeons. She swept the gravel with her paws, doing a little dance.

Pim bundled into himself and looked around at the other rooftops, laid out in grids. It's like a whole other city up here.

"Come see," she said from the edge.

They looked out over the theater entrance, their knees in the gravel and tummies hooked against the cool ledge.

Pim looked down, way down, at the last of the audience filing in. They looked wonderful to him, like princes and princesses.

"What are we looking for?" he asked. Jinny didn't answer.

He watched carefully. He thought, fireworks? It was marvelous that they could look down at everyone, and no one at all would look up to see them. No one would ever guess they were there.

Maybe Father was coming to see Mother, something like that. Something amazing was going to happen.

The audience was all in. No one else was out on the street. He could still hear them way down there, behind the glass doors, buying books and little things, lining up for wine, hanging their coats.

Jinny walked away. He watched her stroll to the other side, just meandering.

Maybe nothing was going to happen. This was all a trick. Pim felt the cold more sharply. He wished he'd known they were going to be on a roof. Maybe this was all Jinny ever did, random moves, pointless destinations, hurry up for nothing. So boring! Maybe she wasn't amazing. Maybe he was as grown up as he'd ever be. This was all there was to do. He'd rather have been in his room alone.

"What are we doing here?" he called to her.

"Shut up." She didn't even look at him.

"How long—"

"Shut up!"

Pim rested his cheek against the stone cornice. He closed his eyes and thought he could feel the rotation of the planet. The planet was a celestial carousel that tipped up and became a ferris wheel, then again a carousel. Over and over, around and around and up and down. In his mind he gazed out from the highest point of the wheeling globe and saw all the distant planets, some sleeping, some waking, some in the bright of day, some close by and others on the distant shore of an uncrossable deep. Then down, onto the carousel, he saw into the ocean, tilted down to its dungeons, and he saw the throng of alien life eating and birthing, hiding and floating in the gloom. Pim thought for the moment, not thought but felt, that everything that existed was alive, or rather, that everything that existed was alive in the same fundamental sense, which might be to say that he himself was not alive in the way he wished he was, but was a lump of soft matter, of dust, and his thoughts were nothing more than a shiver in the electric soup.

Jinny was back.

"Wake up, Pimmy."

"I wasn't—"

"You want to go?"

"Yes."

"Where do you want to go?"

"Home."

"Is that all?"

"Yes."

"You like your room."

"Yes."

"All your projects."

"My work."

"I do, too."

"Really?"

"I love your work."

"You do?"

"Uh huh."

"Which ones?"

"All of them. All of them. And I know you think you're sick. I know you think you have a disease, or something weird, that you're ruined, but you aren't. You don't."

"What? How?"

"I read your diary. It's weird stuff. But you're fine. You're just fine. You're not one of mom's characters, you know, or one of mine! You don't need to worry."

"But that's not..."

"Shut up. Mom's about to come out. I can't really explain this, but there's something

There's something I'm about to do."

"What? Are we leaving? Why did we come up—?"

"Shut up. Listen, Pimmy. I can't tell you everything that happened this time, or what's been going on. Just trust me, okay? It's the right thing. It is. It's ok. I'm happy up here with you. I'm glad you're with me."

They heard the sounds of the audience bundling out onto the sidewalk.

"I'm doing the right thing. Okay, Pim?"

"What."

"Okay? This is me."

"Yes."

"I love you. I love mom, too. And dad. I love dad, too. I love you so much, Pim. I don't want you to worry."

Jinny spied mom below and bounded onto the ledge. She didn't yell. She didn't hesitate. She didn't look back.

But Pim grabbed her jacket, got a perfect grip on the shoulder and held on. He was saving her. He was bracing himself against the ledge, and he yanked back toward the roof. All that came with him was the jacket. She slipped right out. She'd left.

He was sprawled on his back, scraped and jabbed, staring up at the night. Part of him registered the sounds below, but he didn't really hear them. He stared straight up. The stars formed one single, terrible constellation.

He didn't feel anything at all until he stood, not true, because as he rolled to his side and pushed up, he felt the air, the entire sky throbbing, and he stepped toward the ledge, and he looked down through the churning, pounding air.

He saw his mother looking up at him, and the whole heart of the world turned inside out and crushed him with its pounding.

Now, Peter was naked, in his plain fur, shaking with dread, all his good things lost in the garden of the terrible McGregor. He wandered into the road, and he hardly knew where he was going, or how he moved, but he did, toward home, thinking of nothing at all, as if he really knew nothing at all, as if each shoe and each button of his coat had been a part of him, of his memory and his wishes, and all were torn away.

He made it home, where his siblings were busy doing chores or shirking them, lazy or busy with marbles and blocks. Most of them ignored him—those who were young and remembered public diaper changes and swimming without suits. But the eldest two rabbits, Peter's brothers, laughed and jeered at him, then said nasty things.

When Peter didn't respond, neither ashamed nor hurt nor amused, the eldest brother kicked him, called him names, and finally said, "Mother said that if you were trouble once more, you'd have to leave. So go!"

Peter, in his state, didn't take in the full meaning of what his brother had said, but accepted it anyhow, and he wandered from his home, down the road, past the McGregor's garden, and on, and on, alone. There, he thought, I have gone. I am gone. Is that enough?

He walked until he couldn't see any houses or hovels, not in the trees or in the grass. He was naked, the world was naked.

Oh! But then he cursed, he shouted and he cried, because you know what he remembered? What he had left behind?

If anyone ever asks you, what would you take with you to a deserted island, or a desert, or into a locked room for the rest of your life, what would you say?

Food!

A million dollars!

A door!

Candy!

A knife!

An airplane!

Mommy!

Those are all good answers. Do you want to know what Peter wished he had brought with him?

...His book.

In those days, one needed only one book. One book could hold enough stories for a lifetime, and this one had many, plus, it had Peter's own writing, of things he thought could happen differently in the stories, and stories about things he had seen and done. He could remember the book's original stories, there were seven of them, but not his own. The seventh was the longest, and do you know what made him curse again, each day, as he recounted the book to himself, each story, one after the next? He couldn't remember how the last story ended. Not a bit.

After weeks of struggling in the prairie, eating little, able to remember less and less of the story, not more, he resolved to return for his book. Alas, his home was gone, and there was nothing where it had been but a note pinned to a stick in the ground.

It said, "Peter, why did you leave us?"

Chapter Eight

Mr Fin woke with an eye like a typewriter, clacking, whirling metal lashes, tap-t-tap, and the sliding carriage somewhere in his head, tugging, ringing nerves. With his palm, he smacked all the keys, forcing the typebars to lunge at once for the black ribbon. All boggled in mid swing. That kept it quiet for a while, but his eye was sealed shut.

He looked around him through his one good eye. He could see through walls. He could see his toes under the sheet at the end of the bed, and beyond that his dresser, and above that, he could see the framed pictures he'd found in David's boxes, which should be in the other room, and beside these hovered his hat and sweater, hung by the front door, but there was no front door, and his shoes waited beneath them, so close to his naked, sleepy feet. If he turned his head, he saw assembled the random treasures that ornamented all the tables and window sills of his house, not many, he was never like that, but a glass paper weight like the god of marbles, a statuette of some character from the Gita, polished labyrinthine agates and a thumb-shaped jasper, his notebook, opened to a sketch he'd made of The Swan, reading glasses, smoking pipe (did he smoke?), sharpened pencils, and pens.

Everything was right here, now, right up against him. His vision cleared, and instead of the walls rising up and his possessions returning to their places, he saw the dry cream cave of the room he was in, the stainless steel and plastic, the easy-to-bleach linoleum floor.

Once he was dressed, it didn't matter. He went out for his walk, but not so far, just around the yard. A smooth black sidewalk—all void—made a meandering loop to follow through the grass. He assumed that, when he got back inside, David would be awake, waiting for him, and the rest of the house will have returned. He didn't think it through. The air was fresh, late late summerish, and he found a good solid bench along the path, right where he'd hoped it would be. Someone was there, but the bench had room enough for two or three people.

In his eye, the impotently purring typewriter drifted away completely. No more clicking, no whirring. He checked his pockets for a book, crossword or novel, same difference, but found nothing. Would have needed his lenses, anyway.

Vivian was there, on the bench. "You look well," she said.

"Yes, thank you."

"Have you been eating?"

Mr Fin couldn't quite grasp the question. Eating what? When?

"You look well," she repeated. "You look good."

Fin said nothing.

"I'm sorry," she whispered. "You don't mind if I come to see you so often? I don't want to pester you."

"It's good to see you," Fin worked to sound natural, not without difficulty.

"I brought a book, in case you wanted me to read a bit. How would that be?"

"A book? Yes." Mr Fin patted his pockets. His hands were looking, again, for a book. "You have a book?"

"I brought a few."

"Good." Mr Fin thought about this. He wanted to listen, but out here everything was moving too much, too bright and busy. "Inside, I think. We should go inside for that."

As they approached his room, Mr Fin worried that David would be inconvenienced. He did like his privacy.

He stopped in the pale hall. "Maybe not," he said.

"Hm?" Viv put her hand on his arm.

"Maybe not."

"Well, okay. But, well... how about just a chapter? It'll be lunch soon, anyway, I think."

Fin thought about this. "Just a moment." He walked ahead, signaling her to wait, and opened the door to his room.

David wasn't there. Where would he have gone? He stepped in and looked behind the door. Only one bed, anyhow. This was his own room, not David's. He peered down the hall. "It's okay," he said to Viv, without turning, "we've been taking turns, but it's all... it's all clear now."

Two chairs flanked the window, and they each took one.

"What would you like to hear?" she said.

Fin couldn't respond. This was more like the guest room than his bedroom. "This was the..." Here were his things, his bed-stand. "Never mind."

Viv had a small blue tote bag. She dug inside, keys rattling, coin purse, and pulled out three books. It had been a long couple weeks, and getting to this moment had taken much of what patience and persistence she could muster. Still much to do, and she had no idea how to do it, as a friend, as anyone.

Mr Fin's expression had changed. He was staring at the bed.

"I see what's happened. I'm not stupid," his voice was flat, matter of fact.

"Fin," she said. "I'm so sorry," she said.

"How does one do it?"

"I'm so sorry." She was clutching the book. Her eyes were full, face flushed. "Maybe it's just for a while."

"I'll go on, my heart will squeeze out its rhythm." He stopped. He looked at the empty bed. "How did he do it?"

As Virginia opened the door to her home, the carriage rolled off toward the Wash House. She strode up the stairs, saw the scraggly bear leaning motionless against a potted plant, as if dropped there. In her rooms, she changed into house clothes, washed her face, and tidied her desk, letting her fingers linger on the carriage arm of her typewriter. She felt she might be saying goodbye to the machine, and to words, and to the characters, and she felt a deep calm, as though a buzzing she'd grown accustomed to had ceased, and she was plunged into some purer stuff than air. She left her rooms.

She passed by the bear again, stopping to whisper near his head, "Don't give up, dear, don't give up."

Virginia put her ear to the bunnies' door, heard them unsettled in the night, some sleepily crawling into bed, others being a bit silly or twitchy. She peaked in. "Good evening, my dears," she said. Several of the bunnies were surprised, and they jolted in their beds. Virginia smiled. The bunnies said in practiced unison, "Goodnight Mrs Wolf."

A table lamp was still on. Virginia crossed the room to it. "I hope you all had enough to eat ...and that you are very warm ...and very cozy in your beds."

"Yes, Mrs Wolf," they all said in shy song.

"I hope you enjoyed the story this evening."

"Yes, Mrs Wolf." Some did not say it.

Virginia turned the lamp down low. "Right off to sleep you go," she said, pressing the iambs between her lips, as if it were the start of a poem. Many of the bunnies were silent now, but several kept up the game, "Yes, Mrs Wolf." The lamp was out. Some distant light came through the doorway, a shadow of light.

Virginia hummed a tune, waltzing from the lamp toward the door. Along the way, she paused at the foot of each bunny bed and squeezed their toes affectionately. "Goodnight, dear," she would whisper, and "Sweet dreams," and then hum more of her lullaby.

She pulled the door into its frame. As she did, she expected to be overcome with old motherly feelings, a nostalgia and a passion, but she wasn't. Instead, as soon as she'd closed the door, she found that she was panting, her heart pounding in her chest, delighted. She needed a glass of water.

She passed Youngest Bear again as he drifted, wraith-like, at a shadow's pace down the hallway, under a windowsill, ever so slowly closing in. How nice it was to have the house nearly to herself. Just all those little sleeping bunnies, without troubles or worries, dreaming of shiny things, hiding places, the ticking of clocks, warm blankets. They were so simple. The more she thought of them, the more she was reminded of the old days, the very old days, when she was a he who roamed the woods. Living and dying were such easy games then that she spent half her time concocting ways to make her task difficult, complex, beautiful. Virginia said to herself... no, deeper, the self she would have spoken to spoke it to another still further within, or again, another step down, in an almost private, shapeless language, spoke to its quiet sister, mother, or daughter, the one without eyes, without skin, without lips or breath, but only ears, ears alone, a frenzied mind that listened in its dark: "Grey the landscape; dim the ashes; water that murmurs and moves. If I fall on my knees, if I go through the ancient antics, it's you, unknown figures, you I adore; I've hidden you all this time in the hope that somehow you'd disappear, or better still emerge, as indeed you must, if the story's to go on gathering richness and rotundity, destiny and tragedy, as stories should; if I open my arms, it's you I embrace, you I draw to me."

"I sit," she said. The moon came in upon her knees. "The moon comes in upon my knees," she said. She felt a peace come upon her again, and in that, the characters, the fantastical city, all the pieces of story floated, suspended in liquid calm, resolution: all were without desire. She needn't make them move again, never pluck them from the bath and stuff them with motives—power, vengeance, guilt, lust—never string them together with their desires. They rested safely in their motionless world, unwritten, free.

I am the narrator, said her head. I am the narrator, it said again. She had used the phrase the night before, to draw her listeners in, to treat them to her godlike presence. Now, the phrase pronounced itself, less her voice, but some other being coming toward her: I am the narrator. I can tell you certain things about your daughter, about last night (and all the others before it). I can resurrect moments for you. These moments will become you, and her, and the night, and the more you listen—the more you remember—the more you forget: you are overcome by the story. I am the narrator, a constant storm of attention.

The voice went on and on. Where was her quietude? "I sit," she said again. "The moon lays prone across my lap."

Now the characters moved again, the imaginary world opened around her, Orpheus and Eurydice wandering the dead valley, the city mumbling in its fog, Pim and Fin suffering and changing, and the little Pear and the Ogre trapped together, Orpheus chained to a tree, Eurydice clinging to the wall of ice, chained and chased, and the spider working away in the eye of god. I am the narrator, went the voice, I can put the the pieces together, finish the story. Then we'll know.

Virginia rushed to her study. She took down each of her books, her books, the first editions, the crisp, unopened tomes, the publisher's hardcover best with dust jackets vibrating, yelling with color, arranged like an altar above her desk.

She tossed tissues and notebook paper into the waste bin and stuffed the novels in after. She struck four matches at once, tasted the white sulfur blaze slip up through the air to her tongue, almost dropped the fire in. Instead she blew it out with one puff, despised the thin riffles of smoke.

In her mind, the heavy grey and white flakes of her burning books would fall and float through the room, words becoming air, carbon. From the conflagration, a ghost would appear, her ghost, her voice released with the thousand tiny explosions of fire-eaten pulp, her form from the tomb of books, visible, audible. Virginia shut her stinging eyes, waiting for something to well up before her or within her, and she sat waiting, perfectly still, as the lack of fire exhausted her, the slow turmoil of ashen papers not happening, not happening, leaving only this room, cold floor and furniture.

In the morning, there was one less bunny.

Virginia chose what she felt was the stupidest among them. She would not yet devour the intelligent, though the old urges felt the same regardless. She knew, she knew she might eat them all if they stayed for very long. Uncooked, delicious, struggling just a bit: there had been no chase, no cleverness, no disguises. She had opened the door, observed the slow rising and falling, pulsing forms, could see their softness, could smell the days of worry still in their fur. Ah, the smell. When she pulled back the blanket, it was like opening an oven door, the trapped aromas of the body, its outsides and its insides, wafted up sharply and then hovered, heady and complex. The conjunction of this sweet waiting meal and the delight of observing one's own child sleeping just the same way, with the same rich smells: this did not escape her. It drove her on. We say to our children, "I could eat you up!" Virginia the Wolf ate up the bunny child, adoringly, thinking of her very own daughter.

Waking, the bunny must have felt Virginia's grip, perhaps saw her eye, her teeth, her ears, her nose, but the terror was quick and confused. What a perfect way to die: not oblivious but not in prolonged dread—secure in the half-self of waking, then crushed by perfect jaws, crushed by the infinite.

She left no evidence. She had the spare bed removed and the others shifted to hide the gap. But it would not have mattered. What would one expect from a wolf, and who would stop her?

To eat a few lost bunnies seemed, all things considered, harmless. The feeling it gave her was irresistible, and she immediately craved another, as if they all belonged together, as if she would be doing them a favor.

The next night, she stammered through dinner. She broke into sweats. She couldn't look anyone in the eyes. She tried to tell a story, to distract the children from their missing sibling, but found her mind dry, found her mouth stuttering, "um...", "and then," and at last she gave up. Her mouth would not cooperate. "BODt— BA—...Bed-ti-muh," she told the bunnies.

She waited as long as she could. Strolling down the midnight stairs, her head lightening, lifting, at peace. For no one, she acted surprised by the smells coming from the guest room. She crept to the door, opened it carefully, and just peeked in. Well, well.

Yasha saw the wrapped laundry in the Wash House. She was told her brother was sent to be fitted with a casket, a wagon, and a horse, to pull him in a funerary procession. The arrival of a dead body had initiated a complex sequence of rituals and preparations, according to the wolf tradition. That was the story.

"Don't drink the water!" they called to her as she walked off along the water. She stayed the night by the shack, saw the boatman in the morning, and ran. Eventually, she found the Stable House. Already she did not expect her mother to be there, for why would she have stayed here? She only hoped to find out where she had been sent, to know that she was alive, or to see evidence of her brother's mutilation.

The Stable House itself was a relatively simple affair, and the dogs were all in the same sturdy work clothes, all mutts. Yasha suspected they were all male, but it was difficult for her to tell. One of the dogs pointed her in through a red pine door. Unlike the Wash House, this was a place built only for working dogs, for mud and horses. Yasha stood on the raw wood floor in what was clearly the dining hall and office, containing both a long bare table and a cluttered desk. Three dogs, inconvenienced by her arrival, examined her from across the room. Two sidled off while the third strolled to the desk and sat down.

"Come," he commanded without looking away from his ledger.

"Good morning,... sir," Yasha tipped her head and stood a respectful distance from the dog.

He grunted and glanced at her from the corner of his eye, remaining focused on his ledger, moving a pencil quickly, as if sketching.

"I'm looking for my br—er, for my mother. I believe she came here yesterday."

"She did."

"She isn't still here?"

"Isn't."

"Would you be so kind as—."

"Rabbit or hare?" He turned his chair toward her.

"Rabbit, sir."

The dog studied her. "You are a young rabbit?"

She nodded.

"Variety?"

She didn't understand the question. "Yes, sir?"

The dog dislodged something from his teeth and chewed it. "Breed?"

"No, sir!"

He licked his nose and shook his head. "From what village?"

As far as Yasha knew, her village had no name. "I don't know sir. East of here, many days walk. Rabbit village."

"Your mother?" He meant, is that what you want? She understood that much.

"Yes, sir, do you know where—?"

"Left yesterday. They'd taken the body. We were all done. Have to say, I put a shitty horse on it. So, could take a while. To the Tailor House." He chewed something at the back of his jaw. "G'Do up a suit. Can't bury naked, you know?" He reached behind him and drew a small glass jar from a shelf. "Follow the river. But not now. You stay the night in the barn loft. Catch up in the morning." He handed the jar to Yasha. "Don't open less you get really thirsty, and don't drink the river."

Yasha backed away, "I should—."

"It's all set up. Where your mother stayed. Go on." He turned back to his desk.

"I don't want to trouble you... I'll just-."

"Hey!" He barked, as though he was furious, but the emotion left him immediately. He might have smiled. "You stay in the loft. Don't you be out at night... rabbit."

Yasha left as quick as she could. Out on the porch, Yasha realized she was clutching the jar of water like it was a baby.

Pim was waiting for her by the barn door.

"I thought I should help you," he said. He was limiting himself to simple statements. He was hiding here, away from the house, on a past trajectory, perhaps never to return.

Yasha and Pim laid next to each other on the mattress in the loft. The smell of horses was overwhelming, but they adjusted. Propped up on his elbows, Pim said, "I've never been out here. They always brought the horses to the riding ring for us. It's weird." He looked over the low rail at the horses in their stalls. "They just stand there, don't they?"

"I suppose you eat the horses, too," Yasha said, rolling over.

"Of course not." He sat up cross-legged by his pillow. "We eat chicken, or sheep, or ducks, or eggs, or sometimes lambs, and pigeons, and quail, and geese, and squirrels, and little cats, of course, and sometimes other, smaller birds, and pigs, and cows, and things like that. And sometimes mice or opossums, or raccoons, or turtles, or frogs—in soup. But we'd never eat a horse. And I swear, we've never eaten rabbit before. I think it's all just a misunderstanding. I'm really probably wrong, and he's out here, just fine, you know, with your mom." He expected her to say something reasonable, but she appeared to be pouting. "It's just, I know my mother can be pretty, well, scary. It's not her fault." He gulped back tears and blew his nose into his sleeve. "It's dusty up here."

Yasha saw his emotion, but misunderstood. "Why don't you leave? She's mean to you."

"This is my home. All my things," he said easily. Then, "She needs me. I know it doesn't seem like it. But I think she will." He went on uncertainly, "Last night," he stopped, unable to say more, not entirely sure what words he could use.

Yasha turned to look at him. "Her story?"

"What?"

"She read it, her novel?" Yasha insisted.

"Yeah, I guess." Pim was lost.

"What's it about?"

"I don't know. We were on the roof, the roof of the theater, we were there instead."

"Who?"

"Me and my sister."

"You have a sister?"

"She left me there, and she..." He pushed himself through the words.

Yasha waited.

The young wolf let the word come out, letting the sound happen, avoiding the sense: "Jumped."

Yasha sat up, folding her legs.

Pim watched the horses.

"Off the roof? Why? Is she okay?"

It took Pim a while. "She's not okay. It was my fault," Pim said. "I let her." Pim was frozen in time.

"What do you mean?"

Pim was only talking now, saying, not thinking, "I should have stopped her. I mean, a normal person would do anything, anything to stop someone, to stop her. I was right there. It should have been easy."

"What were you doing there?"

"She brought me. Mom was inside, reading. Then she came out, and, she she jumped right in front..." There, his mouth locked up.

Yasha tried to imagine Pim's sister. "What was her name?"

Through his teeth, he said, "Jin."

"Pim," Yasha could already see the cracks in his world, "she sounds terrible. She sounds like a monster."

He was confused.

"Only a monster would do that. Your sister is evil, like your mother. You all deserve each other."

Yasha turned away and stretched out under the blankets.

Pim stayed sitting, dejected, tried to think of things to say as bits of his world tumbled around in his mind.

Virginia had lost track of time, but she could count the days back by the number of bunnies she had eaten. Ask her if it was morning or evening, lunch hour or tea time, and she would have to admit, she was lost. Better, though, time and space were a loom of smells and digestion, her body was the weaver and her limbs and teeth the gears of the world, and better still, when she relaxed, her thoughts swam freely, lightly, gently over the world, just so happy, so happy to be here.

She had eaten enough of the bunnies that, dumb as they were, they would soon begin to take notice, and the rest would have to be done with soon. That, or she would have to quit. Wait and see. She did not expect the mother rabbit to return. How unutterably disgusting life is, she said. We have been taking into our mouths the bodies of dead birds. It is with these greasy crumbs, slobbered over napkins, and little corpses that we have to build. But how delicious, she told herself. Ah, but we could be free of it, she told herself. After, she said to herself. We must be patient, here in the dark, she thought to herself, assuming the dark was metaphorical. She felt her head chiming new voices deep within. New stories, she expected.

She had a leaf removed from the table, and a chair for each missing bunny, so that the table still appeared full. At dinner, she did not eat, but worked with some difficulty to tell a story while the bunnies ate. She wanted them to feel comfortable. She found it difficult to enunciate. Non-phonetic words were difficult to pronounce. The narrative, clear as it was in her head, would not stay put as she struggled to follow it with words.

In the afternoon, she spied the bear-shaped-thing. She stood over him and watched as he ached across the floor, inches at a time. "More power to you, my friend!" she said. "Charge on, oh life!"

She had been so desperate to finish, to draft Jinny home, to see in her world and her characters the missing story. Or secrets. Love or hate, something to pity or despise, it didn't matter, something to explain, something to fix. She was hungry again. She felt so full. She filled her chair, had trouble walking, she was so full. But she was hungry. She thumbed her manuscript, found the last-written line. She clung to it a moment, then let go. The stack of pages fluttered into a clump and slid in several directions across the floor.

She kicked over the waste basket, sending her novels tumbling: a footbridge of stones leading to the unwritten. Now tonight, she said, my body rises tier upon tier like some cool temple whose floor is strewn with carpets and murmurs, rises and the altars stand smoking; but up above, here in my serene head, come only fine gusts of melody, waves of incense, while the lost dove wails, and the banners tremble above tombs, and the dark airs of midnight shake trees outside the open windows. When I look down from this transcendency, how beautiful are even the crumbled relics! What shapely spirals the peelings of pears make—how thin, and mottled like some sea-bird's egg. Even the books strewn down appear lucid, logical, exact; and the horns of the sheep we have left are glazed, yellow plated, hard. I could worship my hand even, with its fan of bones laced by blue mysterious veins and its astonishing look of aptness, suppleness and ability to curl softly or suddenly crush—its infinite sensibility. Immeasurably receptive, holding everything, trembling with fullness, yet clear, contained—so my being seems, now that desire urges it no more out and away; now that curiosity no longer dyes it a thousand colours. It lies deep, tideless, immune, now dead, like the child clutching at books—word for the moon, notes of features; how people looked, turned, dropped their cigarette ends. A, pits of air through bodies, B, book powder, C, the caul of sleep, D, ways of naming death. But now let the door open, the glass door that is for ever turning on its hinges. The shock of the falling wave which has sounded all my life, which woke me so that I saw the world in its last throes, no longer makes quiver what I hold.

In the morning, there was one less bunny.

It became more difficult for Virginia to be who she was and not that other wolf. The difference was simple: the more she ate and thought about eating the bunnies, the more she was aware of her own infinite expanse—how else would she have survived one beheading or burning after another? That immensity was alluring, though she knew that if she lingered too close to it she would be lost, consumed by her own eternal presence: to be everywhere was to be nowhere, and to become the wolf of old would be just another version of the same losses.

So she toyed with that old self and felt the artistry of teasing out her infinite being as she consumed more of the children in their little children's beds. Fortunately for the bear, she did not return to her study. She preferred the window, where she sat very still, escaped into the quiet fantasy at the end of the world, the measureless city in the valley of the mountain of death. The wind careened against the rock and ice like a hundred hammers. Orpheus had to lash Eurydice to his back tightly as they descended. He took time to check every foothold, every crag for solidity, and once prepared to move, waited to feel the wind die away. Numbness burned in his fingers and toes and gripped his face like a mask of stone. They had spent lifetimes in the ice, in the bowels of the universe, but Orpheus felt no joy at the open air, no pleasure in the stale breath of the underworld.

Orpheus woke in a cave of clay deep in the bowels of the cliff city. Voices seeped through the walls, recalling to mind, but without fear, the faces hovering in the ice, and as his eyes adjusted to the fragrant brown of the room, Orpheus's memory returned, in slow beats, without flood or shock, but there it was, on Orpheus's lips, Eurydice's name, then Eurydice's cry, Eurydice's weight, Eurydice's warm blood caked against his back and in his hair, the tangled spine, acrid notches of the body, collided jaws, locking steps, tendons, little fibers rushed up and down the mud walls, slick with the morning, cold with the night.

He pulled himself up and surveyed the room. Not a prison. He followed an open passage to another, similar room, and so on until he had the sensation of moving again through the ice caves, a small clay and stone version of the same haunted halls. He had to duck through the passages, twist to the side to fit through. He had forgotten that he was nearly a god.

Orpheus found an exit. The light of day flared against him, into him and, staring directly into the new morning, Orpheus felt the shades of death burn away in the white hot sun. He faced the slate mirror of the sea, the sky's double, climbing with fractal radiance.

Orpheus woke in the underworld on a straw cot in the damp shade of a mud wall. Climbing up and up and up again, he saw light, and finally, hands against his brow, he gazed out at the ropes of clouds cast across the shale sea, the lacing of blue and violet ether: he was at the line between worlds. Beyond one horizon was the world of monsters, and in the depths, beyond the dark horizon of clay and coal, the wall between existence and non-existence, each host of chaos held at bay by Apollo and Poseidon, by heroes, by the force of water, by winds and words. He could live once more, he could leave, but where was Eurydice?

Orpheus woke alone on the vast plain. He tried to sing, but his voice had left him. When he approached the river to drink, the water's teeth snapped at his flesh. Orpheus woke.

The young bear reached his paws into Virginia's study. His eyes lit up at the sight of the loving books splayed across the floor, and he spent the night crawling to them, absorbing them into his furry arms. When he discovered among them the loose sheets of manuscript, hundreds of sheets, covered with the insect prints of an old, inky typewriter, he felt the future rustling out before him in the lines, laughing to himself about such fortune, such happiness.

Yasha and Pim snacked as they walked in the sun. The path loosely followed the river, ducking out into fields, around trees. Pim was only trying to think of what would rescue Jinny in the rabbit's opinion.

"Rabbit?" he said.

"What?"

"Jinny was always very sweet to me."

"Really?"

Not really, but, close enough, Pim thought. "Yes. And Mother's new stories: they're all from Jinny's stories. She's always on edge because of it. She's trying to sort things out."

Yasha could see what he was doing and smiled, feeling mature. "My name is Yasha," she said.

"Yasha." Pim smiled. "I thought you might have a name."

"Your sister and my brother," she said.

"Oh, yeah." Pim hadn't considered the parallel. "But you have—." He tried to think this through. Was the death of a rabbit the same as Jinny's death? "Did you love him?" He looked for her eyes.

Yasha didn't expect the question, or the answer, "No."

"Oh." Pim smiled. "Jinny said she loved my work."

"You miss her."

Yasha saw a building in the distance, the Tailor's House.

"Is that water?"

Yasha held up the jar. "Yes. You thirsty?"

"Yes." Pim's head was blazing. "Very."

"Have it all. I don't really trust those dogs. I'll drink from the damn river."

Pim poured all the water from the jar into his mouth, down his throat, into his belly and blood.

The Tailor's House was tiny. Inside was room for the Tailor himself, his few tables, and a fireplace. Bolts of cloth and other materials were all balanced in the rafters, and there was no chair but for the Tailor's own stool. He seemed eager enough to answer Yasha's questions. His tongue hung out from between his lips at all times, even as he spoke, slipping from one side to the other, and as he continued work, snipping, paring, mating pieces, he would bite down harder and harder in concentration. Yasha watched him for a few moments, waiting for him to greet her, but he went from one arabesque task to another.

Yasha broke in. "Good afternoon?"

"See, see, see," the Tailor remarked, cutting a dramatic curve.

"Pardon me, but did you just finish a suit for a... a dead rabbit?"

"Dead rabbit, dead rabbit. How dead?"

"Excuse me?"

"How dead?"

"Well, all the way dead!"

"How dead? Inside? Outside? Pieces? Smashed? Crushed? Broken? Drowned? Hanged? Sick? Still-born? Cancer? Heart attack? Bullet wound? Knife wound? Bad blood? Loss of head? Poisoned? Axed? Eaten? Snake bite? Infection? Tongue sores? Spots? Bloody lung? Broken back? Loss of hope? Starvation?—"

"Those two! The last two!" Yasha was relieved to have stopped him.

"Just those two?"

"Yes, I think so."

"Nothing else?"

"To my knowledge, nothing else. Did you see him?"

"Does it matter if I saw him?"

Yasha wasn't sure. "Well, you had to measure him, didn't you?"

"A rabbit is a rabbit, a dead rabbit all the more." He gestured proudly at his table, "Do you see measuring tape?"

She didn't. "But you made him a suit?"

"I made a suit for a rabbit, yes."

"And my mother, she came and picked it up?"

"Who is your mother?"

"Did Mrs Rabbit come and pick it up?" Yasha had raised her voice. He didn't seem to mind.

"Ah. Yes. Of course she did." He held up a black fabric with a variety of holes and curves, like a tangled up musical staff, arpeggios of snipped wool. "He certainly didn't pick it up for himself," he let the material down into a fibrous pile and swept up a needle, "did he?"

"Of course not."

"Not if he was dead."

"Of course."

"As you say he was."

"Yes."

"Lost his hope."

"Yes."

"Starved."

"Yes!"

"All the way?"

Yasha opened the door to leave.

"Wait!"

She jumped in alarm.

He worked quietly with a needle

"Really, unless you can tell me where my mother is..." she began.

"Try this on," said the Tailor.

It was a black vest, buttons made of chalcedony; jade green stitching made circles and stars on the shoulders and pockets. Yasha took it. "It's beautiful," she said, entirely distracted. She was genuinely amazed.

"Put it on."

It fit her well. "It's very comfortable," she said.

"It's yours."

The tailor told her where to go next: the Shearing House, where the body and the coffin would be cleaned and stuffed with wool. Mother had made a great arc, following the river away from the main house, then along a bend back toward it. Finally, at the Shearing House, the river went its own way and a wide gravel road interceded and led back to the house, its stacked rooflines just visible.

Late in the day, Pim and Yasha saw Mother in the middle distance, sitting on a wooden box in the back of a wagon, pulled by a raggedy horse. The Shearing House was at the top of a rise from which she must have just descended. She was sitting tall, looking about. The air was resplendent, and she was aglow. Yasha called to her, and she waved back merrily. They caught up, huffing and puffing, and Yasha climbed into the hobbling wagon.

Mother Rabbit hugged her tightly. "How did you get all the way out here?" she beamed.

"We were looking for you," Yasha said, her desperation bursting.

"Of course. I'm sorry. You didn't need to worry about me." Mrs Rabbit tidied Yasha's fur. "Didn't Mrs Wolf tell you where I was?" She looked into her eyes, brushed her new vest. "Isn't this nice!"

"Mother, is he...?" She pointed into the box.

"Yes, he's all ready for a good burial, dear. I can't tell you how it relieves a Mother's heart. Strange, I suppose."

"But I mean, he's really in there?"

"Oh, darling. Yes. When something dies, it stays dead. I hope you didn't think he was going to get better. You didn't did you?"

"Mother, are you sure he's in there?"

"What's wrong, dear? What's gotten you so..."

"Have you actually seen his body?" She had worked up a panic. Pim kept his distance from the two of them, walking along at the front of the wagon, hand on the mule's back. He remembered the taste of the soup. And what if the box was empty, as he suspected?

Mother was appalled. "After everything," she began.

"We have to open the box, Mother. We have to know for sure that he wasn't—that he— we have to make sure he's there! Did you see him?"

"What has gotten in to you?"

Despite her mother's protests, Yasha was prying at the box with her paws. It was a simple pine box with pegged corners. She got her fingers squeezed under the lid then finally bent it up far enough to see inside.

Orpheus, stranded at the end of the world, awaited the work of its hollow-eyed priests to deliver him Eurydice, his lost love. He was confused and then angry when a cloaked demon brought him a book, covered with flesh, closed around nothing more than a kind of vade mecum. He pushed it away. But the demon priest explained, the book was his love, all that could be saved of her mind was here preserved, here written in the language of the fates. Indeed, when he opened it, it would speak to him, guide him, lead him on to her whom he seeks, for it is her living, waiting being that will summon him through the book. Tearfully, he demanded to know what was done with her body, but the creature went on, unmoved. You will know this is true when you open it for the first time, in the land of the living, and you will be filled with the music of her voice, the taste of her lips will be upon your mouth and travel in your breath to your loins, and you will know at once that you hold her in your hands, at last, that you gaze upon her entirety, and that she is yours.

Now Orpheus grasped eagerly for the book, and the cloaked figure slipped it back into the folds of his sleeve. He gave Orpheus this warning: All I have said is true, and all will come to pass as I have described, if you only forbear to open the book until you have stepped both feet into the light of the living world, for to open her soul here, at the end of all things, on the dry land of graves and in the empty air of ghosts, would cause her instead to be lost forever, and her doomed soul would be stitched with agony into these mute walls and forever curtained from your immortal eyes.

Orpheus wandered for days, weeks, and years, never finding the boundary between the dead and living.

The next day, Virginia had trouble walking, she was so large now: great rabbit-shaped bulges protruded from her sack-like belly. She didn't leave her rooms until the dinner bell chimed. It took her some effort to negotiate the stairs. Her legs and arms felt shortened, and her balance was thrown off by the bodies sloshing in her gut. She wasn't hungry, but she enjoyed going to table. She would tell a story. She would tell the ending, describe the city in its fullness, draw in the ghosts and the heroes, describe the eternal heart of the monster, reveal the eye of god.

She stopped in the archway to the dining hall. At the table already were Pim, the mother, and the young rabbit, and the few remaining bunnies. The table was set accordingly. This might be a little awkward, she thought, but she kept cool, maneuvering as if with elegance to her chair and situating her bottom on the seat. Her belly grumbled a bit. She smoothed it out and covered what she could with her napkin.

"GUD EAVET—" She halted, trying to bring her clumsy tongue into check, half belching the words, acid in her throat. "GO-OD," she placed her palm on the table, focus, "EE...V..EE...UNG!"

Close enough. She smiled broadly and sipped her water. Where had the words gone?

Virginia waved her hand at the table and the guests to indicate, Please Begin. As she lifted her fork, she tried to steal little glances at the rabbits, to ascertain their level of suspicion. Would a mother rabbit have a good accounting of her bunnies? They make so many. A few missing were hardly worth noticing. She held her fork but ate nothing. She picked up her knife and cut a few pieces of whatever-the-loaf-was.

Yasha was hungry. She ate all the vegetables on her plate, then, as if everything was just fine, she said to Virginia, "Won't you tell us a story?"

Virginia was flattered and put down her fork and knife, smiling wide. Oh, to tell stories forever, and never end them or leave them behind. She took another sip of her water, sloshed it around her mouth.

Every one listened intently.

Virginia settled back in her chair, stretched her neck, licked her lips.

But when the wolf opened her mouth to speak, to say, "Once," what came out was a chorus of sorrowful voices, wailing for release, trapped in her terrible belly. She slammed her mouth shut with her hands, paws, but the wailing filled her face like a balloon. Horrified, she leapt up, fell backwards with her chair, away from the gaze of those at the table. She leveraged herself up again, nearly gagging, clenching her jaws. Pim's eyes disturbed her most, he was looking at her, straight at her, her body like this, full of death, stained with the old hunger, and she saw how he was resolved against her, and probably jealous.

Inside her, the alphabet had kept the bunnies alive, taught them to speak and breathe through the gore of digestion, taught them to withdraw inside themselves with her, to hear her voice collected by their bodies as one, to think together and be companions in the dark. They exulted in Virginia's depths with horror and glee: now we can speak! —The thought lifted their screams, speak! That part of the brother that had passed into Virginia worked to unravel her words, to yell even in her mind, because the imaginary friend had seen Jinny, had watched her through Virginia's eyes, and the alphabet had a scream built into it, let it loose inside Virginia. When Virginia felt it inside her, she thought, "Jinny? Jinny, is that you?" and she let go of herself, let her mouth wag open, reached out her arms and shut her eyes.

Yasha didn't spare a moment. She grabbed a carving knife from the table and, finding Virginia's neck, swelling with voices, caught her flesh with the point and drew the blade all the way down her body. Virginia opened like a purse, and out poured all the little bunnies, gasping and gagging, cruelly reborn. Virginia no longer looked like herself. Her form was melting away into puddles and clots of wolfish stew.

Pim was crying out, too, as if trapped, but soon regained his senses. "Buckets! We need buckets!" He leapt onto the table. "Bowls! Use the bowls!" He scrambled along grabbing soup bowls and serving bowls. Then louder, called to the staff, "BUCKETS!" Pim leapt into the muck and swept and scooped up parts of Virginia with his hands. Yasha and Mother gathered up the bunnies.

Two of the staff appeared with buckets but stopped in the doorway. They observed Pim on the table, watched him scrambling to fuss on the floor, scraping particles of Virginia into his palm and shaking them into a bowl. They observed the bunnies huddled in the corner. They saw Yasha who, at the moment, was trying to wipe invisible wolves from her pants. She itched.

The staff dropped their buckets and left, ran through the corridors, echoing their barking against the plaster and stone, howling in the yard with their fingers dug into the grass like claws.

Soon, much of Virginia was contained and sitting on the table, churning a bit, but quiet. Mother and Yasha were in a corner of the room, away from the fray. Mother had pulled down a tapestry and constructed a cove for the children. But the more she inspected them all, the more she wept, for their injuries were not injuries. All the blood was Virginia's. She wept for joy.

Altogether, the bunnies said, "Mama!" and embraced her.

Yasha ran to the window to observe the departure of the servants, saw them fight over the sheep, the victors dragging the braying wool into the trees. The rest galloped after.

In the night, Virginia woke and crawled from the buckets, from the table. She dragged herself to her study and found a needle and sturdy thread. Beginning below her navel, she sewed careful, tidy stitches up across her belly. The needle hurt, it hurt to pull the thread through, but once a stitch was made, pulling it taut was somehow reassuring, a more pleasant pain. Before she finished, she looked for ballast. She couldn't get around the room too easily. Her legs wobbled and she lost her balance. She coughed furiously when things inside her chest shifted. She found a glass paperweight and slipped it into her ribcage. Little else was in reach.

"I can help." It was Pim, in the doorway. "I know just the thing."

Pim gathered the books scattered on the floor. He stacked them in his arms. He went to the shelf, ran his fingers along the notebooks and novels until he came to what he wanted, Jinny's books. He pulled them down in one handful and added them to the stack. One at a time, he slipped the novels and the notes into his mother's chest cavity. He said nothing.

After the last notebook, he took the needle from Virginia's fingers, and he finished the stitching, right up to her neck, where the knife had gone in. He did a very nice job.

"Let's go," he said.

She was heavier than ever now, and leaned almost all of her weight on his back. They took the footpath from the garden, through the bamboo and sage, and staggered out toward the water. Once they heard the river in the distance, it was all they heard.

In the soft mud, Virginia said, "Will you hate me forever?"

Pim didn't want to respond. He said only, "I don't."

She still hung on his shoulders. "How did she do it?" Virginia wanted an answer, but Pim just stared through the water. "I really want to know," she said. "What did you... What did she tell you?"

"She said she loved us."

Virginia could hardly breathe. "I loved her, too." Her face had lost everything.

"It was just... She had to."

"Unvanquished," she said, "Unyielding, what a good life she might have had." She kissed Pim on the head. "Wouldn't she?"

Virginia took careful strides into the water. He watched her. He wanted her to look back. He thought he might receive her last look, that it would be pure, loving. He thought it would elate him and break his heart, too, that he would want to stop her if she looked, but he wouldn't stop her, he would stand there, watching, but he would know that she had thought of him with the water up to her chin, and turned. Somehow it had all been for them, somehow she could free them at this moment. She didn't turn.

I need a howl, she thought, a cry, but still, how much better is silence, so that I hear the watery voice, summoning as I descend.

Mr Fin, on the invisible Swan, floated into the empty harbor.

Sam saw the bound look on his face, and said, "Mind what you are about. Don't go burying yourself alive, or putting yourself where you'll be like a bottle put to cool in a well. It's no affair or business of yours to become the explorer of this, which must be worse than a dungeon."

No sooner had the words appeared between them but Mr Fin had espied in the depths the chasmic opening in the sound.

"Guide me," he said to the sea, "for I have no rope," and down into the water he went.

The water within several meters of The Swan was warm and lit with reflections, but very soon Mr Fin passed through a wall of aching cold, and all things were shades of darkness below, collisions of light above. He found the opening, but already his breath was gone. Rattling horns of air flew up from his nose, then no more, and he waited to see what would happen next.

I felt my consciousness swallowed by the water, by the suffocating pressure, and I was gone. First my feet and hands were gone, then my elbows and knees. Inch by inch, my larger muscles tightened and vanished, then my hipbones. The disappearance reached my ribs and my chest, then finished off my organs. I was nearly weightless, a mere bobbing head on a bone-hook. In layers, though, my head was leaving me, pieces of skull, from the occipital bowl along old fracture lines, and my cheeks and chin softly melted away so that to speak or to struggle lost meaning. The rest of my skull lifted toward the surface as tiny marbles of warmth. My nose wasn't there. All that was left were my eyes in the water, and they didn't seem to mind the cold, but things were getting blurry, and the salt was uncomfortable. One eye closed, though no lid was left to cover it. The other remained, and with that one, I beheld.

A figure came toward me from the chasm. I knew at once it was Hart Crane, the rabbit, though he was not himself. He wore a more human figure, or mostly so. His clean brown fur moved magically in the water, and his ears waved and flapped as he pushed himself lightly through the depths. When he was very close, I saw that where his eye had been bruised before, now the eyeball was gone entirely.

Hart reached out toward my seeing eye, enclosed me in his hand, and fed me into his own empty socket. Now we were as one, and by this symbiosis, I regained my other senses and felt the elasticity of his youth—though none of it was mine, I felt it. Our two separate eyes now turned us toward the hollow eye of the cave, and our body brought us into it, as if a mere thought were enough to command the world. We traveled some distance, straight down, it seemed, absorbing sharp pearls of oxygen through tender vents in our furry body. With difficulty, we commanded our eyes in sync, and the dim world seemed whole enough. I could see other tunnels leading off in all directions from the one we followed until, abruptly, we entered a large chamber, lit by fruit and jellies and nearly empty, with slick silver cast walls of wood. The water here, contrary to expectations, was thin and light, an even mix of water and air. Our feet settled on the floor. In one corner of the room was a simple chair and a small table. Around us, some poor creature had burst into fleshy petals and hovered in its own red ether. Beside the table and chair, cut into the floor, was a sunken area, indeed, the shape and size of a grave. That was the room.

We approached. My eye looked away, on instinct, but Hart looked on and moved us to the lip of the open tomb.

There was no body. I expected to feel relieved. Instead, we mourned together the absence of a body. Where has he gone? Who has taken him from us?

Our body sat and let our fingers find the edge of the grave. Now Hart recoiled as I pressed on, pressed us on toward the hollow space. I remembered as a boy, a friend would hold my arms up behind me as I lay face down on the floor, and then, once my shoulders had been stretched, my arms were lowered, down, down, and it felt like my arms were passing through the floor. Just so, to carry oneself into a grave has that feeling of impossibility, of moving into a non-space, and when I touched the grave's bed with my toe, I felt a thrill that made me giggle just a little, and so I wanted more.

I stretched flat in the open tomb. I felt stories surround me, and these, too, made me smile. Hart, though, removed my eye from his skull, climbed from the grave, and cast me across the watery room. I floated, spinning through the cloud of that other creature for a few moments, observing in pink flashes as Hart took his seat at the table, and, I could see, took up his pencil and pages and wrote everything down in the book, in David's book, and I had to stay there, floating in the blood, spinning slower and slower, and watch him as he continued the work, perhaps with these last moments between us, what I'd done, and he would not look up at me again, because I could see that he would be writing here forever, narrating his life to its conclusion, making sense of that moment when he disappeared.

That was when I recognized the room: its wooden walls gave it away. I saw that the table was not placed on the floor but growing out of it, and the tunnel by which we'd entered was a hollow root, an arm of the tree-bird. I could leave him here, and the book, and they would be together.

Chapter Nine

Who is not beautiful when sleeping? What more pure sleep is there than that of the unborn child? And what more perfect an image is there of the unborn than the film-like pre-dawn envelope of the fish-roe, tender and cold? One hundred lonely wombs still lived, piled soft little wombs like jelly in the grass, sealed up so cruelly in the burnt outer shell of their sisters' eggs, forming a crisp and congealed surface on the mound in the yard.

Fish children are laid out to hatch in the back yard, as a custom. These, we could say, were lucky in that a tree protected them from much harm, though the tree itself eventually went to flame. It is still the habit in some families for the young to eat their way out of the pile—the softened sacs and unfulfilled siblings provided exceptional nutriment. Such may not have been the case with this particular family, but in the absence of parents and physician to wash and care for them during the hatching process, nature offered its expertise.

The first 30 or so to wiggle from the soft interior through the morbid crust were the strongest, and they ate ravenously. Fish children are generally quick-witted. Much of mathematics, for instance, is born into them, along with the rules to many simple games involving cards, stones, tiles, or beads. Instinct gave the survivors, approximately 12 of them after a day had passed, something to busy themselves with about the yard, staring up or staring down, sorting pebbles into rows, sticks into categories: activities that, in the absence of nurturance, distraction, and the sobering patter of adulthood, seemed of divine proportion; for them, the universe was the yard, the materials of the universe were the charred tree, charred house, swing set, grass, tender worms, stringy flies, shovels, trowels, rakes for shaping the air, sorting the garden, murder, eggs to eat. Indeed, everything seemed edible at first. Whatever proved inedible was countable, held pattern, the qualities of a coded landscape, one pattern wedded to another: branches, fence-posts, rocks. Everything touchable was a piece in a game, for them serious and sublime, full of character and premonition: a radiant young world.

All the bunnies said to mother, "Why can't we stay here? Everything is so beautiful and grand. No matter what happened, it feels like home," all with one voice. The bears thought so too.

Pim fell in love with his house, and he went all the places that had been closed to him, looked in all the cupboards. He slept in Jinny's room, looked at her books and her school papers and her clothes. He would not leave the room for days, but slept there waiting to become half himself, half her.

The bears were content to stay there with him. Middle already owned the place.

But Mother said, "We need to get home now. It's been too long."

Eldest Brother was gone, Mother thought, believing him merely eaten, and so there was nothing left to do for him, but for the bunnies, he had been transmuted into the voice that held them together, the alphabet that whispered between their ears. They were not disturbed. They were pleased with the gift.

Mother said, "We need to get home now. It's been too long."

Yasha could not tell what her mother's words meant, where, now, after all this, where home would be, with the way she had been. They would go somewhere else, she imagined, or rebuild from the desolation their home, from the remnants of other places, the fractured homes coughed and shat by the zeppelins.

She said to Youngest Bear, "I forgive you," though she had no reason, only the peace of never seeing him again.

He said slowly, "I could tell you more stories, someday."

"I won't be back," she said. "You'll have no reason to leave here."

"Maybe you will find Mr Crane." He thought for a few long moments. "Will you be safe? There are still the zeppelins."

"Yes," Yasha said, "I don't see any escape from the zeppelins."

"It would make a wonderful story, to go and find him—make a rescue," said Youngest.

Yasha wanted to disagree. This was what horrified her about bears, or about living. "I don't want to hear any more stories."

By the third day after hatching, only four salmon children remained. They had all grown to sufficient size so that none would dare to feed on another. Their equality in size and, evidently, in mind, made them sisters, and survival hardened their sisterly bonds as surely as those bonds were, the day before, the potential source of a safe and rich meal. They took the names that came to mind: One, Two, Three, and Four.

One of the sisters, named Two, had always obsessed herself with the back wall of the house, and it was while tinkering with its forms that she first pressed through the limits of the known world and out of the fog of familiar aromas—she slipped into the second world: the house. The others followed.

The house was typical, but for them it was majestic. They studied the shaped glass, symmetrical furnishings, trinkets, photographs (though these induced a vertigo difficult to endure). They tasted everything. Few things yielded until they eventually discovered the high drama of the kitchen.

Life had meaning again. Though much of the food had fouled somewhat, they marveled at the fruits, the myriad salted grains, the cupboards with boxes and bags. When Two first opened the refrigerator, she gasped and lost her voice for a moment. It was still cool, though there was no electricity, and the colors, containers, glass jars, foils, wraps, and vegetables were a divine shock—compared to a dandelion, a red pepper is a flower beyond comprehension.

All four fish were well grown after a few weeks in the house, eating, sleeping, exploring. Their appetites slowed. Their bodies were strong now, durable, and their hearts pumped more thoughtfully. Now, with time to inquire, they decided that the house held a plan for them, that there was work to be done, that they did not, despite all of its miracles, exist in a finished world.

At the center of the universe was the kitchen, they reasoned, and though empty of food now, it would surely generate more, the way the yard had done, though perhaps much more slowly, given the complexity of the house foods. Somehow the kitchen and the yard were related, but clearly the kitchen was the master of the yard. As for the other rooms of the house, which seemed to lack innate functions, they were more, to the salmon children, like game boards, surfaces and pieces that signified something else, variables—the functions and the rules of which needed discovery. Properly arranged, a harmony might be achieved. Would there be answers? The possibility occurred to them, but they hadn't managed to formulate questions. They surmised, therefore, that the first pursuit of life was the very generation of life's questions.

The four fish focused first on the quality of symmetry. In the room farthest from the kitchen (a bedroom) they laid out all of its items in a grid on the floor. Once arrayed, they rearranged the items by grouping those that expressed more or less symmetry, formal balance. The size of the objects dictated the sizes of the grid cells, and most intriguing to them was the seeming natural occurrence of blanks, that is, empty cells. The obvious two hypotheses: the scheme was in error, or the selection of objects was incomplete. The blanks were either a problem, suggesting that objects with peculiar symmetries existed somewhere to disturb their order, or a prediction—that certain objects existed somewhere to fill in what was lacking. They increased the number of ordering principles, color, straightness and curvature, movement, joints, relative softness and hardness; they worked to overwhelm the possibilities.

Along the way, they discovered objects that seemed so pure that they could not be said to belong so much in the grid as they might represent the various natures that, specified at the end of each row and top of each column, could describe the fundamental characteristics of each cell, the basic formulae—the perfectly straight line, the infinitely bendable line, the marble, the feather—these were more ideas than objects.

The persistence of missing objects thrilled them, and they began to see them in their minds' eyes, and to imagine ever larger grids, ever more encompassing but always incomplete, which explained the necessity of multiple rooms, indeed, suggested that each room might have its own particular elemental structure, its own unique principles. Sitting up at night, around the kitchen table, they discussed the grids as they had established them in each room (there were five), and described with their hands how they might see those grids lift into the air and freely rotate above the table, and they could see the blanks of each grid somehow lining up with the filled spaces of another so that, in the proper arrangement of the five grids, their hands collaborating as if partaking in a complex game of cat's cradle, a kind of super grid was formed, complete, ideal, playable, and they would say to each other the missing things they had imagined in private that day.

(We don't have words for what they would say to each other, at this time.)

During the day they expected the world to come into sharper focus, but it did not. They expected the logical correlation between objects, through the process of including all things, to settle itself into a hierarchy of forms, but it did not. During the night they hatched new plans, new rules, threw out the old, doubted everything.

Three floated the anxiety first. What if the world simply obeys our whims?

No one had a response.

Three's assertion was not readily thinkable, merely a collection of words, an obtuse metaphor.

The resulting anxiety did spark a few ingenious maneuvers. The first was to assume that the images on the walls that depicted the birthing yard (the back windows) were accurate representations at all times of the actual yard. Clearly, noted Four, we should emphasize the correlation of the first sphere of existence, as we see it, as it changes, with the second, the house, and through their balance, she said, through contrasts, and inversions, find the rhythms of all being that form the basis for the five domains, and therefore, the role of objects in relation to living. She was scraping bits of dried mold at the back of the refrigerator into a snack bowl. It had a kelpy aroma. It made her hungry, somewhat careless with her ideas.

One snorted because, she cried, of the problem of the other windows (the front and side): what did they portray? Were these other versions of the yard? The yard in different eras? Would you have us believe that these are other spheres of existence, or other foundations for existence? Take the wrong assumption, she remarked, and you find yourself at the ridiculous in no time.

Four tossed some mold into her mouth and slid the bowl onto the table as she sat. One and Three plucked up some scrapings and chewed.

Two was impassive, her head resting on the table. She was exhausted from moving furniture all day. Her voice drowsy, she said, but that's what they are. Of course that's what they are. But, she lifted her head carefully, as if balancing the thought—an egg or a bee on her shoulder—easily lost, easily disturbed, that's what they are, she said again, but that doesn't mean they are real.

In time, Little Bear wandered back up the river to where the ship lay in still-rusted wavering grasses, where its bulk and hollows had compressed, petrified until it was a solid stone, or so he thought, finding such a stone where he expected the tree-bird.

Little Bear found that the upper surface of the stone fit his back and neck and skull very finely, that there were smooth concaves and convexes where he needed them, and rough bits where, idly, he could scratch, as needed. It wasn't the stone that fit. It was his deflated form that fell neatly into any container. He remembered his youth as a house of ants, and now, having grown used to a certain pace and softness in his manner of living, the pain of those years, all the pains, seemed one small part of growing, and the desire for death that haunted him still seemed not so much what it had been, but instead was only a wish to sleep in the day or night and not wake to the unyielding world, but always be uncertain about the substance of his surroundings. What he wanted, at all times, in all of his days, was his mother's voice reciting the pages from her books, or he would accept the voice of Hart Crane, or the Wolves even, and so on, any voice but his own, the sweetest being those voices given over to the page, lost, unrehearsed and unvarying in their recitation of the familiar lines. These were more than enough.

Such remembered lines drifted now across stories he had not been told, but lived, which rose up from this moment beneath the sky, where he would be for the time being, and the rock, as he had been, he felt, waiting for Hart Crane to arrive. Mute images of himself, somehow in view in his memory, and Hart Crane, as they had wandered into the mountains. Sometimes Hart cast him over his back like a coat, or else the bear hobbled or crawled through the day's heat, the rabbit muttering through his exhausted mouth. These images existed only to fade away from the chance that he might tell them ever to himself or anyone else, if there was ever any one again to tell. He saw his brothers' camp as they had found it, and traced his memory of that day, the odd exchanges between Middle and Eldest and the rabbit, and the voyage they made all together into a cave that ran toward the heart of the mountain, toward, he thought, mother. All too soon, just as they were being enveloped by the darkness, they were attacked, so it seemed, by a sleeping creature, and Crane was consumed by it as it flailed its many limbs and scrabbled up the cave walls, awakened to frenzy and dashing for the safety of the open air. Little Bear was lucky that he fell such that his eyes could see the keyhole of daylight that was the entrance framing the beast, the tree-bird—A Tree Growing in the Mountain's Ear!—as it leaped into the air with Mr Crane in its grasp, or it in his grasp. The bear's first thought had been, oh, Mother, I'm sorry, Mother, please don't be scared.

Now prone in the gray sun, limp as if there were nothing left in him but a handful of sawdust, the bear forgot those days and held close to his chest the manuscript he'd stolen from Virginia's rooms during his time in her house's shadows. The mystery of Princess Yasha's life and death awaited him, ever patient, as she approached the reptilian city coiling down the cliffside, and how, in her glorious perfection she regarded herself, on the first pages, as a pinprick of disaster, a seed of nightmare and ruin, and how, though she thought only of her death, hundreds of pages lay before her, and he fell into bliss between the story to be and the dream of the story that always waited.

Mr Fin woke, feeling that he was next to David on the bed, but when he looked, David was not there anymore, must have gone out, to breakfast perhaps, if it was already so late. The window was cracked, but the curtains did not move. One of those mornings.

Mr Fin wanted to get up, but it was a wish in his head, and his body was not cooperating. Up, he said. Let's get up. He was speaking to his body in his head, and couldn't remember how to make the commands happen in the muscles, he could only speak. He heard kitchen sounds, plastic plates and cups, serving spoons digging in and then at rest again, a clock made of people lined up with trays. It must be a memory, he thought, of the cafeteria at school. The noise stopped, as though the cafeteria door had shut just outside his own door.

He heard knocking in the distance, as if at a neighbor's house. He would not get up to see. It came closer, knock knock, then a pause, then knock knock, closer, possibly his front door, then the same pause, then knock knock, until the sound struck his bedroom door, like a canon shot, then it moved on.

Someone was in the room, standing near his knees. Hello, he thought, but again, no cooperation. Since when is my mouth part of my body, he wondered. I need at least my head.

Some business was being done to his calves, his blankets, his socks. Soon enough, everything felt better. My body is waking up, he thought.

Hello, he thought, once more.

It was a man in white, but it wasn't David. He took Mr Fin's hand and gave it some vigorous rubs and squeezes, then worked his way up the arm. Fin smiled, or thought he did.

The man said, "Your friend left you some books." He indicated with a nod of his head, the nightstand, the books stacked neatly there.

"You think you'll be up to reading? You want me to come back after Hodge and 'Melia?"

He had brought life to Fin's right shoulder and now his thumbs and fingers sorted through the bones and meat of the left. Mr Fin could breathe more easily. Hello, he thought again. And Oh, his lips moved, he could tell.

"Yeah? Alright, then. It'll be about half an hour. I'm thinking you should have your breakfast here soon as I'm done. I'll set you up. Sound good?" The hand's slowed, "How's that feel?" Something about the shoulder bone. "That hurt?"

Maybe it did hurt.

"We'll get you moving today, get you in the shower and everything."

This man had cinnamon breath, thick stubble, the kind that never shaves away, stubble and no face under, surrounded by deeply reddened skin and dark eyebrows. Hands of a god, anyway. Was it Sam, he wondered.

Then he was in the chair, legs crossed, and Mr Fin was propped up in his bed.

The man was saying, "...the old man who fished alone, the name of whom I have no desire to call to mind, saw the town-lands and learned the minds of many distant men, and weathered many bitter nights and days in the deep heart of the sea, amidst the coiled lines or the gaff and harpoon and the sail that was furled around the mast, all in the dark undersea wing of the pluming waters. When he set out again from the witch's island, it was under a sail patched with flour sacks and bedsheets and, furled, it looked like the flag of permanent defeat. He fought only to save his life, to bring his shipmates home. But neither by will nor valor could he save himself, for his own recklessness destroyed him—a child and a fool, he killed and feasted on the cattle of the Sun, and he who moves all day through the heavens took from his eyes the dawn of return...leaving a boy who had been with him before in a doublet of fine cloth and velvet breeches and shoes to match for holidays, who on week-days made a brave figure in his best homespun—hardy of habit, spare, gaunt-featured, a very early riser and a great sportsman. It will be enough not to stray a hair's breadth in the telling of it."

When it was over, Fin said, with little breaths and finger gestures, "Leave me that book," and the man left the book on the blanket by his hip. Will you come back, Hart, he tried to say, but there was nothing for it, and the rabbit was checking on bits and pieces in the room, dials and dust and dangly bits and paper weights, his eyes always busy elsewhere.

Just look at me, he thought, but still grateful, willing to drift away without him. But just look so I can speak again, when I feel I might be able. The door was shut. Where had David gone all morning? Who left the books on the table? He remembered all of them fondly. They were his own. He knew how Odysseus, in this one, listened to the sirens, and he knew in their song how he would forget his son, how he would journey to the underworld to draw the song of the end of singing from the milk-gray waters one dreams of crossing, one day. With that water in his palms, he fed his son's lips and removed the three arrows, stealing him back for as long as he could hold his breath in the dark maze of the gone world. And so, knees on the deck of the black ship, all around him his wide-eyed men wearily peeling wax from their ears, he said, "I heard nothing. I heard nothing. Yet I would have given anything to go on hearing it—oh, to be devoured by that song!"

Imagine the primal wonder, the jaw-dropping splendor experienced by the fish sisters on first discovering the kitchen faucet: running water. It ran rusty and brown at first, belching from deep, possibly damaged pipes. It would not amaze them that the plumbing still worked. But the discovery of this element drew the universe into focus, filled them with a sense of limitless possibility. Imagine, in centuries to come, rabbits in space might be born and die without ever seeing the earth, grass, dirt, or without ever breathing freely in an airy expanse. Then, to find earth, atmosphere, pouring forth from some tube in space, life itself rushing back into the universe!

The sisters, One, Two, Three, and Four, held no memories of the sea, nor legends of water-locked early fish, and they had never swam or felt rain or taken a drink. This ever so soft material amazed them. So they let it run, watched it squirm from room to room. They observed its anti-gravity properties as it lifted bits of this or that, tugged bits of paper around the kitchen floor. It flowed into winding arms and puddles, and they considered that it might be a living creature, stretching into the world, picking things up, smelling, embracing, eating, carousing with the world.

It came up to their knees, and they sat down in it, learned to float.

One of them went under and came up gagging and spluttering, distressed but intrigued.

Gradually they worked out how to swim, noticing a strange pressure around their gills. Faster than it could drain through the door cracks, the house filled with water, right up to the ceiling, and the children floated along with it, not scared in the least, but relieved. Here it comes, they thought, not caring what the words meant.

They could stand on the floor and be covered by water, and move about in the room, swimming here and there, among the objects gradually pulled from their grids by the currents.

They held their breaths, studied the quiet cold interior of the water possessing them. We've been swallowed, they thought, by the secret essence of the universe.

For several days they were timid about staying underwater and slept two nights cradled in the light fixtures. But then Three let herself drift heavily down to the carpet and held her breath as long as she could. Longer. Who knew what would happen next? One and Two watched. Minutes passed. Four swam down and sat beside her, gave her a tap on the shoulder, to see if she was dead. Three opened her eyes, feeling a little groggy. They waited together. Half an hour. An hour. They might live forever, never breathing.

Mr Fin woke with an eye like a sharp rock, wordy, clamoring dreams smashed uselessly against the shore, eyelids washing in and out. The swollen shabby roundness of his face surrounded the eye stabbed through its green grassy center, but nothing else, an island of cheek and jowl—no shoulders, chest, back, thighs, calves, heels, toes... no fingertips. He rolled and saw one arm was still there, not fully attached, but it made a bridge between the mattress and the nightstand, the hand gripping a bottle of pills. He let it go and it sank from view, the pills and nightstand too, all hidden below the tide. Everything could go, drawn in or sunken away, so that he was only the floating island, water lapping against him, and if his eye was a sharp rock, then it scribed the air, and if his mouth was a gaping harbor or inlet, then it had been carved by time and water, and said only that. In this way, he carried David all the way down the hill, past his bench, toward the water. He marched carefully over the petrified wood and blackened green stones and into the soft sand, and all the way in up to his ankles, and knees, and hips, and belly, and his elbows and his chest, and as David took on water, he became light, and eager, pushing in and pulling out in the waves, until he let go.

Water filled the house, and, in just under a thousand years, drank the entire planet of its rivers, lakes, and its oceans. The earth, dry as a bone, mumbled on, its moonish face littered with piles of life lingering together, heads turning as they could until, tired, set free from care, the multitude of last eyes fixed on the furthest point, the opposite of shore, reflecting the bright sidereal sea, long above.

It was not Orpheus, any more, who wandered the dead lands, but Eurydice, the book of the poet under her arm, her legs weary of the centuries. She could see the house filled with water in the distance, but it was too far to go.

She had obeyed, never once opened him, but carried him, wrapped in linen, in search of the living world. Surrounded by thirst, she listened to the house gurgle with trapped seas, saw its giant salmon population carousing in the windows, playing bridge or dice and pouring snacks into little bowls. She went as far as the edge of the village, to the long vanished garden, where the rabbits once lived, and where they lived a second time, through the generation of children with her own voice beneath their skin, and she lay Orpheus's book before her, a solitary dream against the flat earth. She unwrapped him, letting the linen windings fall into the constant dry churning of the air.

She pressed her palm against the book's cover as if it were his chest or his forehead or his cheek, or a door.

Now she was done wandering, and she opened the book.

[Acknowledgements]

I want to thank my gracious friends, teachers, and colleagues who have read the work over the years and given me encouragement and critique. Without my wife, Carin, and my two children, Elinor and Malcolm, this novel would have been finished far sooner and been far less because of it, especially as it would have lacked the influence of their love and brilliance.

[Note]

Some material in this text is drawn without quotation or citation from other sources, including the writing of Hart Crane, Virginia Woolf, Maurice Blanchot, Ernest Hemingway, Homer, Stéphane Mallarmé, and my grandmother. In most instances, source texts have been altered for effect or through a constraint.

—S. H.

[Colophon]

This book has been designed by Rebecca Maslen, Philadelphia.

Title page is set in IKHIOOGLA, designed by "junkohanhero" from dafont.com.

Text is set in Gentium Basic, designed by Victor Gaultney. Gentium is a typeface family designed to enable the diverse ethnic groups around the world who use the Latin, Cyrillic and Greek scripts to produce readable, high-quality publications. It supports a wide range of Latin- and Cyrillic-based alphabets. The design is intended to be highly readable, reasonably compact, and visually attractive.

Created in Adobe InDesign CS5 and 6.

Also Available from Starcherone Books

E. R. Baxter, *Niagara Digressions;* Kenneth Bernard, *The Man in the Stretcher: previously uncollected stories;* Donald Breckenridge, *You Are Here;* Blake Butler and Lily Hoang, eds., *30 Under 30: An Anthology of Innovative Fiction by Younger Authors;* Jonathan Callahan, *The Consummation of Dirk;* Joshua Cohen, *A Heaven of Others;* Peter Conners, ed., *PP/FF: An Anthology;* Jeffrey DeShell, *Peter: An (A)Historical Romance;* Nicolette deCsipkay, *Black Umbrella Stories,* illustrated by Francesca deCsipkay; Sarah Falkner, *Animal Sanctuary;* Raymond Federman, *My Body in Nine Parts,* with photographs by Steve Murez; Raymond Federman, *Shhh: The Story of a Childhood;* Raymond Federman, *The Voice in the Closet;* Raymond Federman and George Chambers, *The Twilight of the Bums,* with cartoon accompaniment by T. Motley; Sara Greenslit, *The Blue of Her Body;* Johannes Göransson, *Dear Ra: A Story in Flinches;* Joshua Harmon, *Quinnehtukqut;* Gretchen E. Henderson, *The House Enters the Street;* Harold Jaffe, *Beyond the Techno-Cave: A Guerrilla Writer's Guide to Post-Millennial Culture;* Kent Johnson, *A Question Mark Above the Sun;* Steve Katz, *The Compleat Memoirrhoids: 137n;* Stacey Levine, *The Girl with Brown Fur: stories & tales;* Janet Mitchell, *The Creepy Girl and other stories;* Alissa Nutting, *Unclean Jobs for Women and Girls;* Aimee Parkison, *Woman with Dark Horses: Stories;* Aimee Parkison, *The Petals of Your Eyes;* Ted Pelton, *Endorsed by Jack Chapeau 2 an even greater extent;* Michael Rizza, *Cartilage and Skin;* Thaddeus Rutkowski, *Haywire;* Leslie Scalapino, *Floats Horse-Floats or Horse-Flows;* Nina Shope, *Hangings: Three Novellas.*

Starcherone Books, Inc., exists to stimulate public interest in works of innovative prose fiction and nurture an understanding of the art of fiction writing by publishing, disseminating, and affording the public opportunities to hear readings of innovative works. In addition to encouraging the development of authors and their audiences, Starcherone seeks to educate the public in small press publishing and encourage the growth of other small presses. Visit us online at www.starcherone.com and the Starcherone page on Facebook. Starcherone Books, PO Box 303, Buffalo, NY 14201.

Starcherone Books is an independently operated imprint of Dzanc Books, distributed through Consortium Distribution and Small Press Distribution. We are a signatory to the Book Industry Treatise on Responsible Paper Use and use postconsumer recycled fiber paper in our books.

Founder Ted Pelton wishes the new editorial board well as they take the reins for Starcherone's 15th year. Bon voyage!